Lady Sarah's Sinful Desires

Lowering his gaze, he looked down at Lady Sarah, who was staring toward the turn in the path with some measure of anxiety. There was a restlessness about her entire body that easily conveyed her eagerness to seek the company of others and avoid being left alone with him.

"Why are you so nervous?" he asked without making a move to follow the rest of their party.

"Because we ought not be alone together," she said. "It isn't proper."

He considered that for a moment before saying, "I'm hardly going to ravish you out here in public where anyone could happen upon us at any given time. Honestly, Lady Sarah, I do believe you're overreacting."

Her eyes met his at that moment, bright and accusing and with the slightest hint of fear. "Am I?"

By Sophie Barnes

Novels

LADY SARAH'S SINFUL DESIRES
THE DANGER IN TEMPTING AN EARL
THE SCANDAL IN KISSING AN HEIR
THE TROUBLE WITH BEING A DUKE
THE SECRET LIFE OF LADY LUCINDA
THERE'S SOMETHING ABOUT LADY MARY
LADY ALEXANDRA'S EXCELLENT ADVENTURE
HOW MISS RUTHERFORD GOT HER GROOVE BACK

Novellas

MISTLETOE MAGIC
(from FIVE GOLDEN RINGS:
A CHRISTMAS COLLECTION)

Lady Sarah's Sinful Desires

Secrets at Thorncliff Manor

Sophie Barnes

AVONBOOKS

An Imprint of HarperCollins*Publishers*

This is a work of fiction. Names, characters, places, and incidents are products of the author's imagination or are used fictitiously and are not to be construed as real. Any resemblance to actual events, locales, organizations, or persons, living or dead, is entirely coincidental.

AVON BOOKS
An Imprint of HarperCollins*Publishers*
195 Broadway
New York, New York 10007

Copyright © 2015 by Sophie Barnes
Map courtesy of Sophie Barnes
ISBN 978-0-06-235885-1
www.avonromance.com

First Avon Books mass market printing: May 2015

Avon Trademark Reg. U.S. Pat. Off. and in Other Countries, Marca Registrada, Hecho en U.S.A.
HarperCollins® is a registered trademark of HarperCollins Publishers.

Printed in the U.S.A.

10 9 8 7 6 5 4 3 2 1

For Erika Tsang.
I couldn't have done this without you.
And for my family.
I love you all so very much!

Acknowledgments

Writing is a continuous learning experience—a journey of the imagination—and because of this, there are moments when I find myself stumbling, overthinking an issue, or simply coming to a complete standstill. Thankfully, I work with an extraordinary group of people who always help me get back on my feet, point me in the right direction, or give me that extra push that I need. Each and every one of them deserves my deepest thanks and gratitude, because when all is said and done, a book isn't the work of just one person but of many.

I'd like to thank my wonderful editor, Erika Tsang, and her assistant, Chelsey Emmelhainz, for being so incredibly helpful and easy to talk to—working with both of you is an absolute pleasure!

Together with the rest of the Avon Books team, which includes (but is far from limited to) copyeditor Judy Myers; publicists Pam Spengler-Jaffee, Jessie Edwards, Caroline Perny and Emily Homonoff; and senior director of marketing, Shawn Nicholls; they have offered guidance and support whenever it was needed. My sincerest thanks to all of you for being so wonderful!

Another person who must be acknowledged for his talent is artist James Griffin, who has created the stunning cover for this book, capturing not only the feel of the story but also the way in which I envisioned the characters looking—you've done such a beautiful job!

To my fabulous beta-readers Codi Gary, Mary Chen, Cerian Halford, Marla Golladay and Kathy Nye, whose insight has been tremendously helpful in strengthening the story, thank you so much!

I would also like to thank Nancy Mayer for her assistance. Whenever I was faced with a question regarding the Regency era that I couldn't answer on my own, I turned to Nancy for advice. Her help has been invaluable.

My family and friends deserve my thanks as well, especially for reminding me to take a break occasionally, to step away from the computer and just unwind—I would be lost without you.

And to you, dear reader—thank you so much for taking the time to read this story. Your support is, as always, hugely appreciated!

LADY SARAH'S
SINFUL DESIRES

Even though I fear for the future, I find I have no choice but to act—indeed, morality and honor compel me to do so, my only consolation being that I will not be facing this battle alone. How great my influence will be remains uncertain, but I must at least try to make a difference.

To those of you who may happen upon these words in the future, please rest assured that my companions and I did what we could, and that even if I were to die tomorrow, it would be with a clear conscience.

The diary belonging to
the 3rd Earl of Duncaster, 1792

Lady Sarah's
Sinful Desires

Chapter 1

In a carriage on the way to Thorncliff Manor
1820

"**D**o you suppose we'll be arriving soon?" Rachel asked with an edge of impatience. "Before leaving the last posting inn, Mama assured me that it would only be another two hours, but according to my pocket watch it has already been one hundred and twenty-seven minutes. To be exact."

Christopher gazed across at his younger sister. "I don't believe Mama has ever visited Thorncliff before," he said, referring to the Countess of Duncaster's large estate, which she had turned into a guesthouse. He and his family would be spending the summer there. "This makes her estimate regarding the duration of this journey exactly that—an estimate."

Rachel didn't look pleased. "I wish everyone would appreciate the importance of precision as much as I do."

"Cook does," Laura said sweetly, directing Christopher's attention to another sister. He had five in total. "I'm sure she would acknowledge the importance of accuracy. After all, there's nothing worse than a cake with too much flour in it."

"Do you have to encourage her?" Fiona asked. As the youngest of the Heartly siblings, she had never developed the sort of patience the rest of the brood possessed.

Christopher frowned, while Rachel's face beamed with newfound pleasure as she latched onto Laura's comment. "Life as we know it would be impossible without adhering to mathematical and scientific principles. Buildings would fall to the ground, dough would refuse to rise, your clothing would be ill-fitting . . . why, I could go on forever about the effect a lack of structure would have on us all."

"Must you?" Fiona asked with an underlying note of dread.

"Why not distract yourself by contemplating the splendor of our destination?" Christopher suggested. As much as he loved Rachel, he had little desire to endure a prolonged lecture on Euclidean geometry or, God forbid, her recent study on the movement of slugs.

"I've heard that Thorncliff is magnificent. Apparently the third Earl of Duncaster wasted no expense when he expanded it," Laura said before Rachel could comment. "My friend Lady Harriet visited last year with her family, and she has assured me that the estate can easily amuse us all for the duration of our three-month stay."

"I've no doubt about that," Fiona said promptly, her eyes lighting, "especially since I've every intention of putting my own time there to good use. I mean to find that jewelry box Grandmamma spoke of when we were little."

Christopher stared at her. "What are you talking about?"

"Don't you remember? She always said her family in France sent heirlooms to England during the revolution to prevent them from falling into the wrong hands. It was all she would have had left of her family after they all perished at the guillotine, but for unknown reasons, the box of heirlooms never arrived. I'm convinced they must be hidden away at Thorncliff. Considering Grandpapa's close friendship with Lord Duncaster, I—"

"Now that you mention it, I do recall her saying something to that effect, but I never really put much weight in it," Laura said. "You know how badly Grandmamma suffered the loss of her family. I always believed her talk of the jewelry box was her way of hoping a part of them had been left behind and would eventually come to her."

"But she specifically mentioned receiving a letter from her sister, the Duchess of Marveille, in France, encouraging her to wait for it—that the duchess had sent it to England and that arrangements had been made for it to be delivered to her."

"Your memory is certainly to be admired," Rachel said, "but I think we must accept that the heirlooms never left France, as unfortunate as that is."

"But in her diary," Fiona insisted, "Grandmamma wrote of a visit Grandpapa made to Thorncliff shortly before his death. She wrote that she prayed her husband would soon return home with *the box*."

"And yet she never received it," Christopher pointed out.

Fiona sighed. "No, she didn't. Grandpapa set sail for France, perishing with the third Earl of Duncaster when the ship went down." She sighed, her expression somber, though her eyes remained sharp with determination. "It's possible the jewelry box is still at Thorncliff, in which case, I've every intention of locating it. You can count on that."

Christopher had no doubt about it. If there was one quality his sister didn't have in short supply, it was tenacity, which was why he was surprised when she dropped the subject completely to say, "I still can't believe Mama and Papa convinced Richard to join us."

Christopher curled his fingers into a fist. "He had little choice in the matter. Oakland will be overrun by workmen the entire summer, and I daresay they'll be busy if Mama's plan to redecorate the entire place in the Greek style is to be fulfilled according to schedule."

"Even so, you must admit that it's surprising," Laura said.

Christopher chose not to comment. Contemplating his younger brother's service to the Crown made him uncomfortable. As Richard's older brother, he'd always felt a certain responsibility—a need to protect him—but the war against Napoleon had left Christopher with nothing but a distinct sense of failure. Reaching inside his jacket pocket, he pulled out his own pocket watch to assess the time. It was one minute after two in the afternoon. He waited a minute before brushing his thumb across the watch face three times.

"There's no point in that, you know," Rachel said. "Good fortune is derived from hard work and common sense, not from silly rituals."

Although her comment was to be expected, it still annoyed Christopher. "I believe in luck, Rachel, and if that means adopting a few oddities, then so be it." Turning away from her, he determined to savor the gentle sway of the carriage as they tumbled along, thankful that his sister chose not to comment any further. The truth of it was that his superstitious nature embarrassed him, for he knew it defied all logic and reason, yet he couldn't seem to avoid the feeling that awful things would happen unless he took certain measures to prevent them. He sighed. The hold it had on him had only increased after passing a tree with two ravens in it in 1815. That year, he'd not only been unlucky in love but his brother had also been captured by the French.

"Do you think Chloe will ever remarry?" Laura asked suddenly, referring to their widowed sister and consequently drawing Christopher out of his reverie.

"Probably not, all things considered," Rachel muttered.

It occurred to Christopher that Rachel might be prettier if she didn't insist on pulling her hair so tightly back. Her sisters ought to offer their assistance, for they all looked pretty with their soft curls framing their faces, but Christopher knew that to suggest such a thing would only invite argument. Rachel had some very stubborn ideas—none of which were likely to get her married.

"It's a good thing her husband died in that duel, or I would have run him through myself," Fiona stated.

Christopher frowned. He wasn't sure if he ought to be proud of his sister's thirst for blood or terrified. Hell, he wished he'd had the opportunity to challenge the late Lord Newbury himself after discovering the man's numerous affairs. In the end it had been the unhappy husband of Newbury's latest paramour who'd seen to the man's demise. "One can only hope that if she does remarry, it will be to a man who deserves her," he said.

Laura's eyes lit up. "Perhaps she'll meet an eligible gentleman at Thorncliff!" She leaned forward, her gaze fixed on her brother. "There might even be a young lady there to—"

"You'd better not finish that sentence if you know what's good for you," Christopher warned.

"There's no need for you to be so touchy," Laura told him primly as she straightened and raised her chin a notch. "I only want what's best for you."

Christopher groaned. His mother and father had told him the exact same thing. Repeatedly. It was the reason he'd avoided sharing a carriage with them to Thorncliff. The last thing he needed was to be trapped with them for six hours while they took turns suggesting potential brides to him. As the eldest son and heir to the Oakland title, he knew he'd eventually marry. He just wanted to wait until he was ready—perhaps enjoy another Season of blissful bachelorhood in the arms of that little opera singer he'd had his eye on. He certainly had no desire to repeat the mistake he'd made five years earlier. "If I may offer a suggestion, dear sister—restrict your romantic musings to the heroes and heroines in those wildly creative novels you're writing and keep me out of it."

"But—"

"No buts," he told her firmly. "I won't allow you to play matchmaker for me."

Folding her arms across her chest, Laura stared back at Christopher, glowering. He knew she was struggling to hold her tongue, and he admired her effort. Truly he did. But there was no telling how long her self-restraint would last. Deciding to steer her attention away from him completely, he said, "All things considered, I think it would be more prudent if I were to find husbands for each of *you*."

"W-h-a-t?" The outburst came from Rachel, which wasn't the least bit surprising. Christopher knew her entire world revolved around math and science. Settling down and starting a family was probably the furthest thing from her mind.

"You're not getting any younger," he said, indelicately addressing the subject their mother had broached so often that it had turned into a regular sermon.

"I'm only eighteen," Fiona said with marked indignation. "Hardly an old maid yet."

"True," Christopher agreed, patting her hand in a gesture he hoped would soothe her. "I admit that your situation is not as urgent as Rachel's or Emily's, who, if I may remind you, are three and twenty and two and twenty, respectively."

"It's good to know that when age is of concern, everyone in this family can be quite precise indeed," Rachel said, her eyes flashing as she pressed her lips together in a firm line.

"Surely you must have considered leaving your scientific discoveries to someone—a legacy of sorts, if you will? Who better than a child, whom you can educate and influence so he or she will share your enthusiasm for . . ." Christopher searched his brain for a suitable word but could only think of " . . . slugs?"

"Since you've developed such a keen interest in my research," Rachel said, the fire in her eyes cooling a fraction as she spoke, "I'll have you know that I intend to publish my work as soon as it is completed. *That,* dear brother, will be my legacy. Husbands and children will only complicate the issue."

"I don't think Christopher intended for you to have more than one," Laura murmured.

Christopher's lips twitched as he fought against the smile that threatened. Appearing to be amused by this conversation would not be to his benefit, trapped as he was with three women in a closed carriage.

"More than one what?" Rachel asked, her head swiveling toward her sister. There could be no denying her irritability.

"You spoke of husbands just now," Laura explained. "As in plural?"

"I . . ." Rachel began. She must have realized that denying her error would be futile with witnesses present, for she crossed her arms instead and said, "Oh! You know what I mean."

"Did you ever consider," Christopher remarked, "that there might be a lonely scientist out there who'd be thrilled to make you his bride? Shared interests and all that?"

"There isn't," Rachel said, her expression so tight she looked positively frightening. "Not unless I am willing to settle for a man who's either thrice my age or one who can barely afford to put food on the table. I calculated the probability of it last year."

"The statistics might have changed since then," Christopher offered.

Rachel said nothing further. She merely glared at him.

"Well, perhaps I will focus on settling Emily's future instead," he said. He wasn't sure why he insisted on continuing this discussion, other than that he took pleasure in teasing his sisters.

"She won't like your meddling any more than you would ours," Fiona said with a seriousness that belied her age. "And don't forget that unlike the rest of us, you're Papa's heir. It's your *duty* to find a wife and start producing children."

Christopher angled his head just enough to stare down at his youngest sister. "And what, pray tell, would you know about that?" he asked.

"Enough to inform you that you cannot accomplish it alone," Fiona declared. Laughter sprang from Laura's lips, and Rachel turned a deep shade of crimson. "You will need a lady to assist."

Hoping to hide the rising sense of discomfort that always came with this particular subject, he assumed his most arrogant tone and uttered the only word that might be considered appropriate in such a situation. "Indeed."

Unwilling to discuss the subject further, he proceeded to stare out the window, forcing his thoughts away from the woman he should have married five years earlier if she hadn't turned out to be a complete fraud.

"That can't possibly be it," Laura said a short while later.

Christopher turned toward the sound of his sisters' voices all *ooh*-ing and *aah*-ing, as if they'd just stepped inside La Belle Anglaise, an exclusive fabric shop in Mayfair. They were all blocking the window of course, preventing Christopher from glimpsing the subject of their excitement until Rachel moved aside, apparently through with her inspection.

Christopher leaned forward, equally amazed. In the distance, nestled against a soft swell of hills, stood a manor . . . no . . . a palace, more splendid than any he'd ever seen. Hell, it put Carleton House to shame with its regiment of marble columns standing sentry before each wing, the central part of the building paying tribute to a Greek temple.

"It makes Oakland Park look like a hovel," Fiona remarked.

Christopher blinked. To his amazement, he found he could not disagree. Thorncliff was indeed a sight to behold, its magnificent size a true temptation that made him eager to explore. "I've read that the original structure was built upon the ruins of a Roman settlement during the twelfth century."

"Truly?" Fiona asked, her voice filled with excitement.

Christopher nodded as his gaze swept the length of the impressive building. "There's even supposed to be a vast network of tunnels running beneath it."

His interest in Thorncliff wasn't a new one. Intrigued by castles since he'd been a young lad, he'd read about the great estate on numerous occasions, and since his parents had announced that the Heartly family would spend the entire summer away from home, he'd looked forward to the prospect with great anticipation. There was also the advantage that here, it appeared, he stood a reasonable chance of avoiding his mother and the potential brides she no doubt longed to press upon him. Smiling, Christopher sat back against the squabs. Salvation was finally within reach.

In another carriage on the way to Thorncliff Manor

Seated between her younger stepsisters, Alice and Juliet, Sarah made a stoic attempt to ignore the disapproving look that sat upon her stepmother's face. Her father was more tolerable, since he'd been reading his newspaper the entire journey and had paid little attention to the rest of the family.

"Is there something you wish to say, Mama?" Sarah eventually asked, unable to stop herself from uttering the question for one moment longer.

Lady Andover's gaze narrowed, but just as Sarah

had suspected, she merely responded with, "Not at the moment."

Speaking of Sarah's sins in front of her young, impressionable sisters was taboo. Later, however, once the girls were out of earshot, Sarah had no doubt that her stepmother's tongue would give her a sound thrashing. After all, it was what Sarah had come to expect after proving herself a disappointment to the Argisle name.

"Would you look at that!" Alice suddenly gasped, supplying Sarah with a much-needed distraction. Leaning forward while Juliet tried to press past her in an attempt to look out the window as well, Sarah just managed to catch a glimpse of the largest building she'd ever seen when her stepmother said, "Do sit back, Sarah. Your sister can't see when you're in the way."

Sarah did as she was told, fully aware that her stepmother had just used Alice and Juliet to her own advantage, for there was a smug smile upon her face as if to say, *I know you do not wish to cause a scandal in their presence.*

Biting back a scathing remark, Sarah remained silent and unmoving while her sisters' excitement filled the carriage. Instead, she reached inside her reticule and stroked the little fur ball within, taking comfort in its heat while she wondered what her stepmother would say if she were to discover that Sarah had brought her pet hamster along with her. Lady Andover would probably find a way to punish Sarah for it, which was all the more reason for Sarah to keep her pet well hidden.

"We're finally here," Alice exclaimed as the carriage tumbled into a paved courtyard and came to a swaying halt. "Just look at that doorway! It must be twice as wide as the one we have at home."

"And beautifully carved too," Juliet said as she strained to look past her sister. "Oh, I can't wait to get inside."

Sarah couldn't help but agree as she stared out at the looming façade, the weather-worn stones suggesting that this great building had borne witness to many things through the ages. It had history.

"Calm yourselves, dears," Lady Andover said. "You may be on holiday, but you are still expected to conduct yourselves properly." She looked directly at Sarah, a warning in her sharp eyes. "There will be no running about. Is that clear?"

"Yes, Mama," Alice and Juliet spoke in unison, their voices filled with disappointment. A footman opened the carriage door and gracefully offered his hand to Lady Andover. She alit, followed by Alice and Juliet. Sarah made to follow them, but she was stopped by her father's staying hand upon her arm. "You will not disrespect your stepmother," he told her softly but sternly. "After all that you have done—the disgrace you have put us through—you have no right. No right at all. Do I make myself clear?"

"Perfectly, my lord."

With a curt nod, he released her, allowing her to flee the stifling interior of the carriage even if she could never escape her shame. A tight knot twisted inside her chest as she watched her sisters climb the steps of Thorncliff. *Please don't make the same mistake I did*, she prayed as she started after them, unbearably aware of her father's stubborn presence at her side. "There's a purpose to this visit," he muttered. "I trust you will remember that."

Looking up into his stalwart gaze, Sarah nodded. How could she possibly forget?

"Good," her father said as they stepped over the

threshold into a massive hall with polished marble floors. At the center, a large wind rose was inlaid in black and gray tones. "I'm glad we understand each other."

Sarah would never know if he said anything further, for her entire focus was riveted upon the marble archways that flanked the sides, the niches that stood above them, filled with poised statues and crowned by towering windows through which golden rays of sunlight cast their glow. Above these, the ceiling curved toward an enormous painting depicting a fray of soldiers, angels and leaping horses.

"Come along, Sarah," her stepmother hissed, the words undoubtedly louder than intended as they rose through the air and bounced off the walls, filling the vast space with bitterness. "Don't stand there dawdling. We're being shown to our rooms now."

On a heavy sigh, Sarah followed her family as they were led to a long corridor by a maid. Though the ceiling here was not as high as in the hall, it was still high enough to make Sarah wonder which poor servant was given the task of dusting for cobwebs all the way up there, if Thorncliff even had a ladder long enough for such a task, or if they just left the spiders alone in the hope that no one would see them. As they walked, Sarah also noted that footmen had been placed at every corner, their expressions impassive as they stared straight ahead, protecting the virtues of young ladies by bearing witness to potential mischief. Or perhaps they served to protect Lady Duncaster's valuables from Thorncliff's many visitors, Sarah mused.

They soon arrived in another hall, this one smaller than the first. A splendid staircase monopolized the space as it rose up, splitting halfway before continuing left and right. Bronze statues of women reaching toward the ceiling, each with a candelabrum in her hand, stood on either side of the base, while tall lanterns reminiscent of the streetlights Sarah had seen in London stood at the very top.

"I daresay I'll lose myself in this place," Alice murmured as she looked up at the ceiling, almost tripping on the steps in the process.

"If you do, I'm sure a maid or a footman will direct you to your room, though I doubt it will even be an issue, since you and Juliet will be in either my own or Hester's company," Lady Andover said, referring to the lady's maid the three sisters would be sharing.

Sarah didn't need to look at her sisters to know they would both be scrunching their noses at such a prospect, for as kind as Hester was, she'd gotten on in years and lacked the energy Alice and Juliet craved. "We would so much rather have Sarah for our chaperone," Juliet said. "Oh please, Mama, can't we spend our days with her instead? You won't wish to run through a maze with us anyway, and Hester prefers to sit in the shade all day."

"Which is very correct of her," Lady Andover said. "Young ladies should stay out of the sun and off their feet as much as possible. They certainly shouldn't be running around like savages. Besides, Sarah will be quite busy during her stay here. She's going to make the acquaintance of Mr. Denison and will no doubt be quite occupied by his company. Isn't that so, Sarah?"

"Quite so," Sarah said, dreading the meeting her father had arranged for her.

"So you see," Lady Andover continued, her breath coming in short bursts as they reached the top of the stairs, "Hester and I will have to do."

"As you requested in your letter, my lady," the maid said as they followed her down a long corridor lined with burgundy runners, "you've been placed conveniently close to each other. The rooms are also quite spacious, so hopefully you will all be very comfortable." Halting in front of a door carved in rich tones of auburn-colored wood, the maid pressed down on the handle until the door swung open. "For the young ladies," she said before crossing to the door opposite and doing the same. "My lord and lady. If you need anything, please don't hesitate to ring the bellpull."

"Thank you," Lord Andover said as he popped his head through the doorway and peered inside the room. "I think this will do very nicely."

Bobbing a curtsy, the maid took her leave while Alice and Juliet escaped inside their room. "I'm sure Hester will be up as soon as she's ensured that the footmen have our luggage under control. In the meantime, Sarah, please see to it that your sisters get some rest," Lady Andover said, her countenance stiff as always. "The journey has been a trying one."

"I will do my best," Sarah promised.

Offering a curt nod, her stepmother said nothing further as she turned her back on Sarah and followed her husband into their bedroom, closing the door behind her and leaving Sarah alone in the corridor. She took a breath, trying to relax and ignore the way her insides shuddered in response to her stepmother's resentment. "Have you ever seen anything so beautiful?" she heard Alice remark.

Entering her room, Sarah had to confess that *she* certainly had not, for as it turned out, they were to share an entire suite of rooms with a comfortable sitting area in the center.

"Never," Juliet replied, echoing Sarah's thoughts.

Ignoring her sisters, Sarah walked across to the window and peered out at the vast lawns, the intricate flower gardens, the maze in the distance and the massive lake upon which, if her eyes did not deceive her, was a sailing ship—a frigate, to be exact. No doubt Thorncliff surpassed every ancestral home she'd ever visited. Nothing compared. Perhaps that was the point of the Thorncliff estate.

Sarah resisted the urge to explore Thorncliff for an hour—longer than she'd ever thought possible. Then, with the intention of taking a look around, she left her slumbering sisters to Hester's watchful eyes.

After descending the stairs, she wandered down a corridor and soon discovered that Thorncliff was filled with guests and servants to the point of overflowing. Her first impression upon visiting a salon wrapped in Chinese décor, where some ladies were having tea, was that she'd probably be unlikely to discover a private space she could claim as her own. This suspicion grew when, after passing a series of other rooms, she found each one to be occupied by somebody else. Though she did recognize a few faces and made sure to offer polite greetings, she had no desire to engage in conversation with anyone, fearing it would only result in unpleasant prying.

Eventually, Sarah decided to head out into the garden in search of a secluded corner where she and Snowball would be able to enjoy each other's company. The poor little creature had spent the better part of the day confined to her reticule and was surely growing restless. But, before arriving at the

French doors that would take her outside, Sarah came upon another door that piqued her interest. It was made almost entirely of glass, and beyond it, she could see nothing but greenery—trees, bushes and ferns mostly, all planted on either side of a tiled path that wound its way between them before disappearing from view.

Reaching out, Sarah pressed down on the handle until the door swung open. A humid heat blending with the smell of wet soil greeted her, and she stepped quickly inside, closing the door behind her with care. Silence, and the relief that came with solitude, washed over her as she reached inside her reticule and retrieved her furry companion. Snowball squeaked, wriggling between Sarah's fingers as she stroked him gently across his back. "I'm sorry," she whispered. "I know you'd love nothing better than to scamper about between these plants, but if I set you down, I'll never find you again." Stepping forward, she started along the path while her gaze leapt from one massive glass window to the next.

Andover Abby didn't have a conservatory, and Sarah had always wanted to visit a house that did. She just hadn't imagined finding one of such incredible size. Why, it had to be at least one hundred yards long, and the width . . . perhaps twenty or thirty? Thinking herself alone and lost in her attempt to calculate an accurate square footage, Sarah instinctively leapt at the sound of a very loud grunt, startled by it to such a degree that she let go of Snowball, who tumbled to the ground and, as one might expect from a curious hamster, chose not to sit and wait for Sarah to pick him up again but raced off along the path as fast as his tiny legs could carry him. Forgetting the sound she'd just heard, Sarah hurried after him, desperate to catch him before she lost him forever in the small jungle.

"Snowball?" Sarah hissed, as if the creature would actually come walking back to her when summoned. Pushing past some wide leaves, she finally spotted the little fellow, sitting quite happily on the edge of the pathway. Heart pounding in her chest, Sarah dropped to a crouch and eased her way forward, desperate to prevent him from leaping off between the bushes. Good heavens, she'd never find him then! With measured breaths, Sarah moved with the silence of a wraith—at least to her own way of thinking— and as tedious and strenuous as the endeavor proved, she knew she had to avoid startling Snowball at all cost. Eventually, she reached him, her hand moving toward him, ready to snatch him up, just as another grunt shook the air.

Snowball darted off beneath a fern, and Sarah swore with vigor. Hands clenched into two tight fists, she prepared to rise and give whatever creature it was that had produced the sound a proper set down, when a voice spoke, saying, "Aren't you a bit too old to be crawling about on the floor?"

Sarah froze. If the grunt had belonged to a pig, she might have understood. A pig would not have been clever enough to know what Sarah was trying to accomplish, but then again, a pig would not have been roaming around a conservatory either. Her irritation grew. Of course her efforts had failed because of a man. Brilliant!

Expelling a deep breath, she unclenched her fists, closed her eyes for a brief second and rose, determined to avoid a quarrel with the foolish individual behind her. She prayed that somehow she'd find the ability to be polite in spite of her annoyance. "Sir," she started to say as she turned toward the dunce, "I will have you know that I . . ." Her words trailed off as he came into view.

Heaven above if the addlepated dunderhead had not been graced with looks that could easily make a roomful of women swoon. Sarah steeled herself. She would not allow his handsome face to affect her. "Where else should I be, all things considered?"

"On your feet?" he suggested, as if he were speaking to a child.

Sarah glared at him. "Obviously," she said. "Why on earth didn't I think of that?"

Idiot.

The man's eyes widened as he leaned back a notch, and Sarah realized to her horror that she'd spoken the insult out loud.

Chapter 2

Christopher trained his features. Surely the young lady—if such a term could even be used to describe a woman who scrambled about on the floor—had not just called him an idiot. The look of horror upon her face confirmed that indeed she had, and as he stood there staring back at her, wondering what she would say next, Christopher considered taking the gentlemanly approach and saying something to save her from further embarrassment. He quickly dispelled the notion. "Do your parents approve of your poor manners?"

"*My* poor manners?" Her eyes glinted. "I . . . I . . . I will have you know—"

"Yes, so you said before, and as a result, my eagerness to discover what it is you wish for me to know is increasing by the second." Then, to prove himself completely unsympathetic, he followed the statement by saying, "By the way, there's dirt along your hemline."

She dropped her gaze, shifted a little, then let out a sigh. "So there is," she said, her tone suggesting that the state of her gown was presently of very little concern to her.

Clearing his throat to fill the silence that followed, Christopher stepped forward, intending to make up for his poor behavior by introducing himself properly. But as he moved toward her, she quickly retreated, the heel of her foot hitting the edge of the path just as a gasp burst from between her rosy lips. One second she was standing upright, and the next she was tumbling backward, arms flailing as she reached for something to grab onto.

He was before her in two long strides, his arm reaching around her back, catching her while her weight carried him forward until he loomed over her, one leg bending at the knee as his booted foot sank into the boxed soil behind her. She sucked in a breath, eyes going wide, and he became instantly aware of their inappropriate closeness.

"What are you doing?" she asked irritably.

"Isn't it obvious? I'm saving you."

"As gallant as that may seem, you wouldn't have had to make the effort if you'd only stayed where you were."

"Are you saying this is my fault?"

"Of course it is. Now if you don't mind, I'd like to return to an upright position." Briefly, Christopher considered dropping her. Thinking better of it, he pulled back instead, bringing them both away from the dirt. He immediately released her, aware that she was looking terribly shocked, perhaps even frightened. "Forgive me," he said as she stepped out of his reach. Bowing, he added, "Viscount Spencer at your service, Lady . . . ?"

"Sarah," she supplied. "Lord Andover's eldest."

"Ah." He studied her a moment, deciding that she must be roughly twenty years of age. That meant she would have made her debut years ago, yet he failed to recall ever meeting her before. How curious, considering that her hair was such a pale shade of blonde it bordered on white and was bound to draw attention. Silence drew out between them, and he became acutely aware of just how inappropriately alone they were. Why the devil hadn't he noticed it sooner? Christ, what a bloody idiot he was for allowing himself to forget how manipulative the fairer sex could be.

He leaned toward her, perversely pleased by the little gasp of distress she exerted, her eyes darting about as if seeking escape. "How did you find me?" he asked. It had to be his mother. Or perhaps one of his sisters? Somehow one of them must have discovered his hiding place and sent Lady Sarah after him.

"Wha-what do you mean?"

"I think you know," he told her gruffly. "You. Me. Alone. All we need now are some witnesses and you can look forward to becoming Viscountess Spencer. But just so you know, I will ruin you before I marry you if that is indeed your game."

She edged away from him, her breaths coming short and fast while her throat worked at getting her words out. "You're mad," she muttered, her hand rising like a shield before her. "Stay back! Don't you dare come any closer."

Studying her, he noted the fear that rose from the depths of her clear blue eyes. Was it genuine? Or just another part of the game she played? Miss Hepplestone had been an exemplary actress, portraying any emotion at will. "You should leave," he muttered, hating the power Miss Hepplestone still held over him after all these years. She'd made it impossible for him to judge people objectively.

"I cannot," Lady Sarah said, not budging an inch in spite of her clear apprehension. She crossed her arms and stared back at him with defiance, eventually saying, "I have to find Snowball first."

Christopher raised an eyebrow. "Snowball?"

"Yes, my lord." When Christopher said nothing further, momentarily distracted by an unexpected curve to her lips, she added, "My pet hamster."

His frown deepened. "Pet hamster?"

Lady Sarah sighed, her posture going from rigid to . . . less rigid. "I am aware that repetition can be useful when acquiring a new skill, my lord, but I fail to understand its purpose at present unless it is to help you with your comprehension?"

Christopher forced his expression to remain still. By deuce if the chit had not just insulted his intelligence. Again. He should be offended, but to his amazement he found her candor oddly refreshing. It was absurd, except that she appeared to be quite serious as she peered back at him with . . . concern? "I suspect you think me obtuse, my lady." She didn't respond in the affirmative, but she didn't deny the claim either. There was something admirable about that. Christopher straightened himself. "I was merely surprised, that is all. A lady with a pet hamster named Snowball is somewhat unusual, wouldn't you agree?"

Her lips parted ever so slightly. For a long moment she remained unmoving, saying nothing, and Christopher wondered briefly if time had perhaps frozen to a halt. "Not to me, it isn't," she finally said.

"No," he agreed as his gaze swept over her. "I don't suppose it is."

Something flashed behind her eyes. Uncertainty perhaps? She sighed again, this time with very clear frustration. Unfolding her arms, she spread them wide, raised her eyebrows and said, "Well? Are you just going to stand there, or will you help me find him? After all, it is your fault he went missing in the first place."

"I don't see how it can possibly be my fault, since I was fast asleep at the time."

"Precisely," she muttered, turning away from him and peering through the greenery.

Apparently, she'd decided that he didn't pose a threat after all, or perhaps finding her blasted hamster was just more important than her own safety. Christopher was damned if he knew. "You're doing it again," he said.

"Doing what?"

Christ, she could be infuriating.

"Speaking in ambiguities. And just so you know, I abhor ambiguities."

"Then let me be clear," Lady Sarah said as she moved along the path, her eyes searching the undergrowth. "When I arrived here, I thought the room was empty. But then there was a sudden grunt, which startled me, causing me to drop Snowball."

"A grunt?"

"Precisely. It was not entirely dissimilar to the sound a pig might make," she explained, "but now that I've discovered you were sleeping in here, I think it's safe to assume you were . . . snoring."

Christopher's lips twitched. "Lady Sarah, did you just compare me to a pig?" He ought to feel affronted. Instead, he found her strangely amusing. *Be careful,* an inner voice warned. He stopped the smile that threatened.

Sarah hesitated, her focus riveted on the undergrowth as she fought the distraction Lord Spencer offered. "I wouldn't dream of it, my lord." She was mortified by each word she'd spoken since making his acquaintance. Really, there was no excuse for it—not even after his unpredictable outburst earlier. To think that he would accuse her of trying to trap him into marriage. What a ridiculous notion. Still, she wasn't fool enough not to recognize a threat when she saw one. Good heavens, he was a handsome devil, with that penetrating gaze of his and that mouth forever promising to smile without actually doing so. It was maddening. *He* was maddening. She had to find Snowball so she could escape.

"I think you did," he said.

Sarah blinked. What was he talking about? Rummaging through her brain, she sought the answer, embarrassed all over again the moment she found it. "To be precise," she said, "I wasn't comparing you to a pig, my lord. I was merely comparing your snore to a pig's grunt. There is a difference."

"I think you just insulted me again," he said, sounding pensive.

Indeed she had, though she was too deep in her own mess by now to right her wrong with a mere apology. Still, she decided to make an attempt at it, since it was clearly the proper thing to do. So she straightened herself and spun toward him, eager to have it over and done with, only to find herself chest to chest with the man. Her breath caught, heat flooding her cheeks as her hands came up of their own volition, grabbing at his shoulders as she tried to steady herself.

He reached around her, holding her still, and she looked up, her eyes meeting his—dark and unyielding. She gasped then, realizing her mistake. They were close—too close—and she was too aware of him, his heat, his strength, his scent. The man was a threat—a danger she had to avoid. Experience screamed for her to beware. She decided to listen. "If you'll please release me," she said, her voice barely more than a whisper. He let her go and she took a step back. "That was terribly careless of me, Lord Spencer. Whatever must you think?"

His mouth was set in a firm line. "That the conservatory appears to be a hazardous place for you, Lady Sarah, considering that I've had to rescue you twice already."

She wanted to look away, to run, hide and retreat. To think that she had silently referred to him as foolish—an addlepated dunderhead—when she herself could hardly be credited with exhibiting much intelligent thought since making his acquaintance. Not that she cared about his opinion. Really, what did it matter if he considered her a clumsy dimwit incapable of keeping her balance? Ignoring the voice that told her it mattered more than she wanted it to, Sarah looked him straight in the eye and said, "Then perhaps you'll be good enough to help me find my hamster so I may leave?" Inhaling deeply, her nose filling with the scent of wet soil, she quietly added, "Please."

"I'd be delighted to," he said, his expression softening. It even looked as though he just might smile this once. Instead he turned away and disappeared around a corner.

Recalling her task, Sarah continued along the path she was on, anxious to find Snowball. What on earth had she been thinking, venturing downstairs on her own in a house she didn't know? And now, here she was, alone with Lord Spencer. It was a situation she of all people should have known to avoid. Really, she was far too curious for her own good—a trait that had led her into trouble on too many occasions.

Hurrying after Lord Spencer, her slippers tapped bluntly against the tiles as she approached the spot where he now stood. "Shh!" He raised his finger to his lips to underscore the need for silence.

Sarah paused, her gaze dropping to the same bit of plant-filled dirt he was looking at. She spotted a streak of fuzzy white fur. Snowball. Holding her breath, Sarah watched as the viscount crouched down slowly, the fabric of his breeches tightening across his thighs as he did so. A shiver spread across Sarah's back. She ought to look away, but it was impossible with her eyes already roaming to the wide sweep of Lord Spencer's shoulders, the tousled coffee-colored hair in need of combing, hands large enough to encompass her own and legs she'd made a stoic attempt to ignore, but couldn't.

And then, like a wolf on the prowl, he lurched forward, hands swooping down on their prey as he tried to grab Snowball. "Damn!" The expletive was swiftly followed by "I beg your pardon, but that's one swift creature you've got there, my lady." Instead of a hamster, Lord Spencer was holding a lump of dirt, which he quickly discarded before shooting to his feet and darting along the path, clearly giving chase.

Sarah rushed after him, almost skidding sideways as the path curved to the right. She nearly collided with Lord Spencer when he came to an abrupt halt. "Blast," he muttered. "I think I lost him."

Sarah studied the ground on both sides of the path, her eyes seeking white amidst the green, or even the slightest movement that would give her a hint of Snowball's presence. "You almost had him before, but then . . ." What was she doing? Was she seriously going to criticize his efforts, when he had agreed to help her?

"Then what?" he asked, hands on hips as he turned a pair of narrowed eyes on her.

"Nothing," Sarah said. Blast her quick tongue. She should learn to keep her thoughts to herself. "Let's keep looking, shall we?"

"Not until you tell me what you were about to say."

Lord, the man was stubborn. "I already told you it was nothing."

He leaned toward her, crowding her with his much larger size. "I think you were about to tell me it's *my* fault your hamster ran off again."

"You obviously frightened him," Sarah said. She was tempted to say, *again* but thought better of it. Already she didn't like the way Lord Spencer was looking at her—as if he was considering marching her back to her parents and asking them to keep her under lock and key.

"As it happens, I am perfectly content with returning to the comfortable chair I was occupying before you woke me," he said as he started moving away.

Sarah couldn't blame him. In the space of half an hour she'd been less than polite toward him, all because he made her feel uncomfortable. But that wasn't his fault. It was hers. "I'm sorry," she said.

He stopped. Turned. One eyebrow rose slowly as he regarded her with his dark eyes. "I beg your pardon?"

Apparently he wasn't going to make this easy for her. Very well then, she deserved it. Straightening her back, she forced herself to remain unaffected by his handsomeness, focusing on a spot beyond his left shoulder. "You were just trying to help, my lord. It was unfair of me to blame you for your lack of success." Her eyes shot to his face. Oh dear. He was going to think she was mocking him now.

The corner of his mouth twitched. "Apology accepted," he said, "even though I suspect it sounded better in your head than it did once you spoke it out loud."

"Quite." Sarah dropped her gaze to the floor, hating how stupid he made her feel—especially since she'd always prided herself on her smart rejoinders. She caught a flickering movement out of the corner of her eye. There, peeking between some fern leaves, nose twitching as he scouted the area, was Snowball.

"Don't move," she whispered. Cautiously, she then eased her hand forward, hoping to coax her little pet from his hiding place. To her frustration, he started backing away from her, forcing her to lean forward even further, until, sensing she would lose her balance, she brought down a hand to steady herself, her fingers pressing through wet soil just as a fern leaf brushed against her cheek.

Patience fled and so did Snowball as soon as Sarah attempted to snatch him. A moment later, she heard Lord Spencer muttering something from behind her. It was then that she became acutely aware of her unladylike position. Fighting the wave of embarrassment that threatened to overwhelm her, she applied her driest tone and said, "Perhaps when you have finished judging me (she could just imagine him rolling his eyes), you'll be good enough to help me up?"

A measure of discomfort filled his voice as he said, "Of course. My apologies," and then she felt his hands on both sides of her waist, gripping her firmly as he gently pulled her back to solid ground. It was a quick endeavor really, and quite efficient, since she was now safely out of the dirt. His hands didn't linger upon her either—indeed, there was nothing in the effort that could be construed as inappropriate in any way—and yet, Sarah could still feel the heat of him upon her after he'd let her go. His touch . . . it had somehow curled its way beneath her skin, warming her insides—an odd sensation, considering his ability to vex her. It had to be his handsomeness, she decided. Against her better judgment, she looked up, her eyes settling on the soft curve of his mouth—a mouth that threatened to smile, even though it resisted—and she inadvertently wondered what it might be like to place a kiss there.

She jerked away from him. Where on earth had that thought come from? She didn't even like this man! Not particularly.

"Are you all right?" Lord Spencer asked.

"Yes," Sarah replied, hating the high pitch of her voice. "Thank you. I um . . . I think he went that way." With a sniff intended to hide her discomfort, Sarah pushed past Lord Spencer and went after Snowball, pretending all the while that her heart was completely immune to the viscount's presence.

"You must be terrified," Sarah whispered moments later when she discovered Snowball in a gap at the base of a fountain. "Come on," she added, hoping her voice would soothe the anxious creature. How awful it must be for him to be chased through a veritable jungle by two stomping giants. Sticking her fingers inside the hole, Sarah coaxed him out toward her, murmuring words of reassurance until she finally managed to scoop him up in both hands while gently stroking his head with her thumb. "Shh . . . it's all right. You're safe now." Remembering she was not alone, Sarah turned to Lord Spencer, her eyes meeting his as she smiled and said, "My lord, we've finally got him!"

Lord Spencer tilted his head and peered down at the subject of their discussion. "*We?* To be fair, you're the one who caught him."

Determined to part with Lord Spencer on good terms, Sarah shook her head. "It was a joint effort." She hesitated a moment before reaching her cupped hands toward him. "Would you like to hold him?"

Lord Spencer eyed her offering with clear apprehension. "I don't think . . ." He straightened, his features hardening as he looked in the direction of the door.

Sarah stilled. Voices were approaching.

Clutching Snowball against her chest, Sarah looked to Lord Spencer, who appeared to be equally aware of their problem, his eyes as dark as when he'd accused Sarah of trying to trap him.

His eyebrows drew together. "Hide yourself," he said, his expression both rigid and cold. "I'll divert their attention. You can come out and leave as soon as we're gone." And then he strode away along the path without another word, leaving Sarah behind with an unexpected pain in her chest.

Chapter 3

Two hours later, Sarah was summoned to a small parlor by her father. A footman showed her in, and as she stepped inside, she realized that her father was not alone. He was accompanied by a man who looked to be of similar age to her father, with a figure that showed a great fondness for food.

Caught off guard, Sarah dipped into a curtsy as the door closed behind her.

"My dear," her father said, his voice more loving than it had been these past two years, "I'm so glad you could join us." She rose, straightening her spine. The man with her father . . . it couldn't be . . . *please don't let it be* . . . "Why don't you have a seat on the sofa beside Mr. Denison so you can become better acquainted?"

Oh dear God, it was.

The man she was meant to marry was as old as her father, making him a good thirty years her senior. His head was balding too, whatever hair that remained there as gray as ash from a burned-out fire. Meeting his gaze, she was instantly struck by the look of pleasure shining in his eyes. She forced a smile, even as her stomach contracted at the thought of what was in store for her.

"I must say I am delighted to finally meet you," Mr. Denison said as she stepped toward the vacant spot on the sofa.

"Likewise," she said as he bowed toward her. She cast a hesitant look in her father's direction. Noting the beaming smile upon his face, she knew it would not go well for her if she complained about this match. Reluctantly, she took her seat, with Mr. Denison beside her.

"I understand from your father that your journey to Thorncliff went well?" Mr. Denison inquired.

Of course her father would not have mentioned the strained atmosphere that had prevailed inside the carriage. "It did."

There was a brief silence, broken by her father's cough. Sarah glanced toward him. He nodded in Mr. Denison's direction. "And you, sir?" Sarah asked Mr. Denison, taking the cue her father had given. "Did your journey pass without incident?" Lord, this was mundane conversation! If only she could be quarreling with Lord Spencer instead.

"My daughters found it rather tedious, but I didn't mind it so much. In fact, I could gaze upon the English countryside all day without tiring of it."

"You . . . you have daughters?" Of course he was bound to have children at his age if he had been married before, which meant he must be a widower.

"Victoria is two and twenty, and Diana will be three and twenty next month. It is my hope that they will be able to make good matches for themselves during our stay here. Since it is my wish—my fondest wish, I might add—that you and I will . . . become better acquainted over the next few weeks, I was hoping you might be willing to help them. They're wonderful girls, both of them. I'm sure you'll find . . ."

Mr. Denison's voice faded into the background until Sarah was oblivious to what he was saying. She could scarcely breathe, her stomach bottoming out as reality hit her: marriage to an aging man she did not know and being stepmother to women who were older than she was. It was unthinkable, yet it seemed that this would be her lot—the price she must pay for her transgression.

" . . . and you are far more beautiful than I had ever imagined," Mr. Denison continued. "To think that I have been given the chance to court you is indeed an honor. Your father had so many positive things to say about you in his letter, and I've already discovered that we have something in common—a fondness for the outdoors!"

Didn't most people enjoy a bit of fresh air and sunshine? It was hardly enough basis for marriage. Sarah's hand curled around the fabric of her gown. Perhaps . . . She glanced at her father, aware that she was about to risk his wrath. "Mr. Denison, has Papa also told you of my scandalous behavior?"

Mr. Denison coughed. "Well . . . he . . . er—"

"I have informed Mr. Denison that you are no longer chaste. He has kindly agreed to accept. Is that not so, sir?"

"Oh, indeed it is, my lord." Mr. Denison's mouth drew into a wide smile. "In fact, I suspect I'll find Lady Sarah's willful nature most agreeable."

For once, Sarah's father looked just as disgusted as Sarah felt. Unlike her, however, he quickly recovered. "Two weeks, Mr. Denison. Will that be enough time for your courtship?"

Sarah stared. It was as if she wasn't even in the room.

"Certainly, my lord. It's more than sufficient," Mr.

Denison said. His laughing eyes looked Sarah up and down.

"Good," Lord Andover clipped. "The sooner we plan this wedding, the better."

"I couldn't agree more," Mr. Denison said. He edged closer to Sarah. "What say you, my dear?"

Nooooo!!!

Realizing that her hands were trembling, Sarah closed her eyes and prayed for strength. "Perfect," she managed, even as her mind began contemplating a speedy escape. Portsmouth wasn't far. Maybe she could board a ship bound for America. If she could find the money to sponsor such a journey.

"Well then," Mr. Denison said, "perhaps you'd like to join me for a stroll in the garden tomorrow. I've been told there's an antique sundial—should prove interesting."

"I'm sure it will," Sarah said politely. Apparently she would not have to plan an escape after all, since she was clearly destined to perish from boredom.

Once again Mr. Denison beamed, offering Sarah a direct view of his teeth. Each was crooked, and one was even missing. She tried not to wince at the thought of eventually having to kiss him. Ga!

Mr. Denison rose. "If you'll excuse me, I'd like to rest before dinner this evening. Thank you for your time, Lord Andover. Lady Sarah, I'll look forward to seeing you later."

Sarah nodded, still struggling to comprehend what had just transpired—that her future had been determined by men and that it didn't look the least bit bright. She'd always imagined she'd marry for love. *Love.* How easy it was to conjure an empty reflection of that emotion with pretty words. Words she'd fallen prey to once with embarrassing ease. No, she would not marry for love. She would marry because her parents were desperate to be rid of her, which, to be fair, was not such an uncommon reason.

Schooling her emotions, Sarah rose, as did her father. "I ought to go and pick out a gown for dinner this evening," she said, grateful that her voice did not reflect her inner turmoil. "I'll want to look my best for Mr. Denison."

"Don't squander this opportunity," her father said, his face drawn in grim lines. "You have your sisters to consider. As soon as you are settled, they'll be less likely to have their reputations ruined by association, if word were to get out."

"It won't," Sarah said. It hadn't yet.

"Still, you'll be your husband's responsibility, and as a married woman living in Yorkshire—"

"I'm going to Yorkshire? For good?" She might as well be going to the moon.

"It's where Mr. Denison has his home—a horse farm with spectacular Thoroughbreds, including ten prime mares, in case you're wondering. Once we breed them with that stallion I bought in Germany last year, we'll produce some fine racers."

"A horse farm," Sarah echoed, feeling weak. Of course her father would leap at the opportunity to form an alliance with a fellow horse enthusiast. Especially if there was money in it, which there would be, considering the best horses sold for somewhere in the vicinity of one thousand pounds, perhaps more.

"And if I don't comply?"

Heavy creases formed upon her father's brow. "We've been over this a dozen times before, Sarah. You were born to procure land, status and opportunity through marriage. Squandering your chance to do your duty . . ." He took a breath, visibly agitated as he stared at her without compassion. "I have done the best I can, under the circumstances, providing a match for you that will benefit this family greatly."

"By sending me off to Yorkshire to live on a horse farm."

"If it's any consolation, I wish I could go in your stead."

"And marry Mr. Denison? I'm sure you'd make a delightful couple. I certainly woul—"

"Watch your tongue, Sarah!" Her father's voice ricocheted off the walls. He paused and took a fortifying breath before continuing. "The important thing is that nobody there will care one way or another about your past—especially not when you're a married woman."

"I'll be out of the way," Sarah murmured. *While you and Mr. Denison will be filling your coffers.*

"It's for the best," her father said, upon which he left the room.

"**Y**ou made the right choice, selecting the blue gown this evening," Lady Andover said as she and Sarah followed the rest of the family down the stairs to supper that evening. "No doubt Mr. Denison will find you pleasing."

"You speak as though I deliberately aim for him to do so," Sarah muttered.

"You continue to try my patience," Lady Andover said. "Your papa and I have been exceedingly tolerant. We have even found a man who is willing to marry you when most would have shuddered at the thought of accepting another's castoff. But rather than show us some gratitude, you treat us with contempt."

"*I* treat *you* with contempt, Mama?" Sarah could scarcely believe the accusation. "You wouldn't say so if you were in my shoes."

"I hope you're not implying that we have been unjust with you or that we've treated you any differently than you might have expected under the circumstances. There are many parents who would have disowned their daughter for what you've done, yet you continuously act as though all of this is our fault, when you have only yourself to blame."

There was a measure of truth to that which Sarah could not deny.

"I doubt I'm likely to forget it, Mama," Sarah said, "but if you wish to maintain some semblance of normalcy and prevent unnecessary gossip, I would suggest we try to pretend I've done nothing wrong. To that end, it wouldn't hurt if you smiled at me on occasion."

Halting, Lady Andover stared at her stepdaughter, her lips stretching into a tight smile. "Will this do?"

Sarah's heart crumpled, but she held her head high as she said, "It's fortunate you're not an actress, since you'd hardly have much success on the stage with such a meagre effort."

"Pretending one's daughter is not a disappointment is no easy task, Sarah, but I do what I must, and so will your Papa. All I ask is for you to follow suit so we can put this mess behind us."

And with that final bite, Lady Andover sailed after her husband and her other, untarnished, daughters, entering the green salon with them while Sarah trailed behind. As much as it hurt, she knew she only had herself to blame. She also knew she had a duty to fix her mistake as best she could for the sake of her sisters' reputations.

Straightening her spine, Sarah followed her family, aware that her arrival had not gone unnoticed. She was being watched by several prominent guests, their curiosity undoubtedly enormous due to Sarah's absence from Society for so long.

Quickening her pace, she hurried past the Duchess of Pinehurst, a dragon outfitted with a pair of quizzing glasses, her attention fixed directly on Sarah. Her Grace was notorious for hunting down brides for her grandsons—of which she had several. Explaining to her that she would rather marry Mr. Denison was not a conversation Sarah wished to endure.

Catching her breath, she looked about, seeking her soon-to-be fiancé, relief flooding her when she failed to find him. Glancing at her parents and younger sisters, she decided to avoid that quarter, since they were now busily conversing with the Earl and Countess of Wilmington. Panic set in at the thought of being questioned by *that* inquisitive couple, so Sarah continued past them, hoping she would soon discover a small nook where she could go unnoticed until they were all called into the dining room.

To her relief, she discovered an alcove with a low bench and a window looking out on the garden. Heading straight for it, she almost reached it when a young lady stepped into her path and said, "I believe I've yet to make your acquaintance."

Sarah froze, her eyes shifting between the dark-haired woman and the window seat that beckoned. "I . . . er . . ."

"Allow me to introduce myself," the lady said with an air of confidence that was difficult not to admire. "I'm Fiona Heartly—the Earl and Countess of Oakland's youngest. And you are?" Lady Fiona tilted her head as she peered up at Sarah with great interest.

There was no getting around it without being rude. Sarah was going to have to introduce herself to someone for the third time that day, so she forced a smile and said, "Lady Sarah—the Earl and Countess of Andover's eldest."

Lady Fiona frowned. "Are you married?" she asked rather bluntly.

Sarah shook her head, not liking the direction in which this conversation was going. "No," she said, deciding to keep her reply short.

"Perhaps you have a fiancé then?" Lady Fiona inquired.

Heavens, but the woman was being forward! Sarah pressed her lips together and fought the urge to run. "Not really," she said. Technically this was true. Lady Fiona's frown deepened. "Forgive me, but I'm simply trying to place you. I made my debut last Season, but I didn't see you at any of the social gatherings. Had you been there, I would have noticed, since I do have a tendency to be quite observant." She narrowed her gaze, and Sarah's skin began to prick. "You're not old enough to be on the shelf yet, which makes me wonder why we've never met before."

"I made my debut two years ago," Sarah explained, "but then Grandmamma died and I went into mourning, which is why I was absent last Season."

"And this year? I do hope you and your family haven't suffered any more losses."

"I . . . er . . . there was no need for me to go to London this year," Sarah managed, hoping her new companion would accept that without further question.

She didn't of course, her eyebrows rising as she leaned toward Sarah. "No need?" she asked.

And now for the unavoidable truth. "My father found a suitor for me before the Season began."

"Oh." Lady Fiona looked very disappointed, but then her face brightened. "Who is he? What's his name?"

Sarah cringed. "Mr. Denison."

Lady Fiona looked pensive. Eventually she shook her head. "I've never heard of him." She studied Sarah. "Have you met him yet?"

"Just this afternoon," Sarah admitted while she prayed for this conversation to come to a speedy end.

"Well?" Lady Fiona asked. "What's he like?"

"Er . . ."

"Is he handsome?" Lady Fiona asked impatiently. Before Sarah could utter a word, she said, "I can tell by your expression that he's not." She looked at Sarah with pity until Sarah felt like screaming. It was all so unfair!

"He's older," Sarah confided. It was clear that she would not be rid of Lady Fiona or her prying questions anytime soon.

Lady Fiona's eyes narrowed. "How much older?"

"I can't say," Sarah said, for indeed she could not. She could only hazard a guess.

"Well," Lady Fiona said, her expression softening with a smile as she took Sarah by the arm and steered her away from the tempting alcove, "if he doesn't please you, then I'm sure we can find someone else who does."

"Wh-what?" Whatever Lady Fiona was getting at, Sarah didn't like it. "My parents insist on Mr. Denison," she said, hoping to dissuade the woman from whatever matchmaking scheme she was contemplating.

Lady Fiona glanced at her with disbelief. "Why?"

"Well . . . I . . . that is . . ." How on earth was she going to explain their reasoning?

"I'm sure they believe they've found a good husband for you," Lady Fiona said as she pulled Sarah along. "But parents' criteria always differ from their daughter's. Considering your lengthy absence from Society, I think you ought to have a look around Thorncliff before making any hasty decisions. There are plenty of eligible gentlemen here. Young and handsome ones even."

"I don't know . . ." Sarah hedged.

Lady Fiona looked at her in dismay. "You cannot mean that you would rather marry an old untitled man you barely know as opposed to a dashing viscount or earl?"

"My parents—"

"Yes, yes. Their opinion on the matter is clear. But what about yours?"

Sarah blinked, and Lady Fiona grinned. "Fear not. We'll find someone better for you than this Mr. Denison fellow, but first I am going to ensure that you make some more friends by introducing you to my family. I have every confidence that you'll enjoy spending time with me and my sisters during your stay here."

Sarah groaned. This was going to be a disaster. Arm linked with Sarah's, Lady Fiona guided her toward their shared destination—a group of ladies chatting amicably with an older couple and a gentleman: a man whom Sarah recognized immediately. Lord Spencer.

Heaven help her! Sarah wanted to dig in her heels and claw her way back to safety, but Lady Fiona had a very firm hold on her arm, and before Sarah knew it, she was brought before the rest of the Heartlys and introduced, all the while acutely aware of Lord Spencer's dark gaze boring into her.

"So you see," Lady Fiona said as soon as the

necessary pleasantries had been exchanged, "Lady Sarah is now back in Society." She gave her brother a pointed look that made Sarah's cheeks flame.

"We're absolutely delighted to make your acquaintance," Lady Fiona's mother, Lady Oakland, said. "I'm sure my daughters will enjoy your company immensely, and if there's ever a need of dancing . . . well, Spencer makes an excellent partner. I do hope you'll keep him in mind."

Sarah nodded, because it was the only thing she *could* do while the Heartly daughters smiled with unabashed glee. Lord and Lady Oakland looked equally enthusiastic at the prospect of pairing her off with their son, while Lord Spencer appeared rather acerbic. Hardly surprising, when it was embarrassingly apparent that his entire family was on a matchmaking spree.

Fleetingly, Sarah wondered if it was possible for her to dissolve into the Persian carpet on which she was standing. And to think she'd been concerned about the Duchess of Pinehurst! The Heartlys might not be equipped with quizzing glasses, but it was clear that they were in possession of something far worse—a keen desire to find the viscount a wife.

"Thank you, my lady, but I'm so out of practice that I really don't have any intention of dancing while I'm here. I'd hate to embarrass my partner by making a cake of myself," Sarah said, hoping to discourage Lord Spencer's wrath. After all, the last time she'd seen him, she'd suspected him of suspecting her of entrapment.

"Good evening, Lady Oakland," came a voice from behind Sarah's right shoulder. She winced, recognizing it as her stepmother's. "Lord Oakland," Lady Andover added. "How delightful it is to see you both here, and with your lovely children, no less."

Lady Oakland smiled politely, while Lord Oakland offered a bow. "We thought we'd escape to Thorncliff while our home is being renovated."

"A wonderful retreat, don't you agree?" Lady Andover asked.

"Oh, without a doubt," Lord Oakland said.

"I see you've met my eldest daughter," Lady Andover continued, her smile unfaltering as she looked about the group of people gathered before her, "but unfortunately I must steal her away. I hope you don't mind."

"Of course not," Lady Oakland said. To Sarah she added, "It was a pleasure making your acquaintance, Lady Sarah, and since we'll be here the entire summer, I'm sure we'll have another opportunity to talk later."

"Thank you, my lady," Sarah told her politely.

"I'm sure she'll look forward to it," Lady Andover remarked, her smile particularly bright as she pulled Sarah away with her. After a few paces, she whispered, "Don't lose focus, Sarah. It is widely known that Lord and Lady Andover are actively encouraging their son to marry. It would be a travesty if they were to pin their hopes on you. Have a care and stay away from them."

There was no opportunity for Sarah to comment on that remark, since they came within hearing of Mr. Denison and Sarah's father, who were busily conversing with two young ladies of a similar age to Sarah.

"How radiant you look," Mr. Denison said, not bothering to hide his interest while his eyes took her in. Sarah shuddered. "If I may, I'd like to introduce you to my daughters."

Forcing a smile, Sarah greeted Miss Victoria Denison and Miss Diana Denison, noting that they were not the prettiest women in the world. "A pleasure," she said, even though it did not look as though they reciprocated the sentiment. Sarah couldn't blame them.

A gong sounded, announcing that it was time for the guests to move to the dining room. Inside, a table long enough to seat a hundred was dressed in white tablecloths and peach-colored floral arrangements. Discovering there were place cards, Sarah drew a breath. It would take forever for everyone to find their seats.

Following her family, she glanced down at the individual cards, reading the names as she passed and wondering at how many she didn't know. It was shocking to think that a mere two years could result in such ignorance of the British peerage.

"I do hope I'll be seated next to you," Mr. Denison whispered behind her.

She politely nodded, continuing along until her mother found her seat, then her father's, then her sister Juliet's, who'd been placed between her father and a young gentleman no more than seventeen years of age. Alice was seated on the other side of this gentleman and possibly next to his father, while Sarah still hadn't found her spot.

"Dash it all," she heard Mr. Denison say. "I'm here."

"Enjoy your meal," Sarah told him, not waiting for his reply as she crossed to the opposite side of the table. She was free—for now. Finally, she spotted her name, elegantly curling its way along a piece of paper.

"Allow me to assist."

There was no need for Sarah to look at the man

who'd just spoken in order to recognize that voice: rich and warm, with a hint of tension. Darting a look in her stepmother's direction, Sarah was met with a stern look of disapproval, as if it was somehow Sarah's fault that she'd been seated next to Lord Spencer. "Thank you," she said, "but I can manage."

"I insist," he muttered, his hands already pulling her chair away from the table so she could take her seat.

The words brushed against the nape of her neck, producing a shiver. Stiffening, Sarah swallowed as she fought to maintain her composure. She would resist him.

"Thank you," she said as she claimed her seat and waited for him to sit down next to her, his leg briefly brushing hers as he did so. The touch sent a tremor racing along her every nerve. "I was actually hoping for a chance to speak with you," she confessed, pleased that her voice sounded normal.

"Oh?"

"After our encounter earlier," she whispered while the gentleman to the other side of her conversed with the lady to his right, "I just . . . well, I wanted to apologize for creating a situation that could have been devastating to us both. It wasn't intentional. That is to say, I'm not trying to trap you."

"No?"

Allowing herself to look his way, Sarah saw that his face was turned toward her and that he was studying her closely.

"Truly, you have no cause for alarm," she assured him, "though I realize it may not appear that way after your mother's recent effort to pair us off and Lady Fiona's blatant insinuation, but I promise you that neither was speaking on my behalf."

"And why should I believe you?" he asked, his eyes searching her for she knew not what. "I know nothing about you other than that you have a peculiar fondness for rodents."

"You say that as if it's a bad thing."

"Wouldn't you rather have a puppy or a kitten?"

Sarah shook her head. "I'm not allowed any pets. My stepmother's allergic."

Understanding dawned in his eyes. "You sneaky little minx," he muttered.

Sarah shrugged. "Snowball doesn't bother anyone as long as I keep him in my room. Besides, he makes me happy."

Lord Spencer snorted. "Happiness is fleeting and highly overrated."

Sarah stared at him while a footman leaned over, filling her glass with wine. "I don't understand you, my lord. You're both young and handsome." When he raised an eyebrow, she said, "There's little point in denying the obvious. You're also in possession of a title—one that's probably attached to a nice piece of property, so unless you've gambled away your fortune, you should be quite well off."

"An astute observation for a woman who claims to have no interest in me."

"My lord, I'm beginning to think you're too arrogant for your own good." She winced. "Forgive me. I should not have said that. I merely meant to point out that you have little to complain about, especially when you also have a large family that clearly cares about you."

"Oh?"

"They wouldn't be so concerned with helping you pick a bride otherwise. I trust you are free to pick any lady of your choosing as long as she is agreeable and accepts your offer?"

"Yes," he murmured, staring at the tablecloth. "Except I have no intention to marry."

"Not ever? Surely you must do so eventually, considering your position."

"If and when I do shall be my own affair, Lady Sarah, nobody else's."

She bit her lip, suppressing the urge to hit him. A punch straight to the shoulder—that ought to convey her annoyance with him. "Your freedom to choose is enviable, my lord, and yet you bemoan it when you should consider yourself lucky instead. Not everyone has your advantage."

Lord Spencer nodded. "True. But did you ever consider that being one of the most eligible bachelors in England can come with its own set of problems? People aren't always what they seem, Lady Sarah. Most will pretend to be something they're not in order to charm you."

"So you're the suspicious sort?"

"I prefer to think of myself as cautious."

"Or perhaps you're just afraid of letting down your guard."

His features tightened, his eyes turning to flint, until Sarah felt like squirming. She should not have said that either.

"Lady Sarah," he spoke between clenched teeth, "are you deliberately trying to provoke me?"

Determined not to let her discomfort show, Sarah said, "Not at all, my lord. I was merely making an observation. Unfortunately I have a tendency to speak before I think."

The corner of his mouth twitched. She detected the hint of a smile. Her muscles relaxed.

"So I've noticed," he said.

Reaching for her glass, Sarah took a sip of her

wine. She shouldn't be encouraging this conversation. In fact, she ought to be closing herself off from any possible connection with him, but there was something about him—something she wasn't quite able to resist. "I've never been known for my good judgment," she admitted. Not the sort of thing you told a man you might be interested in. But she wasn't interested in him of course. She couldn't be. She was going to marry Mr. Denison.

Lord Spencer's expression brightened, though he still refused to allow an actual smile. "I'm beginning to suspect that today was not the first time you found yourself crawling around on the floor."

"A useful exercise when you're looking for something you've dropped."

"I agree."

"You do?"

"Does that surprise you?" He took a sip of his wine.

Was he joking?

"Of course!"

He chuckled, a rich rumble that captured her awareness. "Just because I disagree with your execution doesn't mean I necessarily disagree with the practicality of it." He slanted a look in her direction. "Your maid will have some difficult dirt stains to deal with."

Sarah scrunched her nose. "I confess I wasn't thinking of her." She should have done so though—she should have crouched rather than knelt. Instead, she'd given Hester more work. Guilt took hold of her conscience.

A lull arose in the conversation as footmen arrived with the first course—plates of salmon mousse garnished with dill and caviar, which were placed before each guest. "It appears our hostess has excellent taste in food," Sarah said, hoping to change the subject. Her gaze drifted toward the elderly woman who sat at the head of the table, her gloved hands bedecked by jewel-encrusted bracelets. Sarah had never seen anyone quite like her, for she appeared as though from a different age, her hair set in a style belonging to the previous century. It was most unusual, though in a fascinating sort of way. It made Sarah look forward to making the lady's acquaintance.

"Lady Duncaster is meticulous when it comes to entertaining—especially since everyone here has paid a hefty price in order to attend. I'm sure she wishes to ensure we're all afforded an experience that will live long in our memories," Lord Spencer said, drawing Sarah's attention back to him.

"I find it surprising that a lady of her stature would open her home like this to strangers—and accept payment for it, no less." Scooping a bit of mousse onto her spoon, Sarah took a bite, almost sagging at the exquisite taste and creamy smoothness.

"From what I gather, her ladyship has always had an eccentric streak, with more of a nonchalant attitude as far as Society is concerned." Lord Spencer took a bite of his food, pausing momentarily before adding, "Running a place like this is costly. With no children or grandchildren, I daresay it must be terribly lonely as well. There's no doubt in my mind that turning Thorncliff into a guesthouse is serving more than one purpose, and if you ask me, I admire her all the more for not minding if the *ton* approves of her choice or not."

Sarah nodded her agreement. She'd heard of cases where peers had fallen into terrible debt. God forbid if an earl should make a living at anything other than running his estate or gambling. The fact that it was more acceptable for a peer to increase his wealth at the cost of another's misfortune rather than do an honest day's work went beyond Sarah's level of comprehension, but then again, there was very little about the *ton* that made sense to her. "I must admit that Thorncliff is more extravagant than any other place I've ever visited," she said. "From what I've seen since my arrival earlier today, it will take the duration of my stay to explore it." She took another bite of her food. Heavens, this tasted divine.

"It was founded during the twelfth century by a knight named William Holden. After Holden's service in the Crusades, King Richard the First rewarded him with land, and William began work on what would eventually become Thorncliff Manor," Lord Spencer told her. "Since then, each generation has expanded on it, molding it into the estate it is today."

Sarah couldn't help but be impressed. "How do you know all of this?"

Lord Spencer shrugged. "I have a particular interest in the history of English castles. They intrigue me."

Their plates were whisked away and a new course was set before them; glazed duck accompanied by an arrangement of fruits and vegetables.

"Has that always been the case?" Sarah asked.

Lord Spencer stilled. "Why do you ask?"

The question surprised her. "Because I'm interested."

He looked at her for a moment as if deciding whether or not to believe her. Absurd. Why on earth would she lie about something like that?

Picking up his cutlery, he went to work on his duck. "When I was ten, my family and I visited Brighton. On our way back to London, we passed

Bodiam Castle. It was as if it had been conjured from my imagination—the perfect setting for all the stories I'd read about knights. As soon as I returned home I made a sketch of it, and then a model—the first of many."

"And did you ever manage to visit Bodiam Castle properly so you could explore it?" She took a bite of her food, her eyes straying across the table as she did so. Mr. Denison was watching her with a frown. So was her stepmother, she noted. Sarah chose to ignore both of them in favor of enjoying her evening. She glanced at Lord Spencer. Who would have thought that she would find him entertaining, considering his penchant for cutting remarks and quelling frowns? He was much too serious.

"Unfortunately, I did."

"Unfortunately?"

His eyes seemed to darken. "It was a great disappointment, as is often the case when one's expectations have risen to unreasonable heights."

"I see," Sarah said, for it was the only response she could think to make. Nobody was this caustic by nature. Something must have happened to him to make him so cynical. Sarah couldn't stop herself from wondering what it might have been. "Will you be staying long at Thorncliff?" she found herself asking, even though she knew she shouldn't. She'd met him in the conservatory and had been placed beside him during dinner. It had to stop there.

"The entire summer," he said. "And you?"

"Until my engagement is announced, I'd imagine." She would not allow him to think she had any interest in him, when she didn't. No matter how handsome he might be. She'd known handsome once, and the encounter had ruined her.

"Ah." He raised an eyebrow. "Then you really aren't trying to trap me?"

"You still suspect I might be?" She narrowed her gaze on him. "Please don't tell me you're one of those men who thinks himself so desirable that a woman would find it near impossible to resist his charms. That she would go to great lengths in order to get herself married to him against his own will."

He reached for his wine. "Of course not."

She continued to stare at him while he placed the glass to his lips and drank. "Good Lord," she uttered. "You are!"

"And what if I am?" he said, leaning closer so only she could hear. "Is it so difficult for you to imagine that I am coveted? That young ladies aspire to marry me if for no other reason than to please their over-eager mamas?"

"Your arrogance is unbecoming," she said, even though she knew he spoke the truth. A man with his features and in possession of both title and wealth would never be unpopular. Quite the opposite.

"A matter of opinion," he stated. There was a pause, and then, "Allow me to ask you this: if I had compared your eyes to summer skies when first we met, would you have been flattered? Or would you have wondered about my motives?"

Sarah forced herself to breathe, no matter how difficult the effort seemed. A coincidence. That was all it was. Lord Spencer couldn't possibly know that those exact words, among many others, had compelled her to toss away her innocence two years earlier. She told him the truth when she answered. "I would have thought you the worst possible scoundrel."

"And so you should have if I had indeed said such a thing. Not doing so would be extremely naïve."

Heat rose to her cheeks as she averted her gaze, concentrating on the plate of fruit that had been placed before her. Continuing her conversation with Lord Spencer would prove to be not only pointless but also painful. He was unmovable in his convictions as well as a constant reminder of how utterly stupid she'd once been. But she'd been given a chance to put all of that behind her. And so she would, with Mr. Denison by her side. In exchange, she would trade in all the silly dreams she'd ever had of marrying for love.

Chapter 4

He'd upset Lady Sarah, Christopher realized as the meal drew to an end, but as usual, he'd been unable to halt the bitter words from escaping his mouth, for they reflected the way he felt—a wariness of any young lady who showed an interest in him.

Then again, it had been five years since Miss Hepplestone had disappeared from his life forever. How much longer was he going to put off doing his duty because of the apprehension she'd instilled in him? Forever seemed like a feasible time frame.

Rising, he offered Lady Sarah his hand, assisting her until they stood across from each other. "It was a pleasure," he said politely. His mother had made a great effort turning him into a gentleman. It was about time he started acting like one. "Perhaps I'll see you again soon."

"Perhaps," she said, not meeting his gaze, though she did manage a weak smile as she took her leave of him. And then she was gone, leaving Christopher in the company of the other gentlemen with whom he was meant to enjoy the obligatory after-dinner drink. Crossing to where his father was sitting, Christopher took the vacant seat beside him and attempted to concentrate on the conversation he was having with some of his acquaintances, Mr. Hewitt and the Duke of Pinehurst, about horses. "I've an urge to buy myself a new stallion," Lord Oakland was saying, "and since my wife's birthday is approaching, I'm considering getting her a new mare as well. Don't suppose you'd happen to know of anyone who's selling prime stock at the moment?"

"I'd try Mr. Frick if I were you," Mr. Hewitt said. "He's quite the expert on horses—always has a couple of fine ones up for auction at Tattersalls. Few years back, he began crossbreeding his best Thoroughbred with an Arabian he acquired on the Continent, producing spectacular foals—expensive, mind you, but well worth it if you're looking to please your wife."

"I remember when the two of you became affianced," the Duke of Pinehurst said, changing the subject. He was a stout-looking fellow with more girth than height to his aging figure. He pointed a finger at Christopher. "And I remember when you were born, lad." He sighed. "Seems like only yesterday."

Taking the occasional sip from the glass of claret before him, Christopher listened quietly as the older men in his company began reminiscing about the past. He was only too aware of how soon he was likely to find himself in their shoes. If the speed with which the first thirty years of his life had passed him by was any indication, he'd be a grandfather before he had time to blink. It was frightening, and quickly led to a mood he didn't much care for. Devil take it, he really ought to set his mind to finding a wife.

White-blonde hair and clear blue eyes filled his mind's eye as he pondered Lady Sarah. What was he thinking? He knew little about her—had only just met her—yet she was the first who came to mind as he contemplated his future. Perhaps because he secretly enjoyed the way she scrunched her nose when he annoyed her. Or because of how blunt she'd been with him during dinner. Nobody, not even his sisters, had dared accuse him of being afraid. Not that it mattered. Lady Sarah had already set her sights on someone else and would soon be announcing her engagement.

He was still wondering who the lucky fellow might be when his father rose from his seat along with the other gentlemen, their conversation apparently at an end. "Shall we go and join the ladies?" his father asked him, "or would you prefer a game of cards?"

Getting to his feet, Christopher rose to his full height—an inch above his father. "A game of whist would be splendid." Anything to take his mind off his duty.

By eleven o'clock, Christopher and his father had won most of the rounds. "Gentlemen, I think I'm going to retire," Christopher said, downing the last of his brandy.

"Already?" Mr. Hewitt asked. "How about one last round?"

"You'll have to find another partner," Pinehurst told Hewitt. "I've been ready for bed myself this past hour."

"It's been a pleasure," Christopher said, rising.

With a nod, Christopher's father wished him a good night, as did Hewitt and Pinehurst. Hewitt did not look pleased, probably because he'd hoped his luck would change and that he and Pinehurst would win another round before closing the game. It wasn't likely to happen unless Christopher and his father deliberately allowed it.

Exiting the room, Christopher turned right, in a direction that would lead him toward the stairs. It was an exceedingly long hallway with a series of nooks set into the walls, where vases filled with bursts of lilacs had been placed to their best advantage. The distance between doorways leading into different rooms was at least twenty paces, occasionally twice that, and as he passed each one, he glanced inside, marveling at the vast variety of design between them. He was just about to pass the last room on his right when his sister Fiona stepped out, blocking his path. "We need to talk," she said as she reached for his hand and began dragging him back inside the room with her.

What the devil?

"Have you been lying in wait for me?" he asked. "How on earth did you even know I'd be coming this way?"

"I knew you'd eventually need to go upstairs, and I didn't want to miss you once you did. *We* didn't want to miss you."

Christopher froze. *We?* That's when it occurred to him that the room Fiona had led him into was filled with not only his remaining sisters but with his mother as well. *Damnation!* He turned for the door, determined to make his escape while he could, only to find that Fiona had closed it, locked it, and removed the key during the momentary state of bewilderment he'd endured upon seeing all those familiar faces staring back at him. It was a trap, and he could see no decent way out of it.

"I apologize," his mother said as she patted the seat next to her, "but we knew you'd find a way to avoid us if you suspected us of wanting to speak with you."

"And why do you suppose that is?" he asked as he

strode across to the vacant spot the settee offered and lowered himself onto it. "Surely not because the only subject you wish to discuss with me these days is the acquisition of a wife."

"If you would only make an effort to speak with the young ladies you meet, I'd at least be able to relax in the assurance that you would eventually warm to one of them, but how are you to find a bride for yourself when you insist on avoiding them all?" Lady Oakland asked.

"I did not avoid Lady Sarah during supper, Mama," Christopher said defensively.

Belatedly, he realized his mistake as a hush filled the room and his mother smiled serenely. "Indeed, you spoke to her much longer than I've seen you speak to any other young lady in recent memory. You didn't ignore her, Kip."

True. Lady Sarah was not the sort of lady one ignored.

"And from my own conversation with her," Fiona added, "I found her delightful company. She's well-spoken and pretty, not to mention that there's a gentility about her that's much to be admired."

She's also in dire need of kissing.

Christopher blinked. When the hell had his thoughts taken on a life of their own? He clenched his jaw. "I will not allow any of you to involve yourselves in my private affairs," he said. "I thought I made that perfectly clear during our ride here." Glaring at Laura, Rachel and Fiona in turn, he was only marginally satisfied to see them avoid his gaze. Chloe hadn't been present during that conversation, so he addressed her next, saying, "You, of all people, ought to understand my reluctance to marry."

"Certainly I do," Chloe said. "I know what it is

to lose faith in someone you love. But you are Papa's heir, Kip. You may not want the responsibility that's been placed upon your shoulders, but it's yours nonetheless. Besides, there's every possibility that you'll make a wonderful match and that you'll be happy."

"I doubt it," Christopher muttered, unwilling to fuel their enthusiasm in any way.

"Just so you know, this wasn't my idea," Rachel mumbled.

"Thank you, Rachel," Christopher said. "I'm glad to see that at least one of you has refrained from ignoring my wishes."

"Oh do be sensible," Laura said. "Lady Sarah is very pleasant."

Clearly his sisters had not met the same woman Christopher had encountered in the conservatory or at the dinner table, because *that* Lady Sarah had not been genteel or pleasant when she'd accused him of being an idiot or of being too arrogant for his own good. He allowed an inward smile at the recollection.

"She's lovely," Emily continued, "and not at all like that horrid Miss—"

"Hush!" Lady Oakland narrowed her eyes on her daughter while Christopher gripped the armrest next to him. "We will not speak of that woman ever again. Is that clear?" Dark ringlets bobbed in accordance with Lady Oakland's wishes while all her daughters nodded agreement. Lady Oakland relaxed her posture. "Good." She turned to look at Christopher. "From where I was sitting, it looked as though Lady Sarah was pleased with your company this evening. She smiled at you a great deal even though you insisted on treating her to your stone face."

"My what?" Christopher asked.

"That incessant scowl of yours," his mother explained. "I'm surprised flowers don't wither and die in your presence."

He shook his head. "Really, Mama, I think you exaggerate." But he knew she was right. Smiles were inviting, and he had no wish to invite anyone to do or think or say anything. Regardless, Lady Sarah had favored him with her smile, and she'd been radiant.

"Do I?" his mother asked. Immediately Christopher's sisters shook their heads. They weren't blind.

"Lady Sarah is a proper young lady of good breeding, Kip," his mother went on. "We know she comes from a very good family, and although you were absent when she made her debut, I had the good fortune of attending a dinner at which she was asked to play the pianoforte—she's very accomplished."

Christopher suppressed a groan. This was getting out of hand. "I think you're exaggerating her interest in me. Besides," he added, "she's getting engaged to someone else."

The sooner his sisters and mother left the subject alone, the sooner he could continue upstairs to bed. He was beginning to acquire a headache.

"To whom?" Rachel asked.

Christopher dealt her a deadly look, which had seemingly little effect on her. "What does it matter? The point is that there is no point to this conversation, since Lady Sarah is already spoken for."

"By Mr. Denison," Fiona supplied. When everyone turned to her for an explanation, she shrugged her shoulders. "A minor detail, considering she doesn't wish to marry him."

"And you deduced this how?" Christopher bit out.

Unfazed by his tone of annoyance, Fiona said, "It was clear in the way she spoke of him."

Closing his eyes, Christopher fought for patience.

"Please tell me you didn't question a woman you'd only just met about her feelings for the man she intends to marry."

"Of course I did," Fiona replied. "How else was I to discover if she was worthy of your considerations?"

Christopher groaned. Opening his eyes, he looked at each of them in turn. "Have you completely lost your minds? Do you even hear what you are saying?"

"I believe we're suggesting that you should save Lady Sarah from her undesirable suitor and—"

"Enough," Christopher clipped, cutting off Laura. "Your romantic notions are captivating too much of your time if you imagine there's any chance of such a scenario taking place. It's completely unrealistic and best suited to one of your novels."

"That was rather harsh," his mother said in that tone of hers that made him feel so very small.

He felt as though he'd just kicked a puppy, and by the pained expression on Laura's face, he realized he might as well have. "I'm sorry," he said. "You know I think you're extremely talented, but this . . . it's all too much."

Laura nodded. "I'm sorry too, Kip. I just want for you to find that special someone who will make you happy. We all do."

"I know you do," he said, even though he knew this would never happen. His heart had grown cold after Miss Hepplestone's machinations. A love match had become an impossibility.

"And I think Lady Sarah is our best bet," Lady Fiona said, stubborn as always. "Don't think we didn't notice that you *almost* smiled while you were talking to her."

Of course his sisters had noticed that minor slip in his composure.

"Or that she looked slightly flustered when she was first introduced to all of us," Chloe said. "Especially when she looked at you, Kip."

"I'm sure she was just uncomfortable with being dragged before a group of people she didn't know, who, if I may remind you, practically insisted she be paired off with me in some capacity or other," Christopher said. "What on earth were you thinking?"

"That she was glancing at you a great deal during that particular conversation," Emily said. She frowned. "Are you sure you never met her before this evening? I could have sworn there was a certain familiarity between the two of you, though it did perhaps seem a bit strained."

There was no way in hell he was going to mention his encounter with Lady Sarah in the conservatory earlier in the day. Only trouble lay in that direction. "You're imagining things," he said.

"I don't think so," Chloe said.

Christopher was reaching his limit. "I don't want any of you to interfere," he told his mother and sisters crisply.

"And we won't," Lady Oakland assured him as she offered a far too innocent smile, "as long as you promise to give Lady Sarah a chance."

"She. Plans. To. Marry. Mr. Denison!" Did he really have to educate his own mother on the impropriety of setting his cap for another man's intended, no matter who he might be?

"Tsk, tsk." His mother waved a dismissive hand. "Until Mr. Denison actually proposes . . . he hasn't proposed yet, has he, Fiona?"

"No, Mama," Fiona said, her smile annoyingly smug upon her pretty face.

"Well then," Lady Oakland said, "until he does

and Lady Sarah accepts, there's nothing to prevent you from pursuing her as well. With your title taken into account, not to mention that you'll be the Earl of Oakland one day as well, I think it's fair to say that you have a clear advantage."

"Has it not occurred to you, Mama, that Lady Sarah probably has a good reason for considering Mr. Denison?" Christopher asked. "That he's probably been chosen for her by her parents? Especially if what Fiona says about Lady Sarah's lack of enthusiasm for the man is true."

"Of course it's true!" Fiona looked at him incredulously.

"I can't imagine Lady Sarah's reasoning," Lady Oakland said, "or her parents' for that matter, but I can assure you that once you show an interest, they'll welcome your suit with open arms. They'd be fools not to."

Which was precisely why Christopher was reluctant to have anything more to do with Lady Sarah. Instinct told him that something wasn't right about her willingness to marry beneath her station and that involving himself with her would be synonymous with courting trouble.

"All I'm asking is for you to make an effort to further your acquaintance with her, Kip. See where it goes," his mother said. She made it sound like such a small request, when it was anything but. "In return, we'll stop pestering you about finding a wife, won't we, girls?" All the Heartly daughters nodded their agreement. "Otherwise," Christopher's mother continued, delicately brushing a piece of invisible lint from her skirt, "I fear we'll have no choice but to keep looking for other eligible young ladies for you to consider. After all, it is your duty to marry, so I'd hate to squander the opportunity Thorncliff offers in finding you a potential bride. And before you protest too loudly, you ought to know that your father agrees."

Christopher's mouth dropped open. He was being blackmailed by his own family. A ghastly vision of having all the young ladies who were visiting Thorncliff dragged before him by his mother produced an instant shudder.

"It's for your own good, you know," his mother added, patting him gently on the arm.

Christopher almost winced. "But what if Lady Sarah doesn't want to give *me* a chance?" Good God, he'd lost control of his own future, and all in the space of fifteen minutes if the clock on the mantel was any indication.

Lady Oakland shrugged. "Then at least you can say you've tried. Besides, you've always enjoyed a good challenge, and if she's worth having, she's also worth fighting for. Now," she continued with a spark to her voice that startled Christopher, "shall we ring for a late-night snack?"

Christopher sat in stunned silence for a moment, attempting to comprehend what had just transpired. "Not for me," he finally managed. "I believe I'm going to continue upstairs to bed—which is where I was initially headed." Rising, he waited for Fiona to unlock the door, while he proceeded to wish everyone a good night. They faced him with serene faces, leaving no hint of their scheming nature. God help the men who eventually married them!

Turning on his heel, Christopher made for the door and fled, only too aware of the roaring in his ears. Apparently Thorncliff wasn't large enough to save him from his meddling sisters and mother after all. For that, he would probably have to board a ship bound for America. A drastic measure, to be sure, but one that he was seriously considering by the time he climbed into bed, even though the simplest course of action would probably be for him to nod and play along.

Chapter 5

"Isn't it marvelous?" Mr. Denison said as he studied the ancient sundial sitting on a pedestal in the middle of the rose garden.

Standing beside him, Sarah did her best to hide her disinterest. "Absolutely," she said, her thoughts straying to the conversation she'd had with Lord Spencer the previous evening during dinner. He truly was the most solemn man she'd ever encountered. Not once had he made an effort to charm her. If anything, he'd attempted the opposite, which was probably for the best, since she was not one to welcome pretty compliments. Not anymore.

"Look at how precise that shadow is," Mr. Denison said, interrupting her thoughts. "An ingenious piece of engineering."

Looking down at the flat stone before her, Sarah tilted her head. It was certainly clever, but an ingenious piece of engineering? Hardly. "Perhaps you should buy one for your own garden," Sarah suggested.

"An excellent idea, my lady, although I'd much rather think of it as *our* garden."

Sarah stiffened. "It isn't yet."

"A mere technicality that will soon be rectified."

Straightening, Mr. Denison moved toward her, while Sarah fought the instinct to retreat. "I've been considering your daughters' prospects," she told him hastily. Her words produced the desired effect, halting Mr. Denison in his tracks.

"How efficient of you." His mouth curved with what appeared to be appreciation.

"They are of age, sir, if you'll forgive me for saying so."

He seemed to ponder this. "So are you, my dear." He stepped closer, his laughing eyes taking her in, regarding her in a manner that made her skin crawl. "I'll accept nothing less than a nobleman for my girls. They will be ladies. Is that clear?"

Unsure of how she would facilitate such beneficial matches—or disastrous ones, depending on which side you viewed the situation from—Sarah nodded.

"I'm thinking your dinner partner from last night might be an option," he continued.

"Lord Spencer?" He couldn't be serious.

"And since the two of you are already well acquainted, it should be simple enough for you to put in a good word on Victoria's and Diana's behalf."

Good God. He *was* serious. Or at the very least mad. "As it happens, we did speak of marriage last night." When Mr. Denison's eyes darkened, Sarah quickly added, "I thought I would make it clear to him that I am already spoken for."

"Wisely done, Lady Sarah," Mr. Denison said. "I applaud you."

"As it turns out, however," she continued slowly, "his lordship informed me that he has no intention of becoming affianced to any young lady in the immediate future."

"Ah, but he hasn't met my Victoria or my Diana

yet," Mr. Denison said. "Once he does, he'll be sure to change his mind."

Sarah doubted that but chose not to say otherwise. At present, she was faced with greater concerns, like the fact that Mr. Denison was suddenly much closer than he had been a second earlier. *Please don't touch me.*

Raising his hand, he caught a strand of her hair between his fingers, his lips pursing while he studied it. "I'm lucky your father happened to mention you in passing during his last visit to my farm. We were discussing our new business transaction, and when I told him he'd have to do better than one stallion when I was putting in ten mares, he brought you up."

Oh joy!

"Can't say I have an issue with marrying into the Earl of Andover's esteemed family, even if you are spoiled goods," he said, and Sarah flinched. "After all, we both know that you *must* marry, and since nobody else will have you if they are made aware of your . . . situation . . . it appears you're quite stuck with me. So I do hope you'll appreciate how lucky you are as well. After all, you are acquiring a husband."

It was a struggle not to gape at him. Standing perfectly still, Sarah concentrated on breathing. Dear Lord, this was not someone she could easily run away from but the man who would soon have the right to bed her.

He leaned closer, while the edge of his mouth curved upward. "In case you're wondering, I find myself particularly fortunate to be marrying the sort of woman whose passions run so high that she'd allow a man to have his way with her at a house party."

Swallowing the bile that rose in her throat, Sarah thought of her sisters, her parents, her greatest error in judgment—every reason she had for allowing this man near her. "It wasn't like that," she said, relieved that her voice did not betray the ragged state of her nerves.

Mr. Denison chuckled. "You needn't deny your true nature when you are with me, Lady Sarah, for indeed, I look forward to encouraging your wanton behavior." Leaning in, his lips brushed her earlobe.

"Sir," she managed, "this is highly improper."

"I rather suspect that you like impropriety."

Good God! Was that his tongue against her ear?

"Why, you're practically trembling in your effort to suppress the desire I've evoked in you. You needn't though." Easing away from her a little, he looked at her from behind hooded eyes. "In fact, if I may make a suggestion, we could retreat to a more private location, where I could show you—"

"No!" Unable to take any more of it, Sarah stepped back, her breathing fast and desperate.

Mr. Denison's eyes widened, his entire face contorting into an ugly grimace as he caught her firmly by the wrist and pulled her toward him. "No?"

"Forgive me," Sarah said, suddenly fearful of what he might do next. She glanced around, hoping to find a reason to escape his grasp. Unfortunately a hedge shielded them from the view of others.

"If you're unwilling to submit, then perhaps I ought to reconsider my bargain with your father?"

What a blessing that would be, but with her sisters' futures at stake, it was one Sarah couldn't allow, no matter how much she detested the thought of sharing the rest of her life with the likes of Mr. Denison. "And forgo the handsome compensation you'll receive from Papa on our wedding day?" His eyes sharpened, telling her she'd hit the nail squarely on its head, even though she'd no idea how big her dowry was. Huge, would be her guess, all things considered.

"The amount was certainly tempting, but now that I've seen you . . . well, there's no denying that you're the real prize." He licked his lips while his eyes roamed over her, making her stomach churn. "I've had a prudish wife for much too long, Lady Sarah. Now that she's gone, I've a yearning for a wanton one instead—one who'll give me the sons I crave and whose body I can enjoy to my heart's content."

Sarah gasped. She could not believe he'd just said that to her.

Laughter shook his belly. "You're going to live on a farm, my dear. I suggest you get used to the baser things in life. If you resist . . . well, let's just say that you wouldn't be the first to feel the sting of my hand."

He was a monster. She considered telling her father, but what good would that do? It wasn't a crime for a man to beat his wife, even if it might be frowned upon by some. Lord, there were even men who sold their wives at market if they wished to be rid of them. And her father had determined to be rid of her, so whatever she told him, he'd probably claim she exaggerated the issue. Especially since Mr. Denison had seemed so polite and reserved in Lord Andover's presence.

Sarah took a breath. She needed time in which to examine her options. "I wouldn't wish to make you unhappy," she said, her mind spinning as she sought the right thing to say, "but I would like for us to have a respectable start to our marriage—for it to be devoid of any scandal. After all, you do have your daughters to consider. If you wish for them to marry nobility, as you say, then it would hardly do for anyone to find their father in an indelicate situation with me, even if we are to be married."

He stared at her long and hard before leaning back. "As much as I had hoped our courtship would lead to stolen kisses and . . . so much more, I have to admit that you make an excellent point."

Sarah expelled the breath she'd been holding, her shoulders sagging with relief. "Perhaps I should join your daughters for tea this afternoon so I can get a feel for their accomplishments," she suggested, hoping to steer his thoughts in a different direction.

"An excellent idea," Mr. Denison said as he picked a rose and offered it to her, all traces of lechery gone from his countenance. It was like being with a completely different man from the one who'd regaled her with his lascivious ideas only moments earlier. "Shall we continue along this path? I believe it will take us down to the lake."

They had not gone more than five paces before Sarah heard a voice calling her name. Halting her progress, she felt a wave of relief at the sight of Lady Fiona coming her way, though apprehension swiftly followed when she saw that Lady Fiona was not alone. She was accompanied by Lady Emily and Lady Laura, as well as by Lord Spencer, who was even handsomer than she recalled.

Determined not to favor him with too much attention, Sarah shifted her gaze to his sisters. "What a lovely surprise," she said as she addressed the group as a whole. They couldn't possibly imagine how grateful she was to them for intervening in her stroll with Mr. Denison.

"We hope we're not interrupting a private conversation," Lady Laura said.

"Not at all," Sarah said politely. "Your company is most welcome."

Against her better judgment, she glanced at Lord

Spencer, her cheeks heating when she found that he was looking straight back at her. His handsomeness was clearly having an effect on her—one she shouldn't allow. Shrugging off the shiver that spread across her shoulders, she focused on Ladies Emily, Laura and Fiona, saying, "If you will permit, I'd like to introduce you to Mr. Denison."

"We're delighted to make your acquaintance," Lady Fiona said while Lady Laura and Lady Emily both nodded in agreement. "And since our paths have crossed, may I suggest you join us? We're hoping to make an attempt at the maze."

"Well . . ." Mr. Denison hedged, clearly reluctant to join a larger group.

"Oh, it's going to be such fun," Lady Fiona said, already stepping toward him and taking him by the arm.

"Thank you, but we'd rather not," Mr. Denison said, his hand possessively holding on to Sarah's arm.

It was more than Sarah was willing to bear. "I think a maze sounds splendid," she said. "In fact, I believe I should like to try it with my friends, but if you'd rather not—"

"I understand your daughters wish to marry?" Fiona blurted.

Sarah couldn't imagine how she'd discovered that bit of information or how it might be relevant to the conversation, but when Mr. Denison nodded, Fiona said, "The Duchess of Pinehurst is most eager for her grandsons to marry as well. None have been very successful with the ladies, but it would be a wonderful coup for your daughters—an association with a duke and duchess. Her Grace is presently enjoying a quiet spot in the shade just over there—I'd be happy to introduce you to her if you like."

Sarah couldn't imagine the Duchess of Pinehurst being pleased by Mr. Denison's unexpected company, but she felt the need for a reprieve from him herself and almost jumped for joy when he accepted Lady Fiona's offer. "I'll see you this evening for dinner, my lady," he told Sarah. To everyone else, he said, "A pleasure meeting you," before strolling off alongside Lady Fiona.

Sarah watched them approach the duchess, not daring to enjoy her freedom until he took a seat beside the dragon and Lady Fiona was on her way back.

"Is he not courting you?" Lady Laura inquired as they waited for Lady Fiona to reach them.

"He is," Sarah said, uncomfortable with the confession.

"And yet he won't be seeing you again before dinner?" Lady Laura asked.

Sarah was grateful for it. "He'll probably go back to the house for luncheon before we're finished with the maze, and then he'll take his afternoon rest," she explained.

"How difficult that must be for you," Lord Spencer murmured, his expression completely inscrutable.

His voice, on the other hand, made her heart flutter just enough to remind her of the effect he was starting to have on her. "Are you not aware that absence makes the heart grow fonder?" she asked.

He raised an eyebrow but failed to comment, since Lady Fiona arrived at precisely that moment. "Shall we proceed?" she asked.

Nodding, Sarah fell into step beside her.

"We simply cannot allow you to marry that man," Lady Fiona said as they walked ahead of everyone else. "He's much older than I expected and not the least bit handsome. As a beautiful young lady, the daughter of an earl, no less, you can do so much better for yourself."

Sarah sighed. Lady Fiona's curiosity and eagerness to help where she believed help was needed would be difficult to tackle. "Thank you for your consideration, but—"

"I can think of a dozen more eligible gentlemen who'd be thrilled to make you their wife."

No you can't, Sarah thought sadly.

"Spencer, for instance—"

"Please stop," Sarah said, afraid Lord Spencer might have overheard. The last thing she wanted was for him to think she was secretly scheming to lure him to the altar. "We have nothing in common." She decided not to mention that he also unnerved her with his uncanny ability to look ill-tempered at all hours of the day. But she had to admit that she did enjoy their discourse. Perhaps they could be friends, in an odd sort of way.

Lady Fiona slanted a look in her direction as if to say, *And I suppose you have much in common with Mr. Denison?* Instead she asked, "Why are you really considering marriage to that man?"

Sarah almost choked. "I . . ." She had no obligation to answer that question, especially since she'd only met the Heartlys the day before. Clenching her jaw, she said, "It's a private matter."

There was a moment's silence until Lady Fiona leaned closer and whispered, "If you ever feel the need to discuss it with a friend, I'd like you to know that you can count on me."

"Thank you," Sarah said. She was grateful for the offer, even though it was one she could never accept.

"Isn't Thorncliff marvelous?" Lady Laura asked

as she and Lady Emily came up alongside Sarah and Lady Fiona. "I do hope you're enjoying your stay, Lady Sarah."

"It's a marvelous estate," Sarah said.

"And utterly romantic," Laura said with a conspiratorial smile.

Sarah's cheeks heated in a most impractical way. Aware of Lord Spencer's presence as he followed behind them, she couldn't help but say, "And contrary to Bodiam Castle, Thorncliff is impressive both inside and out."

"A fine observation," Lady Fiona remarked. "Perhaps you share Spencer's interest in English castles?"

Realizing her mistake, Sarah said, "Not really." Determined not to encourage any matchmaking ideas, she chose not to mention the fact that although she'd never considered the issue, she couldn't help but be intrigued by Thorncliff and longed to know more about it.

"I agree with you," Lady Emily said. "It's just nice to be able to enjoy such a wonderful retreat."

"And the opportunity to remain abed all day if I so desire," Sarah added.

Christopher coughed, then raised an eyebrow when Fiona and Lady Sarah turned to look at him. "Are you all right?" Fiona asked.

"Quite," he managed, though he was anything but after Lady Sarah's talk of staying abed. The unbidden vision *that* had produced, of her sprawled out upon the sheets, naked, of course . . . He struggled to think of something—like problems that might occur if crocodiles were found in the lake—that would halt the sudden stirring in his nether region. Could crocodiles even survive in the British climate, or would Lady Duncaster have to bring them inside for the winter? The thought that evoked, of reptiles roaming about the halls of Thorncliff and possibly lounging on the sofas, brought a stupid smile to his lips and then an unintentional chuckle.

"What's so funny?" Emily asked.

Christopher blinked, then schooled his features and frowned. He'd been woolgathering and had failed to realize that his sister had fallen behind and was now walking directly beside him. "Crocodiles," he said.

"Crocodiles?" The note of disbelief was almost tangible.

"Funny creatures, don't you think?" Christopher mused, unwilling to divulge the reason behind his thought process for fear that . . . he grimaced as his mind betrayed his command, offering him an image of Lady Sarah's hair fanned out upon a pillow as she gazed up at him with parted lips, so ripe for kissing. As much as he'd tried not to notice how tempting they were, he wasn't dead, and had consequently failed in his attempt.

"You look a bit tense," Laura said, and Christopher blinked again, surprised to discover that she had snuck up on him as well. "Perhaps you ought to loosen your cravat, lest it cut off the blood supply to your head." She laughed at her joke, as did Emily.

Christopher rolled his eyes.

"Come on," Fiona said when they reached the maze, releasing Lady Sarah and running forward. "First one through wins a green ribbon!"

Laughing, Laura and Emily raced after her, while Lady Sarah looked mildly stunned.

"Mazes tend to bring out their competitive streak," Christopher told her.

"But not yours?"

"As pretty as I'd no doubt look with a green ribbon tied in a bow upon my head," he said dryly, "I think my sisters have better use of it."

The corner of her mouth twitched, and without warning, she suddenly smiled—a bright, beaming smile that reached her eyes, almost blinding him with her radiance. His heart stilled. No. He would not allow himself to be drawn in by her feminine wiles. His sisters and mother might be able to get him to spend more time with her, but he'd be damned if he was going to let her anywhere near his heart.

"You're probably right," she said, her expression sobering.

If only he could make her look happy again. Her beauty had increased tenfold when she'd smiled, her joy threatening to infect him as well. Unwilling to let her affect him in any way, he looked to the puzzle the maze offered.

"Shall we?" he asked, gesturing toward the entrance.

She hesitated, her eyes betraying her uncertainty. Perhaps he'd be able to tell his sisters that his efforts to spend more time with Lady Sarah had failed due to her lack of interest. But then, surprisingly, she raised her chin and nodded. Stubborn little minx. "I suppose we should at least try to follow your sisters," she said. "The longer we delay, the less chance we'll have of winning."

And so he offered her his arm, which she accepted, though he sensed she was regretting her choice to leave Mr. Denison's company. Christopher still couldn't believe she was destined to marry that stodgy old man. It defied logic, but so did many other *ton* marriages. Her arm remained loosely linked with his, her body as far away from his as possible as she hurried forward.

"I get the impression that you'd like to avoid spending time with me," he said after a few moments of silence between them. Spotting his sisters as they rounded a corner, Lady Sarah quickened her pace in an effort to catch up to them.

"Your impression is correct," she said.

Her frankness startled him to such an extent that he found it difficult to comprehend that this was indeed what she had just said. "May I ask why?" he eventually managed.

"Because in spite of your cynicism, I happen to enjoy your company." She sounded sincere. There was even a hint of a smile to her voice.

Christopher frowned, then shook his head, completely befuddled by her logic. "That makes no sense," he finally told her.

"It makes perfect sense to me, my lord, but if you want further explanation, I fear I must disappoint you, for I shall offer you none. All I ask is that you respect my desire to be left alone."

Desire.

The word crept through him, so innocent in her use of it, yet provoking a series of thoughts he ought not to be having. He should know better. Hell, he'd promised himself never to let another woman tempt him ever again. Glancing down at her profile, he could not deny that as much as he tried to resist, Lady Sarah stirred his blood.

His heart increased its pace as her fingers curled into the wool of his jacket. This could not be happening. Worse than that, he could not allow himself to like her, not when he had every intention of simply placating his mother and sisters by engaging Lady Sarah in the occasional conversation. Nothing more.

And yet, all obligation aside, there was no denying that he enjoyed sparring with her—that he liked watching her stand up to him no matter how uncomfortable he probably made her feel. Recalling the unhindered smile that had captured her face when she'd found Snowball, he felt an odd swelling inside his chest. For reasons he could not explain, and against his better judgment, he found himself drawn to her—had in fact looked forward to seeing her again today. Clearly, he was allowing himself to be led astray. It had to stop.

"My lord?"

Her voice brought him out of his reverie, and he realized that his mouth had gone inexplicably dry. "Forgive me," he muttered. "I was lost in thought."

"You stopped very abruptly," she said, "and I feared perhaps I'd upset you. In any case, we ought to hasten our progress if we are to keep up with your sisters. I believe they went that way."

It was then that Christopher realized how alone they were. Again. Indeed, if it weren't for the occasional squeal of laughter sifting through the air, there would be no evidence of anyone else's presence. Lowering his gaze, he looked down at Lady Sarah, who was staring toward the turn in the path with some measure of anxiety. There was a restlessness about her entire body that easily conveyed her eagerness to seek the company of others and avoid being left alone with him.

"Why are you so nervous?" he asked without making a move to follow the rest of their party.

"Because we ought not be alone together," she said. "It isn't proper."

He considered that for a moment before saying, "I'm hardly going to ravish you out here in public where anyone could happen upon us at any given time. Honestly, Lady Sarah, I do believe you're over-reacting."

Her eyes met his at that moment, bright and accusing and with the slightest hint of fear. "Am I?"

Noticing that a lock of her hair had come undone and was trailing down the side of her neck, Christopher reached out, catching it between his fingers. Her breath caught, and it was as if her whole body shuddered in response. Christopher stilled, his eyes locked with hers. Then hesitantly and with utmost care so as not to startle her any further, he placed the tips of his fingers against the side of her neck and felt her pulse. It was leaping in a frantic rhythm, not from any passionate response, he wagered, judging from the look of panic she was presently bestowing upon him, but because she did not trust his motive.

Damn. He scarcely knew his motive himself, other than that he'd succumbed to the urge to touch her—had accepted the excuse her hair had offered. Retrieving his hand, he stepped back. "What on earth do you imagine I might do to you that you would be so thoroughly alarmed?"

Her chin rose a notch as she stared back at him boldly, her composure seemingly restored by some miracle. "The worst, if you must know."

"Good God, I would never," he blurted.

She held his gaze. "You would not be the first man to make such a claim, my lord, but since you yourself have been blessed with sisters, I'm sure you can appreciate the value of a woman's reputation."

Christopher flinched. She was absolutely right, and though he hadn't done anything truly inappropriate, he'd certainly thought about it, and that was almost just as bad. "My apologies," he said. "I've no desire to make you feel uncomfortable, and since I do not wish to marry at present, as you well know, then it goes without saying that I will try to avoid any compromising situations. Which is why I cannot help but wonder if it isn't really me you fear but yourself?"

Why the devil would he say something like that?

Her jaw clenched and she grew rigid, as if she was struggling to remain calm. Christopher braced himself for the biting remark he knew would come, except it didn't. Instead, Lady Sarah closed her eyes, no doubt eager to block him out. She took a deep, shuddering breath, then raised her chin. Her eyes opened and she looked to the sky. Christopher followed her gaze until he found himself admiring a couple of swallows who appeared to be caught in a playful chase.

"There's something to be envied in the freedom of birds," Lady Sarah said. She sounded detached, as if she was speaking to herself rather than to him. "What I wouldn't give for the opportunity to fly away from it all."

"You wish to flee?" When she didn't respond, he said, "Is it because of Mr. Denison?"

Abandoning the swallows, Lady Sarah looked at him for the longest moment, studying him with her clear blue eyes, until she finally spoke. "Have you ever done something regrettable, my lord? Something that suggests exceedingly poor judgment on your part, and for which you will never be able to forgive yourself?"

The question gave him pause, not so much because of how unexpected it was but because of what it told him about Lady Sarah . . . and because of its importance. He sensed that if he told her he had not, it would put an immediate end to their newly established acquaintanceship, while if he spoke the truth, it would bring them closer somehow. "Yes," he said simply.

She waited a moment, but then she nodded, as if deciding she would believe him. When she made to continue along the path, Christopher caught her gently by the arm, halting her progress. "Lady Sarah," he told her seriously, "it's impossible for me to imagine what kind of burden might be troubling you, but I do know how difficult it can be to feel as though you've acted stupidly—to fear the judgment of others if they were to discover your folly." She tried to pull away, her face increasingly devoid of emotion with every breath she took, as if she was building a wall between them. Persistent as ever, Christopher slipped his hand down around hers and raised it to his lips, kissing her gloved knuckles before saying, "You needn't confide in me. Not ever. But I would like for you to know that as unlikely as you may find it, I am your friend, if you wish it. So are my sisters."

Her whole demeanor seemed to change in response to that promise, and she suddenly smiled wide and beautifully. "Thank you," she said, those gorgeous eyes of hers dancing with joy. "You are most kind."

Her happiness in response to such a small gesture filled him with pleasure, and it struck him that it was harder for him to train his emotions around her today than it had been yesterday. Somehow, she'd reached inside his chest with her confession and spoken directly to his heart.

Retreat, his inner voice told him.

Pushing aside the compassion that muddled his brain and weakened his defenses, Christopher tried to consider Lady Sarah objectively. She was not like Miss Hepplestone, he decided, or any other young lady he'd ever met, for that matter. He hadn't lied when he'd told Lady Sarah that women coveted him, chased him even, to the point where one such woman had delivered the performance of a lifetime in her attempt to wed him. None of it had been genuine, and Christopher had never felt more used or humiliated.

But with Lady Sarah it was different. She made no attempt to seek his company or to try and charm him. In fact, the only interest she'd shown in him had had nothing to do with his title or wealth but rather with his passion for castles. Additionally, she had made it clear to him and to Fiona that she planned to marry Mr. Denison.

This gave him pause.

"May I ask you a personal question?" he asked.

"Of course, though I cannot promise I'll give you an answer."

He liked how direct she was, even if it did occasionally lead to a blunt comment. "Fiona says that you do not wish to marry Mr. Denison. Is that true?"

Her expression turned from openness to wariness in an instant. "I don't believe I've told your sister anything of the sort."

"She can be very observant."

Lady Sarah nodded stiffly. "Mr. Denison is not my first choice, he is a practical choice—a suitor picked for me by my father in order to facilitate an alliance."

"What sort of alliance?"

"To be blunt, my father has a particular fondness for horses, and Mr. Denison, it appears, is in possession of some fine ones. Crossbreeding will prove financially beneficial to them both, and since I'm not getting any younger, I have decided to help Papa achieve his goal and accept Mr. Denison's offer when he asks."

"You say he's not your first choice though. Might I

ask who that fortunate individual would be?" Christopher asked. For reasons he couldn't explain—simple curiosity, no doubt—he needed to know who had captured her heart and why the man had not married her.

"It's inconsequential."

The words were spoken so bitterly that they brought Christopher to an immediate halt. "I don't believe that," he said.

"Then believe this," she told him, her blue eyes shimmering like pools of water, "the man I loved was not the man I thought him to be. Who I marry no longer makes a difference."

Thoroughly surprised, it took Christopher a moment to gather his wits. He hadn't imagined meeting someone who'd suffered a similar situation as he had, let alone a young lady. Intrigued and feeling strangely linked to her now, he longed to question her about her experience—to ask her how she'd survived the ordeal—but it was obvious that the confession had been a difficult one for her to make, so he chose not to press her.

"Then we have both survived the pain of a broken heart," he told her instead, feeling the need to share a little of his own past with her, and to make her aware of the similarity between them. She would understand, better than his family did, for they found it impossible to comprehend why he'd continued to pine for a woman who'd never existed.

He hadn't been able to help it though, in spite of his anger. To his way of thinking, it was almost as if Miss Hepplestone had murdered his one true love and he had helplessly mourned her for well over a year. When he'd finally decided the time had come for him to move on, his parents and sisters had taken it upon themselves to throw as many eligible young ladies his way as possible. If that wasn't enough reason to regret venturing back out into Society, he wasn't sure what was. Of course, the more eager they'd been to help him make a proper match, the more determined he had become to thwart their attempts. He was stubborn that way.

The same ought to be true of Lady Sarah, especially since his mother had given him an ultimatum that offered no reprieve from wife hunting during his stay at Thorncliff. He ought to leave. Against his better judgment, Lady Sarah stopped him from doing so. At first, he'd recognized in her the same reluctance to trust others that he had felt in the wake of Miss Hepplestone's departure from England. Now, after what Lady Sarah had just told him, he wanted to know more about her.

They continued to make their way through the maze, twisting and turning in an effort to find the exit. There was something addictive about the woman at his side, he realized, perhaps because she was so apprehensive at times that the moments she smiled were to be cherished.

"Will you tell me who broke yours?" Lady Sarah asked when they arrived at the end of the maze.

They'd shared a companionable silence for several minutes, so the question was one he hadn't expected. "Only if you will reciprocate." Christopher found himself holding his breath as he waited to see how she would reply.

Glancing about, she raised her hand and waved, and Christopher saw that his sisters were seated in the shade of a tree, waiting for them. Lady Sarah started in their direction with measured steps, her gaze slightly lowered. "I fear I'm not ready for that yet," she said. "It's possible I never will be."

"Well, if you ever change your mind, I'd be happy to listen."

She snorted a little before blurting, "Of all the people in the world, you're probably the last person I'd wish to share my troubles with." The weight of her words must have hit her just as hard as they did Christopher, for she immediately clasped a hand over her mouth, her eyes wide with shock. "Forgive me," she gasped. "I meant no offense by that. It is just . . ."

His heart thudded in his chest. Instinct told him to leave her unspoken words alone, but he couldn't seem to stop himself. "Just what?" he asked.

"The thought of you knowing me that well frightens me." She looked away from him, her voice muffled as she continued to speak. "If you must know, it's because I should hate for you to think less of me."

"I daresay that would be quite impossible, Lady Sarah, though I am curious to know why our paths have never crossed before."

For a brief second, she looked perplexed—as if she wasn't comfortable with the question. Eventually she said, "Following Grandmamma's death a little over a year ago, I chose to remove myself from Society while I mourned her. I was still young, so it didn't seem the sort of thing that would make a difference, but it does mean I'm not as accustomed to mingling with the aristocracy as I ought to be, having had only one Season."

"Well, I think you're doing splendidly, though it does explain why we haven't met before. I was abroad traveling the Continent two years ago, which is when I suspect you must have made your debut."

"Indeed," she murmured, eyeing him warily as they approached his sisters. Stopping a short distance away, she said, "I know we've only just met, but I was wondering if I might impose on you for a favor?"

"What sort of favor?" Her tone coupled with her evasive gaze made him wary.

"You won't like it, I'm afraid, but Mr. Denison is looking to get his daughters settled and has asked me to assist." Cold dread seeped through Christopher's veins, starting at the top of his head. "After seeing me in conversation with you last night, he's decided that having you for a son-in-law would suit him splendidly."

"I'm sure it would," Christopher said, "though I do believe I'd likely jump into the Channel and swim for France before allowing such a thing to happen."

"I understand, and have made him aware of your disinterest in marriage, but he insists."

"I hope you're not implying that this favor involves me getting leg-shackled." That would certainly be an outrageous request to make of any man.

"Of course not." She looked as though she might cross her arms. Instead she placed one hand on her hip. "I would never presume to suggest such a thing, but if you could make an effort to talk to them a little or perhaps take them for a walk—"

"A walk is out of the question. There's no time limit to it and few possibilities for me to extricate myself in case I wish to flee their company." What was he saying? He should tell her she was being entirely too forward. Which she was.

"A brief inquiry about their day then?"

"I won't enjoy it." He'd seen Miss Victoria Denison and Miss Diana Denison at breakfast that morning, his interest piqued by their association to the man whom Lady Sarah intended to wed. Neither, as it turned out, was very attractive or refined.

"It would help me a great deal," Lady Sarah told him quietly.

"Allow me to think on it," he said. Of course he

would do it. Especially since he sensed her concern with the issue. Clearly it mattered to her a great deal, though he'd yet to figure out why. But even if he was willing to assist her, there was no need for him to look like a green lad being led about by a woman he'd only just met. Contemplatively, he continued toward his sisters while Lady Sarah thanked him, her voice filled with gratitude.

"Shall we walk back to the house?" Laura asked, rising to greet them. "We can have tea and strawberry tarts on the terrace."

"If only we could have *choux à la crème* instead," Christopher said, recalling the treat he'd discovered at a small intimate café in Paris.

"You might as well give up on that," Emily told him as she collected the bonnet she'd removed from her head.

"*Choux à la crème?*" Lady Sarah inquired with a quizzical expression when they were once again alone, trailing after the rest of the group at a pace that even a snail would lose patience with.

"It's a delicious cream-filled pastry," Christopher explained. "When I returned from my travels, I tried to explain what it looked like to Mama's and Papa's cook, but her attempt at making it was such a failure I chose to avoid repeating the effort."

"A pity, if it's your favorite."

Christopher shrugged. "I'm sure I'll return to France one day, if for no other reason than to acquire the recipe."

"Have you been to many countries?" Lady Sarah asked.

A gentle breeze tugged at her hemline, offering Christopher a subtle glimpse of her ankles as he followed the movement. They appeared to be slim and delicate. Diverting his gaze, he tried not to ponder what the rest of her body might look like if it were uncovered. "A fair number, I suppose, though not nearly as many as I'd like. Italy was among the most remarkable—its beauty and history are unforgettable."

Lady Sarah nodded. "I'd love to see the world beyond England one day, but it's harder for a woman to travel abroad than it is for a man. In all likelihood, I'll remain here forever."

Looking down at her upturned face, Christopher couldn't help but notice the sadness that filled her eyes. Schooling his features to hide his concern, Christopher decided not to question her further about her decision to marry Mr. Denison. Considering how briefly he'd known her, he'd already invaded her privacy enough. Instead, he would have to step back and allow her the freedom to confide in him when she was ready to do so.

"**I** saw you in Lord Spencer's company this morning," Sarah's stepmother told her later when they were having tea together in the Indian salon. Sarah doubted her stepmother was enjoying it any more than she was, but they'd both agreed that they must remain cordial with each other if they were to prevent gossip.

"His sisters were there as well," Sarah said.

Setting her cup aside, Lady Andover gave her daughter a pointed look. "Are you suggesting that the ladies present held greater appeal than his lordship?"

"No. He is a striking man, Mama, and I confess that I do enjoy his company immensely. What I meant to imply was that you needn't concern yourself about my reputation. He and I were not alone."

"Not even in the maze?"

Sarah felt the heat rise to her cheeks. Of course Lady Andover would ask the one question Sarah wished to avoid answering. Steeling herself, she told the truth. "We were separated from the others for a short while. Nothing happened."

"And you expect me to believe that, given your history?"

Anger flared to life within her. "I do, Mama, especially since you know I have never lied to you, though in hindsight, I sometimes wish I had."

Lady Andover sat back against her chair and gave Sarah a hard stare. "You have quite the backbone when others are not within earshot." When Sarah said nothing, her stepmother continued in a steely tone. "Did I not warn you to stay away from the Heartlys? Your future is not with them. It is with Mr. Denison, to whom you should be eternally grateful. You should be spending your days with him instead, unless of course you wish for him to change his mind about you."

It was exactly what Sarah wanted. Unfortunately she was well aware that people didn't always get what they wanted and that she wouldn't either.

"I'm sure Papa's business arrangement with Mr. Denison, along with my dowry, are incentive enough for Mr. Denison to make me an offer once our courtship draws to an end."

"How vulgar of you to say such a thing."

"I don't see why, when it is obviously true."

Lady Andover scoffed. "I'm sure Mr. Denison also appreciates your feminine beauty and realizes that you . . . oh don't look so horrified, Sarah. A woman's ability to encourage an amorous response in her husband is a strength. Wield it correctly, and you'll soon have Mr. Denison dancing to your tune."

Sarah shuddered. She wasn't sure she could handle any more "amorous responses" from Mr. Denison without being violently ill, never mind a lifetime supply of it.

Her stepmother's eyes pierced Sarah like needles while her mouth curved in a smirk. "Besides, unlike most young ladies, it's nothing you haven't tried before. I'm sure Mr. Denison will be ever so pleased by your experience on your wedding night. Really, Sarah, there's nothing for you to worry about at all." Heart bouncing about her chest, Sarah definitely disagreed. "But in order for any of this to transpire and for your sisters, whom I know you love and adore, to have the bright futures they deserve, you must make every effort to encourage Mr. Denison and to stay away from the Heartlys. Especially from Lord Spencer. We simply cannot risk the possibility of him making an offer."

Sarah fought not to roll her eyes. "He scarcely knows me, so I find that prospect highly unlikely, especially since he does not wish to marry. He has also been made aware that Mr. Denison is presently courting me and that I intend to accept his eventual proposal, but"—she held up her hand to stay her stepmother's words of protest—"if Lord Spencer decides to ignore all of that and make me an offer, which he won't, I shall simply decline."

Lady Andover nodded. "You'd better, because if you don't and end up married to a man who's expecting an innocent on his wedding night, his anger will know no bounds. He will no doubt take vengeance on all of us, including your sisters."

Hope seemed to flee before Sarah's eyes as she said, "For your information, Mr. Denison asked me to help him get his daughters settled. He has set his sights on Lord Spencer, so you needn't worry, Mama. I will do my duty."

"And I shall be keeping an eye on you," Lady Andover remarked. "Is that clear?"

"Perfectly," Sarah ground out. Thank God for Thorncliff's many distractions and her stepmother's fondness for piquet. If luck would have it, the countess would be too busy playing cards to bother herself with her stepdaughter's affairs. Lord knew Sarah could do with the reprieve.

Chapter 6

The following morning, Sarah awoke early. So early, in fact, that it was still dark outside when she rose from her bed, groaning as she considered the day that stretched before her. Mr. Denison was supposed to take her rowing, but the thought of being trapped in a boat with him was extremely unappealing. Perhaps she could feign a megrim, but her stepmother would probably find that suspicious, since Sarah was never ill and had always loved being out on the lake at home.

Looking out the window, she was tempted with the chance to escape her worries, if only for a moment—to feel the freedom of being outside as the sun rose over the lake and the birds began to chirp. Picking out a lavender-colored gown, she got dressed, stepped into her slippers and snuck quietly out of her room.

Downstairs, Sarah was met by the steady ticking of clocks in various rooms. The house was still sleeping—not even a servant preparing the dining room for breakfast was to be found. Reaching the French doors leading out onto a patio, Sarah was surprised to find them unlocked. Opening the right side, she stepped nimbly out into the crisp morning air, grateful she'd brought a shawl along to warm her. She pulled it tight across her shoulders as she closed the door behind her and started in the direction of the lake. The darkness had begun to brighten, and by the time she reached the lakeside, the first rays of sunshine shimmered upon the water.

Drawn to a path leading off to one side, Sarah followed it as it curved away between a copse of trees before leading toward a wide span of dew-covered grass, crushed beneath the solid weight of gray granite benches. Realizing she might as well have gone barefoot, since her silk slippers were almost soaked through, Sarah considered removing them as she stepped forward, until she realized, quite unexpectedly, that she was not alone. A man stood to the far right of her; he was tall, and cast in relief against the now orange glow of the sky. His back was toward her, but that did not prevent her from determining his identity, though even if she'd been in doubt, her heart rate would have told her he was none other than Lord Spencer.

Of course it would be him of all people, she mused, as she watched him quietly from a distance. Fate did after all have a fondness for mischief. Knowing she ought to resist the temptation of sharing his company in solitude, Sarah turned to leave, but she had scarcely done so when she heard his voice, clear across the distance. "Will you not even greet me?" he asked.

Her breath hitched, and she was thankful he wasn't close enough to hear it. Slowly, she turned to find him looking back at her, his face cast in shadow as the sun peeked out from behind the maze on the opposite side of the lake. "Forgive me, my lord, but we are alone, and we really shouldn't be. It isn't proper."

"Perhaps not, though I daresay none shall be the wiser, since everyone is still abed and will no doubt remain so for the next two hours." He tilted his head. "What brought you outside so early?"

"I couldn't sleep," she confessed.

"I see." They both remained unmoving, not uttering another word until he finally said, "I really wish you'd make up your mind about staying or leaving. The anticipation is difficult to bear."

His stark expression coupled with the note of sarcasm made Sarah smile. "As long as you promise to remain on your best behavior, my lord, I daresay I'd like to watch the sunrise from here."

"I won't bite, if that is what you fear."

For some peculiar reason, his words evoked a delightful shiver accompanied by a rush of heat in the pit of her belly. Bothered by the silliness of it, Sarah took a fortifying breath and moved toward him with hesitant steps. "Are you usually awake this early?" she asked as she came to stand beside him.

He nodded. "It's my favorite time of day—the birth of a new dawn as light pushes away the darkness and life rises from its slumber." Turning toward the spectacular radiance of colorful light, he slipped something between his fingers, adjusting it until, with a sharp jerk of his upper body, he tossed it out over the water. The stone skipped numerous times before sinking below the surface, leaving rippling rings in its wake. "Care to try?" he asked as he offered her a perfectly flat stone.

"I confess I don't know how," she said as she stared with longing at his offering.

"I didn't ask you if you did. I asked you if you'd like to try."

For two years her true nature had been boxed

away and labeled Unsuitable. She took the stone from his hand. "I'd love to," she said.

"In that case, let me show you how." His hand was upon her wrist, pulling her toward him before she could voice a protest as he tried to position her correctly. "Turn sideways, like this."

Sarah's heart slammed against her chest as she struggled for breath, not to mention some measure of calm. With her back toward Lord Spencer's chest and his hand upon hers while he tried to place the stone correctly between her fingers, she could feel the heat radiating off of him and penetrating her skin. Dear God, she could not think straight when he was so close.

Yesterday, distraught by Mr. Denison's unsavory advances, she'd confided in Lord Spencer as much as she'd dared, which had not been much. Even so, she'd left his company feeling as if a thread had been spun between them, perhaps because he'd refrained from pressing her for answers. Instead, she'd been free to divulge as much as she'd wished and he'd respected her refusal to tell him more, just as she had respected his.

"That's it. I think you've got it," he murmured, his breath tickling the side of her neck and teasing her senses. "You're going to turn away from the lake and then back toward it in a fluid but rapid motion, like this." And then, before she managed to quell her ragged nerves, he guided her through the motion until the stone slipped from between her fingers and flew through the air, skimming the water in a couple of leaps.

"I did it!" Thrilled by the results of her effort and the fact that she'd actually managed to skip a stone on her first attempt, even if Lord Spencer should really be the one to take the credit, Sarah whirled around, eager to share her victory with him, and almost lost her footing in the process.

Lord Spencer grinned, his smile wide as he caught her about the waist. "Easy does it! You wouldn't want to fall in and get wet."

Sarah stared at him—at the unhindered amusement crinkling the corners of his eyes and at the dimples forming at the corners of his mouth. Truly, the man was likely capable of converting nuns with that smile. It ought to be illegal. "Certainly not," she said, intensely aware of his unexpected closeness, the sturdy feel of his hand as he shifted it to her lower back, the fresh scent of soap suggesting he'd recently bathed. Perhaps last night before bed?

"You really ought to stop doing this, my lady." His eyes sparkled as he spoke. Gone was the guarded expression she'd grown accustomed to.

Sarah sagged, feeling weightless. A woman could easily lose herself in those eyes. "Doing what?" she asked, her voice sounding breathless.

"Falling into the arms of unsuspecting gentlemen. They might get the wrong idea."

Pulling her upward, Lord Spencer narrowed the distance between them, and as Sarah gazed back at his handsome face, more particularly at the delicious curve of his mouth, she couldn't help but wonder if he might kiss her. Indeed, she secretly hoped he would, even though she knew she shouldn't. Longed for it, in fact, as the air grew heavy with intimacy . . . expectancy . . . desire. Or at least that was how *she* perceived it. As it turned out, he had only been trying to set her back on her feet so she wouldn't fall over again like the dim-witted female she was. It was clear that Lord Spencer's handsomeness was confusing her senses.

"Right you are," she said, hoping her embarrassment wasn't too obvious and that she hadn't looked as though she'd been begging for kisses as he'd held her in his arms. Lord, she'd never outlive the humiliation!

Crouching down, Lord Spencer sought out two more stones, rose to his feet and sent them flying across the water in quick succession while Sarah stared in amazement. "You must have had a lot of practice doing that," she said after counting well over ten skips.

Lord Spencer chuckled. "I confess I find the exercise soothing. My grandfather taught me how to do it when I was little, and I've been doing it ever since—always trying to beat my own record."

"And what's that?" Sarah asked curiously.

"Twenty-five."

Sarah shook her head in wonder. "And I only managed a measly two."

"For which you should be very proud," Lord Spencer assured her. "It took me several attempts before I could skip a stone even once, but Grandpapa insisted I should keep at it. He told me there's no reward to be had without effort and that the best things in life are worth struggling for."

"He sounds like a very wise man."

Lord Spencer nodded. "I was very fond of him, perhaps because he always had time to spare for me. He taught me how to whistle with a blade of grass as well—not the sort of thing you might expect from an earl. But he was not the haughty sort, and neither was my grandmother. I believe my family has benefitted greatly from it and that it's provided us with a closeness many families of the *ton* lack."

Sarah envied that. She'd never felt particularly close to her parents, and now . . . now she felt as if a vast chasm lay between them. And although she loved Alice and Juliet dearly, her need to protect them from the truth meant denying herself and them the sort of closeness sisters ought to share. Speaking of Lord Spencer's grandfather, she realized how much she missed her own—a serious man who'd always saved a few smiles just for her. "My favorite childhood memory is flying a kite with my grandpapa when he and Grandmamma took me out for a picnic one summer. The air was warm with a gentle breeze, and I remember the sound of bees buzzing about the wildflowers while we enjoyed our lunch on a large blanket."

"Your sisters weren't with you?" Lord Spencer asked.

"They were too young at the time, so I suppose they must have remained home with Lady Andover and Papa—or with their nanny." Staring across the lake, Sarah welcomed the memory. "We had pancakes for dessert that day, with strawberry jam. Grandmamma and I went for a walk and picked a large bouquet of flowers while she talked about the birds we spotted. She knew everything there was to know about birds—that was her passion. Later, while she took a rest, Grandpapa surprised me with a kite he'd ordered from London. It was so beautiful— bright red with elegant long ribbons."

"Do you still have it?"

"No. I'm not sure what happened to it."

"Your sisters never got a chance to try it?"

Sarah shook her head with regret. "Grandpapa died the following year, and Papa never took the time. He's always been very busy."

Lord Spencer tilted his head a little, the smile he'd given her earlier nothing more than a memory. "I couldn't help but notice that you didn't refer to Lady Andover as 'Mama.' Is she not your real mother?"

"You've clearly forgotten your Debrett's," Sarah said as she pulled her shawl up over the curve of her shoulder, cocooning herself in its warmth.

He tossed another stone out over the lake. "I can tell you the names of everyone currently married and who their heirs are, but when it comes to daughters and previous husbands or wives, I confess I have a tendency to forget."

"Unless you're interested in their family history because they happen to own a fascinating castle."

Sticking his hands in his pockets, he nodded. "There is that."

Sarah took a deep breath. "My mother left when I was a baby. According to Papa, she offered no explanation. One day she was just gone, and although he searched for her, there was no news of her whereabouts until she showed up in the Rhône four years later."

"A harsh truth to have to tell a child," Lord Spencer muttered.

"He didn't have to," Sarah said. "In fact, I know he planned to protect me from it, but I overheard him discussing the facts with Lady Andover while they were courting. He specifically requested that she treat me well—that I was not to suffer from any feeling of rejection the truth might cause."

"And did Lady Andover live up to her responsibility?"

"I believe she tried, or that she would have done had I not known the truth." Sarah hesitated. She'd already told Lord Spencer more than she'd ever shared with her friends. Was it wise to continue?

"What do you mean?"

Tempted to share her innermost feelings, Sarah said,

"I was hurt by all the lies that she and Papa told me. When I eventually confronted them, they said they'd acted in my best interest, but I disagreed. Since then I've given them both more trouble than they bargained for, I think, always trying to escape them by seeking refuge on the roof or in my den in the woods."

"You had a den in the woods?" He sounded pleasantly surprised.

"Of course," she said, enjoying his reaction.

"So did I." He glanced down at her. "But mine was more of a fort. My brother and I . . ." He paused, inhaling deeply as he looked away. There was a moment's hesitation before he said, "We played some wonderful games there as children, fighting off our invading sisters with wooden swords and projectiles—pig bladders filled with water or mud."

Sarah laughed. "They must have been furious with you."

"I suppose they were on many occasions. We teased them a great deal."

Staring up at him, she caught her breath. "You're smiling again," she whispered.

"Am I?"

Her heart beat faster. She nodded. "It suits you. You should do it more often."

"I'll keep that in mind," he said, turning once again serious. Shifting his gaze, he looked out across the water.

Deciding she would not allow his reaction to bother her, Sarah did the same, while silence stretched between them. They stood like that, side by side, as the sun rose higher and higher until Sarah became aware of Lord Spencer's hand wrapped around her own. When that had happened, she couldn't say, but it felt both right and soothing, and although she knew she probably ought to pull away, she did not feel compelled to do so.

"Do you read, Lady Sarah?" Lord Spencer suddenly asked.

Sarah blinked. She'd been lost in her thoughts for a while. "If you're inquiring as to whether or not I know my letters," she said with amusement, "then the answer is yes."

"Are you fond of twisting other people's words? Or do you simply enjoy torturing me?" he asked. Lowering his gaze, he turned his head toward her, his dancing eyes the only hint that he was teasing her.

"Only you," she replied, not bothering to hide her smile, "and in answer to your question, I do read on occasion—I find Shakespeare's comedies particularly enjoyable."

"I confess I'm more partial to the Greek classics—there are some wonderful stories there. Romantic ones too, if you find such literature tempting?"

I find you tempting.

She shook her head, dispelling the silly idea. "I used to," she said in answer to his question. "When I was younger, I often dreamed that my life would be like a fairy-tale and that one day I'd have my happily ever after, but then . . ." She swallowed convulsively at the recollection of dreams dashed as a world filled with liars and scoundrels had been revealed to her. " . . . I grew up, I suppose. We all have to eventually."

"So there will be no dashing prince to whisk you away on his magnificent steed?"

"Don't be absurd," she told him lightly, determined to hide her pain, her heartache, her dread of marrying a man who would not treat her well. The last thing she wanted from Lord Spencer—or from anyone else, for that matter—was pity. "A prince needs a princess, and I am anything but."

"You're right," he agreed, studying her. "But instead of telling me what you're not, why don't you tell me what you are?"

Words tumbled through her head, all of them describing a girl who no longer existed. She missed that girl. "I no longer know," she said, because she did not want to tell him she was scared, or embarrassed, or that she'd lost herself to guilt.

"Then tell me who you used to be, and perhaps we can try to find you together."

A wave of emotion crashed over her. Why did he care? It would be so much easier if he didn't. Her heart beat restlessly in her chest. "Outgoing and adventurous." She paused before admitting, "Happy."

"In spite of your strained relationship with your parents?"

She brushed aside a bothersome strand of hair. The thread between them tightened. "I've never been the sort of person to sit and feel sorry for myself while life went on around me. Instead, if happiness had vanished from my immediate surroundings, I would go looking for it."

"And did you always find it?"

"Yes. Even though it often came at a price: a grazed knee, trouble with a farmer for letting a pig out of its pen, a scolding from my father . . ." *Ruination.* Pulling away, she crossed her arms over her chest. It was too much—her awareness of him too acute. If she wasn't careful, she'd find herself falling for this man, and she could not afford for such a thing to happen. She wouldn't survive it.

An eyebrow rose, but he did not look censorious. "So you were the hoydenish type?"

She shrugged. "To say otherwise would be a lie."

"Honest through and through," he muttered. "I like that."

"Have you made any sketches of Thorncliff yet?" she asked, directing the conversation away from herself. If she were completely honest, she would tell him the truth about herself this instant, but that would mean the end of a promising friendship—a friendship she wasn't quite ready to give up.

"There hasn't been much time, though I was thinking of starting today—this afternoon, to be exact."

"It seems like a lot of work," Sarah said as she glanced toward the house. It was partially hidden from view by trees and bushes, but she could still catch a glimpse of the towers at each corner. "It's an intricate building with a lot of details—particularly around the windows. How long do you think it will take you to make the model once your sketches have been completed?"

He shrugged. "A year, I'd imagine. I have to carve the plaster casts first, and that takes time. One mistake and I'll have to start over."

"I'd offer to help, but the only thing I've ever carved was a bird, which ended up looking quite peculiar after I accidentally cut off its beak. I sliced the tip of my thumb in the process. Who knew a finger could bleed so much? It was quite impressive."

"Not as impressive as having a stone lodged in your forehead, I'll wager." Bowing toward her, he brushed aside his hair to reveal a puckering scar an inch above his left eyebrow.

"How on earth did you manage that?"

He straightened. "I was out for a ride one day when I was about ten, perhaps eleven. My hat was knocked from my head by a low-hanging branch, and when I leaned over, attempting to pluck it from the ground with my whip—a much simpler task than actually dismounting—I lost my balance and fell smack on my face."

Sarah gasped. "How awful!"

"There was a pretty bad graze too, but that was gone within a week."

"It adds a dangerous edge to your appearance." She pursed her lips. "I was wrong to call you arrogant, Lord Spencer, for it is clear now that the ladies have no choice but to swoon at your feet."

"I never said they swoon at my feet," he amended with a furrowed brow that caused Sarah's stomach to tighten. "Nevertheless, I shall take your comment for what it was surely meant to be—a compliment. Even though I don't see you swooning."

She was beginning to fear that she might. Tilting her head defiantly, she said, "I am made of sturdier stuff, my lord."

That made him laugh—a deep rumble that tickled her insides. Heaven help her.

"I fell off a horse once as well," she admitted. The memory still terrorized her. "I haven't ridden since."

"Really?" He looked and sounded equally surprised. "But everyone rides."

"Not me." She shuddered at the very idea of it. "You couldn't pay me enough to get onto one of those unpredictable beasts."

His eyes sharpened. "Not even if I tell you that I'm planning a surprise for you?" Taking her by the arm, he started leading her back toward Thorncliff.

What was he doing? What was *she* doing? She was supposed to be spending time with Mr. Denison. Instead she was allowing Lord Spencer to creep beneath her skin. *Resist him,* she told herself. *Resist the temptation he offers.*

She was beginning to suspect the effort would be futile, especially since he'd made no effort to charm her with compliments or platitudes. He wasn't the type. But that didn't mean this surprise he spoke of wasn't a means to achieve the same goal as a compliment might. Appreciation was swiftly replaced by suspicion. After all, he was a man. He was also aware of her intention to marry Mr. Denison. So then why was he asking her questions that made it seem as if he wished to encourage a deeper friendship with her? And why was he arranging surprises for her? She could think of only one explanation.

Forcing him to a halt, she turned and faced him. "Lord Spencer, are you trying to seduce me?" He might not wish to marry, but that didn't mean he was opposed to a liaison.

He stumbled a little "God no!"

She frowned. "You needn't sound so appalled." As if she were the last woman on earth he'd ever consider.

"Of course I'm appalled! How can I not be when you just asked me if . . ." He shook his head. "I'm a gentleman, Lady Sarah. I would never try to lead you astray."

He sounded sincere, and she found that she believed him. Her curiosity got the better of her. "May I ask about the nature of this surprise?" she asked.

"If I told you, then it wouldn't be much of a surprise, now, would it?"

Sarah scrunched her nose, conceding the point. "If it involves riding, you might as well forget it."

"We'll see. You've a few days to decide if you're courageous enough to find out what it is, but you will need to get on a horse in order to do so."

Sarah did not like the thought of that one little bit, but the idea that he'd been thinking about her enough to consider planning a surprise for her warmed her heart. Eyeing him, she warned herself to beware. Really, could there be anything more tragic than falling for yet another man with whom she had no hope of spending her future? *Friends*. That was all they could ever be.

They climbed the steps to the terrace in silence, though there was nothing awkward about it. If anything, it felt comfortable—as if they'd known each other for years and found no need for unnecessary conversation.

Eager for breakfast, Sarah hoped the servants would have some food ready for them in the dining room. She hastened toward the French doors, but a staying hand stopped her. Puzzled, she looked up at Lord Spencer, whose brow was set in a frown as he regarded the ground before them. "What is it?" she asked, unable to comprehend the reason behind his apprehension.

"You should watch where you're going," he told her simply. Then, with a nod toward the house, he released her and continued on his way.

Surprised by his peculiar warning, Sarah watched as he reached the door, opened it and waited for her to join him. Her gaze returned to the ground before her, curious to discover the reason behind his odd behavior. Surely she must have missed something. But there was nothing except a crack in the tiles, and then it struck her. Raising her gaze, she studied Lord Spencer, who appeared to have grown rigid in a manner that spoke of mild discomfort. "Are you superstitious, my lord?"

He shrugged ever so slightly, as if aiming for an air

of nonchalance, though he failed miserably in that regard. "I wouldn't be the first, and I doubt I'll be the last," he muttered.

"No. You probably wouldn't," she agreed, intrigued to discover that the Earl of Spencer was governed by irrational fear—that he had a flaw. Well, perhaps it was more of a quirk, really, but what surprised her was her own reaction, for rather than think it strange, she found it utterly endearing.

"And if you must know," he said as she reached his side and stepped over the threshold, "it's not limited to stepping on cracks."

"No, I don't suppose it would be," she said, amused by his resolve to defend himself even though an accusation had yet to be made.

"I do many things in threes."

"Like cutting up food?" When he failed to respond, she chose to clarify. "When I was seated beside you at dinner the first evening, I noticed that you cut your orange slices into three equal parts."

"Yes . . . well . . . one can never be too thorough." He expelled a sigh. Sensing that he had come to a halt, Sarah turned toward him. He offered a sheepish smile. "I know it's illogical. My sister Rachel has certainly told me so repeatedly. I just feel that there's no harm in adhering to these notions unless, of course, someone happens to be standing directly behind me when I throw spilled salt over my shoulder."

Sarah felt her lips twitch, but she made a deliberate effort to remain serious. The last thing she wanted was for him to suspect her of having a laugh at his expense, which she wasn't. But there truly was something undeniably charming about his self-conscious confession. For the first time since she'd made his acquaintance, he looked awkward and apprehensive, perhaps even a little concerned with what she might think of him now. It was all very silly in a way, that he should be embarrassed by his superstitious nature. But it was clear that he was, and Sarah felt a sudden overwhelming need to assure him that not only was it perfectly normal—after all, it was hardly an oddity, considering how many Englishmen crossed their fingers for good luck or hung a horseshoe outside their home—but it added character as well. If anything, he had just become all the more interesting. "You're quite right," she said. "I suspect it would be unpleasant to get salt in one's eye, so it is very correct of you to apply caution when . . . acting on this need of yours to ward off bad luck."

He stared back at her, then straightened himself, growing a full inch taller in the process. Crossing his arms, he said, "Lady Sarah, are you . . ." Closing his eyes for a spell, he looked as though he might be reconsidering his words, but then his eyes opened and he asked bluntly, " . . . are you mocking me?"

"Heavens no!" It bothered her that he might think so. "Indeed, you ought to know that I always touch wood after saying something the Fates might choose to meddle with, I never walk under ladders . . . not that I've been given much opportunity to avoid doing so, but it does seem like something one ought to avoid. Also, I make a deliberate effort not to voice my dreams out loud for fear that once I do, they'll have no chance of coming true." Not that they would anyway, considering how impossible they were. What a pity she hadn't been wiser when she'd attended the Gillsborough house party.

"Lady Sarah?" a faint voice prompted. Her vision sharpened just as Lord Spencer asked, "Are you all right?"

"Yes," she said, with a definitive nod for good measure. She would not allow him to suspect that anything was amiss—that she was unworthy of his friendship.

Please. Let me have this without him judging me.

He frowned. "You look a bit pale. Perhaps we should see if breakfast is ready."

Feeling increasingly hungry, Sarah immediately agreed and had just accepted his arm when a loud crash sounded farther down the hallway. Looking in the direction of the sound, Sarah saw that a maid was kneeling on the floor, frantically gathering up the items she'd been carrying while three young ladies hurried toward the dining room, giggling like girls straight out of the schoolroom as they looked back over their shoulders at the maid.

Pulling away from Lord Spencer, Sarah marched toward them. "Did you cause her to drop her tray?"

The women could not have been more than sixteen years of age, yet they looked at Sarah as though she had no business breathing the same air as them. "I don't see how that is any of your concern," a pretty blonde stated. Sadly, her character did not match her looks.

"Have you no compassion?" Sarah asked. She had no idea who these young ladies were other than that they seemed to be future Lady Andovers in the making. "No decency? The least you can do is apologize."

They looked incredulous. Then one of them, a slim brunette, said, "But she's a maid." She looked toward the kneeling woman. "It's her job to do what she is doing, just as it is our job to make a smashing match for ourselves." Looking beyond Sarah, the little shrew proceeded to bat her eyelashes at Lord Spencer while attempting a sultry smile most courtesans would have been proud of.

Good God!

"Watch yourselves or you'll be unmarried and breeding before the year is out," Sarah hissed in a low whisper for only them to hear.

"Oh?" The third one, with light blonde ringlets, asked, her eyebrows arching as she stared hard at Sarah. "And I suppose you speak from experience?"

They exploded in a fit of laughter while Sarah struggled to still her trembling hands. Balling them into fists, she turned away, her head held high by some miracle as she went to the maid and lowered herself on the floor beside her. "Allow me to help you," she said as she reached for a piece of broken porcelain and placed it on the tray.

"Oh, you mustn't, my lady," the maid said, her voice quivering a little as she piled the pieces of shattered teacups back onto the tray.

"That was badly done," Lord Spencer's voice spoke behind her, addressing the three young ladies. "You ought to be ashamed of yourselves."

"We were just having a bit of fun," one of the ladies complained. Sarah decided to focus on the shards of porcelain.

"Perhaps I should have a word with your parents about your deplorable behavior, not only toward Lady Duncaster's maid but toward Lady Sarah as well. You are in no position to speak to her with such disrespect."

A muttered exchange of words followed, and then the closing of a door. Sarah sighed. At least her chest wasn't clenched as tightly as it had been earlier. Footsteps thudded against the floor. "Here's another piece," Lord Spencer said as he bowed over Sarah. She felt his hand upon her arm, and then he was helping her to her feet. "I've asked a footman to come and assist, so please, allow me to ensure that you are well cared for—your hunger appeased."

"Thank you." She accepted the arm he offered.

"That was very kind of you, what you just did," he said as they walked away from the maid. The footman Lord Spencer had summoned arrived to help.

"I consider offering help a natural response to someone in need."

"And yet it isn't. Not when we consider the different ranks within our Society."

Sarah's temper flared. "Are you telling me that because she is a maid, she is less deserving of assistance? That you and I are too important to help her?"

"No. But I believe most peers would have called for someone to assist rather than offer assistance themselves." Lowering his voice, he said, "In case you were wondering, I quite liked how domestic you looked just now. More importantly, you've proven yourself most charitable—a trait I happen to admire a great deal."

"Thank you, my lord, but—"

"Lady Sarah," he said, expelling a very exasperated sigh. "Are you not aware that a gentleman ought to be allowed the courtesy of complimenting a lady without too much resistance?"

Biting her lip, Sarah chastised herself for her stubbornness. "Please forgive me, my lord. Your words of praise are most appreciated, I assure you."

He frowned slightly but said nothing further, nodding his approval instead.

With heightened spirits, Sarah allowed Lord Spencer to lead her through to the dining room, where an elaborate buffet, complete with sausages, bacon, kippers, eggs, toast and a variety of preserves had been prepared. Six footmen stood ready to assist, and since Sarah and Lord Spencer were the first to arrive, Sarah had no doubt that their requirements would swiftly be met.

Now that she was aware of Lord Spencer's propensity for threes, it didn't escape her notice that he added three pieces of bacon to his plate alongside his eggs, or that he stirred his coffee three times in a clockwise motion after adding a splash of milk and three spoons of sugar. Smiling quietly to herself, Sarah was busily buttering her toast when Lord Spencer rose to his feet in an unexpected hurry and said, "Good morning, my lady."

Raising her head with a jerk, Sarah drew a sharp breath at seeing her hostess staring down at her with a distinct air of curiosity. "Good morning, Lady Duncaster," Sarah said with immediate haste, hoping she didn't sound too dim-witted, considering the slight pitch of her voice. "I hope you don't mind us getting a head start on the food, but we were both up at an unreasonably early hour and couldn't resist the temptation of such a wonderful assortment of dishes." Inhaling deeply, she tried to slow the pace of her tongue, which was practically tripping over itself. "We'd be honored if you would care to join us."

"My dear Lady Sarah," the countess said as she looked from Sarah to Lord Spencer and then back again. "There is very little need for you to concern yourself or for you to be so wary of me, for that matter. In fact, I am really quite ordinary, in spite of my eccentricities, which I daresay are numerous. That aside, however, your family and Lord Spencer's are paying good money for a luxurious getaway. If it is your wish to venture down into the kitchen and rummage through the cupboards in search of a midnight snack, then by all means, don't let me stop you. This may be my home, but after turning it into a guesthouse, I have relinquished all expectation of receiving the same considerations that would have been my due had I not done so." Her lips drew into a wide smile. "That said, I'd be delighted to join the two of you for breakfast if I may. I simply love becoming better acquainted with my guests. I've had little opportunity to speak with you, Lady Sarah, and although your grandparents were dear friends of mine, Spencer, I'm embarrassed to say that I know next to nothing about you." She then took a seat across from Sarah and beckoned for a footman to pour her some tea.

Lord Spencer resumed his seat and Sarah took a bite of her toast, pausing only for a moment in stunned surprise as a generous slice of cake topped with a thick layer of whipped cream was placed before Lady Duncaster. The countess must have realized how unusual this seemed, for she did not hesitate in explaining that this was her preferred food in the morning. "If it were up to me, I'd eat nothing else throughout the day, but my physician has cautioned me that it's not the best for my health and that I ought to eat the occasional meat, fruit and vegetable, though the mere thought of doing so makes me shudder. I've agreed to a compromise though, requiring that all such meals are accompanied by jam or preserves—something with which to sweeten each bite."

"I can't say I'd enjoy that myself," Lord Spencer remarked as he carefully cut his bacon to pieces, "but I do admire you for sticking to your preferences."

"Why? Because of what others might think or say?" Lady Duncaster asked as she scooped up a large spoonful of cake and popped it into her mouth.

Lord Spencer stilled, and Sarah turned toward him, keen to hear his reply.

"Precisely," he said.

With a low chuckle, Lady Duncaster dabbed her lips with her napkin and took a sip of her tea. "Look at me, my lord. I am dressed no differently than I was forty years ago, though my hair has thinned dramatically since then, which is why I have taken to wearing wigs that were *au courant* before I was even born."

"You're not fond of the modern ones?" Sarah asked, taking the chance she'd been given to pry a little.

Lady Duncaster snorted. "They're so horribly plain, whereas this one, for instance . . ." Raising her hand, she gave the pile of cigar-shaped curls on top of her head a little pat. "What can I say? I consider this an intricate work of art. Don't you agree?"

"I suppose so," Sarah hedged. "Either way, I think it suits you splendidly."

Lady Duncaster smiled. "I know it's unusual—that most people view me as something of an oddity because of it—but it's what I like, so I see no reason to change it."

"Have you always disregarded other people's opinions?" Lord Spencer asked.

Lady Duncaster turned her eyes toward the ceiling in contemplation. "No. Not always. There was a time when I adhered to protocol and never veered from what was expected of me. But then one day it occurred to me how miserable I was and how desperately I longed for a bit of excitement in my life." Lowering her gaze, she looked to Sarah and Lord Spencer in turn. "When Lord Duncaster was alive, God rest his soul, we took great pleasure in traveling together to faraway destinations. In fact, it was a long sea voyage from India to England that initially brought us together." She sighed deeply as if lost in a distant time, but then she blinked and her gaze sharpened. "Really, if you ever have the opportunity to leave England and see other places, I highly recommend the adventure such a journey offers. Thankfully, my husband and I brought so many wonderful memories of our travels back home with us, which is part of the reason why I could never see myself leaving Thorncliff.

"Here, amidst the many mementos, I can recall with fondness the greatest love of my life—a man without whom I scarcely know what to do with myself." Her hazel eyes shimmered a little with momentary bleakness, but then her entire demeanor turned challenging as she raised her chin and said, "What others may think of me is inconsequential— particularly now that I am in my dotage. Besides, they're certainly willing to forgive my eccentricities in exchange for coming here."

"Well, I have to say I like you all the better for it," Lord Spencer told her.

Sarah smiled, as did Lady Duncaster. "There's nothing wrong with having a bit of personality," the countess added, "though I do believe the *ton* frowns upon those of us who dare to put it on open display. Too bad, I say." And with that, she raised her teacup in salute.

Half an hour later, the threesome had finished their meal, while the din within the room had risen significantly due to the arrival of many more guests. "If you'll please excuse me," Lord Spencer said as he, Sarah and Lady Duncaster strode out into the hallway, "there's a matter I'd like to attend to, though I do hope to see you both later."

"We shall depend upon it. Shall we not, Lady Sarah?" Lady Duncaster asked.

"Indeed we shall," Sarah agreed, reluctant to let him go, since it brought an end to a pleasant morning and reminded her that she was to spend time with Mr. Denison. Perhaps she could avoid her future husband for just a bit longer?

Hope bloomed as Lady Duncaster took her firmly by the arm and guided her through to the stairs, where Sarah's parents were presently descending along with her sisters and Hester. "We were wondering what happened to you, Sarah," Lady Andover said with a fleeting glance in her daughter's direction before looking toward Lady Duncaster. "May I compliment you once again on your beautiful home, Lady Duncaster? It is a remarkable work of architecture."

"Thank you, Lady Andover. You are most kind," Lady Duncaster said. "I trust you are comfortable in your rooms?"

"Oh, indeed we are," Lord Andover said. "There is nothing with which we can find the slightest displeasure."

"I'm happy to hear it," Lady Duncaster said. "As for your query regarding Lady Sarah—it appears she and I are both early risers, for which I'm most grateful. She kept me company during breakfast, and in return I have promised her a tour of the gallery."

"How terribly kind of you," Lord Andover said while his wife beamed with pleasure. Undoubtedly, they would have been less pleased to discover that Sarah had been sharing Lord Spencer's company. Lord Andover looked at Sarah. "Just don't forget about Mr. Denison. I understand you're supposed to be meeting him in an hour for a tour of the library and that he's also taking you rowing this afternoon? That ought to be fun."

"I'm sure it will be," Sarah said tightly. "In fact, I can hardly wait."

Her father must have registered the sarcasm, judging from his immediate frown. Before he could comment, however, Lady Duncaster said, "Since you have an appointment, Lady Sarah, we'd best be on our way if you're to see the gallery first." To Sarah's parents she added, "Please excuse us, but we'd hate to leave Mr. Denison waiting. Just go on through to the dining room and you'll find your breakfast there."

She and Sarah waited until Sarah's family had continued on their way, then they started up the stairs. It wasn't until they reached the landing that Lady Duncaster said, "I know it's none of my affair, Lady Sarah, but I cannot understand why a young woman of noble birth, such as yourself, would pay any attention to a man like Mr. Denison. Forgive me for being outspoken, but I've always had a tendency to attack an issue with directness, so if there's anything you'd like to share—a burden weighing heavily upon your shoulders—I will keep your confidence. Have no fear of that."

The comment caught Sarah off guard. She was not accustomed to having her problems addressed so plainly by others and had in fact hoped they would go unnoticed. "It is kind of you to concern yourself about me, my lady—"

"Oh, kindness has nothing to do with it, my dear," Lady Duncaster said as she guided Sarah along a corridor. "I am an old woman with little to occupy my mind. It is why I chose to fill Thorncliff Manor with people.

"Have you any idea how empty this place is when it's just me and the servants? It's frightfully depressing really. No, my inquiry is entirely based on pure curiosity and the hope that your story will distract me from the fact that I have lived my last adventure long ago and have only the end looming before me."

"You speak as though you're well into your eighties," Sarah said, feeling quite distressed on behalf of her hostess, "when you appear to be not a day over fifty-five."

"Ha! You are sweet to say so. Why, I feel younger already."

They soon arrived in a long, sunny room with tall ceilings embellished by stucco cherubs, flower garlands and flowing ribbons cast in gilded plaster. Displayed along the length of the left wall were paintings—the usual ancestral portraits—though they appeared more vibrant here, aided by the bright light spilling through the windows opposite. "Please forgive me, my lady," Sarah said as they went to stand before a painting of a man wearing a breastplate, his chin adorned by a pointy beard, "but I would prefer not to speak of my troubles. It would serve no purpose but to tarnish your opinion of me."

"I doubt that very much, considering my own colorful past, but I respect your wish and will press you no further. However, I do suggest you keep in mind that our transgressions are always far worse in our own minds than they are in actuality."

"I must disagree with you there. The *ton*—"

"Disapproves of most things that fall outside a particular set of rules. That is not to say your actions, whatever they may have been, are not to be frowned upon. But you are still young, and it would be a shame for you to let past errors deprive you of a happy future. Especially if you regret what you did and are unlikely to repeat the mistake."

If only it were that simple, Sarah thought as they

moved on to the next painting. It was of a lady with hard eyes and a sharp chin, her lips set in a petulant pout, as if she could think of a dozen things she'd rather be doing than posing for a portrait. Set outdoors, she wore a heavy leather glove on one hand, upon which was perched a falcon. "Some things are beyond repair," Sarah said, aware of the pain that laced her words.

"Certainly," Lady Duncaster agreed, "but instinct tells me you're a good person, Lady Sarah, and that you don't deserve to be punished forever."

"Perhaps," Sarah said, wishing the conversation would draw to a speedy end.

"Lord Spencer seems to enjoy your company," Lady Duncaster pointed out as she drifted onward. The manner in which she spoke suggested that she suspected a blooming romance between them.

"We are friends," Sarah said, following her, "scarcely more than acquaintances, really, considering we did not know each other prior to coming here."

"Hmm . . . there is no chance you will choose to share your secret with him then?"

The question brought Sarah to an abrupt halt. "Absolutely not!" *Good heavens.* The very idea of doing so was preposterous, not to mention that she could scarcely believe Lady Duncaster, whom she had only recently met, was being unbelievably forward, both in her suppositions and in her suggestions.

To her dismay, Lady Duncaster responded to Sarah's indignation with a light chuckle, the creases about her eyes deepening with the effort as she turned to face her. "Are you aware that George and I were not supposed to marry? In fact, I had been promised to his best friend."

"That must have been terribly difficult."

Lady Duncaster raised an eyebrow. "Duty-bound to marry one while your heart belongs to the other." She studied Sarah closely. "The passion with which you responded before suggests that you will consider confiding in Lord Spencer sooner than you think, my dear. Indeed, I do believe that you will find yourself without much choice in the matter." Her smile was secretive as she moved on, leaving Sarah stunned and feeling uncomfortably uncertain about her life as she knew it.

"Come along, my dear," Lady Duncaster beckoned, drawing Sarah out of her reverie. "I hope you will excuse my frankness, but I rarely have the opportunity to speak openly, since most of my peers think I'm playing with half a deck of cards for the most part. I hope you're not too offended by everything I've said to you this morning."

"No," Sarah said. "Indeed, I find your candor refreshing, though perhaps a bit surprising. You're different than how I'd imagined." An older version of herself, Sarah decided.

Lady Duncaster nodded thoughtfully, then turned to regard the painting of a handsome man, perhaps in his midforties, with dark hair curling softly about his brow and a pair of chestnut-colored eyes. His jaw, though angular, wasn't cut in hard lines, and the edge of his mouth was drawn upward, as though he was about to laugh. "This is my George," the countess said, "forever youthful in the artist's portrayal of him, while I am condemned to wither with age. If everyone in the world were fortunate enough to know the kind of love we shared for each other, then they would be truly blessed."

Gazing up at the painting while Lady Duncaster

spoke of her husband, Sarah felt her heart ache for the countess. "It is so unfair that you must go on without him," she said.

"I used to think so, but he was a great deal older when he died than he was in this painting, and truthfully, nothing lasts forever. We all know it—we are aware that our days are numbered—yet we are still surprised when they draw to an end. Now that I am standing at the end of mine, though I may still have a good ten years ahead, I will tell you this: life is much shorter than you can possibly imagine, Lady Sarah. Eventually, all that matters is how you chose to live it, and I daresay that once you get that far, nobody will care one way or another, except for you." She hesitated a moment before saying, "His father died at sea, you know."

"How?" Sarah asked, realizing belatedly that the answer was not only obvious but that she was asking Lady Duncaster to volunteer more information than she might be willing to share. "Forgive me," she added hastily, "I did not mean to pry."

"Whyever not? There's nothing wrong with being curious, you know." With a final glance in Lord Duncaster's direction, Lady Duncaster moved on, her arm linked with Sarah's. "He was on his way to France in . . . 1797, if I recall. George and I were spending the Season in London, while George's father had decided to remain at Thorncliff, which had been his preference since his wife's death. Unbeknownst to us, he decided to go on a sea voyage. We never knew exactly what happened, but the ship sank, taking everyone with it, including Lord Spencer's grandfather."

"How tragic," Sarah said, astonished to discover such a connection between the two families.

"George blamed himself for his father's death,

which is probably why he became so obsessed with finding that silly treasure."

"Treasure?"

Lady Duncaster sighed. "There is no substance to it of course, other than a grieving man's desire to uncover his father's secrets—secrets which have no basis in reality."

"You're sure of this?" Sarah asked, curious to know more about this new, intriguing subject.

"Of course I'm sure, though I was careful in keeping that opinion to myself. George needed a purpose, you see, and hunting for imaginary treasure seemed as good as any."

"But how do you know it doesn't exist?" Sarah asked.

"Because George's father was a very serious man, Lady Sarah. He was not eccentric, by any means, which is probably why he always frowned upon my position as his daughter-in-law, though I do believe he accepted me eventually. He was the very pillar of propriety, you see, never once acting beyond the bounds of what was deemed acceptable by the *ton*. But then, quite unexpectedly really, his behavior grew increasingly peculiar. He withdrew from Society, began traveling a great deal and became fixated on remodeling Thorncliff, insisting it needed more marble and higher ceilings. The roof in the foyer, for instance, was raised ten feet during the last years of his life."

"And it looks magnificent," Sarah said, "but I fail to see why your husband would have thought it had anything to do with a treasure. Surely Lord Duncaster's father was merely trying to give himself something to do—his travels were probably nothing more than visits to various craftsmen."

"I agree with you," Lady Duncaster said, "but when his father died and George began organizing his belongings, he happened on a letter his father had received from Lord Spencer's grandfather. It was tucked away inside a book. George almost missed it, but after reading it, he became obsessed with the idea that his father had secretly been a treasure hunter and that his bounty was hidden away on the estate."

"What did the letter say to put such an idea in his head?"

Lady Duncaster sighed as she waved her hand dismissively. "Something about having to take one final voyage and to beware the north wind. It was all rather cryptic, but there was one specific thing that stood out, because at the end of the letter, Lord Spencer's grandfather told George's father to ensure that *the wealth* had been placed in safekeeping."

"That does sound a bit peculiar, though hardly enough to make an assumption about a hidden treasure," Sarah mused.

"My thoughts exactly," Lady Duncaster agreed, "but George had a vivid imagination, and I suppose he needed a project with which to pass the time, so he began searching for the treasure he believed his father had hidden at some time during the rehabilitation of the estate. To his great disappointment, nothing was ever found."

"I see," Sarah said. "Well, that is a pity, I suppose. It would have been wonderfully exciting if there really had been a treasure to find at Thorncliff."

Lady Duncaster smiled. "I agree. Unfortunately that isn't the case, for if there were, it would have been uncovered during the recent renovations I made to the estate. I must admit I was hoping to find something so I could prove my George correct in his hypothesis. Instead we must accept that it was never anything more than the fabrication of an aging man and that the letter was probably in reference to some investment Lord Spencer's grandfather and George's father had made together."

"I'm sorry," Sarah said.

Lady Duncaster nodded. "Me too, but that hardly helps, does it? No, I think a ball would do a better job of it."

"A ball?"

"Oh indeed! I shall host one on Saturday for all my guests and perhaps some of the local gentry too. What do you think, Lady Sarah? Wouldn't that be splendid?"

"Indeed it would," Sarah said as, without thinking, she took Lady Duncaster's hand between her own and gave it a little squeeze.

Sitting in the shade of an oak tree that afternoon, Christopher tried to concentrate on a window detail he was drawing, satisfied that his trip to Portsmouth earlier in the day had gone better than he'd expected. At least he'd managed to send the letter he'd written—a key element in the surprise he now *had* to prepare for Lady Sarah, thanks to his impromptu remark. What the hell had he been thinking?

That you wanted a reason to spend more time with her.

A picnic would have done the trick if he hadn't said he was "planning" it. Her expectations would be bigger now. He had to think of something grand. And he had. He'd even happened upon a gift for her—something he was sure she'd appreciate.

His charcoal slipped and he muttered a curse. He didn't want this—this stupid concoction of human emotions that she had created in him. It was his own fault for asking too many damn questions. Remaining indifferent had been easier before, but now, with each answer she'd given him, every little thing she'd said, he'd felt a commonality with her, along with an unexpected urge to give her something to look forward to.

"I admire your patience," Fiona said as she plunked herself down beside him, scattering his thoughts. "Looks like your next project is coming along very nicely."

"No thanks to you," he grumbled.

"What? Is Lady Sarah distracting you, Kip? How promising." She chuckled as she stretched out her legs.

He swatted her arm. "Not really. I'm determined to resist her charms just to spite you."

"Ah! So you admit that you find her charming?"

He glared at her. "Not in the least."

"Don't be ridiculous," Fiona insisted. "Lady Sarah is perfectly lovely. If you say otherwise, I won't believe you."

"Then don't," he muttered. "Whether you believe me or not is clearly inconsequential, but just so you know, I intend to repay all of you for this."

"I shudder in fear," Fiona said, looking not the least bit concerned. Instead, she glanced out across the lake. "She doesn't look very happy at the moment, does she?"

"Who are you talking about," Christopher asked, even though he knew the answer well enough.

"Lady Sarah of course," Fiona replied.

Christopher nodded. It was no coincidence that he'd picked a spot where he could keep an eye on her while Mr. Denison rowed her around the lake. As polite as he'd been the one time Christopher had met him, Christopher couldn't ignore the feeling that there was something unpleasant about that man.

"Do you suppose he might be blackmailing her parents?"

Christopher started. "Why on earth would you suggest that?"

"Because it makes sense," Fiona said. "Or maybe Lord Andover gambled Lady Sarah away. He's not exactly known for his brilliant card play."

Christopher gaped at his sister. "Honestly, I don't know where you get your ideas, but it just so happens that Lady Sarah has told me the reason. It has to do with breeding racehorses."

Fiona did not look convinced. "Are they arguing now?" she asked, abandoning the topic. "It looks like they might be."

Returning his gaze to Lady Sarah's boat, Christopher saw that Mr. Denison was leaning toward Lady Sarah, his back rigid as he spoke, while she was leaning away from him. Christopher clenched his hand. The charcoal snapped.

"You ought to interfere," Fiona said.

"It's not my place. Besides, they're out on a lake. It's not as if I can just walk up to them."

"As a gentleman you really should—"

"That," he clipped, with a nod in Mr. Denison's direction, "is the man she's decided to marry. She's made her choice, Fiona, for whatever reason. More importantly, he also happens to be her parents' choice."

"I know you detest any mention of Miss Hepplestone, but I remember you eagerly rushing to assist her with the tiniest of things—things she was perfectly capable of handling on her own—even though she was completely undeserving of your help or of you."

"Don't think I haven't forgotten," he bit out.

"I know you haven't," Fiona said with quiet understanding. "But you are still allowing her to deny you a happy future. To this day she is skewing your vision of anyone who gets too close to you." She sighed. "I like Lady Sarah, and—"

"Why? What reason do you have? You've known her for exactly three days, which is entirely too little time for you to have decided that she will make a fine addition to this family. I certainly haven't." But in spite of his protestations, he couldn't help but admit that he liked Lady Sarah as well. At least not if he was being completely honest with himself. He was just afraid of making the same mistake twice.

"You forget that I'm an excellent judge of character and that I didn't like Miss Hepplestone from the beginning. The problem was that you wouldn't listen to what I had to say."

It was true. Fiona had only been twelve years old when she'd warned him against the woman he'd fallen in love with. He hadn't taken her seriously.

"As for the length of time you've known her," Fiona added, "it's the same duration of time that she's known Mr. Denison, and she is considering him. Besides, since you don't plan to marry for love anyway, I hardly think it matters how well you know her as long as she is who she claims to be, which she *is*. Add to that her pleasant demeanor, her candor and her beauty, and you've found a woman more suitable to be your wife than any other I can think of."

Perhaps Fiona was right. After all, it was common practice among the *ton* to marry without considering whether or not you'd get along with your spouse in the long run. What mattered was prestige, forming alliances and accumulating wealth. Everything else was secondary, and since all he really needed was to produce an heir, his presence would only be necessary in the bedroom—a thought that appealed a great deal as he looked out across the water at Lady Sarah.

That morning, when she'd slipped and he'd caught her, she'd looked so kissable that he'd barely been able to resist the temptation her lips had offered. But if he married her, he'd be able to enjoy those lips, along with the rest of her, every single day. The rest of the time he'd be free to visit his club, build his models and enjoy the company of friends. It was certainly worth thinking about.

"**D**id you mention my daughters to Lord Spencer?" Mr. Denison asked.

"I did," Sarah said, grateful she could offer an honest reply.

"And did you speak favorably of them?"

"Of course!"

"Why hasn't he spoken to them then?"

Feeling like a naughty schoolgirl being chastised, Sarah sat back a little. "I'm sure his lordship has been busy with other matters. Furthermore, he is under no obligation to show an interest in Victoria or Diana simply because I have suggested it. And since he doesn't wish to marry, if you will recall, I think we should give him more time."

"I'm of the opinion that you weren't persuasive enough. Don't think I haven't noticed the way you look at him," Mr. Denison said as he pulled on the oars. After meeting Sarah in the library two hours earlier and informing her that he knew she'd break-fasted with Lord Spencer, he hadn't let the subject go.

"And what way might that be?" Sarah asked, ex-asperated by his accusations.

"Like he's the handsomest man you've ever set eyes on." The right oar splashed against the surface in an awkward motion.

"I cannot deny his good looks," she said, even though she knew that to do so would be a mistake.

Mr. Denison's face reddened. "Perhaps I should remind you that you'll be marrying *me*!"

"I can assure you I haven't forgotten that fact." How wonderful it would be if she could, just for a little while.

"And I don't like to share," Mr. Denison warned as he leaned forward. Relaxing the oars, he took her hand.

Instinctively, Sarah retreated, leaning away from him. That too was a mistake. His eyes darkened into black thunderclouds. "Don't worry, my dear," he murmured as his thumb stroked along her wrist, "I have no doubt that he will be removed from your mind as soon as I take you to bed. In fact, I think you will beg me for more once I put my tongue to work on your body."

It was becoming increasingly difficult for Sarah to keep from gagging. Her stomach roiled at the awful image he evoked, of the two of them as lovers. In-stinct told her to run—to jump overboard and swim for shore—but then what? She had nowhere else to go, nobody to turn to and not nearly enough money to start a new life on her own. There wasn't even a convent for her to seek refuge in anymore. Henry VIII had made sure of that when he'd disbanded them all during the sixteenth century. Silently, she cursed the former monarch and the influence he was having on her life almost three hundred years after his death.

"I can just imagine how it will be between us," Mr. Denison continued, his lips parting as he dropped his gaze to her breasts. "Did your former lover make you shiver and tremble with pleasure?" Before she could manage a reply, he said, "I can see from your shocked expression that he did not. No wonder you're so reluctant to let me near you after such a disappointing experience. Fear not though. I'll give you everything you require. I'll—"

"Please stop!" Good God, she couldn't stand to hear another word. "You're clearly a very passionate man, but I am a lady, Mr. Denison, and while I may have had one indiscretion, I fear I'm still quite inexperienced in these matters, as you yourself have just noted. So please, do try to restrain yourself until we are legally wed."

"You drive a hard bargain," he muttered, eyes boring into her. "Knowing you're not a virgin and that you're going to be mine is driving me mad with need, but if you prefer a traditional courtship, then I suppose I can accommodate your wishes for a little while longer."

"You are most kind," Sarah said. She almost sagged with relief when he released her hand and continued rowing, their conversation focused on mundane topics like the weather, the beauty of the estate and on gossip relating to other guests.

When she and Mr. Denison returned to shore and disembarked a while later, Sarah found Lady Fiona striding toward them with a bright smile on her face. "What an excellent day for boating," Lady Fiona said. "I trust you had an enjoyable tour of the lake."

"We did indeed, my lady," Mr. Denison said, tipping his hat in greeting.

Moving to Sarah's side, Lady Fiona fell in step beside them as they started back toward the house. "I'm sorry to intrude on you like this, but I was actually hoping to take a walk with Lady Sarah so that she might advise me on a private matter."

"No need to apologize," Mr. Denison said. "I'm planning to enjoy my afternoon rest now anyway, so I shall leave Lady Sarah in your company." Turning toward Sarah, he said, "I've enjoyed our time together immensely and look forward to seeing you later."

"Likewise," Sarah said, hoping her tone didn't sound too flat. She watched him take his leave, then breathed a sigh of relief before turning to Lady Fiona. "You look very happy today."

"I find it difficult not to be," Lady Fiona said. "Surrounded by Thorncliff's vast expanse of greenery, flowers, birds and overall beauty that's only accentuated by the marvelous weather we've been having, I cannot be anything but absolutely content."

It was difficult for Sarah not to be affected by Lady Fiona's positive state of mind. With a smile, she said, "You spoke of a private matter before. Would you like to tell me how I can assist?"

"I must confess I may have exaggerated my need for your advice for Mr. Denison's benefit." Lady Fiona slanted a hesitant look in Sarah's direction. "Truth be told, I really just wanted your company."

"So . . . you lied?"

"Can you forgive me?"

Sarah chuckled. "Of course." They strolled toward a group of large oak trees with wide canopies that stood to one side of the lake. As they neared,

Sarah saw that someone was sitting beneath one of them—a man with his head bowed over a book that he'd propped up against one bent knee. Wearing a wide-brimmed hat, Sarah didn't recognize him until he looked up, arresting her with his penetrating gaze and that vexing hint of a smile that he casually wore with aplomb. It made her heart beat a little faster.

"Spencer!" Lady Fiona said. "What a surprise, finding you here."

He frowned, leading Sarah to believe that it was no great surprise at all. Catching the sparkle in Lady Fiona's eyes and the hint of mischief about her lips, Sarah was even more convinced that the woman had deliberately contrived to bring them together. Already planning an excuse to return to the house so she wouldn't intrude on Lord Spencer's privacy, Sarah considered telling the Heartly siblings that she'd just been reminded of a previous engagement when Lord Spencer stood up. "Won't you join me?" he asked.

Sarah studied him briefly, then looked to the ground where he gestured. The wide blanket he'd been sitting on would provide enough space for them all. Sarah was tempted, but she held herself back, unsure of allowing herself the joy of his company.

"What a lovely idea," Lady Fiona said as she stepped toward the blanket. "There's a brilliant view of the house from here, as well as of the lake, and with the shade from the tree I daresay we'll manage to keep our fair complexions. Come sit, Lady Sarah, and you'll see what I mean."

Unwilling to disappoint and more than a little tempted to spend her afternoon with Lady Fiona and most especially with Lord Spencer, Sarah lowered herself onto the blanket.

"What are you working on?" Lady Fiona asked her brother when they were all seated.

Having taken a seat beside Lord Spencer, Sarah could practically hear him grinding his teeth and tried not to smile at the knowledge that he was thoroughly annoyed with his sister. "Just a sketch," he said, glaring at Lady Fiona.

Unable to resist, Sarah said, "Might I have a look?"

Ever so slowly, he turned his eyes on her, as if considering all the possible excuses he could give in order to not grant her wish. How curious. "There's nothing much to see—just rough preliminary drawings of Thorncliff."

"Why don't you let me be the judge of that?" Sarah asked, more curious now due to his reluctance.

After a long moment he sighed, shook his head and reached for the book, handing it to Sarah. He watched as she opened it, contemplating all the ways in which he was going to murder his sister for this. Not so much for engineering an opportunity for him to spend more time with Lady Sarah but for bringing Lady Sarah's attention to his sketchbook. Drawings, in his estimation, were personal—a visual expression of the artist's innermost thoughts, and while most of his sketches were works of precision, lacking any emotion, there was one that he feared might divulge too much.

Carefully, Lady Sarah turned the first page, revealing a detail of Thorncliff's main entrance. "This is very intricate," she said. Her finger drifted across the paper, drawing Christopher's attention to the delicate structure of her hand. "Are there really two dragons perched above the door?"

"Yes," he said, unable to ignore the fruity scent of her. He leaned slightly closer so he could explore it further. Citrus, perhaps? He cleared his throat. "Each is holding a gilt flag. They're quite an atypical feature for an English manor, which is why I want to be certain I include them in the model."

"Spencer loves originality," Fiona said. And then, "Please excuse me a moment. I see Lady Genevieve over there, and I would so like to inquire about the gown she wore last night to dinner—it was very exquisite. I'll be back in just a moment."

Spencer watched her go, exasperated by her conspicuous attempt at getting him alone with Lady Sarah, not that he minded such an outcome in the least. It was the method that bothered him. "If you turn the page, you'll see that there are also tiny dragons peeking out from below the roofline."

"So there are," she said, studying the images. "I quite like them, I think." Lifting her gaze, she met his, her cheeks coloring as she did so. Hastily, as if attempting to appease a shock of nervousness, she brushed aside a stray lock of hair and looked away.

No doubt Lady Sarah was affected by his close proximity, which in turn sent a coil of awareness spiraling through him. He leaned in once more, pretending to study his work as well. Instead he studied her; the pulse beating like the wings of a timid bird against the curve of her neck, soft skin that would feel so smooth to the touch, a spray of tiny freckles dotting the bridge of her nose. What was it about her that fascinated him so?

"You're incredibly talented, my lord. The realism is astounding." She hesitated a moment before saying, "But I fear the perspective may be wrong here."

Ah yes, her directness.

She tapped her finger against the page. "These windows don't seem to make sense. Perhaps the proportions are wrong?"

"Are you certain?" Dragging his eyes away from the corner of her mouth, he studied the drawing he'd made that afternoon of Thorncliff's façade. Admittedly, something looked slightly off.

"The problem is here, I believe. The roofline doesn't slant enough as it moves off into the distance. If you make it narrower here"—she moved her fingers to illustrate her vision—"I think it will look more accurate."

"But then that tower will appear lopsided."

"Not if you continue your line from here . . . to here. Hand me your charcoal and I'll show you." She held out her hand, then wrinkled her nose. "If you'd like me to, that is. I've no wish to impose."

He handed her the charcoal, his fingertips briefly brushing her palm. She stiffened a little, then relaxed as she set to correcting his mistake. "There. I think that's better. Don't you agree?"

"You are most astute, my lady," he told her sincerely, for he was indeed impressed by her ability to weed out such a tiny error that, once corrected, made a huge difference to the drawing as a whole. "I don't suppose you'd be willing to help me with the rest of my drawings?"

"I'd be happy to," she said, but just as quickly as her smile had appeared, it faded as she said, "although, considering I am being courted by Mr. Denison, it might be unseemly of me to keep your company on a regular basis."

Even though it shouldn't have, given his own reluctance to pursue a serious relationship, he couldn't help but feel a bit disappointed. "I understand," he said, "but if the model I make turns out crooked, you'll be the one to blame."

She laughed at that, which pleased him. Seeing her

happy was like listening to birds sing or watching the sun rise—a spectacular gift of nature. It also made him long for closer contact with her, prompting him to nudge his shoulder playfully against hers.

"Lord Spencer," she chastised in a bubbly tone with no attempt to hide her humor, "you are being entirely too familiar."

"Does it bother you?" he risked asking.

She pursed her lips. "No, unless, contrary to what you told me yesterday, you are indeed trying to lead me astray." She raised one eyebrow, and Christopher immediately saw that hidden beneath her attempt at amusement was a very serious question.

"Upon my honor, I would never," he assured her, even though he knew he'd quite like to. But wanting and doing were two separate things. "As I've said, I have no interest in marriage."

"That doesn't quite answer my question."

"I'm a gentleman, Lady Sarah." He was sorely tempted to be a scoundrel. "I would never try to lead any woman astray. Will that suffice?"

She studied him a moment, then nodded. Returning her attention to the sketchbook, she turned the page and immediately drew a sharp breath. Christopher's blood thundered through his veins. "Is that . . ." Her words caught as she stared down at the picture he'd drawn of her. "I look so animated."

"Is that a compliment?"

There was a pause, and then she looked at him with deep emotion swimming in her eyes. "Absolutely."

A rush of warmth swept over him even as the fear of her discovering the true depth of his admiration for her dissipated. Surely she would see what the picture revealed, for he'd captured not only her looks but her spirit as well.

"I should like to see your model of Thorncliff once it's completed," she said, her cheeks flushing as she carefully closed his sketchbook and set it aside.

"Perhaps I'll invite you and Mr. Denison for a visit to Oakland Park, since you will likely be married by then."

Her throat seemed to work convulsively for a moment, reminding him that this was not a match she wanted. Even so, she offered him a faint smile. "I should like that very much. Thank you, my lord."

Perplexed by the sudden wave of anger that assailed him, he told her simply, "Think nothing of it. Your company would be greatly appreciated."

Chapter 7

"Will you partner with me for a game of whist?" Lady Duncaster asked Sarah that evening after dinner when they were joined by the gentlemen in the large Italian salon adjacent to the dining room.

"I'd be delighted to. But who will we be playing against?"

A devilish smile captured the countess's lips. "Lord Spencer and Mr. Denison. They're waiting for us over there at that table."

Following Lady Duncaster's gaze with foreboding, Sarah found the gentlemen seated across from each other, each with a drink placed before them. She was going to need one herself if she was to endure the upcoming game. "How could you do this?" she whispered as she rose to her feet and fell into step beside Lady Duncaster.

"I have a particular penchant for mischief," Lady Duncaster said conspiratorially.

"Thank you, but this is the sort of mischief I can do without." To keep company with the man she desired and the man she would marry, aware that they were not one and the same, and that they never would be, called for more endurance than Sarah believed herself capable of. "A brandy, if you please," she told a footman as she took her seat at the table.

"Strong stuff," Lord Spencer remarked, shuffling the cards.

"Lady Sarah is a strong woman," Mr. Denison said as he took a sip of his own drink, his eyes glistening in a manner that made Sarah squirm.

"I hope I didn't imply otherwise," Lord Spencer said.

"I'll have a brandy as well," Lady Duncaster told the footman, "and a cheroot."

The gentlemen stared. Lady Duncaster looked at them with incomprehension, while Sarah tried to control her smile. The countess was still quite capable of shocking her companions, it would seem.

"My lady," Mr. Denison eventually said, "would you not prefer some snuff? I have an excellent one that you're more than welcome to try."

"Thank you, but I have no intention of inhaling foreign substances into my nose, when it not only makes me sneeze quite uncontrollably but also has been observed to cause swelling and excrescences."

"Are you sure?" Mr. Denison asked, looking dubious.

"The physician John Hill claimed so, and that's got to be fifty or sixty years ago, which is why I choose to abstain completely," Lord Spencer said. "One might think, logically speaking, that inhaling the smoke from tobacco through the mouth would be equally harmful."

"Perhaps, but until medical evidence proves it, I see no harm in enjoying the occasional cheroot," Lady Duncaster said, "more so when I'm as old as I am."

"Quite," Lord Spencer agreed.

"However," Mr. Denison said, "even you must admit that for a lady to smoke in public, more so in front of a young unmarried lady whose delicate sensibilities are—"

"Did you not just say that Lady Sarah is a strong woman?" Lord Spencer inquired.

"Of course," Mr. Denison said. There was the brief hint of a scowl before he trained his features and smiled. "Nevertheless, it isn't proper."

"He is correct on that score," Lord Spencer said, addressing Lady Duncaster, while Sarah felt increasingly like a small child that everyone felt the need to protect. It vexed her.

"So he is," Lady Duncaster said, "but everyone knows how eccentric I am, so I'm sure they'll forgive me. As for Lady Sarah, if my smoking offends you, please don't hesitate to say so and I'll abstain without issue."

Piqued, and with the most bizarre temptation to irk Mr. Denison and Lord Spencer for their delicate treatment of her, Sarah said, "I have no issue at all, my lady."

There was a pause, and then, gathering his wits, Lord Spencer dealt the cards. The ladies' drinks arrived and a cheroot was lit for Lady Duncaster. Holding it expertly in one hand, she held her cards in the other, her poised elegance suggesting that she was not a novice when it came to smoking.

But while Lord Spencer seemed to have accepted their hostess's quirk, Mr. Denison continuously glanced toward her with disapproval as the game progressed. Nothing more was said, however, until Lady Andover approached a while later along with her friend, Mrs. Penbrook. Immediately, Lady Andover said, "I do not wish to interrupt your game, Lady Duncaster, but I couldn't help but notice that you are"—she lowered her voice to a whisper—"smoking, not only in public but in front of Lady Sarah."

Turning her head toward Lady Andover, Lady Duncaster blinked. "So I am."

Lady Andover set her mouth in an angle of distinct disapproval. "Might I ask you to stop?"

"This is her house, Mama," Sarah said, embarrassed that her stepmother would dare to comment so openly on a point of etiquette.

"While that may be true, Lady Sarah, we are not exactly her guests. Are we?" Cringing at the implication that they were customers, Sarah wished there was something she could say to stop Lady Andover from saying anything further. Unfortunately, the woman was determined to make her point. "Therefore, I would appreciate it if the rules of Society could be adhered to so Lady Sarah is not subjected to the sort of things that unmarried ladies should be protected from."

"I did try to tell her ladyship," Mr. Denison said as he beamed at Lady Andover, much like a puppy awaiting its treat.

"I'm pleased to hear that one of you was being sensible," Lady Andover said, patting the proverbial puppy on its head.

"Lord Spencer agreed with Mr. Denison," Sarah said. Even though she had not approved of him doing so, she suddenly wanted to force her stepmother to acknowledge his efforts to adhere to correct behavior as well.

"You chose to ignore both gentlemen?" Lady Andover asked.

Straightening her spine, Lady Duncaster said, "Since Lady Sarah is of age, I thought I would allow her to choose."

"And I suppose she had no issue with it," Lady Andover said, looking to Sarah.

"Of course not," Sarah said, meeting her step-mother's eyes with a steely gaze.

Sighing, Lady Andover shook her head. "Why am I not surprised?"

"With respect, I will bow to your wishes," Lady Duncaster said as she waved a footman over and handed him the offensive cheroot.

"Thank you," Lady Andover said. "Your consideration is much appreciated."

"And since that is the case, perhaps you will allow us to continue our game?" Lord Spencer inquired.

Spearing him with a hard look that had seemingly no effect, Lady Andover gave a curt nod before walking away, her arm linked with Mrs. Penbrook's.

"Well, that was rather awkward," Mr. Denison said a short while later. "I told you smoking was a bad idea."

"So you did," Lady Duncaster agreed, her eyes fixed on her cards.

They continued playing until the ladies had won twice and the gentleman three times. "If you'll forgive me, I believe I'll take myself off to bed," Mr. Denison said.

"I'll look forward to going for a ride with your daughters tomorrow," Lord Spencer said.

Sarah tried to hide her surprise. He'd told her specifically he didn't want to spend time with them—that the most he would do would be to engage them in a brief conversation—yet he was taking them riding now? Why? Unable to ask him about it, she held her tongue and wished Mr. Denison good night.

"Spencer," Lord Oakland said, approaching. He greeted the ladies before addressing his son once again. "Since you're done with your game, I was hoping to discuss some estate business with you before retiring."

"Excuse me, ladies," Lord Spencer said as he stood up. He bowed to each of them in turn, thanked them for the game and wished them a good night before following his father to a quiet corner at the other end of the room.

"I'm sorry about Lady Andover's interference earlier," Sarah said now that she had a chance to speak to Lady Duncaster in private.

"Think nothing of it," Lady Duncaster told her kindly. "Your stepmother was right and I was wrong. There's nothing more to it."

"You could ask her to leave," Sarah suggested. "The way she spoke to you was quite inappropriate."

"Then you would have to leave as well, would you not?" The countess's gaze drifted toward Lord Spencer. "You would no doubt marry Mr. Denison without further ado and lose your chance for true happiness."

"I already lost that chance long ago," Sarah murmured.

Lady Duncaster shook her head. "This is Thorncliff, Lady Sarah. Have a little faith, will you?"

Unwilling to discuss the subject further, Sarah forced a smile and nodded.

When she returned to the suite of rooms she shared with Alice and Juliet later that evening, Sarah quietly bid her sisters good night before entering her own bedchamber and closing the door behind her. Her thoughts were still on the awful experience she'd had with Mr. Denison out on the lake. Thankfully, it seemed she'd managed to dissuade his advances for now, but for how long? And once she became his wife, he'd have the right to do as he wished with her. It was a nauseating idea, to say the least.

And then there was Lord Spencer. He'd casually

joined her and Mr. Denison for tea on the terrace that afternoon, ignoring all of Mr. Denison's attempts to be rid of him. Chuckling at the memory, Sarah turned toward the bed and came to an immediate halt at the sight of a large object sitting in the middle of the floor. It was covered by a faded green piece of cloth. A note rested on top of it, and Sarah spared no time in picking it up, curious as to what it might say.

Please accept this gift as a token of my admiration and with the fondest memories of playing hide-and-seek with the little "rodent" who will soon reside within. I hope he will approve of his new home.

Your friend,
Lord Spencer

Sarah read the note again and then a third time for good measure before setting it aside and approaching the object. Since coming close to losing Snowball in the conservatory, she had kept him mostly in the small box she'd brought along in her trunk. There were holes in it for air of course, but it was still a tiny place for Snowball to spend his time in when Sarah was away from him.

Curious to see what Lord Spencer had given her, she reached out a hand and plucked away the fabric covering the gift, unveiling a large wooden-framed box with glass on all sides and a wooden lid with holes in the top. Inside, some hay had been placed in one corner, while segments cut from two slim branches had been placed at angles, creating ramps for Snowball to climb.

A smile touched Sarah's lips, spreading wide until she had no doubt that she was grinning like an imbecilic fool. She didn't care in the least. What Lord Spencer had done for her, or more precisely, what he had done for Snowball, deserved her deepest gratitude, and as she took the tiny creature out of the small box in which he'd been placed and set him down in his new habitat, she knew she'd have to find a way to repay Lord Spencer's unexpected kindness.

Chapter 8

"Isn't it exciting?" Lady Andover asked the following day in reference to the upcoming ball, which had been announced that day at luncheon. She was having tea with her daughters in a shaded corner of the terrace, while her husband had gone for a ride with Mr. Denison. "And to think that Lady Duncaster has been considerate enough toward the children to arrange a separate room in which they may dance with their governesses and maids in attendance is quite remarkable. It will give the two of you a wonderful opportunity to practice the steps your instructor has taught you," she said, addressing Alice and Juliet.

"Just as long as I won't be paired off with an eight-year-old," Alice said, looking not the least bit thrilled with the prospect.

"Nonsense, my dear," Lady Andover said, waving her hand dismissively. "You will dance with your sister."

Alice and Juliet exchanged a glance and groaned. Sarah didn't blame them. They'd been dancing with each other for over a year now and were surely eager to partner with boys their own age. Not much chance of that happening anymore. Sarah had wrecked such an opportunity for them, though she herself was of the opinion that a girl in search of ruination would not be deterred by an overbearing parent. "It is certainly an evening for us all to look forward to," Sarah said, even though she did not enjoy the prospect of dancing with Mr. Denison.

Later, when her sisters decided to join a game of croquet being played on the lawn, Sarah's stepmother leaned forward in her seat. "How are things progressing between you and Mr. Denison?" she asked.

Reaching for her teacup, Sarah raised it to her lips and took a sip. If only it were filled with stronger stuff. Like brandy. "Fine," she managed.

"Really? You don't sound convincing, Sarah."

Setting down her cup, Sarah forced herself to look Lady Andover in the eye. "What do you expect? He's old enough to be my father."

"And you were hoping for a young and handsome gentleman, I suppose?"

"I was hoping I'd have a choice."

"Well, you don't. It was difficult enough for your father to find one man willing to marry you, never mind two. And don't be discouraged by his age, Sarah. There are benefits to having a more mature husband."

Whatever those benefits might be, they eluded Sarah.

"It's just . . ." Sarah hesitated, suddenly overcome by emotion now that she was faced with the chance to confide everything she'd learned about Mr. Denison's character. She drew a shaky breath. "He's said some very troubling things to me."

Lady Andover frowned. "Such as?"

Encouraged, Sarah lowered her voice to a whisper. "He clearly has certain . . . expectations." Closing her eyes briefly, she struggled to go on. "Expectations of a physical nature, Mama."

"Well of course he does," Lady Andover said. "He's a man, and you're to be his wife."

"But the things he has said to me . . . the implications . . ."

"You're practically an innocent, Sarah. I'm sure you're making more of this than necessary, and considering what a nice man Mr. Denison is, you're doing him a great disservice by implying that he's done something wrong."

"He threatened to strike me if I give him trouble!"

"You must have shown him your willful side, then. I have warned you about that. Repeatedly." She sipped her tea while Sarah stared at her. "Just be a good wife, and I'm sure he'll treat you well. He's told me he cannot wait to show you your new home."

Any hope Sarah had of avoiding the future her parents had prepared for her shattered. "You don't care about me at all, do you?"

Lady Andover straightened herself. "I've loved you as best I could, considering you were not my own flesh and blood. You were very difficult as a child, always scampering about and doing things a little girl oughtn't do, like climbing trees and getting your gowns muddy. Frankly, I wasn't surprised to learn that you'd lost your innocence."

"Mr. Harlowe assured me that he would marry me," Sarah said in a voice so small it was barely audible.

Lady Andover shook her head. "Considering your very own mother abandoned you, I find that extraordinarily naïve."

Sarah winced, pained by the hateful comment. Anger was swift to follow. Stiffening her spine, she raised her chin a notch and said, "Perhaps if you had done your duty and shown an interest in me, advised me and warned me that men will say whatever they must to get what they want, then maybe things would have been different."

A deprecating smirk curled Lady Andover's lips. "You're a grown woman, Sarah. It's time you took responsibility for your own actions."

"And so I shall," Sarah said, her chest tightening as she rose to her feet and stared down at her stepmother. "But it still won't absolve you of your careless disregard toward me."

"Sarah," Lady Andover hissed, "you—"

"I can only hope that Alice and Juliet will be better served by you than I have been," Sarah added, and then, without waiting for a reply, she walked away, glad to have finally vented some of the things that had been on her mind for years.

"**H**ave you seen Lady Sarah today?" Laura asked as she cast her fishing line into the lake. Her face was shaded from the hot sun by the wide brim of her straw bonnet.

Christopher shook his head. He'd waited for her that morning, hoping she would join him for another sunrise, but she had not appeared, and eventually he'd returned to the house, where he'd breakfasted with the Earl of Woodford—a quietly reserved gentleman who'd arrived at Thorncliff a few days earlier. Christopher hadn't lingered in the dining room, thinking he might run into Lady Sarah in the garden a little later instead, but she had remained absent, while his mind had remained full. Of her.

He would probably have seen her at luncheon, now

that he thought about it, but he'd missed that meal, since, upon returning to his room with the intention of taking a short rest after his obligatory ride with Miss Diana and Miss Victoria, he'd actually fallen asleep for two full hours. What irked him the most was that she was probably spending time with Mr. Denison instead, for Christopher had not seen him either.

"Not yet," he told his sister now. Once he'd made the decision not to sit around waiting for Lady Sarah to make an appearance, he'd eagerly agreed to take Laura out in a boat so she could make a go at fishing, which was apparently something she'd wished to try for a long time. Besides, he liked to row. It soothed him, and soothing was something he definitely required, considering how agitated all thought of Lady Sarah made him these days. Had she even liked the gift he'd sent to her room for her to discover? "I quite like her, in case you're wondering," Laura said.

Christopher eyed her carefully. Yesterday it had been Fiona, and now it was Laura. He sighed. The last thing he wanted to do was encourage any of his female relations to start making wedding preparations. That would certainly be putting the cart before the horse. "I didn't realize you'd spent enough time in her company to form an opinion," he said, watching with interest as one mayfly chased another across the water, rippling the surface.

Laura didn't respond immediately, her attention seemingly fixed upon the point at which her fishing line pierced the water, but then she turned her head toward him, squinting a little against the sun as she said, "It's true that I haven't had the opportunity to speak with her much, but I have seen her in your company. She pleases you, Kip—I know this because your expression has eased a little since making her acquaintance. On one occasion I even saw you smile."

"She's quite outspoken," he said. "I like that."

"Hmm . . ." Laura smiled. "I think she likes you too. You're not the only one who appears more animated than usual when you are together."

"But Mr. Denison—"

"Doesn't stand a chance compared with you."

"How can you be so sure?"

Laura grinned. "Oh, you know me, Kip. I'm a veritable romantic, so there's always the chance that I'm reading too much into it, though I will say this: Lady Sarah initially struck me as a somber sort, but when she's with you, her face brightens with a radiance that threatens to outdo the sun. Mr. Denison does not have that effect on her."

"I can tell you're a writer, Laura. Your words are most poetic." *And uplifting.* Picking up the oars, Christopher started rowing them back toward the lakeside.

"Is that the end of our expedition, then?" Laura asked.

"Yes. Sorry about that," he said.

"But I haven't managed to catch any fish yet."

"Perhaps you can make another attempt from land. At any rate, I find there is a lady with whom I need to speak."

"Does she by any chance have white-blonde hair and light blue eyes?" Laura's voice was practically ringing with laughter as she spoke.

"She might," Christopher acquiesced.

"Then by all means, don't let me stop you. Row as fast as you can!"

Putting all the strength of his arm muscles into the

effort, Christopher proceeded to do precisely that, reaching the shore much faster than he'd anticipated, which resulted in a jolt that almost threw his sister overboard. "Forgive me," he said, offering her his hand in order to help her disembark.

"I can manage from here," she said as soon as they were safely back on steady ground. "In fact, I see a lovely spot over there below that weeping willow. I shall fish from there." And then she strode off with a brisk pace that brooked no argument.

Turning toward the house, Christopher scanned the garden as he crossed the lawn until he spotted Lady Sarah's sisters keeping company with their maid. He hurried toward them, tipping his hat in salute as he approached the two young ladies. "Good afternoon," he said.

"Good afternoon, Lord Spencer," they both replied, beaming with beatific smiles, while the maid acknowledged him with a simple, "my lord."

"I was hoping to have a word with Lady Sarah. Do any of you know where I might find her?" he asked.

"We left her with Mama on the terrace almost an hour ago so we could join in a game of croquet," Lady Juliet said. "She might still be there."

"But if she isn't, I know she was planning to visit the orchard this afternoon, so you might want to look for her there," Lady Alice supplied.

"Thank you, ladies," Christopher said, "your help is much appreciated."

But when he arrived at the orchard after a pointless trip to the terrace, he found the place empty. Not even a lonely gardener could be seen. For the first time since his arrival at Thorncliff, Christopher wished the estate was not so large and that it would be both quicker and easier to locate people.

Sighing with disappointment, he crossed toward a cherry tree and reached up, plucking an almost ripe cherry from one of the branches. He popped it in his mouth, flinching a little in response to the tart flavor. As much as he loved the fruit, he had to admit that they weren't quite ready for picking. Well, he might as well go back to the house, he supposed. In all likelihood, Lady Sarah would be there relaxing in one of the salons while he wore the grass thin looking for her outside.

He'd just started back toward the entrance of the orchard, when a loud "I've got it!" reached his ears.

Christopher froze. He knew that voice and the lady it belonged to. Lady Sarah was indeed somewhere close by, though he failed to see her even when he crouched lower so as to look below the branches of the many trees. Moving in the direction from which her voice had come, he passed between neat rows of apple trees and pear trees until he reached the far end of the orchard where a low stone wall separated it from the meadow beyond. And there, sitting amidst a field of clover, was Lady Sarah, with a great big grin on her lovely face. Christopher almost forgot to breathe, so taken was he by her natural beauty, but just as he was about to make his presence known to her, she turned her head until her eyes met his, and her smile immediately broadened, if such a thing were possible. Laura was right, Christopher realized. Lady Sarah did indeed welcome his company.

"Lord Spencer," she said, moving to rise. "You've certainly found me in quite a state."

"Please don't get up on my account," he said. "You look so lovely there—like a fairy queen from a magical tale. Allow me to join you instead."

"Your compliment is welcome, my lord, but are

you sure? I wouldn't want you to ruin your clothes on my account."

"Are your clothes ruined?" he asked as he climbed over the wall and went toward her.

Her expression was a little sheepish when she replied, "I've acquired a few grass stains that won't be gotten rid of too easily."

"May I see?"

"Certainly not," she laughed as he plopped down beside her, "they're on my bottom."

He tried to school his features even though he couldn't help but say, "It wouldn't be the first time I've had the pleasure of viewing you from that particular angle."

She looked momentarily taken aback, and for a second he regretted his attempt at lighthearted humor. Perhaps he'd gone too far? But then the most extraordinary thing happened. Her laughter deepened until her eyes began to water, and he suddenly realized that he was laughing as well.

"Lord Spencer," she said as soon as she'd gotten herself under control once more, "I don't mean to shock you, but it does look as though you're enjoying yourself." Before he could respond, she added, "I'm sorry for not thanking you sooner for that wonderful gift you sent up to my room yesterday. Snowball is extremely pleased with it, as am I, but you see, I have been delaying our meeting again until I'd found something with which to repay you."

Christopher's heart gave a little shudder. He'd been in her thoughts, and she was grateful for the gift. It took him a moment to realize how pleased he was by this, and what that signified. She mattered to him, as did her opinion. What had begun as a casual endeavor to please his family was rapidly turning into something more. Shockingly, the idea didn't frighten him at all. "I'm happy to hear you're pleased with it, but there's really no need for you to offer anything in return. I merely thought it might be nice for your hamster to have a bit more space than your reticule offered, so when I saw it in a shop window in Portsmouth, I decided to buy it."

"It was incredibly thoughtful of you," she said, "undoubtedly the most thoughtful gift I've ever received, which is why I really must reciprocate."

"As I said, there is no need," he told her. "Your delightful company is more than enough."

"But I insist," she said, her smile growing mischievous.

Ah, how he'd love to kiss those lovely lips. Perhaps he should. Especially since it would probably remove all thought of Mr. Denison from her mind. He leaned toward her, drawn by her vigor and mesmerized by the joy that lit up her eyes.

Something green popped up between them, and Christopher instinctively drew back, his eyes focusing on the tiny plant she was holding between her fingers. It took him only a fraction of a second to see what it was, and when he did, he was struck by an overwhelming fondness and appreciation for the woman sitting before him. To think that she had crawled through a meadow in order to find a four-leaf clover for him broke all remaining defenses.

"I know it isn't much," she told him hastily as he took it from her. Her smile had dimmed, and she sounded almost shy as she spoke. "But I thought it was something you'd appreciate."

"I can think of nothing better," he said as his eyes met hers.

The idea of potentially doing as his mother wished and marrying Lady Sarah settled more firmly. She was kind and giving, prepared to do her duty and marry the man her parents had selected for her, even though he wasn't to her liking. She concerned herself about others even though—as he'd gathered from conversations he'd had with her—nobody had ever concerned themselves much about her. Instead, she'd been abandoned by her mother and practically ignored ever since.

His heart beat steadily in his chest. Lady Sarah deserved better than what Mr. Denison had to offer. She deserved to be swept off her feet and revered, but would Christopher be able to do so? Could he potentially love her?

The question brought him up short. Not only did she warrant deep affection but she no doubt craved it as well. Unfortunately, he wasn't sure that he would ever be able to give her what she needed. "I shall have it framed so I may carry it with me as a token wherever I go," he said. Simple letters strung together to form words. They weren't nearly enough to impart to her how touched he was by her gesture.

"You do me great honor," she said, and the meekness with which she spoke left him without a choice. He simply had to respond, not with words but with a caress that would show her the true depth of emotion she stirred in him.

Reaching up, he brushed his fingers lightly against her jawline until the palm of his hand was pressed against her cheek. Her eyes fluttered shut on a sigh, and she leaned against him, her breath tickling his skin. Had he not been desperate to taste her lips, he might have been content to stay like that forever, for there was something so intimate yet calming about the current state they were in.

But it was far from enough.

He faintly wondered if even a kiss would be,

though his role as a gentleman cautioned him against considering anything more for the present. And so, with the greatest anticipation, he bowed his head, determined to place his lips upon hers, when the most vexing sound pierced the air—her name being called by Lady Andover.

"I am here, Mama," Lady Sarah announced, dutifully scrambling to her feet and almost bumping her head against Christopher's in the process.

Sitting back on his haunches, Christopher groaned his irritation before jumping to his feet as well and helping Lady Sarah back into the orchard, arriving at her side just as Lady Andover emerged from between the trees. "Sarah, I . . ." Her eyes lit upon Christopher and instantly narrowed. She clearly didn't like him, which he found to be absurd. He was a viscount after all, and heir to an earldom, though judging from the way Lady Andover was looking at him he might as well have been a common criminal.

He was well aware that from her perspective, he might even be worse than that, considering he'd just been discovered in a very secluded part of the property and in the company of her stepdaughter. Lord only knew what the lady might do if she so much as suspected what *he* had just been about to do with Lady Sarah. Murder him, no doubt. "Forgive me," he said, deciding that an apology was always a good way to begin. The only problem was that he wasn't entirely sure how to complete it.

Thankfully, he did not have to, since Lady Sarah spoke up, saying, "I came in here to look at a particular group of trees, Mama. You know my interest in grafting. Apparently one of Lady Duncaster's gardeners is quite adept at it. In any event, I grew too hot beneath my bonnet, so I set it aside on the wall, just there, but then the wind took it and . . . well, I was very grateful when Lord Spencer arrived and offered his assistance."

Lady Andover didn't look too convinced, but apparently she decided not to challenge Lady Sarah. Instead she nodded and looked toward Christopher. "That was most kind of you, Lord Spencer, but if you'll please forgive me, I must ask Lady Sarah to come with me. Mr. Denison has returned from his ride and is most anxious for her company."

"I'm sure he is," Lady Sarah said, her eyes fixed on her stepmother.

"Well, you mustn't keep him waiting, Sarah. It isn't polite," Lady Andover said.

There was a pause. Christopher looked from one to the other, noting their strained expressions. Perhaps he should say something?

"We should also discuss your choice of gown for the ball on Saturday," Lady Andover said flatly.

"Ball?" Christopher searched his brain for the mention of such an event but found nothing.

"It was announced at luncheon," Lady Sarah explained. "I believe you were absent."

So she'd noticed. How encouraging.

"Yes, well," Lady Andover said as she latched on to Lady Sarah's arm, "there's a lot to be done if we're to look our best. Not a moment to lose!"

"I have no doubt that you and your daughters will look absolutely ravishing, Lady Andover," Christopher assured her. "Indeed, I can think of no reason why you would not."

"Thank you," Lady Andover replied crisply. Bidding him a good afternoon, mother and daughter then set off together, though Lady Sarah did glance back at him over her shoulder. Christopher responded with a wink, and as she turned away, he could tell she was smiling.

Chapter 9

~~◦◦◦~~

Reaching for his tinderbox a couple of days later, Christopher ignited a wood splint and lit an oil lamp. It had been two days since he'd managed to have a private word with Lady Sarah. Somehow, Mr. Denison had constantly been hovering nearby. But after receiving a positive reply to the letter he'd posted from Portsmouth, confirming that his idea could be implemented without delay, Christopher had written a note to Lady Sarah informing her that her surprise would be ready today. Looking at his fob watch, he saw that it was almost four o' clock in the morning, allowing him fifteen minutes in which to get ready and go meet her. Dressing with haste, he completed his toilette by dabbing a bit of sandal-wood oil below his jawline, then snatched up his beaver hat and left his room.

Ten minutes later, he rendezvoused with Lady Sarah in the conservatory. She looked stunning, with a few soft tresses of pale hair falling below the brim of her bonnet, her eyes clear with suspense of adventure and her lips as lush as he remembered them to be. The excitement of being alone with her and of doing something inadmissible together—the risk involved—made him feel like a young lad sneaking out of his dormitory at Eton.

"Are you ready?" he asked.

She nodded. "I can't believe I allowed you to talk me into this. What if we get caught?"

"Then I suppose I'll have to marry you," he joked.

"I'm beginning to think this might be a huge mistake."

Worried she might change her mind after all the preparations he'd made, he said, "Nobody will be the wiser. They're all asleep, and I promise you that I have no ill intentions toward you—I shall remain on my very best behavior."

"Do you swear it?"

He looked at her steadily. "I do."

She exhaled slowly. "Then let us make haste, for I confess I'm quite eager to discover what it is you have planned."

"We'll cut across the grass," he said as they stepped out into the garden, the air crisp with predawn freshness. "Ready?" He offered her his hand, which she accepted as she gazed up at him with her sparkling blue eyes.

"Ready," she assured him.

It was a brilliant moment—one Christopher knew he would later look back on with great sentimentality.

They ran toward the lake, Sarah skipping occasionally in order to keep pace with Lord Spencer's longer strides while her skirts swirled about her legs. More than once, she felt as though she might tumble to the ground, but his firm hold on her hand held her steady, carrying her forward until they were out of sight of Thorncliff. It was both liberating and a reminder of how carefree she'd once been.

By the time they reached the horses, she found herself

quite breathless. But then apprehension overcame her as she took in the large creature that would carry her toward her destination, and she retreated a few steps.

"You needn't worry," Lord Spencer said in a calm voice. "I'll lead your horse so she cannot run away. Nothing bad is going to happen to you today, Lady Sarah. You have my word on that, as a gentleman."

The manner in which he spoke was so convincing. "Can we ride at a trot?"

"I've allowed enough time for that, so yes." He took her hand in his and met her eyes. "The last thing I want is for you to feel nervous about this in any way, so if you don't think you can manage it, then—"

"I'll do it," she said with a deliberate nod. She might have had a bad experience with horses in the past, but Lord Spencer had somehow managed to set her at ease. Additionally, she really wanted to see what he had planned, and perhaps prove to both of them that she could overcome her fears.

"Thank you for trusting me," he said with a gentle squeeze of her hand that made her shiver.

Removing his hand from hers, he then untied the horses' reins from a nearby tree, leaving her momentarily bereft until she felt him grasp her by the waist. A strong sensation of weightlessness followed as he lifted her up into the saddle of a speckled mare. She could not recall the last time she'd felt so self-assured. It was all thanks to him, of course. He'd done this for her, and for that she owed him her thanks.

"I believe we should be there in half an hour," he said as he swung himself up onto his own horse, grabbed the reins belonging to hers, and started toward the copse of trees where the forest began. "That ought to give us just enough time to get everything ready before the sun rises."

"Won't you tell me what I'm to expect?" she asked as she followed him along a well-trod path.

"No. I want to see your expression when you discover what I have planned for us."

His boyish enthusiasm, so apart from his usual austerity, was unmistakable, increasing Sarah's curiosity tenfold. Whatever did he have in store? The best she could come up with was a special vantage point from which to watch the sun rise, so when Lord Spencer eventually led her out into an open field where a massive balloon sat waiting, Sarah could only gape in awe.

"You told me once that you envied the freedom of birds. Unfortunately, I cannot give you wings, Lady Sarah, but I can take you up in the air if you're willing to be a little daring."

"I . . ." Sarah could scarcely think of what to say. No words would ever be capable of conveying her gratitude, her amazement or her indescribable surprise at what he was willing to do for her—the lengths he must have gone to in an effort to make this happen, all because of a comment she'd made. Her heart thrummed with a mixture of joy and anticipation. "If I'd been given infinite time in which to wonder what you were up to, I doubt I would have considered this. It is, without a doubt, the very best of surprises."

Her praise clearly pleased him, for he gave her a rare smile that melted her heart as he helped her down from her horse and guided her toward a large group of men who stood waiting. "Lady Sarah," he then said, "I'd like to introduce you to Mr. James Sadler—an experienced balloonist—and his son, Mr. Windham Sadler. They have very kindly made their balloon available to us today and will be helping us with our ascent."

"Thank you, gentlemen," Sarah told them, unable to hide her enthusiasm. "I cannot tell you how excited I am to be given such a unique opportunity."

"The pleasure is ours, my lady," Mr. James Sadler said. "I'll be riding up with you while my son will remain down here to help the rest of the men control the ropes."

"The ropes?" Sarah asked, curious to know everything there was to know about their upcoming adventure.

"There are four," Mr. James Sadler explained, pointing out each of them. "My men will use them to keep the balloon anchored so we don't drift away. I tried that once, and it took me a devil of a time to get home again. My understanding is that you'd like to return to Thorncliff at a decent hour, which is why I think it best to avoid any chance of drifting. So, if you're ready, I should like to begin, seeing as his lordship has explained to me his desire to watch the sun rise from way up high."

"Well?" Sarah asked as she turned to Lord Spencer, barely able to contain her excitement. Nerves danced around her belly, but she chose to ignore them, confident that everything would go smoothly, since Lord Spencer had made the arrangements. She knew he'd never risk her safety.

Having pulled out his pocket watch, Lord Spencer was busily staring down at the face of it. "One moment," he said, holding up his hand in a staying motion. "Five minutes past five," he eventually said as he swiped his thumb across the watch face three times. Returning it to his pocket, he then offered Sarah his arm and guided her toward the sturdy basket below the balloon.

"Another superstition?" Sarah inquired as he

placed his hands upon her waist and began lifting her into the basket.

"My most prevalent one." The corner of his mouth twitched. "I wouldn't dare to go flying without heeding it."

The statement made Sarah a little less sure of herself. She looked to Mr. James Sadler, who was following Lord Spencer into the basket. "This isn't dangerous, is it?" she inquired. "I mean, there's no real risk of any of us getting hurt?"

The balloonist glanced at Lord Spencer before returning his gaze to Sarah. "If I must be truthful, my lady, I should tell you that it's not entirely without risk. I myself have had a few accidents, but I wasn't anchored securely to the ground when they happened. Considering our precautions, I have every confidence that you'll be back on solid ground, safe and sound, within the hour."

Nodding, Sarah swallowed whatever apprehension she had and grasped one of the ropes linking the basket to the balloon. Against her other hand, she felt a brush of warmth and instinctively turned her head to find Lord Spencer staring down at her with an inscrutable expression. "Hold my hand," he murmured as Mr. Windham Sadler called out orders and the basket gave a little jerk. "It will ease your anxiety," he added, when she hesitated to do as he suggested.

It was not the least bit proper, but neither was sneaking out of Thorncliff unchaperoned, Sarah decided. Besides, she had no illusion about Lord Spencer's motives, since he did not wish to marry. Additionally, he had assured her that he would never try to seduce her, and while she secretly wished he might err from his gentlemanly ways just once, she believed him. Friends; that was all they were—all they would ever be. Her fingers grasped Lord Spencer's, and she immediately savored the comfort he offered as his hand closed around hers, reminding her that they were in this together.

Gradually, they rose, putting first one foot, then five, fifteen, and eventually thirty feet between themselves and the ground. They traveled up above the treetops, where birds remained dormant, until they reached such a staggering height that Sarah was able to glimpse Thorncliff far away in the distance, placed firmly against the sprawling dips and curves of the English countryside. "This is undoubtedly the most incredible thing I have ever experienced," she whispered.

"I'm glad you think so," he told her, giving her hand a gentle squeeze as he stepped up behind her, his arm coming about her waist, securing her against him.

It felt natural, in spite of the giddy flutter in the pit of her belly. He was strong, his chest a solid wall against her back, and he was warm, sheltering her against the chilly dawn air that cooled even further as they rose higher.

"How can I ever thank you?" she asked in wonder as a glow emerged upon the horizon.

"You've already given me a clover." His words whispered softly against her cheek, stirring to life an awareness that made her insides quiver.

She laughed in response to his statement. "It seems such a paltry offering in the face of all this."

"Hmm . . . and yet it was picked with a great deal of consideration. For that reason alone, its significance is priceless." He paused for a moment before saying, "You once asked me who broke my heart. I think it's time for me to be completely honest with you."

Sarah felt her chest tighten. "I'd be honored to share your confidence." If only she could reciprocate.

Expelling a deep breath, Lord Spencer began relating the details of his relationship with a certain Miss Hepplestone while Sarah listened intently to every detail. With each word he spoke, she could feel them growing closer—a similar sensation to the one she'd felt in the maze, and then later by the lake that morning when he'd taught her how to skip stones. It was almost as if their souls were reaching out and embracing each other, which was unlike anything she'd ever felt with anyone else before.

When he stopped talking, Sarah leaned her head back against his shoulder and said, "You mustn't blame yourself for falling prey to her scheme. You lost your heart to a woman whom, from what you've just told me, most men would eagerly have married. Unfortunately, she was nothing more than a fabrication created by Miss Hepplestone with the sole purpose of deceiving you. *She* is the one who's to blame, my lord. Not you. Never you."

"I was a fool," he said, his words a plain statement of fact.

"We've all done foolish things at one time or another. You should be thankful that you discovered the truth before it was too late and that you didn't end up married to her."

"And so I am." Lowering his head, his cheek touched hers. "Will you share your own foolish exploits with me? Somebody broke your heart, Lady Sarah. Tell me who it was."

She stiffened, her nerves wrought with tension. "What would be the point?"

He didn't answer. Instead, he fell silent while shades of red spilled across the sky. His confession had brought them closer, and then she'd broadened the distance between them by refusing to reciprocate. Standing there with him so close, yet so far away, Sarah desperately wished they lived in a different time, when her one foolish mistake would not matter nearly as much—a time in which she and Lord Spencer could explore the deep connection developing between them, and where they might have a chance of being together.

Returning to the house later, Sarah inquired about Lord Spencer's work as they strolled across the lawn. "Will you include the gardens in your model of Thorncliff?"

"Of course. The manor would not be complete without them."

"So you'll even construct copies of the ship and the maze?" She couldn't help but marvel at his attention to detail.

Lord Spencer nodded. "I plan to. Yes."

"But what will you do with it once it's complete?"

He looked puzzled. "What do you mean?"

She spread her arms wide. "Please don't tell me you plan to hide all these models away from the world." To be so passionate about something and not share it seemed wasteful.

"I don't exactly hide them—"

"I'm pleased to hear it."

"But I don't exactly put them on display either."

She halted her progress. "Whyever not?"

"For someone who hasn't even seen my work, you seem surprisingly confident that anyone else would have an interest in, or even appreciate, the models for what they are."

"You doubt yourself," she told him matter-of-factly. Before he could respond, she said, "I think it's natural for any artist to fear censorship."

"I'm not an artist, and I don't fear censorship," he protested. "When I complete my model of Thorncliff, I'll have ten in total. Of course I've considered the possibility of an exhibition, but I doubt anything will ever come of it. My models are a hobby, Lady Sarah, hardly worthy of anyone else's perusal."

She raised an eyebrow. "And you say you don't fear censorship." He did not look amused. "I think an exhibition of your models would be a grand way to introduce the public to the incredible architecture of English castles."

"Why are you so insistent on this?" he asked testily.

"Because I believe in you and the ability you have to do something more with your 'hobby' than you think possible," she told him hotly.

He stared at her, then shook his head. "You are being absurdly stubborn right now."

"I'm trying to be supportive."

"I appreciate that, Lady Sarah, truly I do, but until you've actually seen one of my models, you really have no idea if I'm deserving of your support or not."

She decided not to argue even though she was certain his models couldn't be anything short of brilliant—not if his drawings were any reflection of his skill.

As he guided her forward, they approached the house and, to Sarah's surprise, almost collided with a young lady who was hastily rounding a corner just as they were stepping up onto the terrace. Sarah recognized her immediately as Mary Bourneville, a young lady of roughly her own age, whom she'd met during her first Season and with whom she'd felt the possibility of a strong friendship—a friendship she'd stopped pursuing after the Gillsborough house party.

"Forgive me," Lady Mary gasped, a startled expression crossing her face. "I was just returning from an early morning walk—the weather's so lovely this time of day."

"Indeed it is," Lord Spencer said.

Lady Mary smiled brightly. "Well, if you'll please excuse me, I must return upstairs to see to my aunt." And then, before Sarah could manage a word of greeting or ask Lady Mary if she'd like to join her for breakfast, Lady Mary hurried inside, leaving Sarah alone with Lord Spencer once more.

They stood for a moment in silence until Lord Spencer finally said, "I'm beginning to suspect that Thorncliff Manor might be overrun by adventurous females."

Sarah gave him a sidelong look. "She was only going for a walk, my lord. There's hardly much adventure in that."

Shaking his head, Lord Spencer began guiding her toward the door. "I agree," he said, "but if that is all that young lady was doing, I'll eat my hat."

After breakfast, Sarah joined Mr. Denison on the terrace for a game of checkers. Thankfully he refrained from making any more lewd remarks and treated her just as politely as he did everyone else.

Her thoughts throughout it all, however, remained on Lord Spencer. Their outing had been a marvelous success even though she'd failed to be as open with him as he'd been with her. Thankfully he'd refrained from pressuring her, veering away from the topic entirely by inquiring about her favorite color, flower and food while comparing her choices to his own. She'd learned that he wasn't fond of strawberries, which had surprised her. Everybody loved strawberries, though apparently not Lord Spencer.

Stop thinking about him, Sarah. He's not for you.

"Diana and Victoria were thrilled with the ride they took with Lord Spencer the other day," Mr. Denison said as he moved one of his pieces forward, capturing one of Sarah's.

"I'm glad to hear it," Sarah said. If that were true, there wouldn't be a painful knot in her stomach. Selecting a piece, she moved it toward the king's row, capturing three of Mr. Denison's pieces along the way.

"You're very good at this," he said.

Sarah didn't think she was particularly skilled at the game, but she thanked him politely for the compliment. "Lord Spencer has also offered to put in a good word on behalf of your daughters with some of the other gentlemen here, so hopefully an offer will be forthcoming for at least one of them before you depart."

"You've spoken to him again, I take it?" Disapproval was very apparent in his tone.

"It's been difficult not to, considering the task you've given me."

Mr. Denison captured more of her pieces. "As long as you keep your encounters brief, I see no issue with it—especially not if you are working in Diana's and Victoria's best interests."

"How magnanimous of you." Annoyed by Mr. Denison's high-handedness, Sarah was pleased to capture his remaining pieces with her king.

He pushed the game aside and leaned toward her, his elbows resting on the table. "Let's not forget that I arranged for him to take them riding. Not you."

Sarah had meant to ask Spencer about that, but she hadn't wished to ruin their time together with talk of

Mr. Denison and his daughters. "Of course," she said, bowing her head in order to avoid an argument.

But as the day wore on and she was denied the chance to keep anyone else's company, Sarah couldn't help but wonder what it might be like to push Mr. Denison into the lake. Fantastic, she decided, if only she had the courage.

Chapter 10

⧵⧸◦⧵⧸

"**W**ill you be joining us for the picnic today?" Juliet asked Sarah the following morning. "The weather is marvelous, and we would so love having you along."

"As would I," a male voice spoke at Sarah's right shoulder. Turning, Sarah faced Mr. Denison, attempting desperately to feel something for him besides distaste. When he held up a bouquet of lovely roses, she managed a smile and thanked him with grace. He offered her his arm, which she dutifully accepted.

"A picnic sounds lovely," she said as they walked out into the entrance hall, where servants stood ready with bonnets and gloves. Locating hers, Sarah handed her roses to a maid and set her bonnet on her head. She prepared to tie the ribbon when Mr. Denison said, "Allow me."

What could she do? Publically protest? Doing so would humiliate him, so she allowed the intimacy, her feet firmly rooted to the ground while his fingers grazed her chin in a manner that showed deliberation. "I cannot seem to resist you," he whispered.

Clamminess overcame her entire body.

"Ah! Mr. Denison and the lovely Lady Sarah!"

Sarah's heart quickened—an automatic response, it would seem, whenever Lord Spencer arrived. Pulling on his gloves, he looked at each of them in turn. "I take it you're going on the picnic?"

"Indeed we are," Mr. Denison said, straightening himself in a manner that drew attention to his portly belly. "In case you were wondering, my daughters have decided to remain here and have a go at the maze. Perhaps you'd care to join them?"

"I believe they will be enjoying Mr. Everett's and Mr. Donahue's company today, so I'm for the picnic. Fine weather for it," Lord Spencer noted. Gesturing toward the door, he allowed Sarah and Mr. Denison to lead the way. But as they stepped out onto the front step, where the sun spilled over them, he continued past Sarah, his hand unmistakably brushing her elbow, where his fingers seemed to rest for the briefest of seconds. Sarah gasped, completely disarmed by the unexpected gesture.

"What is it?" Mr. Denison inquired as he guided her toward an awaiting carriage.

"Nothing," she murmured, the heat from Lord Spencer's hand still present upon her skin. "It's merely hotter today than I expected."

"I'll meet you there," Lord Spencer called as he swung himself up into the saddle of a fine-looking horse. The statement was general, yet Sarah sensed that it was directed specifically at her, more so when the rogue looked straight at her and winked. A flutter erupted in the pit of her belly, to which Sarah muttered an oath. Why couldn't Mr. Denison affect her so? Looking to her supposed beau, she scrunched her nose. There were just about a million answers to that question. None of which would make the slightest difference in the end.

"**L**et's play a game," Lady Fiona suggested when everyone had finished their lunch and the footmen had packed away the food. Sitting on a large blanket next to her sister Alice, Sarah stared out over the countryside, enjoying the view from the hilltop.

"What sort of game?" Juliet asked, curious.

"How about cross questions and crooked answers?" Lady Fiona said, her eyes gleaming.

"Oh yes," Alice said, "I love that game!"

"Who will participate?" Sarah asked.

"You may count me out," Lady Andover said, to nobody's surprise.

"I don't enjoy games," Mr. Denison said. Yawning, he swatted away a fly.

"Neither do I," said Lord Andover.

Lady Duncaster looked as though she was tempted to roll her eyes, but she refrained, while the Oaklands informed everyone that they would go for a stroll instead.

In the end, the players included Alice, Juliet, Lady Fiona, Lady Laura, Lord Spencer, Lady Emily and Sarah. Deciding the youngest player should start, they all listened with interest as Alice turned to Juliet and asked, "What is the use of a pig?"

Smiling, Juliet declared, "To be carved and eaten for supper!"

Turning toward Lady Emily, Juliet then asked, "What is the use of a husband?"

"To supply security for the woman he marries," Lady Emily replied.

The game continued until Lord Spencer asked Sarah, "What is the use of a hot air balloon?"

"To allow us the pleasure of flying with friends," she said, her cheeks heating in response to his unexpected reference.

"Shall we see what we've come up with?" Lady Fiona asked after everyone had had a go. "Lady Alice, why don't you give us your question and your answer. And don't forget that if you cannot remember what they are, you must forfeit the game."

"That won't be a problem for me," Alice said. "The question asked of me was, what is the use of a velocipede, to which the answer is, of course, to be carved and eaten for supper!"

Everyone laughed at the silliness of that.

"I rather like mine," Juliet said when they'd gathered their wits. "The question asked of me was, what is the use of a pig, to which the answer is, of course, to provide for the woman he marries."

More laughter erupted, barely ceasing at all as the rest of the questions and answers were mentioned. "Tell us yours, Lady Sarah," Lady Fiona urged her when everyone else had had their turn.

Not daring to glance in Lord Spencer's direction, Sarah raised her chin and said, "Very well, the question asked of me was, what is the use of a hot air balloon, and the answer is, of course, to risk life and limb in the stupidest way."

"Of all the ones we've had, that's the only one that makes any sense," Lady Laura said, while everyone else agreed. Beside her, Sarah could sense Lord Spencer's presence like a giant wall of discontent. "It appears as though our game has had a sleep-inducing effect on some of our companions," Lady Fiona said with a nod toward the Andovers, Lady Duncaster and Mr. Denison. Facing Sarah, she said, "Will you join me for a walk, Lady Sarah?"

"I'd be delighted to," Sarah replied, grateful for the chance to remove herself from the powerful awareness of Lord Spencer.

But as she rose and went to where Lady Fiona was

waiting for her, Lady Fiona said, "You should come as well, Spencer. I haven't seen nearly enough of you lately, and I find that I miss your company."

"Might I come along too?" Alice asked.

Relieved by her sister's proposition, Sarah was about to say it was a wonderful idea when Lady Laura said, "I was thinking you and I would make daisy chains together with Juliet. We can go on another walk later."

Deciding she would much rather make daisy chains with Lady Laura, Alice settled back onto the blanket and began picking the flowers closest at hand.

"May I offer you my arm?" Lord Spencer asked as he came up beside Sarah.

She was half tempted to refuse, fearing the feel of his arm beneath her hand would be too overwhelming a sensation in spite of the fabric lying between them. Knowing how impolite it would be of her to do so, however, she swallowed and accepted his offer while trying desperately to ignore the tight knot forming in her belly. Somehow, without being able to explain how it had happened, he'd become increasingly important to her.

"Lady Duncaster told me earlier that there's a path beyond the trees over there that slants down the opposite side of the hill toward the remnants of an old church," Lady Fiona said, leading the way.

"Sounds intriguing," Sarah said, her curiosity piqued.

"Did I mention that Lady Sarah has an adventurous streak not entirely dissimilar to your own?" Lord Spencer asked his sister.

Looking over her shoulder briefly, Lady Fiona said, "I wonder if it's ever landed you in as much trouble as it has me."

"I've had my fair share of misfortunes as a result," Sarah said, unwilling to be dishonest even if her response did invite more questions.

"Now *I'm* intrigued," Lord Spencer said. "Care to elaborate?"

"I caught a terrible cold one year after I insisted on going for an afternoon walk when the weather promised rain. I should have stayed home, truth is."

"I fell from a rafter in the barn a few years back because I thought myself capable of crossing it without losing my balance," Lady Fiona said. "I was terribly lucky that fresh hay had been brought in that morning and lay in a huge soft heap beneath me."

"Good heavens," Sarah exclaimed, struck by how tragic Lady Fiona's daring exploit could have proven otherwise.

"She was thoroughly scolded, as I recall," Lord Spencer said, "and rightly so. Mama and Papa got a terrible shock, but thankfully you only hurt your wrist a little."

"I was confined to my room for an entire week," Lady Fiona said, "and not allowed any dessert."

"But I took pity on you after a couple of days and snuck a few cakes up to you," Lord Spencer said. He slanted a look in Sarah's direction. "How about you? Were you ever punished for your hoydenish ways?"

Yes!

Filled with discomfort, Sarah nodded her head. The Heartlys were such good people, while she was not. She did not deserve their kindness or Lord Spencer's attentions. She deserved Mr. Denison. "I received similar treatment to Lady Fiona in return for my disobedience," she said. "Unlike her, however, I did not have an older brother who was willing to bring me cake."

Lord Spencer laughed, and Sarah breathed a sigh of relief. Hopefully they could move on to more light-hearted topics now. She decided to make the attempt. "Lord Spencer tells me he enjoys making replica models of castles, Lady Fiona, but since I cannot rely on his opinion, as subjective as it is, I was hoping you might offer yours."

"Are you seriously asking my sister to tell you whether or not my work is acceptable?" he asked with mock indignity.

"I am," Sarah said primly.

"While I'm present?"

"Would you rather we gossip about you behind your back?"

"I'd rather you not gossip at all," he said, frowning down at her. But his eyes sparkled. "My greatest concern is for Lady Fiona's appreciation of the arts." Lowering his voice to a loud whisper, he said, "She hasn't much taste as far as that is concerned."

"I heard that," Lady Fiona said, coming to a halt at the edge of the hill where the path led down between rows of hedges toward a ruin, just as she'd described. Tilting her head, she looked at Sarah with very serious eyes. "Shall I tell you the truth about my brother's little diversion?"

"Little diversion?" Lord Spencer muttered. "Kill me now, why don't you?"

Sarah tried to contain her laughter, but it was to no avail. Lord Spencer's horrified expression forced the mirth out of her until she overflowed with it. Unfazed, Lady Fiona said quite simply, "His models are splendid, Lady Sarah, with the very finest of details. In truth, he is extraordinarily talented."

A moment of heavy silence followed. Clearly, Lord Spencer was dumbfounded by his sister's proclamation. Sarah, on the other hand, realized she wasn't surprised at all. There was something determined about Lord Spencer that suggested he was the sort of man who would complete to perfection any task he set for himself.

"I can see I've left you speechless," Lady Fiona said. Tugging on the bow of her bonnet, she unfastened the silky ribbon and plucked it from her head to reveal her dark brown curls. A moment later the bonnet went sailing through the air until, somewhere further down the hillside, it struck the ground and tumbled into some bushes. "Oh dear."

"What on earth did you do that for?" Lord Spencer asked with clear exasperation.

"I didn't do anything," Lady Fiona said. "The wind snatched it right out of my hand!"

"The wind?" Lord Spencer regarded Lady Fiona as if she'd just arrived from another planet. Shaking his head, he released Sarah's arm and started in the direction the bonnet had traveled.

"Don't trouble yourself, Spencer," Lady Fiona said, rushing ahead of him with such haste that the two almost collided. "I can easily fetch it myself. It won't take long, and when I return, we can go and explore the ruin." She was off in a flash before anyone could offer a protest.

"It's not the least bit windy, is it?" Sarah asked as she and Lord Spencer watched Lady Fiona descend the hillside toward the bushes below.

He shook his head. "I daresay she threw it very deliberately."

"Ah." There was little point in asking why his sister would do such a thing. Especially since it would only lead to more uncomfortable conversation. "Does she know that you have no intention of marrying at present?"

He was silent a moment. "I believe she's hoping to change my mind."

Sarah dared not ask if Lady Fiona was proving successful in that endeavor. She was afraid that nothing, not even *she,* would sway Lord Spencer's resolve to maintain his bachelorhood. If that was the case, she preferred that he say nothing at all. In the greater scheme of things, it made no difference whether or not he would actually consider a future with her, but to her, it mattered a great deal. Somewhere, deep inside, a fondness for him had begun to bloom, and she did not think she could bear the idea of not affecting him equally. "She does have some firm ideas," Sarah said, opting for a noncommittal response.

"I ought to set my mind to finding her a husband," Lord Spencer said, surprising Sarah. "Her sisters are older and ought to marry before her, I suppose, but her boldness concerns me. Another year or two and I fear she'll ruin herself in some mad romantic endeavor."

"I thought Lady Laura was the romantic one."

"She writes about romance, Lady Sarah, but she has a sensible head on her shoulders and has never veered from propriety. Fiona, on the other hand . . . she's too spontaneous."

Sarah hesitated a moment before asking her next question, her fingers curling into tight fists as she did so. "And if Lady Fiona were to risk her reputation for the sake of love? Would you not do everything in your power to help her overcome whatever scandal she might invite?"

The astonished expression he gave her made her insides tremble. Had she said too much? Given herself away? "Has she said something to you that might suggest such a disastrous outcome?"

"No. Of course not," Sarah told him hastily. "I am

merely wondering how a man like you might react, that is all."

His jaw clenched. "I should say that my father would have to take responsibility, but I can assure you that I would be grievously disappointed in any of my sisters if they did not prove themselves more sensible than to toss aside their prospects without the promise of a permanent attachment."

"And yet you yourself have admitted to being led astray by emotion," Sarah said, her anger rising in response to his hypocrisy and the hurt he unknowingly dealt her with his words.

"When I confided in you, I did not intend for you to use the knowledge as a weapon against me." His voice had grown quiet. "Rest assured, I have suffered great humiliation for my stupidity, but it is a fact that men are freer than women to enjoy relationships with the opposite sex without altering their marriageability significantly."

Sarah stared off into the distance. He would never accept what she had done, which, as much as it pained her, also made her grind her teeth. How she hated this world she lived in—the unfairness of it and all the bloody rules that served to cage and restrain. Abandoning all hope of altering Lord Spencer's mind, Sarah nodded faintly and made an effort to return to a more companionable state. "Shall we see what's keeping your sister?" Surely Lady Fiona could not still be searching for her bonnet.

He studied her briefly before offering her his arm, a wave of heat surging through her the moment she accepted. She pushed the troubling sensation aside, determined not to ponder all the what-ifs. Lord Spencer had no wish to marry, and even if he did, she would not be good enough for him. If she had any common sense left in her, she would accept Mr. Denison's hand in marriage once he asked and forget about Lord Spencer forever.

Later that day, however, her resolve to do so wavered as she met Lord Spencer's gaze during dinner, painfully aware of the flush that rose to her cheeks. Placed diagonally across from her at the table, he'd raised his glass in her direction with the barest hint of a smile, their earlier disagreement clearly forgotten. But her father, who was seated beside her, immediately requested her attention in a discussion that he and her mother were having about the number of salons at Thorncliff. One claimed there were seven, while the other insisted on eight. When the argument was finally settled and Sarah looked back in Lord Spencer's direction, she found him conversing with his sister, Lady Newbury, who was seated to his right, forcing him to turn away from Sarah as he spoke.

Once the meal was completed, Sarah accompanied the rest of the ladies to the music room, exiting through a door that prevented her from coming within speaking distance of Lord Spencer. However, rather than following her stepmother to one of the sofas and taking a dutiful seat beside her, Sarah walked across to one of two chairs standing in a corner adjacent to a tall window. It was an excellent spot, really, Sarah decided as she sat down and looked out at the garden beyond, for although it was getting dark, torches had been lit, illuminating all the pathways for anyone desiring to go for an evening stroll.

"Is this seat taken?" a soft voice asked.

Turning her head, Sarah found Chloe Heartly, the Countess of Newbury, gazing down at her with kind eyes. She was a petite lady with auburn-colored hair, an elegant nose and a bow-shaped mouth, who was dressed in a lavender-colored gown that complemented her complexion.

"No. It is not," Sarah said. "Would you like to join me?"

"Only if you don't mind," Lady Newbury said.

"Not in the least. Indeed, I would welcome the company."

As soon as Lady Newbury had taken her seat, she gestured for a maid to bring them both some tea. "I hope you'll forgive me for speaking plainly, Lady Sarah," she said as soon as they were both alone again, "but since you're surely aware that it is no coincidence, my seeking you out like this, I might as well get on with it."

Sarah stilled, the edge of her teacup touching her lips. She took a hesitant sip, returned the cup to its saucer and gave Lady Newbury her full attention. "You may tell me whatever you wish," Sarah told her, "and you may be as candid as you like. I promise not to be offended . . . unless you wish to liken me to a farm animal. There's a good chance I might disapprove of that."

"I can see why he likes you," Lady Newbury remarked with a hint of mirth. "You have a delightful sense of humor."

"I'm also exceptionally good at egg and spoon races."

Lady Newbury laughed. "I'll have to see that to believe it. Perhaps I should have a word with Lady Duncaster—see if it can be arranged."

"I think it would be wonderfully diverting. Especially if it were to be an afternoon event with other contests as well, like a sack race, hoop throwing . . . apple bobbing. There could be prizes for the winners." The thought was so appealing that Sarah could hardly contain her enthusiasm. How wonderful it would be to just play and have fun—to be distracted from reality.

"Then it's settled," Lady Newbury proclaimed as her dainty fingers reached for a biscuit, "but it's not really the reason why I sought you out."

Sarah straightened herself in her chair while Lady Newbury nibbled on her biscuit. "Do go on," Sarah urged her, curious to discover her meaning.

Leaning toward her, Lady Newbury lowered her voice to a hushed tone, just above a whisper, and said, "If you don't mind, I would like to understand your interest in Mr. Denison."

Her voice was pleasant, yet Sarah couldn't help but discern a distinct edge to it. She felt her hands tremble, while her skin grew hot and prickly. The candor had caught her completely off guard. "And if you'll forgive me," she said, her voice catching, "that's a very personal question."

"Indeed it is," Lady Newbury agreed. She studied Sarah with unrelenting curiosity. "Rest assured that the only reason I'm asking is out of concern for my brother. He tells me he enjoys your company—an irregularity in his behavior, since he has not been known to enjoy the company of any young lady in recent memory."

"What are you trying to say?" Sarah's heart thundered in her chest.

"Is it not clear, Lady Sarah? Spencer is in need of a wife, and the only woman he seems interested *in* is you. But rather than make yourself available to a deeper attachment with him, you maintain your courtship with Mr. Denison, insisting that he is the man you will marry even though he is far beneath your station."

Drawing a breath, Sarah closed her eyes in anguish. Had Lord Spencer told his sister all of this? He must have. "Your brother is aware of my reasoning," Sarah said.

"You mean he is aware of your father's interest in Mr. Denison's horses?"

Bleakly, Sarah nodded.

"Surely your father could simply buy the mares he's interested in from Mr. Denison?"

"Marrying me off will prove less costly in the short run with greater returns for the future."

"I'm sorry," Lady Newbury said. "I wasn't aware that your family faced financial difficulties. But if that is the case, I understand your father's reasoning even less." She held silent a moment before saying, "If the issue is with your dowry, then I'm sure Spencer will assure your father that there is no need for one and that he will provide you with whatever you might need."

Most would consider talk of financial matters vulgar. Unfortunately for Sarah, Lady Newbury did not, and the more she spoke, and the more she theorized, the guiltier Sarah felt. "It isn't that," she suddenly blurted, unable to restrain herself any longer. "I mean, it isn't just about horses."

Lady Newbury stopped talking, her eyes fixed on Sarah for the longest, most unbearable moment. Eventually, her expression softened, flooding with kindness. "Whatever troubles you may be faced with, rest assured that I will keep your confidence if you so desire. I know what it's like to be alone and how welcome a friendship can be."

Expelling a shaky breath, Sarah attempted a smile. "Thank you, my lady, I—"

"Please call me Chloe."

"If you will call me Sarah."

"I would be honored," Chloe said.

The offer to share some of her pain with someone else was extremely tempting. "Promise me you won't speak a word of what I am about to tell you to your brother?"

"You have my word on it," Chloe told her seriously.

Gathering her courage, Sarah glanced around, careful of who might hear what she was about to say. Nobody was close enough if she whispered, and so she said, "It is true that Mr. Denison is my parents' choice. It is to be an arranged marriage—a marriage I am duty bound to enter into, though not only for the reason I have given Lord Spencer."

The color of Lady Newbury's eyes intensified, but she did not look alarmed. She merely tilted her head a little before asking, "Then why?"

"I cannot tell you the specifics," Sarah said, knowing she'd already said too much, "or more precisely, I *will* not. My entire family—my sisters' prospects— everything depends on my silence. Good heavens, if you only knew . . . you'd think me the worst possible match for your brother."

"And yet you do not strike me as a woman with ill intent, but rather as someone who might have behaved foolishly on one occasion, for which you have decided to torment yourself for the rest of your days. As for my brother, he's a good man, Lady Sarah, and certainly deserves to make a fine match for himself. But wouldn't you agree that he also deserves the chance to make an unbiased decision?"

Sarah nodded, uncertain as to where this conversation was heading. Lady Newbury couldn't possibly approve of her after what Sarah had just told her.

Lady Newbury frowned as if considering something. "How will he be able to do so unless he has all the facts?"

Sarah sat back, her chest tightening with apprehension and . . . undeniable fear. She felt as if Lady Newbury had just dragged her seat to the edge of a cliff and proceeded to tilt it over the precipice. Lord help her, she could feel herself sliding toward the abyss. "I am not an option."

"So you say. But what if he disagrees?"

"A moot point, since I cannot possibly reveal to him all my reasons for marrying Mr. Denison." *Least of all to him.* The thought of willingly subjecting herself to his disapproval was unthinkable.

He would despise her in every conceivable way if he knew the sort of woman she was.

"You're afraid of how he will react." It wasn't a question but an observation mirroring Sarah's own thoughts.

"Terrified," Sarah confessed. She reached for her teacup but abandoned that idea, since she knew the tea would now be tepid, in which case there was little point in drinking it at all.

"Which suggests his opinion matters a great deal to you . . . perhaps because of your feelings for him?"
Feelings.

Closing her eyes briefly against the rush of emotion that threatened to topple her straight into the abyss, Sarah envisioned Lord Spencer in her mind's eye. She'd developed a fondness for him in the short time she'd known him, perhaps because he'd made no attempt to seduce her—had offered no flowery prose, no praise to her beauty, and no examples of the endless suffering he would endure if she failed to return his undying affection.

Looking inward, she contemplated the contents of her heart. There could be no denying the effect he'd had on her since their first encounter or the fact that she looked forward to seeing him every day when she awoke. "I like him a great deal," she said.

Chloe nodded. "Then you consider him a friend?"

"Of course!"

"Then you know what you must do," Chloe said. "More to the point, I will not allow my brother to lose his heart to an illusion, which is precisely what I fear may happen if you don't show him your hand." She bit into a biscuit before adding, "You're clearly a damsel in distress, Lady Sarah, which makes you extremely hard to resist for a man as valiant as Spencer."

Sarah's heart thumped loudly in her chest, and she became aware that she was clutching the fabric of her skirts between her fingers, twisting it so tight that the creases would be near impossible to remove. "I don't know that I'm strong enough or brave enough to face such a challenge." She spoke to herself more than to Chloe. "But you are right. Lord Spencer ought not develop a tendre for a woman whom he no doubt considers to have an unblemished past, so I will make you a promise. I will not further my relationship with him unless I am prepared to tell him everything."

"That sounds perfectly reasonable to me," Chloe said. Reaching out, she placed one hand over Sarah's. "I can only guess what your secret might be, Sarah, but I'd like you to know that I admire your courage, both in being prepared to make an unfavorable match for the sake of your family, and also for your willingness to do what is right, even if it won't be easy. I can assure you, however, that the worst thing you can possibly do is to continue building a relationship—any relationship—on the foundation of a lie, even if it's one born from omission."

"One sometimes has the tendency to get carried away on wishes that cannot be sustained if we reveal all there is to know about ourselves."

"Tell him your secrets, Lady Sarah, I implore you. Spencer is an understanding and forgiving man as long as he doesn't feel he's being cornered or having the wool pulled over his eyes. Speak with him if you think there's even the slightest chance that the two of you might have a future. I'm certainly fond of you already and I've barely spent more than half an hour in your company. By that rationale, he must be veritably smitten."

When Sarah awoke the following morning, she rose quickly, padded across the carpet and flung open the curtains to reveal a day bathed in sunshine, with a blue sky overhead.

After finishing her toilette, she exited her room to find Juliet reclining in one of the armchairs that stood in the sitting room. She was busily reading a book, though she immediately looked up in response to Sarah's arrival. "Good morning," Sarah said, incredibly pleased to find her sister just so. There was something reassuring about it—a familiarity that struck Sarah as comforting in the way most things associated with pleasant childhood memories tended to do.

Juliet smiled sweetly, while her book dangled from her fingers, the author's voice momentarily suspended. "Hester is seeing to Alice's hair at the moment, but she should be ready shortly. Will you join us for breakfast?"

"I'd be delighted to," Sarah said. "To be honest, I'm feeling quite famished."

But regardless of how hungry she was, Sarah could barely get through the meal fast enough, even though she was reluctant to leave before her sisters were finished eating as well.

"We were thinking of going for a ride a little later," Alice said as she sipped her tea. "Lady Fiona says the shops in the village are rather quaint and worth a visit. She's offered to take us. Perhaps you would like to come too?"

"It's very kind of you to consider me," Sarah said, "but there are a few things I'd like to see to today."

Her sister was not afforded the opportunity to ask about the specifics regarding these *things,* since Lady Fiona, Lady Laura and Lady Emily arrived in the dining room at that moment and immediately joined the group. "I don't suppose you've seen Spencer yet," Lady Laura inquired once she'd filled her plate with toast and bacon. "He's usually an early riser, and since he's quite the expert on the Greek epics, I thought I'd ask him if he can think of a reference for me to use in the novel I'm writing—something to do with love everlasting."

"What about Penelope and Odysseus?" Sarah offered.

"I considered them myself," Lady Laura said, "but I was hoping for something less obvious. Everyone knows about Penelope and Odysseus . . . it's just too predictable."

"You have a point there," Lady Emily said. "If you're looking for a more obscure reference, I'm sure

Spencer will be able to help you. My own knowledge extends only as far as the myths portrayed in paintings, which aren't all Greek."

"I confess I won't be much help either," Sarah said. "When it comes to Greek epics, I've only read the beginning of *The Iliad*. My interests have always drifted more toward Shakespeare and Fielding."

"I wish I had the patience to write a novel," Alice remarked. "What is yours about?"

"Well," Lady Laura said as she casually stirred a spoon of sugar into her tea, "my heroine is a very willful young lady—a hoyden, to be exact. My hero, of course, falls madly in love with her because of how different she is from the other women of his acquaintance, even though his family is quite opposed to the idea."

"It sounds terribly romantic," Juliet sighed.

"Oh, I assure you it is," Lady Laura said, "and a vast improvement on my attempt at writing a gothic novel. After reading Polidori's *The Vampyre* last year, I thought I'd attempt something similar. Eventually I had to admit I lacked the flair for that sort of style. I'm far more comfortable with my current work."

"I look forward to reading it," Sarah said. Noting that Lady Duncaster had arrived, she excused herself to the Heartlys and to her sisters, wishing them a pleasant ride to the village, and made her way over to the buffet table, where the countess was eagerly selecting a piece of apple pie. "Good morning," Sarah said, siding up to her.

Lady Duncaster turned at the sound of Sarah's voice, her eyes brightening and her cheeks dimpling as she smiled. "Why, Lady Sarah. How good it is to see you again. Will you join me for breakfast?"

"I'm afraid I've already eaten, my lady, but I was

hoping to ask a question of you. Lady Newbury and I were discussing the possibility for an egg and spoon race. I was wondering if she might have mentioned it to you yet."

"Actually, she did ask me about it when I passed her in the hallway earlier. Sounds like a marvelous idea to me. Shall we see if we can manage to do it tomorrow? After all, we're having the ball on Saturday."

"Quite right," Sarah said. She watched Lady Duncaster fill her plate, then said, "I realize this is short notice if we're to have the race tomorrow, but I was thinking that it could be fun to consider other events as well where contestants can win prizes. I'd be happy to help with ideas."

"You're suggesting a game day?"

"Well, yes. I suppose I am. If it's not too much trouble."

"I think it's a splendid idea, Lady Sarah. Perhaps you and I can discuss the details after breakfast so I can inform the servants?"

Agreeing that they would meet in the blue parlor half an hour later, Sarah left the dining room in search of some paper and a quill for taking notes. She then headed toward the blue parlor. She'd just entered the room when a soft voice spoke her name. Turning toward it, she saw Lady Mary coming toward her with hesitant steps. "Lady Sarah," she said, her eyes straying from Sarah's as if to ensure that they were alone, "I was hoping to speak with you in private for a moment."

"I was just awaiting Lady Duncaster," Sarah said. "Perhaps you'd like to keep me company until she arrives?"

"Thank you. I'd appreciate that a great deal."

Saying nothing further until they were both seated

on a light blue sofa, Sarah waited for Lady Mary to broach the issue she wished to address, but when she held silent, Sarah eventually said, "It's a long time since we've seen each other. I hope you'll forgive me for not writing as I told you I would, but with Grandmamma's passing so soon after my first Season, life was turned upside down for a while. Eventually it seemed too much time had passed, given our brief acquaintance."

"It's quite all right," Lady Mary said. "You're not the only one to blame for our lack of communication these past two years, since I could just as easily have written to you, but my own life took a turn when Papa was named the new governor-general to India and he and Mama traveled there. It was decided that I should remain here with my aunt, since I'd have a better chance of finding a suitable husband in England rather than abroad." She sighed. "Unfortunately, Aunt Eugenia prefers to avoid large crushes, so I'm pleased with her decision to spend the summer here, as it allows me the opportunity to meet other people."

"And to find a potential husband," Sarah suggested with a knowing smile.

Lady Mary's eyes widened. "That is what I wish to discuss with you, since I know how it must have appeared to you and Lord Spencer when you saw me hurrying through the garden at dawn the other morning."

"At least you were alone," Sarah told her. "The same cannot be said about me."

Lady Mary nodded. "I confess I did wonder about that later. Eventually I decided that he must be courting you."

Sarah shook her head. "We're just friends, so I

would appreciate your discretion. If you would please refrain from telling anyone that you saw us outside alone together, I'll avoid any mention of seeing you."

"I would be ever so grateful," Lady Mary said.

Placing her hand reassuringly over hers, Sarah said, "I'm glad we had this conversation, for I truly do believe the two of us can be fast friends, and if there's ever anything you'd like to discuss with me— anything at all—you may rest assured that I will never judge you."

Lady Mary sighed. "You're very kind to say so, but—"

"Lady Duncaster," Sarah said, noticing the countess had appeared in the doorway and wishing to warn her friend from saying something she might regret. "I ran into an old acquaintance of mine in the hallway and invited her for a chat while I awaited your arrival. Have you met Lady Mary?"

"Oh yes," the countess said, "though it's a long time ago. Her grandmamma was a dear friend of mine. You parents are in India now, are they not?"

"Yes," Lady Mary said. "I am visiting Thorncliff with my aunt."

"That's right," Lady Duncaster said with a thoughtful nod. "Now that you mention it, I do recall seeing Lady Foxworth at dinner. Always was a bit of a bluestocking, that one. Does she still have a penchant for mathematics?"

Lady Mary chuckled. "She's tutoring me, though I fear my skills, or lack thereof, are a great disappointment to her."

Lady Duncaster snorted. "Never mind. I'm sure you have other interests that she would be equally inept at. That's the beauty about differences."

"Yes," Lady Mary murmured, drawing Sarah's attention to her flushed cheeks. "I'm sure you're right." Rising, she added, "If you'll both please excuse me, I know you were planning a private conversation, so I'd hate to intrude. Besides, my aunt did say she was hoping to take a walk down to the Chinese pavilion with me—apparently the architecture there has some geometric elements she'd like to explore."

"Well, I've no idea about that," Lady Duncaster said. "I had it built solely on the basis of its esthetic qualities and the memories it provides me of my travels to China with my late husband."

"Regardless of its purpose, it looks like a most impressive structure, even at a distance, so I'm looking forward to getting a closer look," Lady Mary explained.

As soon as she had departed, Lady Duncaster said, "She's such a lovely young lady, though I do believe she could benefit greatly from your acquaintance, Lady Sarah. She's far too timid and . . . nervous. A bit of confidence would do her a world of good." Then, without waiting for Sarah to offer a response, she dove straight into the subject they were there to discuss by saying, "Do you suppose we could also have a pie eating contest tomorrow?"

"That will probably be very messy," Sarah said, considering it. "I think it's a wonderful idea!" She made a note of it on the paper. "Perhaps a balance beam could also be placed on the lake. The ladies won't want to compete in such an event, but I'm sure they'll be amused to watch the men trying to stay dry."

"Why, Lady Sarah," Lady Duncaster mused, "how positively mischievous you are. Whoever would have thought?"

Sarah grinned. "I hope you'll tell me if I go too far."

"No need for that, my dear."

"Right. I'll make a note of it then, along with the egg and spoon race, which I'm rather looking forward to myself. A three-legged race will also be popular, and for the children we should definitely have blindman's bluff."

"What about an archery contest?"

"Archery? Don't tell me you have a secret stash of bows and arrows."

Lady Duncaster shrugged. "It's not so secret really. In fact, I was quite fond of the sport when I was younger."

"You're not afraid of someone getting hurt? Unless the contestants are experienced archers, I fear it might be too dangerous."

"Not if we use dull arrows," Lady Duncaster said as she clasped her hands together with eager excitement. "We'll award points on the distance traveled."

Sarah was still skeptical about it, but Lady Duncaster seemed quite determined to have her idea brought to fruition, so Sarah wrote it down.

Picking up her teacup, Sarah took a slow sip. "There's something else I'd like to ask you as well," she said. "I was wondering if I might impose upon your cook one day."

"Is there something specific you'd like her to make?"

Sarah paused for a moment before saying, "Lord Spencer mentioned that he was introduced to a dessert called *choux à la crème* during his travels in France—a sweet pastry filled with some sort of custard. He said it was one of the tastiest things he's ever tried, and upon his return to England, he described it to his parents' cook in the hope she could replicate it. Unfortunately her efforts did not achieve the result Lord Spencer was hoping for."

"Is it fair to assume that the Oakland cook is English?"

"She is indeed."

"And you think because mine is French she'll be more successful?"

Setting down her teacup, Sarah nodded. "Perhaps she knows what a *choux à la crème* is, which I daresay would be a good start."

"Well, you're welcome to ask her, my dear, and if she does know, then by all means have her make some. I love trying new food." Her eyes held Sarah's. "Seems to me you're growing increasingly fond of Lord Spencer."

A flush rose to Sarah's cheeks. "Yes, I am." She would not deny it.

"I can tell from the way you look at each other. It's quite apparent that he's very fond of you as well."

"Not only is he a perfect gentleman," Sarah said, "he's also extremely thoughtful and entertaining to talk to. We have the most engaging conversations."

"Better than the ones you have with Mr. Denison?"

"Forgive me," Sarah said, feeling somewhat disloyal. "How terribly ill-mannered of me to praise Lord Spencer when I should be complimenting Mr. Denison."

Lady Duncaster waved her hand dismissively. "My dear, you would have to be blind not to appreciate Lord Spencer's charms. Let's face it. Mr. Denison hardly compares, which is why I'm all the more sorry for your determination to marry him." She paused as she regarded Sarah with a knowing expression. "My husband was also the most wonderful man I ever met."

"I never said—"

"Oh, Lady Sarah. You didn't have to. It's in the way your eyes sparkle whenever you speak of him."

"I didn't realize."

With a nod of understanding, Lady Duncaster

leaned back against her seat. "George and I were very fortunate to marry for love, Lady Sarah. If there's any possibility that you might do the same, I strongly urge you to do what you can in order to make it happen." She laughed, not with humor but with sadness. "It's very odd, knowing George is no longer with me—that I'll never hear his voice again or find him striding through a door in search of me—and that I've somehow managed to go on without him. There's an emptiness within me. No, that's not the right word . . . hollowness is better suited when it comes to describing the peculiar vacancy that's taken up residency in my heart and soul. It helps to fill the house with people."

"You were fortunate," Sarah said, her eyes watering at the pain Lady Duncaster had been forced to endure by losing her husband. "Most people of our set marry for convenience and then go on to live separate lives. A love match is rare."

"And yet it does look as though you have the chance to make one." A pleasant smile stretched its way across Lady Duncaster's face. "That makes you lucky as well, even if you choose to turn your back on it, though I daresay doing so would be incredibly foolish."

"I suppose it would be," Sarah agreed for the sole purpose of making the conversation easier. She didn't want to talk about Lord Spencer or the potential for falling in love with him anymore. Her heart ached at the very thought of it, of how impossible it would be for her to even consider marrying him without him discovering that she wasn't the innocent young lady he thought her to be. He'd resent her, and living with that for the rest of her life would be so much harder than sharing a future with somebody else.

Chapter 11

The following day, after luncheon, the guests congregated on the lawn, where the egg and spoon race was scheduled to start the game day. Taking her position next to Alice and Juliet, who'd been looking forward to that afternoon's events with great enthusiasm, Sarah held her spoon steady, balancing the egg that lay on top of it, as she waited for the sound of a whistle to announce the start of the race, which consisted of eight competitors, including Lady Fiona.

The instant the whistle sounded, Sarah leapt into a run. The egg wobbled precariously as she moved into the lead, but once she'd gained the advantage, she found a steady pace that kept the egg stable. Now all she had to do was reach the chair that had been placed at the end of the track, circumvent it and return to her starting position. The task was easily accomplished, to the great disappointment of her sisters, who soon decided that the apple bobbing contest was far more to their liking.

"You weren't exaggerating about your egg and spoon racing skills," Chloe said as she approached Sarah with Lord Spencer at her side.

"I rather pity the other contestants," Lord Spencer

said with a hint of amusement. "They didn't stand a chance."

Sarah smiled at both of them. She felt exultant, not only because of the win but also because she'd clearly impressed Lord Spencer, the way he'd impressed her with skipping stones. It felt wonderful, considering that carrying an egg a hundred feet could hardly be compared to playing Beethoven's *Für Elise* with flawless accuracy. Her talent was quirky at best, yet it was clear to her that Spencer approved, which in turn made her insides melt. "Perhaps I should join my sisters in bobbing apples. I'm terrible at that, since I can't seem to help myself from breathing through my nose, which in turn makes me cough and sputter."

"In that case, I'd advise against it," Mr. Denison said as he sidled up to Sarah. He greeted Chloe with an elegant bow. Raising his chin, he acknowledged Lord Spencer with a polite nod.

"You don't care for games, Mr. Denison?" Lord Spencer inquired.

"Not when they result in foolish and unladylike behavior," Mr. Denison said.

Lord Spencer's brow furrowed. "Are you saying that Lady Sarah would be foolish and unladylike if she were to participate in the apple bobbing contest?"

Sarah cringed. She did not want him to intervene on her behalf lest it result in Mr. Denison saying something untoward, which Sarah considered a real possibility. Mr. Denison had not been pleased to discover that Lord Spencer's ride with Victoria and Diana had failed to cement a deeper acquaintance. He had in fact complained about it incessantly the previous day, going so far as to blame Sarah for Lord Spencer's lack of interest in his daughters.

Chloe chuckled. "Honestly, Spencer, must you

be so serious? Mr. Denison is only trying to protect Lady Sarah's reputation."

"Precisely," Mr. Denison said. He caught Sarah's eye and smirked. "After all, a lady is nothing without her reputation. Is she, my lady?"

If a fiery pit of eternal suffering had opened up in the ground at that moment, Sarah would happily have jumped straight into it. That Mr. Denison would deal such a blow to her in front of Chloe and Lord Spencer was beyond the pale.

Struggling to maintain her composure, she said, "How right you are, Mr. Denison. I only thought my sisters might appreciate the opportunity to get back at me for beating them so thoroughly at the egg and spoon race, but I see now that it would be most unwise."

"Do you see how fortunate I am?" Mr. Denison said, addressing Chloe and Lord Spencer. "To marry a lady who's sensible enough to defer to her husband's better judgment is indeed a blessing."

At this, Chloe opened her mouth, closing it again when Sarah met her gaze and shook her head. The last thing Sarah needed was for Mr. Denison to disapprove of her friends and insist she stay away from them.

Lord Spencer, on the other hand, quickly remarked, "While I see your point, I do think I would like to encourage independent thought in the lady I marry."

Mr. Denison didn't even try to hide the look of amusement that settled upon his face. "You say so now because you're still a bachelor, Lord Spencer, but I can tell you from experience that there is nothing more trying than an opinionated wife."

"An interesting perspective," Lord Spencer murmured, "though I would imagine that her opinion of you would be of some relevance."

"Which is why I have every intention of assuring her affection by seeing to her every need," Mr. Denison said.

The double entendre wasn't lost on Sarah. She feared it might not be lost on Lord Spencer either, for his eyes narrowed into two fine slits as he stared back at Mr. Denison.

Worried one of the men might say something regrettable, Sarah said, "I still think the apple bobbing might be fun to watch."

"Wouldn't you prefer to see the archery contest?" Mr. Denison asked. "Word has it Lady Duncaster plans on competing, which is certainly something I'd like to witness."

"A splendid idea," Lord Spencer said.

Sarah nodded her head in agreement.

"As much as I would like to join you, I think I'd prefer a seat in the shade along with a cool glass of lemonade," Chloe said. "Congratulations once again on your win," she told Sarah before biding Mr. Denison a pleasant afternoon and turning toward the refreshment tent.

"Well then," Lord Spencer said, swatting away a bothersome fly. "I do believe we ought to make our way over to the large lawn if we're to watch the archery contest."

"I'll bet you ten pounds Lady Duncaster wins," Mr. Denison said.

Lord Spencer slanted a look in his direction. "I'd be a fool to accept such a wager, since I have every confidence in the lady."

Mr. Denison snorted. "She's quite peculiar, but I daresay it's impossible not to like her."

"I'm surprised you think so," Lord Spencer muttered. "After all, she does belong to the more opinionated variety of women."

Sarah groaned. If only Lord Spencer would stop provoking Mr. Denison. She had no doubt that he was doing it deliberately. And of course Mr. Denison responded to each of Lord Spencer's thinly veiled criticisms with rejoinders that, however polite they sounded, soon conveyed Mr. Denison's growing dislike for Lord Spencer.

"Shall we compete against each other on the balancing beam?" Lord Spencer asked once the archery tournament had been completed with Lady Duncaster as the winner. For some reason he'd accepted Mr. Denison's wager and now appeared eager to even the score. "All you have to do is knock me into the water, unless of course I knock you down first."

"Sounds like a fine bit of sportsmanship, my lord. I do believe I'd enjoy the chance to prove my stamina." Taking Sarah's arm, Mr. Denison started toward the lake with a loud chuckle.

"I admire your confidence," Lord Spencer said dryly as he followed behind them.

So did Sarah. Surely Mr. Denison did not imagine himself capable of beating Lord Spencer? It was certainly possible for a man to be physically fit at the age of five and forty, but one need only take one glance at Mr. Denison to realize he was anything but. His large stomach proved it.

Arriving at the lakeside, they joined the group of spectators, many of whom were busily placing bets on the two gentlemen who were currently competing. Sarah recognized one of them as the Earl of Montsmouth, because she'd danced with him once, a long time ago.

Standing on the balance beam that had been linked between two rafts so it could stay afloat out on the lake, Montsmouth held the baton with which he was supposed to topple his opponent into the water.

"Please put me down for five pounds on the Earl of Chadwick," Lord Spencer said to the Duke of Pine-hurst, who'd taken charge of the betting book. Mr. Denison, of course, immediately made a counter bet of seven pounds on the Earl of Montsmouth.

Sarah tried hard not to roll her eyes, a chore that was proving increasingly difficult. "Is Lord Chad-wick a friend of yours?" she asked Lord Spencer.

"We studied at Eton together and later at Cambridge, so I've known him for many years and consider him the very best of friends. He's quite fun and much more charming than I. The ladies simply adore him." Lower-ing his head, he whispered close to her ear, "Which is why I haven't introduced you to him yet."

"What was that?" Mr. Denison asked while a wave of heat engulfed Sarah's entire body.

Leaning forward so he could meet Mr. Denison's eye, Lord Spencer said, "I was just saying that it will be entertaining to see which one of them gets wet."

Mr. Denison grunted. "Chadwick will," he said.

Concentrating on the competition, Lord Spencer didn't respond. For which Sarah was grateful. She wasn't sure how much longer she'd be able to stand the competitive remarks between the two of them. Thankfully both would soon be out on the lake and she would be offered a short reprieve.

She watched as Montsmouth pressed Chadwick backward, convinced that Chadwick would lose his footing and stumble. He didn't. It was as if the soles of his boots were glued to the beam of wood beneath him. He crouched low and flung his baton sideways, hitting Montsmouth just below the knees and knocking him off balance. A loud splash followed and then an eruption of voices as the crowd cheered the victor.

"I suppose we're even now," Mr. Denison said gruffly. "I won the bet with Lady Duncaster, and you've won the one with Lord Chadwick. Shall we see which one of us wins against the other?"

Sarah considered saying that Lord Spencer hadn't had much of a choice in the archery contest, but she thought better of it. It would serve no purpose other than to make it look as if she was supporting Lord Spencer, when her loyalty ought to lie with the man she was going to marry. Even if she could barely stand him.

Lord Spencer and Mr. Denison waited until Chadwick and Montsmouth had been rowed ashore. Congratulating Chadwick on his win, Lord Spencer and Mr. Denison then climbed into the boat and were quickly taken out to the two rafts, where footmen handed them each a baton.

Sarah could hardly stand to watch. Worst of all, she wanted Lord Spencer to win. "Would you care to place a bet, my lady?" Pinehurst asked.

"One pound on Mr. Denison," she told him dutifully. Her parents hadn't given her the usual allowance before coming to Thorncliff, which, Sarah suspected, was meant to encourage her to find Mr. Denison all the more appealing. She could scarcely afford the one pound, never mind the prospect of losing it, which of course would be inevitable.

"He does look a bit top-heavy, don't you think?"

Stifling a grin, Sarah turned her head to find that Lady Fiona had joined her. "I can't believe you would say such a thing about your own brother."

Lady Fiona's lips twitched. "Don't be daft. You

know perfectly well who I'm talking about." They watched as the two men stepped out onto the balance beam from either end, moving toward each other with careful steps. "There's bound to be a very big splash when Mr. Denison falls in and—"

The splash came sooner than expected.

"Oh dear," Sarah muttered. Dead silence followed a number of gasps, and then, an explosion of uproarious laughter.

"Oh," Lady Fiona said, clutching her stomach. She could not control her mirth. Or perhaps she simply didn't bother trying. "Poor Spencer! To lose an opponent so quickly can't be very rewarding."

Still standing on the balance beam, Lord Spencer bowed to the crowd onshore while Mr. Denison splashed around in the water. Sarah squinted. "Good Lord," she murmured. "I don't believe he knows how to swim."

Lady Fiona instantly stopped laughing, as did everyone else. Concerned comments wove their way through the crowd. Somebody called for help. Another splash sounded, and Sarah saw that Lord Spencer had dived into the lake and was swimming toward Mr. Denison, who was now spending more and more time below the surface than above it. Reaching him, Lord Spencer grabbed onto Mr. Denison, hauling him upward, but it was clear from Mr. Denison's frantic movements that he was in a state of panic. Worse than that, it looked as though he was trying to climb onto Lord Spencer, thus pushing Lord Spencer down.

"Dear Lord, they're both going to drown at this rate," someone muttered.

Sarah's heart stilled. She could not breathe. If anything happened to Lord Spencer . . . *Please, God, let him be all right.* The footman with the boat started rowing toward them as Mr. Denison cried for help, splashing frantically while pushing Lord Spencer under. When the footman eventually reached the pair, Lord Spencer was holding the limp body of Mr. Denison in an armlock while treading water.

"Is he dead?" Fiona asked in a low whisper.

"I don't know," Sarah said. She watched silently as the footman hauled Mr. Denison into the boat, then helped Lord Spencer up into it as well. As soon as he was safely inside, she released a deep, shuddering breath.

"What happened?" Lady Duncaster asked, arriving at the scene just as the rowboat hit the embankment and men stepped forward to help Lord Spencer and Mr. Denison back onto dry land, laying the latter flat on the ground. Lady Fiona immediately ran forward to fling her arms around her brother, just as Sarah longed to do. She'd never been so relieved before in her life.

"Apparently he couldn't swim," Lord Spencer said, accepting a towel from a nearby footman.

"Of all the foolish things," Lady Duncaster said. She leaned over Mr. Denison and peered down at him. "Looks like he's still breathing."

"He ought to be fine once he comes to," Lord Spencer said.

"I take it you knocked him unconscious?" Lady Duncaster asked.

"I had no choice."

"Well, I daresay nobody will blame you, given the circumstances," Lady Duncaster said. Sarah disagreed. She was quite certain Mr. Denison would blame Lord Spencer a great deal.

Lady Duncaster gestured to a couple of footmen.

"Would you please ensure that Mr. Denison is carried up to his bedchamber and that he's given every comfort he requires?"

"Yes, my lady," one of the footmen said, immediately seeing to her request with the help of two other footmen.

"Thank you," Sarah said as she approached Lord Spencer. "Had it not been for you, Mr. Denison might not have made it."

"I appreciate you saying so, my lady, but the truth of the matter is that anyone would have done the same," Lord Spencer said. "It was nothing."

Sarah disagreed, but she was not about to argue the point in front of all these people. Instead she nodded, agreeing to join Lady Fiona for a glass of lemonade on the terrace while Lord Spencer went in search of some dry clothing.

That evening, after enjoying a lovely piece of music performed by Lady Emily at the pianoforte, Sarah quietly left the music room with the intention of seeking solace in her room. She needed to think—to untangle all the thoughts and emotions Lord Spencer and Mr. Denison were causing. It was impossible to do so in the company of others without turning into a frustrated mess.

"Lady Sarah!"

Rather than halting and turning toward the voice that had spoken, Sarah quickened her pace, determined to avoid sharing Mr. Denison's company any further. Since recovering his senses, he'd deliberately sought her out and proceeded to criticize Lord Spencer in every conceivable manner. "He knocked me out," he'd said, his voice pitching with outrage. "What sort of man does that?"

"I believe he was trying to save your life," had been Sarah's reply, "as proven by the fact that you are still alive."

"No thanks to him, I tell you. He was deliberately trying to push me under."

"I don't see why he would have swum to your rescue if that had been the case."

"To hasten my demise of course! Had that footman not pulled me from the water when he did, I'm convinced I would have drowned. I owe that fine young chap a debt of gratitude."

Sarah had stared at Mr. Denison in utter dismay. Of course it was natural for him to be in a state of shock after what had happened, but was he mad? "Are you suggesting that Lord Spencer tried to kill you?" she'd asked very carefully.

"I'm not saying he was, but I'm not saying he wasn't, either. He clearly doesn't like me or my daughters." His eyes had narrowed. "Though he certainly seems to have a fine interest in you."

"You're quite mistaken," Sarah had said, not liking the angry look in Mr. Denison's eyes.

"I think not," he'd said. "In fact, I'm beginning to suspect that he might be planning to steal you away from me, but I won't allow it, I tell you. In fact, I forbid you from having anything further to do with him."

"You . . . you can't do that."

"Really?" He'd leaned close to her, his lips almost touching the lobe of her ear. "Then perhaps I'll just discourage his interest by telling him about your past, shall I?"

"You can't do that either." Her hands had trembled, not so much from fear as from anger. "If word gets out, the deal will be off. Papa will withdraw his offer."

"Are you so certain about that? The way I see it, Lord Andover will be especially glad to be rid of you if anyone discovers how willing you are to lift your skirts."

The insult had burned, but she had held her head high and said, "You may threaten me all you like, sir, but I would urge you to consider that treating the woman you'll be spending the rest of your life with unkindly might not be the wisest decision."

Turning, she'd walked away from him, deaf to whatever else he'd said.

Rounding a corner now, she glanced around in desperation. Another hallway intersected the one she was in. Making a sharp turn, she raced toward the first available door on her right and flung it open, closing it softly behind her as she entered the dimly lit room that would be her salvation.

"What a pleasant surprise."

Catching her breath, she spun toward the deep masculine rumble and quickly located Lord Spencer. He was leaning over a table, hands pressed into the surface to support his weight. A stray lock of hair fell across his brow, the corner of his mouth dimpling as he looked back at Sarah. It was clear that he'd been studying a large piece of paper that lay spread out before him, until she'd disturbed his privacy.

"Please forgive the intrusion," she said, immediately cringing in response to the breathiness of her voice. She sounded as though she was foolishly fawning over him, which perhaps she was, a little bit. It was difficult not to when the man had chosen to remove his jacket, provoking an image of careless abandon that did something wicked to her insides. Her heart fluttered uncomfortably in her chest.

"There's nothing to forgive," he said, straightening. He studied her a moment. "Are you hiding from someone?"

"Of course not."

The door opened behind her and Sarah whirled aside, her back pressing up against the wall as the door hid her from view. "Lord Spencer," Mr. Denison said. He paused, and Sarah imagined him glancing around the room. "Sorry to bother you, but I was looking for Lady Sarah. Have you seen her?"

"Not since dinner."

Another pause followed. Sarah's heart raced with the dread of potential discovery. "Well," Mr. Denison said, "I'll bid you good night then."

"Good night, Mr. Denison," Lord Spencer said.

The door swung shut, leaving Sarah face-to-face with Lord Spencer. Crossing his arms, he raised an eyebrow.

"Very well," Sarah muttered. "I wasn't completely honest when I told you I wasn't hiding."

"Hiding from the man you plan to marry is not very promising." He tilted his head. "Did he say something to upset you?"

"No." She shook her head, hoping to dispel such an idea and the catastrophe it might lead to. Diverting attention away from herself, she asked, "Are you feeling all right after what happened earlier?"

"I'm fine. Thank you for asking."

Crossing the floor, she glanced down at the table before him. "Is that a plan of Thorncliff?"

His eyes narrowed. He was still for a moment, then finally relaxed his posture. He nodded. "Lady Duncaster was kind enough to let me borrow it." He gestured toward a large piece of velum containing a partial drawing. "I'm trying to copy it, since it will make it easier for me to complete my model later."

"An ingenious method for maintaining the correct proportions." She leaned forward, studying the plan. "I'm guessing we must be here, in this room?"

"Correct." His voice sounded slightly raspy as he placed his finger against the velum and outlined a section of the house. "Here is what remains of the original structure—the part built by William Holden. It contains the armory, the interior courtyard that once provided the main entrance, and the ballroom, which originally served as the great hall."

"I wouldn't have realized unless you told me," Sarah said. She'd seen the ballroom, the floors made from polished white marble, the bottom part of the pale blue walls trimmed with moldings, the top part filled with mirrors.

"It's been remodeled many times throughout the ages, most recently by Lady Duncaster and, before her, by the late earl's father, who favored rococo." Moving his hand, he pointed to another portion of the plan. "During the fourteenth century, the kitchen was moved to its current location and this staircase was added. It's since been masked by a cabinet to prevent anyone from making note of it. Apparently the first Duchess of Duncaster considered it a blight upon her fragile senses to view a staircase used predominantly by servants."

Sarah couldn't help but laugh. "She must have found life very difficult if the mere sight of a staircase was capable of distressing her."

"From what I gather, she was very high in the instep. She loved the grandeur of Thorncliff but hated being surrounded by servants. She was the sort of lady who expected all the work to be carried out without her having to witness it."

"A difficult task, I'd imagine, considering the size of this place and the number of servants required."

"I agree," Lord Spencer said. Stepping away from the table, he crossed to the sideboard and poured himself a measure of brandy. "May I offer you some port, or perhaps some sherry?"

Sarah longed to accept his offer, but she'd made a promise to Chloe and . . . "I should probably leave," she said, eying the closed door. "Our being alone like this is not the least bit proper."

"And yet it seems to be turning into a common occurrence." He gestured toward the carafes before him. "I repeat. Port or sherry?"

It was tempting. Too tempting. "Perhaps a small sherry. But then I really must go."

The edge of his mouth tilted. "I take it you've chosen to reclaim your adventurous spirit?" Turning away, he poured her a glass.

His voice swept through her, warming her senses. "Since that particular conversation, I've made some considerations and have decided that I do not wish to lose any more of myself."

"I'm pleased to hear it." Crossing to where she stood, he gave her her glass. "I simply fail to understand how you hope to accomplish such a feat by marrying a man you do not like."

Sarah promptly choked on the small sip she'd taken. "Forgive me," she said, accepting the handkerchief he offered and dabbing at the liquid now staining her bodice.

He said nothing, and when she raised her gaze, she found him looking at her intently. Heated, she took a deliberate step back. "I like him well enough," she lied, determined not to embrace the undeniable attraction unfolding between herself and Lord Spencer.

Disappointment filled his eyes. "I suppose that's why you hid from him, because your fondness for him was too much to bear? Come now, Lady Sarah.

Why are you lying to me?" He took a step toward her, setting his glass on the table as he did so.

Sarah retreated once more. If only she'd left when she'd had the chance, she would not be having this impossible conversation. "Because I enjoy the liberty of our discussions and do not wish to darken them with thoughts of an unavoidable future. When I am with you, I . . ." The words caught in her throat. She'd said too much. Far too much.

Lord Spencer advanced, forcing her farther back until she found herself pressed against the wall. "When you are with me you . . . ?"

"Please don't come any closer," she whispered, her heart in utter turmoil. If he closed the distance, if he kissed her, if he showed her what she had no choice but to sacrifice . . . she feared she would not be able to stand it.

"I asked you a question, Lady Sarah." He honored her request and remained where he was.

With shuddering breaths and quivering lips, she met his gaze, confounded by the pure sincerity that shone there. "When I am with you, I feel beautiful, respected and admired without having ever received a direct compliment. You've shown an interest in me when those closest to me did not."

"And Mr. Denison has not? The man is a fool if he doesn't—" Unable to answer truthfully when Lord Spencer was studying her so closely, she'd looked away. "Lady Sarah." His voice was low and careful. "I asked you before if he's said something inappropriate to you, and you said no. Were you telling me the truth?"

She couldn't lie to him, but neither could she meet his gaze without dissolving into a pool of tears. "He has made it clear that he looks forward to our wedding night with great anticipation."

There was a stretch of silence before Lord Spencer said, "Any man would do so if he were marrying you, and ordinarily a woman would be flattered by the ability to provoke such a reaction in her future husband. But, considering your powerful reaction right now, I suspect he may have phrased his longing for you in an undesirable manner."

"He said the most outrageous things to me," Sarah said, unable to stop herself from succumbing to the note of sympathy in Lord Spencer's voice. If only she could tell him everything.

"Considering your innocence, he should have restrained himself better."

Innocence.

One simple word to remind her of what she'd squandered. Regret filled her, as did guilt, because here she was, allowing Lord Spencer to think that Mr. Denison had wronged her most grievously when in fact it was her own bloody fault.

She didn't deserve Lord Spencer's kindness, his sympathy or his affection. "Thank you, my lord. Your insight has been most helpful." She moved to step past him, but he blocked her path with his arm.

"Is your situation so impossible that you are completely incapable of entertaining other offers?"

"O-other offers?" Heavens, she sounded like a complete nitwit.

"From other gentlemen." He leaned closer until she could scarcely breathe. "From someone you might find more pleasing."

A nervous laugh escaped her. "I don't suppose you're referring to yourself?"

His eyes darkened, the air around them thickening with a strange kind of tension that made her stomach whirl and her legs feel weak. "Don't tell me you're not aware of what's between us."

"You mean the easy camaraderie we share?" Lord, she felt nervous, the worst part being that she could think of no way to stop it. Her mind was in a muddle and her heart was turning cartwheels in her chest.

"There is that," he said, his eyes darkening even further as he placed his right arm on the other side of her, fencing her in, "but there's also this."

Panic rose up inside her when she realized his intent. "My lord! I—" His lips brushed against hers, silencing whatever protest she'd planned to make. Aware of how wrong this was, no matter how wonderfully right it felt, she struggled against the many sensations assailing her mind, her body and her senses. It was like swimming upstream in the middle of a torrential downpour.

Moving closer still, he deepened the kiss, his hands moving to cup her face while he pushed up against her, his firm chest pressing into her soft curves, stirring embers to spark a flame within her treacherous body. She felt his tongue glide across her lips and she practically melted, her breasts swelling against her confining bodice until all thought of telling him this could not happen fled to the far corners of her mind.

Gasping for breath, she invited him in, stunned that the feel of his tongue stroking hers would inspire a need to be touched elsewhere—a scandalous prospect that spoke to her conscience in a quiet whisper. *Do not encourage him to want that which he cannot have. It isn't fair.*

Placing her hands flat against his chest, she pushed at him gently. It was enough.

"You taste even better than I had imagined," he said, remaining close—so close she could smell the brandy on his breath, along with a hint of tobacco from earlier.

Sarah clenched her hands, determined to stay strong. "As I told your sister, Lady Newbury, earlier this evening, it is my duty to marry Mr. Denison. I cannot consider anyone else."

For a moment he looked as though he failed to comprehend what she was saying. Then he leaned back, adding distance and leaving her bereft. "Allow me to have a word with your father."

Sarah blinked. She could not believe what he was saying. Was Lord Spencer seriously so interested in her that he would abandon the bachelorhood he coveted in favor of making her an offer? It seemed unfathomable, yet it was essential for him to make a fine match once he married. From his perspective, she seemed like a perfect candidate. "It will not matter," she said.

"Why not? If your father's concern is with the deal he was planning to make with Mr. Denison, I'm sure a solution can be found. I am a wealthy man, Lady Sarah—I'll buy Mr. Denison's horses if need be. All of them."

"You can't be serious?"

"Perfectly so." He ran his hand along the length of her arm. "Surely your father will reconsider your future when he discovers that a viscount would like to compete for your hand."

"A very handsome viscount, I might add," Sarah couldn't help but say.

He looked at her with great intensity, his chest rising and falling, as if he was battling conflicting emotions. Eventually he shook his head. "Do you have any idea how many women I've spoken to over the years? None have engaged my mind as well as you have. They haven't challenged me to think of sharp rejoinders, whereas you . . . I can hardly ever guess what you will say next."

"I often say what I oughtn't."

"And I adore that! It's an exceptional quality—one that has brought me great amusement on multiple occasions." He took her hand in his and raised it to his lips, placing a tender kiss there. "I cannot promise you love, but I can assure you that I will respect you and that I will cherish your company forever if you agree to become my wife."

She took a sharp breath. Oh, how she longed to pretend she had the option to choose. "I'll never forget your kindness," she said, tugging on her hand until he released her, "but you're asking the impossible." Turning away, she made for the door.

"If that's a challenge, Lady Sarah," he called after her, "you ought to know that I love a good challenge. Rest assured, I will rise to it, and I will win."

Stepping out into the hallway, she seriously considered telling him the truth, knowing that however much he'd despise her for what she'd done, it would have the benefit of setting him free.

Chapter 12

When Christopher awoke on Saturday morning, his first thought was of Lady Sarah and the conversation he'd had with her two days earlier. She'd avoided him since then, always insisting upon the company of others whenever he was near so that they wouldn't be left alone with each other. She'd also refrained from joining him down by the lake in the morning, even though he'd sent her a note and a flower, inviting her to do so.

What he'd said to her was true. He did enjoy her company and the conversations they'd shared, and he found that he missed her—especially after speaking with her father. That conversation had gone much better than he would have expected after everything Lady Sarah had told him.

Stretching out until his legs tangled with the sheets, Christopher smiled up at the ceiling. There was to be a ball this evening, and he had every intention of claiming a dance with Lady Sarah. She would not be able to deny him then—not in front of so many people.

Rising amidst the shadows of the predawn morning, Christopher spent half an hour doing his routine exercises before washing up and quickly dressing without disturbing his valet, who slept in an adjoining chamber. Snatching up a small round frame he'd bought in town the previous day and which now contained his clover, he placed the item carefully in his jacket pocket, ensuring that it would be kept within reach. Perhaps if he carried it with him, he wouldn't be so concerned about attracting bad luck, since the clover would undoubtedly balance things out. Was that why Lady Sarah had determined to find one for him? he wondered. How remarkable that she had made the effort. He'd tried to find one himself on many occasions, but he'd never been met with any success.

Once out in the hallway, he paused in front of the next door down from his own, his hand rising with hesitation as he wondered whether or not to knock. On a deep intake of air, he decided to make a go of it, then waited for the voice that would grant him entry. "Who is it?" his brother asked from somewhere within.

"It's Kip," Christopher replied, keeping his tone as low as possible so as not to disturb any of the other guests.

There was a hollow pause, and then the grating sound of a key being turned in the lock. The door remained closed as usual though, and Christopher waited a respectable moment before opening it, allowing his brother enough time to retreat, if that was what he desired to do. "I wasn't sure if you would still be awake," he finally said upon entering, knowing that Richard habitually slept during the day and remained up all night, surrounding himself with darkness. Even the bedchamber attested to it. Only one oil lamp was lit, though it was turned all the way down, emitting a low glow for the sole purpose of orientation.

"The sun isn't up yet," Richard said from his position by the window, where he glanced out through a narrow parting between the curtains.

"No," Christopher told his brother's back. He didn't move farther into the room, knowing that Richard would not approve. "I was hoping I might convince you to take a walk with me in the garden. The air is at its best this time of day, and you can be back before the sun rises. Nobody will see you."

"You cannot be certain of that," Richard remarked in a low timbre that stabbed at Christopher's heart. His voice held a mixture of pain and defeat. "Even you were surprised the other day, I saw, by a certain young lady out for a morning stroll."

There was a hidden question there that Christopher chose to answer. "Lady Sarah," he said. "I enjoy her company immensely, which is somewhat peculiar, considering my reluctance to let another woman into my life, but she has proven herself to be kind and selfless. Since I must marry eventually, I cannot help but consider her. I believe she would make a fine viscountess."

"You're sure of this?"

"Of course I am, or I would not suggest it."

There was a low grunt of reproach before Richard said, "Forgive me, Kip, but you of all people have every reason to second-guess a person's true character."

Christopher stiffened. His brother was right, but Christopher knew Lady Sarah to be the person she claimed to be. "Her parents arranged an unfavorable match for her—one she was quite determined to agree to due to her father's insistence. Apparently Lord Andover has a weakness for horses and was keen on making an alliance with a man in possession of some fine mares—a venture that would also offer Lord Andover a large income, which was probably why Lady Sarah doubted her father's willingness to consider other options.

"But after speaking with Lord Andover yesterday, I believe I managed to convince him that allowing his daughter to marry me would result in a certain prestige that Mr. Denison cannot provide. When I added that I'd be willing to pay for the acquisition of any five horses Lord Andover might desire, his interest increased dramatically. In short, he has given me permission to court Lady Sarah."

"All this trouble for some horses," Richard murmured.

"It would seem so."

"I do not mean to add doubt, but it seems dubious to me. Why wouldn't Lord Andover have tried to obtain such a favorable match for his daughter to begin with? Surely he must have been able to find a gentleman of good standing who might have been willing to make a similar deal to what you have suggested."

"From what I understand, Mr. Denison's horses are quite particular."

"And from what *I* understand, Mr. Denison is a nobody, perhaps a wealthy nobody, but a nobody nonetheless, while *she* is an earl's daughter."

"Are you suggesting there's something I don't know about?"

"I think you ought to ask Lady Sarah that. Wouldn't you agree?"

A wince escaped Christopher's throat at the very idea of it. He'd come to the conclusion that Lady Sarah was everything he wanted in a wife—smart, funny, generous, kind . . . and with looks that would dazzle him forever. He didn't want to consider that she might be flawed—that there was a chance of her being anything other than the woman whom he'd come to admire. But if there was something that she and her parents were keeping from him . . . something that might even affect his own family by association . . . he had a duty to uncover it, however much he might regret doing so. "Yes," he said simply. "I do."

Keeping the left side of his face hidden from view, Richard turned his head, his right eye meeting Christopher's across the distance. "I don't envy the position you're in as heir—this rush everyone's in to get you married so you can start producing an heir of your own." He laughed grimly. "Fortunately, I doubt I'll ever have to fight off any eager mamas or their troublesome daughters. What a relief!"

"Richard, I—"

"Don't say it, Brother. We both know it had to be me."

As if that made it any bloody easier. All Christopher could think of was that if he'd at least been there on that battlefield, perhaps his brother wouldn't have been captured. Perhaps Christopher could have protected him. Instead, the unthinkable had happened, and Richard had been broken as a result of it. Laura was right. It was surprising that he had agreed to come to Thorncliff with them. "I will visit you again tomorrow," Christopher told Richard quietly.

Richard nodded before glancing away, and Christopher exited the room, his heart aching for the young man whose future had been compromised because he'd served his country. It wasn't fair, regardless of what one might expect from war. No. It was a downright shame.

Standing on the lakeshore a short while later,

Christopher couldn't help but hope that Lady Sarah would join him, for he knew that if anyone could lift his spirits out of the gutter where they presently resided, it was she. Ah, but he knew she would not come. She'd taken to avoiding him after he'd kissed her and told her of his intentions. What puzzled him was that Lord Andover must have spoken to her by now about the conversation he'd had with Christopher, but rather than seek him out now that her obligation to marry Mr. Denison no longer existed, she maintained her distance.

For the sake of his own peace of mind, he would have to inquire about the reason. Lord, how he dreaded that conversation and all that it might reveal. He didn't want to discover any unpleasant secrets about Lady Sarah. He wanted her to be as perfect as he thought her to be. Yet there was that nagging little voice of uncertainty that warned him to take heed—especially since the picnic, when she'd been shockingly outspoken about the fanciful notion of following one's heart regardless of the consequences.

With that in mind, Christopher determined to confront her at the first available opportunity so he could question her more closely. His aim was to get all the facts out in the open before he made the same mistake he'd made five years earlier. That meant she would have to tell him about the man who'd once broken her heart.

But when Christopher returned back inside, he was met by Lady Duncaster, who invited him to join her for breakfast, along with his parents. Gradually, Christopher's sisters began trickling into the room along with a few other guests until, by the time he took his leave, the dining room was at least half full. He had yet to see Lady Sarah and the other members of her family arrive.

Too distracted to focus on his sketches of Thorn-cliff, Christopher decided to make good use of his day by visiting the stables. As he approached, he saw that Chadwick was standing a few paces apart from the door leading into the stables, riding crop in hand. Striding forward, he greeted Christopher with a bright smile. "Good morning," Chadwick said. "I'm glad to see you looking well after what happened the day before yesterday. Terrible business that. Don't know what that man was thinking, competing at something that would probably have cost him his life had you not been there to save him."

"His pride got the better of him, I suppose," Christopher said as he fell into step alongside Chadwick. "It was beyond foolish, but at least we both survived the ordeal. What of you, my friend? How are you faring today?"

Chadwick grinned. "When you failed to join me for after-dinner drinks last night, I ended up retiring surprisingly early and have awoken at a most unusual hour."

"You mean before nine o' clock?"

"Nine? That was years ago. I now have a tendency to stay abed until eleven. But, to my astonishment, I find I quite like waking up to the sound of birds singing. Indeed, I'm beginning to understand your fondness for it."

"I've always considered it the best part of the day."

"And you may be right about that."

Finding a stable hand, Christopher asked the man to saddle a horse for him. "There's a fine Thoroughbred by the name of Arion, who recently won the Ascot gold cup."

"I know the horse well," Christopher said. He'd bet good money on that horse and won. "I'd no idea he ended up here at Thorncliff."

"Her ladyship acquired him for a handsome sum so her guests would have a proper horse to ride," the stable hand said. "So there's him, and the one being prepared for Lord Chadwick: Aragorn, who won the Newmarket race last year."

"Good Lord, she must have spent a fortune on both of them," Christopher muttered.

"I cannot say, my lord, but I'd be happy to saddle Arion for you."

"I'd appreciate that," Christopher said. The man went to see to the task, and Christopher turned to Chadwick. "Her ladyship certainly knows how to cater to her guests. I can't say I'm not impressed."

"Admittedly, I wasn't sure what to expect when I decided to come here. I have to say that it's certainly all it's cracked up to be. The gardens alone are incredible, and then of course there's the smoking room, the billiard room and the wine cellar. Lord, have you seen the wine cellar, Spencer? I daresay I could stay down there for days just enjoying the sight of it!" Aragorn was brought out, and Chadwick took the reins. "I gather that there's to be a ball this evening. Hope you asked your valet to polish your shoes."

Christopher grinned, a bit giddy from his friend's enthusiasm, which was always so contagious. "My valet doesn't need telling. When I return to my bedchamber later, my evening clothes will be laid out for me." He glanced at Chadwick. "I'm glad I ran into you—your company is much appreciated," he said as Arion was brought out as well. Placing his foot in the stirrup, he swung himself up into the saddle and followed Chadwick out onto a dirt road that would lead them past the forest to the fields beyond.

"I thought I should tell you that you're looking more like your old self," Chadwick said after a short while.

Glancing across at his friend, Christopher found him looking back at him with a bit of a gleam to his eyes. He'd met him at the tender age of thirteen, during his first day at Eton, and had quickly bonded with him over a prank involving a ferret. Since then, their goal had always been to outdo each other, though they had decreed that they would do so in a gentlemanly fashion and that their behavior would never be an insult to their names in any way.

This had become especially important as they'd grown older and developed an interest in women. So many of their peers had seemed to think little about a young woman's honor, unless she happened to be nobility. Spencer and Chadwick, however, had always considered it their duty to treat all women, including their mistresses, with the greatest respect.

"You were always so positive and carefree until that horrid woman came along and ruined your happiness," Chadwick was saying. "Thank God you're rid of her!"

"Thank God indeed," Christopher muttered.

"So will you tell me what's brought about this sudden change in your demeanor? When I last saw you at the Flintworth Ball, you were scowling at everybody."

Knowing how shocking his response would be, Christopher schooled his features and said, "If you must know, I happen to have made the acquaintance of a certain young lady."

"Surely you jest!"

"I would never," Christopher told him seriously.

There was a moment of silence. "I'm very happy for you," Chadwick said at last. "After five years, I was beginning to think you'd given up on marriage completely. You must introduce me to this lady who's encouraged you to risk your heart again."

"What makes you think I'd be risking my heart?" The idea of doing so came with a wave of nausea. "This is a practical decision, since Richard's unlikely to have any children. Whether I wish it or not, I do have a duty toward my family, and I intend to see to it. As to the lady in question, you met her yesterday at the lake."

"Lady Sarah?" Chadwick frowned unexpectedly. "Wasn't her arm linked with another gentleman's?"

"The man, whose name is Mr. Denison, is not a gentleman. He is simply a minor inconvenience now that her father has allowed me to express my interest in her."

"She's been absent from Society for two years, Spencer. Doesn't that strike you as odd?"

"What strikes me as odd," Christopher said, suddenly irritated by his friend's comments, "is that you would remember her after not having seen her for so long."

Chadwick shrugged. "I won't deny that I had an interest in her at the time." He shot Christopher a look, one eyebrow rising. "Do you know, for a man who claims his heart is not invested, you look rather put out by that idea. Rest assured, I never treated her with anything but respect."

"How good of you to point that out," Christopher muttered. Perhaps this ride had been a mistake.

"In fact, I doubt she'd remember me, considering how popular she was." His frown deepened. "Nobody had a chance with her though. Not after she met Harlowe."

Christopher bristled. When a careless letter between the Marquess of Harlowe and Jean-Baptiste Drouet, Comte d'Erlon, had turned up, revealing a collaboration between the Marquess and Napoleon's army during the war, the Marquess had been brought before the House of Lords and found guilty of treason. After being stripped of his title and his lands, the marquess had enjoyed a brief prison sentence before his public hanging at Newgate. "What do you mean?"

"He charmed her, I suppose, but then his criminal actions were brought to light and he was dragged away from the Gillsborough house party in irons. I wasn't there myself, but I understand that it put a very abrupt end to an otherwise pleasant event."

It also explained why Lord and Lady Andover had kept Lady Sarah away from the marriage mart and were now desperately trying to marry her off to someone like Mr. Denison, who probably wouldn't care about Lady Sarah's connection to Harlowe.

"I'm sure it did." Christopher paused briefly. "Tell me, Chadwick, did Harlowe ever make an offer for her? Was there a brief engagement I ought to know about?"

"No. I can't say he wasn't planning to propose, since he probably doubted anyone would discover the crimes he'd committed years earlier. It truly was a blessing for the Andovers that Lady Sarah avoided marrying him."

"Yes. It most certainly was. Shall we race?" Christopher asked Chadwick as they trotted out onto an open field. Even though he wished that Lady Sarah had confided in him, he understood her reasons for not doing so, considering his own reluctance to tell her about Miss Hepplestone. There was some relief to be found in knowing the truth—to understand the sort of obstacle that prevented her from considering him as a husband.

Leaning forward in his saddle, Christopher urged

his horse into a fast gallop alongside Chadwick. He
would speak to his father, of course, but in general
he could see no reason why Lady Sarah shouldn't
become his wife as long as he was willing to accept
that she had once been charmed by Harlowe. Which
he was, since nothing significant had come of it.

It was approaching eleven o'clock by the time they returned from their ride, dismounted and strode along
a gravel path that took them through the garden
toward the flagstone terrace in front of the house.
A few people were congregated there, enjoying cups
of tea or glasses of lemonade, depending upon their
preferences. As Christopher and Chadwick walked
up the steps, Christopher recognized Emily's voice
and instinctively turned toward it, only to find her
reclining on a wicker love seat with Lady Sarah at her
side. Fiona and Laura were similarly seated across
from them. "Come," Christopher said to Chadwick,
"let's go and greet my sisters."

"And the lovely Lady Sarah is there as well, I see,"
Chadwick remarked, his voice low enough to be
heard only by Christopher.

Once they stood before them, Christopher offered a bow of greeting, as did Chadwick, who
made a show of praising all the ladies to the heavens and bowing over each of their hands. This was
his usual style of behavior with the fairer sex, yet it
rankled Christopher to see it applied to Lady Sarah.
Biting back a childish remark, he seated himself on
one empty chair while Chadwick claimed the other.
Christopher chided himself for his possessive reaction, as he had no right. Not yet, at least.

"We were having the most fascinating conversation just now," Fiona said, excitement clear in every manner of her being. "Did Lady Sarah tell you that Lady Duncaster spoke to her of the treasure?"

This again.

Christopher stopped a groan as he looked across at Lady Sarah. "No. She did not."

Her smile was adorably bashful. "I didn't have the opportunity to do so. When last we met, I was so occupied by the picnic and the good company I was in that it completely slipped my mind." A blush rose to her cheeks, and she looked away from Christopher, her focus on his sisters instead. She had wisely decided not to mention their private encounter with each other in the green salon the other evening. There was no doubt in Christopher's mind that she was thinking about it though. *He* certainly was.

"Surely Lady Duncaster must have told you something that can help us in our search?" Fiona pressed.

"*Your* search, you mean?" Emily muttered.

"I'm afraid not," Lady Sarah said. "In fact, Lady Duncaster is convinced it doesn't exist."

"Then why would Grandmamma mention it in her diary?" Fiona asked, directing a very pointed look at all of them.

"She made a direct reference to it?" Lady Sarah asked, sounding understandably surprised.

"Not precisely," Laura said, offering Fiona a reprimanding look. "There is merely an entry about Grandpapa going to Thorncliff to retrieve a box. Nothing more."

"That's not exactly how she phrased it," Fiona complained.

"It's close enough," Laura insisted, while Rachel shook her head, no doubt bothered by her sisters' lack of precision.

"Did your grandmother include any more details?" Lady Sarah asked. She'd edged forward in her seat and was looking very keen, with her eyes expectantly trained on Fiona.

"Only that Grandpapa promised he would return the following day, but for some mysterious reason he decided to board a ship in Portsmouth with Lord Duncaster instead." Fiona looked at them each in turn. "Don't you see? It's clear they were up to something, or Grandpapa would have delayed leaving or at the very least have sent Grandmamma a note of explanation."

Christopher frowned. It was one thing to indulge his sister's imagination and the longing she had to uncover a grand treasure, but to openly discuss the tragic death of their grandfather like this wasn't something he could allow. Before he could put an end to the folly, though, Chadwick said, "Something urgent must have occurred for both of them to leave with such haste."

"Precisely," Fiona exclaimed, "and if I could just find out what it might have been, perhaps I'll find the treasure. There has to be a link somehow."

"Or none at all," Emily told Fiona kindly. "After all, Grandmamma wrote that Grandpapa came here in order to bring back a box. I'm sure Lord Duncaster would have had it waiting, so if they did leave in haste as we suspect, it ought to have been discovered by somebody. Unless of course Grandpapa took it with him, in which case it's probably resting on the bottom of the English Channel."

"I don't believe that's the case," Fiona insisted. "I'm confident it's somewhere here, and I intend to find it."

"But it does seem a little odd that Lady Duncaster found nothing on the entire estate when she renovated it last. From what I understand, the work was extensive," Lady Sarah pointed out with a hesitant glance in Christopher's direction.

He realized then that she'd noticed his reaction to the conversation and was trying to discourage Fiona from getting too caught up in a dream that would likely disappoint her. He was grateful to her for that.

"I have to confess that you make a good argument," Fiona said, biting her lip.

"Well then, since that's settled, I would like to be the first to request a dance from each of you ladies this evening," Chadwick said with a smile bright enough to outdo the sun. "If I may?"

Christopher stiffened. He didn't mind his sisters dancing with Chadwick—indeed, he was Christopher's friend and as such a respectable gentleman. Besides, they knew him so well that he was practically family. But Lady Sarah . . . Christopher held his breath while each of his sisters promised a dance to Chadwick—a quadrille, a country dance and a cotillion. Good Lord, maybe he was losing his head and his heart over her. The surge of panic he felt was certainly acute.

"Which dance would you prefer, Lady Sarah?" Chadwick finally asked, while Christopher tried to slow his beating heart. He attempted a smile in an effort to hide the scowl he could feel creeping across his forehead.

Her eyes met his with a look of concern, and Christopher immediately realized her predicament. She'd stayed away from him for two days, most likely due to fear. Or, considering her response toward him when he'd kissed her, perhaps she felt as drawn to him as he was to her but didn't believe in the possibility of their sharing a future together. Except now she had to consider Chadwick, whom she could not turn down without being rude, even though Christopher sensed that she wanted to. "If I may," he said, deciding to help not only Lady Sarah but himself as well, "I would suggest dancing a reel with Chadwick, and if you are amiable to the idea, I would be honored if you would consider partnering with me for the waltz."

Her eyes widened a little, her smile a bit tighter than he would have liked, no doubt because he'd taken her choice away from her. A mistake, he supposed, but a necessary one if he was going to prevent Mr. Denison from claiming the most intimate dance of the evening.

"An excellent suggestion," Lady Sarah said, her expression softening as she turned to Chadwick. "I shall look forward to it."

"He does dance the reel to perfection," Laura said. "I daresay you won't be disappointed."

"My only concern is that *he* might be," Lady Sarah said with a hesitant glance at Christopher. "I haven't danced at all these last two years."

"No need to worry," Christopher told her, forcing her to look at him. The apprehension that shone in the depths of her clear blue eyes was unmistakable. "We'll help you through it."

A puzzled expression crossed her face, as if she wasn't sure he was speaking of the dance or of something else entirely. He'd been speaking from his heart, in reference to the troubles she faced—troubles that he would at long last be able to help her overcome.

"Lady Sarah," he said as he held out his hand toward her. "Perhaps you would care for a stroll in the garden?"

She was looking up at him with a guarded expression, and he could sense her attempting to find an excuse that wouldn't embarrass either of them. Eventually she said, "That would be lovely. I'm sure your sisters and Chadwick would like to join us though. We can cross the Chinese bridge to the pavilion out on the island perhaps. Have you ever seen anything quite so exotic in an English garden before?"

And just like that, Lady Sarah was wandering off with the Heartly sisters at her side, amicably talking to them while Christopher and Chadwick followed behind. Somehow, he would have to find another opportunity to get her alone so he could confront her about her past and about her father's approval of him as a suitor.

"I'm sorry to disturb you," Sarah said when she was ushered into Lady Duncaster's private sitting room later that afternoon and found her ladyship dressed in the most peculiar outfit.

Lady Duncaster's face lit up, and she pirouetted around with one foot off the ground. "Isn't it wonderful?"

Sarah blinked. "I'm not sure I know what it is."

"Pantaloons!" Lady Duncaster placed her feet in a wide stance so Sarah could see that the billowing fabric constituted a pair of legs rather than an oddly shaped skirt. "I learned to wear these when I was living in India with my parents, long before I met George. They're extremely practical and far more comfortable than any English clothing I've ever seen."

"And on top . . . is that a shirt of some sort?" Sarah asked as she studied Lady Duncaster's garment with interest.

Lady Duncaster held out her arms. "It's a tunic that I can put on over my head without anyone's assistance. Again, it's very practical and doesn't require the use of that awful corset."

"It's very flattering as well," Sarah told her honestly.

Lady Duncaster beamed. "Thank you, my dear. Now, what did you wish to discuss with me?"

"I was actually hoping you might be willing to take me on a tour of the tunnels beneath Thorncliff. I understand they're quite extensive."

Lady Duncaster's mouth tilted. "Looking for a bit of adventure?"

"Something like that," Sarah said. What she truly wanted was escape from her parents, Mr. Denison and Lord Spencer. Especially after Lord Spencer had kissed her, forcing her to consider him in a way she'd previously tried to avoid. But there was no avoiding it now, with the memory of his lips pressed against hers forever ingrained in her mind.

"Then let us explore," Lady Duncaster said as she twirled toward a Chinese screen, gesturing for her maid to assist her. "I'll only be a few moments." When she reappeared, she was dressed in a fashionable gown, showing no signs of the hoydenish appearance she'd exhibited when Sarah had first arrived.

"How are things progressing with Mr. Denison?" Lady Duncaster asked as they stepped out into the hallway and made their way toward the stairs.

"As expected, I suppose," Sarah told her, unwilling to lie.

Lady Duncaster slanted her a look. "And with Lord Spencer?"

Sarah's heart made an odd little flutter. "He has proven himself to be a good friend."

"I see."

She didn't say more, yet Sarah felt as though Lady Duncaster had said everything with those two words. Discomforted by it, Sarah kept quiet as they descended the stairs and turned down a long hallway until they arrived at the interior courtyard that had once been part of Thorncliff's façade.

"It's so beautiful," Sarah said, stopping to enjoy the sound of water splashing from the fountain that stood in the center. At the opposite corner from her, partly concealed by some potted plants, stood an older woman with a paintbrush in her hand, which she occasionally flicked across the canvas in front of her.

"Yes. I've always loved this part of the house," Lady Duncaster said, her voice muted as if deliberately trying to preserve the peace the space offered. "It reminds me of an Italian villa." Looking at Sarah with sharp eyes, she asked, "Do you know what makes it most special?"

Sarah shook her head. "No," she whispered.

"The imperfections," Lady Duncaster told her seriously. "The uneven paving stones, the way the steps over there have been worn by age and how some of the lions at the base of the fountain have cracks in them. If it weren't so, this courtyard would not be so much different from all the rest—it would not be as special because it wouldn't have the same degree of character."

"Why do I get the distinct impression that you're not just talking about the courtyard?"

Lady Duncaster chuckled. "Surely you can work that one out on your own. Lord Spencer! Won't you join us?"

Sarah stilled, her skin tightening around her entire body as she turned around to face the man she'd been hoping to avoid. Her breath caught. Heaven help her if he didn't somehow manage to look even more handsome than he had earlier in the day when he'd joined her and his sisters on the terrace along with Lord Chadwick. She forced herself to remain calm, but it was to no avail. She attempted a smile instead.

"I'd be delighted to," Lord Spencer said as he approached. His eyes warmed as they swept over Sarah, producing a shiver along the length of her spine.

I will remain sensible, she told herself, even though she feared he might already have muddled her brain with his mere presence. Annoying man.

"Lady Sarah would like to explore the tunnels below Thorncliff, and since you've shown quite an interest in the old place yourself, I thought you might like to come along," Lady Duncaster said while Sarah secretly prayed he'd say no.

Of course he didn't. "How intriguing," he said. He looked at Sarah again, which promptly heated her skin.

Offering both ladies an arm, he placed himself between them. Sarah had no choice but to accept. Rather than avoiding Lord Spencer, as she had hoped, she would be spending her afternoon in close proximity to him instead. Thank God Lady Duncaster would be there to chaperone.

But when they reached the bottom of the stairs leading down to the wine cellar and continued through another doorway, their path lit only by the lantern Lady Duncaster carried with her, Sarah couldn't help but wonder if this adventure of hers had not been one of the worst ideas she'd had in a long time. The light was weak, fading swiftly to a hazy gray that turned to black within a couple of feet of the lantern, and when Lady Duncaster occasionally shielded the light with her body, it was like plunging into a dark hole.

Damp and chilly, the tunnel they'd entered lent no comfort of any kind, making Sarah all the more aware of the warmth emanating from Lord Spencer's body as he walked behind her. She tried to dislodge her awareness, but this was of course impossible.

"During a number of wars, including the Hundred Years' War, some of the rooms down here served as living quarters for soldiers, while others contained supplies," Lady Duncaster said. Entering through a low archway, she shone the lantern around the room so they could see.

"It must have been awfully cold for them down here—especially during the winter," Sarah said. Lord Spencer brushed against her side as he stepped inside the room after her. Caught off guard by the flip of her belly, she stifled a small gasp.

"Of course they would have had furs to keep them warm, but it was generally thought that as long as the soldiers weren't too comfortable, they'd be more eager to stay active," Lady Duncaster said.

"It probably also helped preserve the food," Lord Spencer remarked.

"Very true," Lady Duncaster said as she went back out into the tunnel. "In fact we still use some of these rooms today for that exact purpose—the ones that are closer to where the new kitchen is located."

Determined not to be left alone with Lord Spencer, Sarah hurried after Lady Duncaster. "How long is this tunnel?" she asked.

"When it was last measured, I was informed that it's just under seven hundred feet in length, attaching to another tunnel that runs due south, exiting through a postern almost two miles away, a short distance from the sea." Halting, Lady Duncaster raised her lantern to illuminate a sign on the wall that read

Brokenst with an arrow beneath it. "Signs like this have been placed at regular intervals along the tunnels to allow for some sense of direction. Of course the place names aren't all as accurate as they used to be. This one ought to say Brokenhurst now, but I find I don't feel comfortable about replacing them. This one's my favorite," she said a moment later as their tunnel opened into another one.

Lady Duncaster raised the lantern, allowing Sarah to read *Isle of Wight* on one sign and *New Forest* on the one below it, with arrows pointing in opposite directions. "Incredible," Sarah murmured.

"Are there other tunnels leading off of this one?" Lord Spencer asked, sounding equally intrigued.

"There are several," Lady Duncaster said, turning back in the direction from which they'd come. "One leads toward an abandoned monastery, while another leads only God knows where. I've had most of them closed off to prevent anyone from wandering down here on a lark and getting lost."

"It must have been dreadfully tedious to dig all these tunnels back then," Sarah said. "I can't even imagine anyone completing such a feat nowadays."

"There is a record somewhere that suggests it took almost three hundred years to complete the entire network," Lady Duncaster said.

Sarah was speechless, admiring the patience and tenacity that would have been required. "Are these rooms similar to the first one you showed us?" she asked as they passed several consecutive archways.

"Yes," Lady Duncaster said, holding the lantern toward the room so Sarah could look inside. She couldn't get a clear impression of the room's size, though, since the light failed to reach the walls. Stepping back, she was just about to continue after Lady

Duncaster when she felt an uneven protrusion beneath her right slipper, which seemed to slide sideways as she lifted her foot. Ordinarily, she would
have thought it a stone, but it made a soft metallic
sound that gave her pause. Wondering if someone
might have dropped something on a previous visit
to the tunnels, Sarah halted her progress and was
just about to call for Lady Duncaster to do the same
when Lord Spencer, blinded by the diminished lighting, walked straight into her.

"Forgive me," he said, catching her swiftly by the
waist to stop her from falling.

The heat from his palm, pressed flat against her
belly, seeped through her many layers of clothing,
making her body hum with pleasure. A gasp escaped
her, and she swore she heard his chest rumble.

"I must speak with you," Lord Spencer whispered
in her ear.

"Lady Duncaster," Sarah said loudly, unnerved by
the sparks of pleasure that the touch of his breath
against her bare neck evoked. She heard him curse
beneath his breath as the lantern light grew stronger
and Lady Duncaster returned. "Would you please
be kind enough to shine the light on the ground? I
stepped on something just now and would like to
make sure it's not something important."

"Of course, my dear," Lady Duncaster said as she
lowered the lantern.

Bending down, Sarah saw a brief sparkle. It vanished again as the lantern moved sideways. "Wait,"
she said. "Move the light a little to the left."

Lady Duncaster did as Sarah requested, revealing a
tangled cluster of what appeared to be small pieces of
glass, except they seemed to catch the light in a way
that suggested they might be something else entirely.

Scarcely believing what she suspected she might have found, Sarah reached down and scooped the item up into her hand, where she rearranged it neatly until there was no doubt about what it was.

"Good heavens," Lady Duncaster remarked, her voice conveying a mild state of shock. "It looks as though your sister, Lady Fiona, might be right after all, Spencer. I'd recognize that earring anywhere." Lifting it from Sarah's hand, she held it up so each of the finely cut diamonds could split the light from the lantern in a dazzling flare of color. Lowering the earring, she looked at Lord Spencer and Sarah in turn. "This belonged to Her Grace, the Duchess of Marveille."

"Are you telling me that her jewelry arrived at Thorncliff after all?" Lord Spencer asked in a tight voice.

"It would appear so," Lady Duncaster said. She shook her head. "I never would have thought it, but there's no mistaking this earring. I borrowed it from Her Grace once for a dinner aboard the *Endurance*."

"The ship on the lake?" Sarah asked.

A smile graced Lady Duncaster's lips. "The very same one that carried me from India to England on the voyage where I fell in love for the first and last time. George bought it for me for our tenth anniversary when he discovered that it was being decommissioned. It's been on the lake ever since."

"Fiona will be delighted," Lord Spencer said.

"I know she will," Lady Duncaster said, "but I'm not sure it would be wise of us to tell anyone about our discovery just yet. The house is filled to the brim with guests, and while most of them are comfortably wealthy, there are others who aren't quite as well off as they'd like to appear."

Sarah didn't bother questioning Lady Duncaster's knowledge of her guests' financial situation. Instead she asked, "But how can they be here if they cannot afford it?"

"I suppose some of them are hoping to try their luck at the gaming tables or other bets, while others might attempt to make a beneficial match for themselves. The point is though, that if word gets out that the treasure exists, I fear there may be people, servants even, who will tear this house to pieces in an effort to find it."

"I understand your reasoning completely," Sarah said, watching as Lady Duncaster handed the earring to Lord Spencer and asked him to put it in his pocket. "Your great-aunt wanted your grandmother to have this. Hopefully we'll find the other one to match so that you may give it to someone who deserves it." Looking briefly at Sarah, she turned around and continued through the tunnel.

Cheeks burning, Sarah hurried after her. She was acutely aware of Lord Spencer's heavy footfalls behind her, of the masculine strength he exuded and of her own fluttering heart.

Remember your promise to Chloe, she told herself. *Remember Mr. Denison.*

Her body revolted at the very idea of it.

"There is an important matter I would like to discuss with you privately, if you think you can spare a moment," Christopher told his father later.

Lord Oakland, who was exiting the music room with his wife on his arm, stopped to eye his eldest son with grave consideration. "Your mama and I were planning to go for a ride in the carriage—have a look around the countryside and neighboring villages." He glanced down at his wife. "But perhaps we can postpone the excursion for half an hour, my dear?"

"I have to go and fetch my bonnet anyway," Lady Oakland said, her assessing gaze resting upon Christopher's face. His mother had always been very astute when it came to his troubles—he'd never been able to keep them from her. "I'll meet you out in front at say . . . three o' clock? Is that enough time?"

"I believe so," Christopher said. "Thank you, Mama."

With a warm smile, Lady Oakland patted Christopher on the arm as she glided away, disappearing around a corner. "Well, then," Lord Oakland spoke assertively, "shall we try to find a vacant salon?"

A short while later, Christopher found himself seated in a magenta-colored room with white floral patterns rising toward the ceiling from above each window and door. The furniture, consisting of two large sofa swings suspended from intricately carved wooden frames by thick chains, added a distinctly Indian feel—or so Lord Oakland claimed. Christopher had no doubt it was true, for he'd never felt more foreign than he did right now amidst piles of silk cushions stitched in shimmering metallic tones and strewn about the floor.

Trying to ignore his current surroundings and the distraction they offered, since he knew he was short on time, Christopher sat down on one of the sofas, disturbed by the swaying movement it offered, and faced his father. "If I were to court a woman who might have had a past association with a traitor, would you be against it, or would you trust my decision and give me your blessing?"

"Surely we're not discussing Lady Sarah?" Lord Oakland said, his voice both grave and pensive.

"We are indeed," Christopher confessed.

Lord Oakland frowned. "I see." His frown deepened. "Treason is a very serious offense, Spencer."

"I am aware of that," Christopher said. "But is it fair that she should suffer just because she allowed the attentions of a man she did not truly know? Is her situation really so much different from my own?"

"I gather she was not aware of her beau's transgressions?"

"Of course not! How can you even suppose such a thing?"

"Calm yourself. I'm only trying to get all the facts." Lord Oakland studied his son. "You're certain of her innocence though? That she did not collaborate with this man?"

"It was Harlowe, Papa," Christopher said as he leaned back against a plump cushion.

"I suspected it might have been." There was a moment's silence before Lord Oakland said, "Have you confronted her with your knowledge about this past connection of hers?"

"No."

"You should, because I'll tell you this much, Spencer; I find it highly unlikely that Lord and Lady Andover would insist on marrying their eldest daughter to a man like Mr. Denison if her only fault was that she'd once encouraged the attentions of Harlowe."

"There's also the matter of Lord Andover's interest in Mr. Denison's horses. I believe this to be the real incentive for the match."

"However keen Lord Andover may be on horses, I very much doubt Mr. Denison's are enough to prompt the earl to offer up his eldest daughter. If you ask me, there's something more to it. And don't forget that while you were absent from England at the time, your mother and I were not. Harlowe was a marquess and considered most eligible, so we would have known if he and Lady Sarah had formed an attachment, since we were hoping to pair either Laura or Emily with him."

"Thank God you didn't."

"For which we may have Lady Sarah to thank. But since nobody else knew what Harlowe had done at the time, I don't think anyone would fault Lady Sarah even if she *had* become affianced with him, which again suggests that her connection to Harlowe cannot be all there is to it, unless of course she was aware of his transgressions and chose to turn a blind eye because of some misplaced sense of duty."

"I don't believe she would have done that."

"Which takes us straight back to the question of what might have led to her parents' disinterests in arranging a more favorable match for her."

Christopher sighed. "I cannot imagine."

Lord Oakland raised an eyebrow. "Well, forgive me for saying this, Spencer, but you certainly know how to pick them, don't you?"

Christopher stiffened in response to the reference to Miss Hepplestone. "Lady Sarah is different," he said. "She's not a charlatan."

"That may be true," Lord Oakland muttered, "but from what I've seen of her, she seems quite prepared to marry Mr. Denison. It makes no sense unless there's something else we do not know about. My advice to you would be to find out what that something might be and how great a threat it may pose to this family."

It wasn't what Christopher wanted to hear, but he knew his father was right. "I'll do what I can, Papa. I assure you."

Chapter 13

That evening, Lady Sarah couldn't help but feel as though she was out of place amidst the opulence of the Thorncliff ballroom. She was standing in a small group consisting of Chloe, Lady Ravensby, the daughter of the Duke of Hefton, and Lady Forthright, the daughter of the Earl of Rentonbury. Only twice before had she entered a crowded ballroom dressed in her evening finery, but that was so long ago now and overshadowed by such heartache that she would rather forget all about it. Yet here she was, dressed in a silk ice-blue gown, her necklace and earrings set with diamonds and her hair arranged elegantly at the back of her head, twined with silver ribbons. Hester really had outdone herself, and as a result, Sarah had danced four sets already. Only two more remained, the last one being the waltz.

Her stomach clenched at the thought of being held in Lord Spencer's arms. When Mr. Denison had asked to partner with her for the waltz and she'd had to mention Lord Spencer, Mr. Denison had gone into a quiet rage, which Sarah had found incredibly distressing. And then of course there was her father! Lord, she'd never been so angry with another person in all her life. Apparently, he'd had a very cozy conversation with Lord Spencer the day before, yet her father had failed to mention it to her until that very evening as they'd descended the stairs to the ballroom. That he would allow Lord Spencer to court her if *she* agreed, forcing *her* to deal with the increasingly persistent viscount, was not fair. "You could have made up a story to dissuade him," Sarah had said.

"You're probably right," Lord Andover had said, "but he put me on the spot, and I could think of nothing plausible after he offered to buy five horses of my choosing. At least this way I've bought you some time to consider a good excuse."

Unfortunately, Sarah had failed to think of anything that would dissuade a man like Lord Spencer, other than the absolute truth.

"Are you enjoying your visit here at Thorncliff, Lady Sarah?" Lady Forthright asked. A close friend of Chloe's, she'd married quite young. Although she wasn't a beauty by any means, her eyes were unusually sharp and assessing—the sort that added character.

"Very much so," Sarah replied. She had met Lady Forthright during her first and only Season and had liked her a great deal, had even imagined the two of them might be friends, but Sarah had chosen not to pursue any new friendships after disaster had struck. Instead, she'd secluded herself at Andover Park. "It's such a magnificent home, don't you think? We're all very fortunate that Lady Duncaster chose to open her doors to us."

"We certainly are," Lady Ravensby agreed. She was another friend of Chloe's and very much in love with her husband if the playful smiles she kept sending across the room to him were any indication. "Why, just look at all the decorations up there beneath the ceiling and the chandeliers shimmering with . . . oh, there must be at least a thousand candles, don't you think?"

Sarah had to agree as she stood there looking up at the light dancing off countless pieces of crystal.

"I hope I'm not interrupting," a familiar voice inquired.

Lowering her gaze, Sarah found that Lord Spencer had joined them.

"We were just admiring the magnificence of the Thorncliff ballroom," Lady Ravensby said as she smiled prettily in his direction. "Wouldn't you agree that it is the loveliest you have ever seen?"

"I certainly would," he replied, his gaze resting steadily on Sarah. Her skin grew warm, her stomach collapsing in on itself until she grew restless. Bowing toward her, he said, "It's almost time for our dance, Lady Sarah."

"Indeed it is," Mr. Denison said crisply as he materialized before them, banishing the nervous excitement Lord Spencer had stirred and replacing it with angst. "But before she does, it is my turn to partner with her for a cotillion." Holding out his hand, he waited with a grim expression for her to accept, which she did with great reluctance, allowing him to lead her away from the one man who'd managed to achieve what she would have thought impossible before coming to Thorncliff—he'd made her open her heart again. She trusted Lord Spencer not to hurt her, which only made her hate herself so much more for the pain she would surely cause him in return.

"I thought I told you not to keep his company anymore," Mr. Denison hissed as they broke away from the other dancers to turn about as a pair. "Yet you persist in your folly."

They danced back, linking hands with others and moving in a circle before breaking off again. "I could hardly deny him the dance when he asked me in front of his family. It would have been unforgivably rude."

"You could have told him you'd already given it to me," he snapped.

Sarah knew he was right, but she hadn't wanted to do that. In fact, just the thought of Mr. Denison holding any part of her other than her hand made her skin crawl.

They proceeded to dance a series of elaborate steps consisting mostly of tiny skips, preventing Mr. Denison from commenting further, but as soon as he had the opportunity a couple of minutes later, he said, "The way he looks at you is most disagreeable. In fact, it forces me to wonder if you might have allowed him the sort of liberties that you have been denying me."

Appalled indignation rippled through her, tightening her muscles until she grew completely rigid. "How dare you?" she asked once the dance had ended and he was leading her over to where Lord Spencer waited.

"A man can dare a great deal when the lady has no choice but to submit to his demands." Placing one hand against her back as he pushed her forward, he slowly stroked her spine. "Don't worry," he whispered, "I'll drive all thought of the viscount from your mind soon enough."

They arrived before Lord Spencer, whose eyes were like a pair of dark thunderclouds. "I trust you enjoyed yourselves," he said more politely than Sarah would have expected.

"Oh yes," Mr. Denison said happily, without the slightest hint of his dislikeable character. "Lady Sarah is such an exquisite dancer."

"Then I am even more pleased to have the honor of dancing the waltz with her," Lord Spencer said, offering her his arm. "Shall we?"

Grateful for the opportunity to remove herself from Mr. Denison's presence, Sarah nodded as she accepted Lord Spencer's offer. She was acutely aware of the anger that simmered beneath Mr. Denison's smile, hating how uncomfortable it made her feel and dreading what it might lead to.

"Is everything all right?" Lord Spencer asked as he led Sarah toward the dance floor. "You seemed a little put out just now."

"It was nothing," she said, unwilling to discuss Mr. Denison's vile comments. Knowing Lord Spencer, he'd probably do something heroic, like challenge the man to a duel. As tempting as that idea might be, she could not allow it.

"I only want what's best for you, Sarah." The lack of the honorific felt most endearing. "And I hope that you feel comfortable enough to confide in me whatever troubles you might have so that I may help you overcome them."

They took up their positions for the waltz, his hand coming to rest against her lower back. Heat entered her body at the point of contact, coursing through her in little skips and jumps that left her giddy. "Thank you, my lord." If only she didn't sound so breathless. "Perhaps I will take you up on that offer once the dance is over." She owed him the truth, no matter how much it pained her.

The music started and he took a step backward, pulling her with him until they were spinning around the dance floor. "You've no idea how happy that makes me." A warm glow emanated from his eyes. "I've spoken to your father, you see, and he has given me permission to court you. You needn't concern yourself about Mr. Denison anymore."

"You are exceedingly kind, my lord, to even consider me after our brief acquaintance, but there is something about me that you do not know—something that will change everything between us and make you regret ever suggesting such an attachment."

To her surprise, he didn't look the least bit alarmed. In fact, his smile broadened, and he pulled her closer, allowing her to revel in his musky scent and the strength flowing through him. He was in his prime—a fine specimen of male perfection.

"If it's Harlowe you're concerned about . . ." She tripped in response to that awful name, her heart knocking against her chest, while the palms of her hands grew clammy. "You needn't worry, unless of course you knew of his crimes and—"

"I did not," she managed, still trying to recover her scattered nerves.

"I didn't doubt it for a second, but all things considered, I had to ask." He spun her toward the center of the floor. "You should know that it doesn't matter to me that you might have been interested in him. After all, he would no doubt have made a fine husband if he'd been more honorable."

"But he wasn't," she said. On the one hand, she had no wish to crush Lord Spencer's fine impression of her, but on the other, she wanted it all to be out in the open so she could return to reality—a place where only men like Mr. Denison would want her and where she had no means by which to escape him.

"No. But he is the reason why you were planning to throw your life away on Mr. Denison, isn't he? Because you and your parents didn't think anyone would want to associate with a woman who'd shown an interest in a traitor. You might have been right. But I've gotten to know you, and I've realized that if anyone in this world deserves to be happy, it is you."

Sarah shook her head. "My lord, I—"

"You have many commendable qualities, Sarah. Your incredible kindness and consideration toward others—your selflessness—are much to be admired. And there has always been an easy repartee between us, even in the beginning, when you were quite determined to vex me."

"I vex you? My lord, I do believe it was the other way around."

He chuckled, a rare sound that she wished she could hear more often. "You continue to prove that you are delightful to be around, and I for one can think of no better lifetime companion."

Heart fluttering in her chest while heat nipped at her skin, Sarah focused her attention on the dance. Somehow she had to finish it without succumbing to panic. She inhaled deeply to calm her nerves before saying, "I thank you, my lord, but I fear you might think too highly of me."

"Impossible." His voice was controlled, as though he held a tight rein on his emotions. "This past week has been the best in recent memory, and all because of you. I don't think I need to tell you how much I enjoy your company, for I daresay you feel the same about me." She jerked her head toward him, unbalanced by his candor. He smiled warmly in return, and she realized immediately that she'd shown him her hand. There would be no point in denying his observation other than to prove herself a liar. He squeezed her hand gently with his own, then added, "I'm not generally demanding, Lady Sarah, but when it comes to you, I *will* do whatever I have to in order to win you."

They passed a blur of onlookers, and Sarah glimpsed the terrace doors—large and inviting. Fleetingly, she was struck by the mad idea of making a dash for them. *Freedom.* Would such a thing ever be hers? Or would she always be bound by duty? Once upon a time, it had been to marry well. Now it was to avoid doing so. If only for once in her life she could make a choice that wouldn't spell disaster—one that would grant her a chance at the happily ever after she'd longed for since she was a little girl.

The dance came to a close without her knowing how it had happened. She'd been in a daze, only now aware that Lord Spencer was guiding her toward the refreshment table. "What the . . ." Coming to a standstill, Lord Spencer gazed down at the treats laid out on silver platters. "Those look like *choux à la crème,* but they cannot possibly be. That is, I cannot possibly believe Lady Duncaster's cook would just happen to have made these." Amazement filled his eyes as he looked at Sarah. "It's too great a coincidence."

"I'm sure you're not the only person in England who enjoys them, and Lady Duncaster does have a fondness for cake."

His eyes narrowed. "Did you say something to her?"

Sarah shrugged. She hadn't done it because she sought his favor but because she wanted him to be able to enjoy his favorite treat once more. "I may have mentioned your partiality in passing."

"You amaze me," he said with wonder.

"Why don't you try one?"

Slowly, he broke eye contact with her and picked up one of the pastries. Studying it briefly, he took a bite, his expression turning to one of pure pleasure. "It's perfect," he said before taking another bite, "absolutely perfect."

"I'm glad you think so," she said, unable to stop herself from grinning in response to his undeniable state of euphoria.

"Keep this up and you'll have me wound around your finger for the duration of our marriage."

His words were like a bucket of ice water, reminding her of their previous conversation, except he'd gone from talking about courting her to referencing an inevitable future with her as his wife. It had to stop. "I'm sorry," she whispered, knowing he wouldn't understand, "but I cannot marry you. I—"

"Lord Spencer," Lady Andover said, cutting Sarah off as she came to stand beside her. "I must say you dance splendidly."

"Thank you, my lady," Lord Spencer said, his expression set in firm lines.

Pain filled Sarah's chest as she looked up at him. It was as if a chasm had opened between them, and she suddenly felt more alone than ever before. In that moment, she desperately wished things could have been different between them, and she bitterly resented how silly she'd been to squander her future on a man who'd cared nothing for her.

"If you'll forgive us, my lord," Lady Andover said, "there's a pressing family matter that I must discuss with Lady Sarah in private."

"Of course," Lord Spencer clipped. He met Sarah's eyes and bowed stiffly. "It was a pleasure."

Swallowing her heartache, she watched him walk away before following her stepmother through one of the doors leading out into a long hallway. "What is it, Mama?" she asked as they approached one of the salons.

A smile touched Lady Andover's lips. "You'll see soon enough."

There was something about her stepmother's tone that Sarah didn't like, and when the door to the salon was opened and Sarah was ushered inside, she quickly saw that she'd been right to feel wary.

"What is going on?" Sarah asked upon finding both her father and Mr. Denison present.

Lady Andover closed the door behind her.

"It seems Lord Spencer is proving to be something of a problem," Lord Andover said. "And you don't seem capable of diminishing his interest, as I'd initially hoped."

"I've scarcely had any time to do so since you informed me of his intentions," Sarah complained.

"But there is one solution that ought to discourage him," Lord Andover said.

"And what is that?" Sarah asked numbly.

"We shall merely have to hasten things along a bit," Lady Andover remarked.

"Your courtship with Mr. Denison is hereby over. He will make you an offer within the next few minutes which you will not refuse, upon which your engagement to Mr. Denison will be publically announced."

All warmth left Sarah's body in that instant. It was of course what she had known would eventually happen, but now that it was becoming a reality, she felt as if she was being carted off to the sacrificial pyre. "What if I do refuse?" she found herself saying, astonished by how level her voice sounded.

"Refuse?" Lady Andover screeched. "Are you mad? You cannot refuse!"

Expanding on this, Lord Andover said, "Without an income or a husband to support you, you would soon become destitute."

"Not if I were to marry Lord Spencer," Sarah insisted.

"You can't," Mr. Denison said.

"He's right," Lord Andover agreed. "Consider Lord Spencer's wrath when he discovers that the woman he married isn't a virgin! There's no telling what he might do or how it might affect your sisters."

It was the same argument as always, but it was a compelling one. "Very well then," Sarah said, stiffening her spine with resolve. "Let's get on with it."

"We'll give you a bit of privacy," Lord Andover said, crossing to his wife, who was already exiting the room, leaving the door only slightly ajar for the sake of propriety.

"I must say I'm rather pleased with this outcome," Mr. Denison said as soon as they were alone, approaching Sarah like a weasel seeking out its prey. He stopped before her, so close that Sarah could smell his breath—an unpleasant scent that reminded her of sour milk. Her stomach roiled. It didn't help that Mr. Denison brushed his fingers against her cheek and cupped her chin. "Will you marry me, Lady Sarah?"

"Perhaps if you ask me properly, I might consider giving you the answer you want."

He laughed mockingly. "For a woman in your position, I hardly think you've any right to make demands." His gaze dropped to her mouth. "But maybe all you need is a bit of incentive."

Flinching, Sarah jerked away, but he anticipated her movement and was swiftly upon her, grabbing her by the arms and holding her in place as he bowed his head toward her.

"Stop right there, sir!"

Mr. Denison froze, his mouth twisting into an ugly grimace as he turned his head toward Lord Spencer, who stood in the doorway with Sarah's parents behind him. "This doesn't concern you, my lord," Mr. Denison sneered.

Raw fury burned in Lord Spencer's eyes. "I disagree," he said, his voice cold and frighteningly calm.

Being as close as she was to Mr. Denison, Sarah didn't miss the first traces of doubt as they spread their way across his face.

"You are intruding upon my proposal, Lord Spencer. Please leave this instant."

Ignoring him completely, Lord Spencer looked at Sarah. "Is this what you want?"

"I . . ." She couldn't lie to him. "No," she confessed.

"It doesn't matter what she wants," Mr. Denison said. "This is a business arrangement between myself and Lord Andover. You have no right to question it."

Lord Spencer turned to Lord Andover. "Why would you do this to your daughter? Don't you see what this man is like? He won't treat her well, and she will suffer for it."

"In other words, her marriage would not be so different from most others," Lady Andover said.

"And considering she's not much better than a whore, I—"

Mr. Denison did not finish that sentence before Lord Spencer had taken two long strides toward him and grabbed him by the throat, pulling him away from Sarah and forcing him up against a wall. "Apologize," he growled.

"Why should I," Mr. Denison gasped. "It's the truth!"

Sarah stood completely immobile, her heart beating loudly in her ears while everything slowed to a near halt. This couldn't be happening, and yet it was.

"Hold your tongue, Denison," Lord Andover barked, "or so help me God I shall have no choice but to call you out for your insolence."

"You needn't trouble yourself on that score, my lord," Lord Spencer said while Mr. Denison clutched at Lord Spencer's hands, frantically trying to dislodge them. "I am calling him out myself for the damage he has done to Lady Sarah's honor. We shall duel with swords at dawn."

"No," Sarah said, her whispered word unheard by those around her. She watched, horrified, as Lord Spencer released Mr. Denison and stepped back.

Mr. Denison gasped. Sarah's parents said nothing, no doubt equally disturbed by this turn of events. Lord Spencer turned toward Sarah. "I hope you will forgive me, but I could not allow him to speak of you like that without seeking vengeance on your behalf." She shook her head, unable to utter a single word. "When this is over, I will make an offer for your hand—one that I hope you will accept."

She stepped back, distraught by what had just transpired. She'd lost her chance to tell Lord Spencer the truth before things had gotten out of hand. Now he would be risking his life for a woman who didn't even deserve his friendship. She'd unintentionally deceived him, believing at first that they would never be more than acquaintances. After all, her path had been determined, and he had been so set against marriage. It had been clear, so she'd delayed her confession in the hope that he would never have to know. Now it was too late.

Shifting her gaze, she looked to her parents for guidance, but she received no help from their defeated expressions. "I can't," she told Lord Spencer, watching as incomprehension stole into his eyes. "Forgive me, but I cannot marry you, my lord. I . . . I simply cannot."

His jaw tightened. "Leave us," he said, his eyes not leaving Sarah's.

"My lord," Lady Andover said, "I do not think that it would be wise to—"

Lord Spencer jerked his head in Lady Andover's direction. "Considering what I've just witnessed—your lack of concern for your daughter's well-being—I would caution you against questioning me right now."

After a moment, there came the muffled sound of everyone exiting the room, leaving Sarah uncomfortably alone with Lord Spencer.

Chapter 14

Heart pounding in her chest, Sarah struggled for courage, knowing that she was about to lose Lord Spencer forever. It wasn't easy, and for that reason, she hesitated as she drank him in, determined to savor this final moment of joy that came from his closeness . . . before she distanced herself from him forever. But when she finally parted her lips, determined to do what she must, he took her completely by surprise and lowered his mouth over hers.

No.

She must not allow him to do this. Oh God, why would he kiss her now, when she'd been so close to telling him everything?

His hands slid down the curve of her back, and he stepped closer until their bodies were flush against each other, his lips carefully touching hers—warm, soft, tempting. She gasped in response and his tongue took advantage, stroking her deeply in an intimate demand for interaction. Her hands rose between them, flattening against his chest. It took every ounce of her willpower to deny herself the pleasure he offered and push him away. It had to be done though. Her feelings for him would not allow her to deceive him a moment longer. He had to know the truth, even as his eyes took on a look of bewilderment.

"You respond so well to my advances, Sarah, and yet you continue to push me away," he said, his forehead coming to rest against hers. "Why?"

Her breath shook as she inhaled. "My lord . . . I . . . we cannot continue down this path until you know everything there is to know about me."

Drawing back a little, he stared at her. "Then tell me and let's be done with this madness. Christ, Sarah . . . if you only knew how much you affect me. I did not come here looking for an attachment. Indeed, I was determined to resist my parents' attempts to find me a match because I didn't think I was ready. But then I met you, and it was like a breath of fresh air blew into my life. You've changed me with your sweetness, your generosity and your determination to be positive even though your future looked so bleak. But I can offer you a better future, so why do you continue to resist me? I've already told you that your affiliation with Harlowe is of no consequence to me. And once you marry me, you'll be a viscountess, Sarah. As my wife, nobody would dare call your character into question."

"I wish it were that simple." Stepping past him, she removed herself from his reach before turning toward him again, needing to put some distance between them if she was to complete her task. "Unfortunately, I can never be the sort of woman you require in a bride. I'm not pure, my lord. Do you understand?"

Silence stretched between them as they stood there, staring back at each other across the distance. The corner of his mouth twitched. "You're not pure," he said, as if he needed to repeat the statement in order for it to sink in. When he spoke again, his voice was strained as he said, "I want you to tell me exactly what happened."

Swallowing against the knot that had formed in her throat, she looked away from him. "It happened two years ago, during my first . . . and only . . . Season. My parents paraded me around London, introducing me to everyone who mattered. I attended the necessary balls, and I met Harlowe, over whom I lost both my head and my heart." Lord Spencer muttered something incoherent in response to that, and she paused, aware that her hands were trembling. Balling them into fists, she persevered, adding, "He began sending secret love notes to me, and whenever I would come across him, he would always whisper words of endearment in my ear. Truth be told, he was both charming and attentive. He showed great interest whenever I would speak to him, and his compliments were always plentiful. In hindsight, I realize I should have been more cautious, but he made so many promises to me and—"

"Did he mention these promises to your parents?" Lord Spencer asked in a harsh manner that made her flinch.

"No. When I suggested he do so, he said that what we had should be savored, that once we made our tendre for each other public, we'd lose the privacy that made our relationship so romantic. He said he didn't want to lose that fairy-tale magic until it was absolutely necessary, and given my inexperience, I did not disagree.

"When the Season came to an end, my family and I were invited to attend a house party at which he was also present. We continued our flirtation with discretion, but then one evening, when the rest of the guests were enjoying a musicale, he asked me to excuse myself under the pretext of having acquired a headache and being in need of some rest. In my eagerness to encourage his favor, I did as he requested and returned to my bedchamber. I waited there for about ten minutes before he arrived, professing his undying love for me and assuring me that he would speak to my father the following day and ask for my hand in marriage. He kissed me then, and before I understood what was happening, he was telling me how lovely I was, that he'd never met a woman more beautiful and that he could not help himself from doing what he then proceeded to do. I said nothing to stop him, for he had promised me the world, and in my naiveté, I believed him."

"Bloody bastard!"

Sarah winced. "The following morning I awoke to a great disturbance in the house. The magistrate had arrived, along with the local constable and two tough-looking men whom I suppose they must have hired to restrain Harlowe if necessary. There was a lot of yelling, mostly by Harlowe, who professed his innocence. The magistrate said that that was for the court to decide, upon which Harlowe was practically dragged from the Gillsborough home."

"And your popularity plummeted, I suppose?"

"People had seen us together on numerous occasions. When it eventually became known that Harlowe was guilty of treason, I became a pariah. And then of course there was the issue regarding my innocence—or lack thereof. Even if a gentleman would have asked for my hand, I would not have been able to accept."

"So your parents found Mr. Denison for you—a

man who wouldn't care about any of it." There was no mistaking the anger that marked Lord Spencer's features. No. It wasn't anger, it was rage.

How on earth was she to manage telling him the rest? A cold dread descended upon her at the thought of it, and she closed her eyes, knowing she would never succeed as long as he was dwarfing her with his presence. "There's more," she whispered, aiming for complete disclosure. Whatever happened between them from this moment onward, it would be with the knowledge that he was aware of just how ruined she was.

"You cannot be serious," he said, taking a step back and increasing the distance between them.

Piece by piece, her heart was breaking. Just moments ago, he'd captured her lips in what would have been a passionate kiss had she not dissuaded him. Now he wanted nothing to do with her. Oh, how swiftly words could alter one's perception. "I conceived," she told him quickly, eager now to be done with this awful ordeal. "I had no choice but to confess everything to Mama, and although she was furious with me, she agreed to help me for the sake of my sisters. I traveled to Scotland with the intention of remaining there until after the child was born so it could be given away to a caring family, but then I miscarried and . . . well, when I returned home, everything was different. My parents hated me, particularly since my wrongdoing prevented me from accepting an offer of marriage from an eligible gentleman, and because of the potential damage I'd done to my sisters' prospects."

"I cannot pretend I do not understand their reasoning," Lord Spencer said, his voice sounding awfully distant and hollow. "As for me, it appears I have an uncanny ability to fall for women who aren't what they appear to be."

"I never said I was anything else," she told him, annoyed by the derision he was displaying. "On the contrary, I tried to dissuade you from seeking my company."

"By striking up a friendship with me and then proceeding to avoid me? If anything, that only sparked my curiosity."

"Then what, pray tell, should I have done, my lord? Risk my entire family's reputation by telling a virtual stranger that I am a light skirt?" He said nothing in return, which only made her feel worse, if such a thing were possible. Her chest ached and her throat had grown tight. "Forgive me, but as much as you despise me right now, I hope you will appreciate my reason for not sharing this information with you sooner. I did everything wrong, and I can assure you that I am paying the price daily—more so now that I've met you—but I will *not* allow my sisters to suffer because of my poor judgment. Please promise me that you will keep my confidence, I beg you, and in return I will leave your family alone."

His censorious gaze remained heavy upon her, like a monolith threatening to squash her. It was the first time she'd shared the events that had led to her ruin in such detail, and she hated the way her voice had quivered as she'd spoken.

"It will be difficult to explain to my sisters your sudden reluctance to share their company," he muttered.

Sarah choked back a sob, valiantly steadying her tone before saying, "I'm sure you'll find a way, now that you know how necessary it is to do so."

He sighed as he passed a hand over his jaw. A curse followed, and then, "I cannot deny my anger right now, for I feel it in every pore of my body, but I will say this—I admire your strength and your courage. If your regard for me is even half of what mine was for you before you made me privy to this . . . this catastrophe, then I cannot fail to recognize how difficult it must have been for you to be so brutally honest with me. I thank you for that, even though I wish you would have confided in me sooner. But, I understand your reasoning well enough and will do what I can to keep it a secret. You have my word on that, as a gentleman."

"Thank you," she said, her voice sounding pitifully weak.

"However, I will ask a favor of you in return," he said as he stood there studying her with eyes of flint. "Especially since it appears that I am to fight a duel tomorrow on your behalf."

"Surely you can renege."

His jaw tightened, and she imagined he must be grinding his teeth. "A gentleman does not renege after issuing a challenge. It is a matter of honor, Lady Sarah."

She nodded bleakly, knowing that he was absolutely correct. "I'm sorry."

"As pointless as your apology is, I thank you for it." He paused for a moment before saying, "Now, will you grant me a favor in return for keeping your secret?"

Every word he spoke was like a punch to her stomach. "Of course," she said, her head still held high by some unknown force.

"In that case, I wish for you to tell me the absolute truth about your feelings for me."

He couldn't be serious. And yet there was no denying that he was—frighteningly so. Sarah shifted her gaze to the door, momentarily caught between choosing the cowardly path to flee, and doing what he asked of her. The absolute truth, he'd said. She closed her eyes and focused on trying to control her breathing. Each nerve felt raw, and yet he demanded more. Very well then, she would lay her heart completely bare so that he might crush it at his will. "I have never regretted the choice I made to offer another man my innocence as much as I've done this past week, for I will now live out the rest of my life alone, longing for that which could have been mine had I not tossed my future aside in a moment of folly."

"You were young and impressionable though." There was a question there, as if he was wondering how she'd respond to such a statement.

"That is no excuse."

He nodded, dashing whatever might have remained of her dreams.

"No, it isn't. You should have known better," he told her gruffly. "But Harlowe was a cad and . . . I swear . . ." A strangled sound escaped him as he paced back and forth before turning on her abruptly. "How could you do this?"

"I thought myself in love," she said calmly, though her insides were in a tumultuous uproar.

"Love," he said at length, his posture rigid as he stared her down. A soft pitter patter of raindrops fell against the window, and Lord Spencer straightened himself, saying curtly, "I suppose that explains everything. If you'll excuse me." And then he turned and walked away, while Sarah stared after him in desperation.

Oh God, what have I done?

Chapter 15

Christopher was livid, not only with Sarah, for tearing apart the image he'd had of her as everything he'd ever longed for in a potential wife, but also with himself, for not recognizing the nature of her true character sooner. But even when he'd wondered why she would even consider marrying a man like Mr. Denison, regardless of the story she'd fed him about her father's interest in Mr. Denison's horses, he'd thought Sarah incapable of ever having exhibited such poor judgment that it threatened any chance of him sharing a future with her. He'd been wrong, and for the second time in his life, he'd made a serious error in judgment.

Damn it all to hell!

Christ, he needed a drink. But as he approached the foot of the stairs, his pace slowed until he came to a halt, his mind swirling with everything Sarah had told him. He blinked as he stared back at the long hallway through which he'd just come. There was laughter at the end of it, leaking from the ballroom, where guests still amused themselves, compounding his melancholia.

Drawing a deep breath, Christopher started up

the stairs, unable to ignore one important fact: Lady Sarah had told him everything after all, though perhaps not immediately. But she'd had good reason for that, as she had explained. Unlike Miss Hepplestone, who'd lied and manipulated her way into his affections, Lady Sarah had tried to distance herself from him—a task that could not have been easy, considering his own determination to seek her company. Indeed, she had always insisted that she would marry Mr. Denison. It even appeared as though she and Mr. Denison had been on the verge of becoming affianced when Christopher had chosen to interfere. Clearly she didn't want to marry that man, yet she had been willing to do so for the sake of her family. His steps grew heavier until he reached the top of the stairs.

When he'd insisted on pressing his suit, she'd finally told him the truth, providing him with all the facts and, in so doing, giving him a choice, something Miss Hepplestone had been determined to deny him in her deception.

Raking his fingers through his hair, he considered going back to Sarah and apologizing for his behavior. Hell, he'd forced her to reveal her feelings for him. She had done so, even though, he knew, it had been difficult for her to accomplish such a feat on the heels of her other confession.

The knowledge that he'd hurt her didn't sit well with him, but everything she'd told him had torn him apart inside. If only he'd met her years ago so he could have prevented that scoundrel from taking advantage of her. If only Harlowe, that bloody bastard, was still alive so he could run him through for ruining her.

Christopher's fingers flexed at his sides as he stood on the landing, longing to go back and offer her comfort. The last thing she needed from him was further punishment, no matter how much the truth pained him. It was clear that she'd been shamed by her youthful folly, even though she wasn't solely responsible for what had happened. Her parents should have offered better guidance. They should have done a better job protecting her from scoundrels. Instead, they'd only given her grief, laying all the blame on her shoulders. It wasn't right.

Christopher drew a ragged breath. He really needed that drink, and then he would have to clear his head and give this entire debacle some serious thought. He continued on his way, resisting the urge to turn back to the lady who'd come to fill his every thought.

With everything he now knew about her, the urge to claim her had increased tenfold, not only because he'd been made aware that she had no virtue to protect but also because he felt an elemental need to sever the connection she had between lovemaking and Harlowe.

But if he went to her, he feared he'd lose control and take her at his will and without any thought for what might happen after. To ask her to be his mistress would without a doubt be an insult, but to ask her to be his wife . . . in light of all he knew, would such a thing be possible? He wasn't sure that it would, which was precisely why he had to let her be for the moment and stop himself from acting rashly.

Five minutes later, he was seated in Richard's room with a glass of brandy in his hand, aware that he'd already broken his promise to Sarah but knowing the problem at hand was too enormous for him to deal with on his own. He needed another person's unbiased opinion.

Standing by the window as usual, with his back toward Christopher, Richard gazed out at the darkness beyond through the narrow parting between the curtains. "I cannot offer much advice, since I have no desire to sway your decision," he said, "but perhaps it would help if you were to consider what *you* would tell *me* if our roles were reversed."

Christopher took a long sip of his drink as he contemplated that. "If you were in love with—"

"In love?"

"Yes, damn it. I love her, Richard. I don't know how the bloody hell it happened or when, but there it is." He hadn't thought it possible and had even said as much to Chadwick, as well as to Sarah, but he also recognized that he wouldn't feel as strongly about her confession as he did if he felt anything less.

"Are you certain?" The curiosity in Richard's voice was difficult to ignore. "After all, it wouldn't be the first time you claimed to be in such a state over a woman. We both know how the last time ended, but once that harridan had finally left for America, you quickly recovered from your state of besottery."

"Besottery? That's not a word, surely."

Richard grunted, and Christopher imagined that he was probably tilting his mouth and slanting an eyebrow in that self-satisfied look he'd always exhibited whenever he'd said something original. "Consider it a new one," Richard muttered. "The point is you were just as sure back then that you'd met the woman you were going to spend the rest of your life with as you are now."

"That's not true," Christopher said. "In fact, having had that previous experience, I'm now quite capable of distinguishing between love and infatuation. When it comes to Lady Sarah . . . I would give my life for her without blinking."

"You would, or you would have?"

"I would."

"Then your regard for her hasn't altered in spite of what she's told you?"

The answer was simple. "No," Christopher said. He paused before adding, "That doesn't mean I'm not angry or disappointed. Truth be told, it hurts like the devil to know that another man has bedded her—more so when I consider how grievously he wronged her. This is not the same as her having had a previous husband who died and left her a widow. *That* I would be able to accept with greater readiness, but this . . . an impressionable girl seduced by a selfish scoundrel like Harlowe. It doesn't bear thinking about."

"What will you do?"

Christopher wasn't sure. As it was, he felt terrible about sharing Sarah's secret with his brother, but he knew Richard could be trusted, since the only person he spoke to these days was Christopher—he'd even dismissed his valet after the man had dared to comment on the scarring.

Drumming his fingers against the armrest, Christopher studied his brother's back. "If our roles were reversed," he eventually said, "I would probably urge you to follow your heart, provided the scandal could be contained and would not risk harming the rest of our family."

"And can it be contained?"

"I'm not sure," Christopher muttered as he reached inside his pocket and drew out the framed clover. He had to be honest with himself, especially as heir to his father's title. It wouldn't do if Sarah's history got out, and with ties between her family and his, her sisters would not be the only ones affected by it. "Unfortunately Mr. Denison knows as well, and he is not the sort of man who can be trusted."

"Then I'd best wish you luck, Brother," Richard said without turning away from the window. "I hope you eventually get what you wish for."

A knock at the door made Sarah flinch, and when she heard her father's voice asking if he could come in, she cringed. She'd returned to her bedchamber a half hour earlier, hoping that sleep would soon overcome her and save her from all the distressing thoughts that plagued her. Unfortunately, it had not.

Rising from her bed, she went to the door, opened it and stepped aside, allowing her father entry. "However difficult this situation must be for you, Sarah," he said as he closed the door behind him, giving them privacy, "I can assure you it's just as hard for your mother and me."

Sarah doubted that, and she had no qualms about saying so. "Really?" she asked. "Then I'm sure you must know what it feels like to be cut off from everyone because you fear they might discover your darkest secret? The pain of having to tell the ones you love that you do not measure up to the person they thought you to be? That you're not worthy of marriage or indeed of any form of happiness?"

"You brought this on yourself, Sarah. You have no one else to blame," he told her sternly.

"Perhaps not, but you have no right to pretend you can possibly understand what it feels like. Whatever disappointment you have in me, however much you may resent the choice I once made . . . it doesn't even come close to matching the way I feel about myself right now."

Her father stiffened. "You really care for Lord Spencer, don't you?"

It wasn't something she'd wished to discuss with her father, but she had no desire to lie to him either. Closing her eyes as weariness pressed against her from every angle, she told him simply, "It doesn't matter. I ruined my chance of marrying him years ago, before we even met. I'll have to live with that regret for the rest of my life, Papa. Just contemplating it is unbearable."

"How do you suppose your mother and I feel?" he grated out. "You are our eldest daughter, Sarah. We had such grand plans for you, only to watch you toss them all aside for a hasty romp."

The vulgarity of his words shocked her. "It wasn't like that, Papa."

"No? You were ruled by lust, Sarah, nothing more."

"I thought myself in love! Indeed, I thought that I would marry him. He certainly promised that he would marry me, but then the criminal charges were brought against him. I must confess that I am glad in a way that I did not bear his name when that happened. Lord help me, I was so naïve, and so very foolish."

"There's no denying that." Her father sighed, looking suddenly much older than his forty-eight years. "I've no desire to continue arguing with you. It's tiresome, Sarah."

"I agree with you there, sir," she told him testily, though the edge of her tone had dulled significantly. A pause rose between them, growing awkward until Sarah eventually filled it by saying, "Lord Spencer still plans to duel Mr. Denison tomorrow. I tried to stop him, but he insists that it is a matter of honor—that he cannot renege even though I made it clear that I am not worth fighting over."

Lord Andover's eyes sharpened. "You told him the entire truth?"

"I wished to impress upon him the importance that he disassociate himself from me."

"Then I will pray he can be trusted, Sarah." Crossing to the window, Lord Andover glanced out at the garden. "As for your future, I have given it some thought. I will try to convince Mr. Denison to marry you, but if he's changed his mind, we'll need to make other plans. You cannot remain at home any longer, Sarah. While your mother and I were hoping to get you settled in some capacity, we may have to consider other options."

"Like what?" Sarah asked, uncertain of what her father might suggest.

"I wrote to your uncle, Mr. Bentley, before Christmas, inquiring if he might consider taking you on as a governess for his three children."

"But Mr. Bentley is in Cape Town!"

"Precisely." Lord Andover looked at her steadily. "By the time I heard back from him, I'd managed to secure a match for you with Mr. Denison, which I believed you would find more favorable, since it would allow you to remain in England."

"But can't I become a governess in England?" she asked hopefully, attempting to sound amicable. After everything she'd put her parents through, she doubted they'd grant her much of a say in the matter, but she was determined to try. "Or perhaps a lady's companion?"

Her father spun around to face her, his eyes a deadly shade of black. "Don't you see? People would always wonder why an accomplished lady of breeding ended up in such a lowly position. And where there is curiosity, an answer soon follows. We cannot risk anyone discovering the truth about you, when Juliet will be making her debut next year."

"I realize that, Papa."

"It's settled then," Lord Andover told her ominously. "If Mr. Denison still wants you, which I pray he will, since I'll otherwise have to find a way of shutting that eager mouth of his, you will marry him without hesitation, and by God you will smile when you do so. If, however, he's had a change of heart, we will begin arranging for your immediate departure for Cape Town. Either way, I trust you'll manage to show a bit of gratitude in return for the lengths Lady Andover and I have gone to on your behalf."

"Gratitude," Sarah muttered faintly.

"Indeed, Sarah, you ought to be eternally grateful for the restraint I've managed to exhibit whenever I've been forced to contemplate this horrid affair. Don't think I didn't consider turning you out or having you horsewhipped on more than one occasion. Bloody hell!"

Silenced by her father's burst of anger, Sarah nodded grimly. He was right, of course. She had acted deplorably, had squandered her prospects, and now it was time to pay the price. She should indeed be grateful that her father was willing to try to get her settled, even if it would mean marrying a man she did not care for, who'd be far below her station and who would not treat her well. That failing, there was Mr. Bentley in Cape Town and his three children, a position she supposed she could align herself with during the two months it would no doubt take for her to arrive there. "Thank you, sir," she told her father stiffly. "Your generosity is greatly appreciated."

With a grunt, he drew himself up to his full height so he could stare down at her with proper intimidation. "I should certainly hope so, Sarah. There are many papas who would not be as tolerant of a willful daughter as I."

He took his leave then, closing the door behind him as he left. Sarah stood for a long time after, hands trembling as she stared at the spot where her father had stood while he'd condemned her.

Chapter 16

By the time Sarah awoke from her restless slumber the following morning, it was twenty minutes to five. Panic coursed through her veins as she flung the coverlet away and leapt from the bed. She dressed with haste, almost forgetting to put on her spencer in her rush to get to the dueling field before it was too late.

Hurrying downstairs, she passed a clock and glanced in its direction. Only five minutes to go. She would never get there on time—especially not if she had to go in search of brandy first, as she'd wanted to do in case either man suffered an injury.

Deciding to abandon the idea, since they could just as well return to Thorncliff if medical attention was required, Sarah prayed that the gentlemen would be late as well so she could make a last attempt to stop them. Perhaps they'd overslept or would spend some time discussing rules before the duel began. As doubtful as either of those scenarios were, she couldn't help but hope.

But when she dashed breathlessly out onto the field after following a trail through the woods at a near run, she saw that Lord Spencer and Mr. Denison were already engaged, their rapiers clanging together in the still morning air as they attacked and parried. "I'm too late," she murmured, mostly to herself. She'd known she would be the moment she'd woken, but she'd still clung to the hope that she might arrive on time, although she'd stood little chance of stopping the duel even then.

"You shouldn't be here," Chadwick said, striding toward her. His brows were drawn together in a hard line that seemed misplaced on the otherwise cheerful earl.

"I had hoped to arrive sooner," she said, undeterred by his comment.

"To what avail?"

"Why, to try and stop this foolishness."

He studied her assessingly. "There is nothing foolish about a man defending a lady's honor."

She winced at that. "Not even if he gets himself killed?"

"That's not going to happen here today. Neither man has any interest in causing the other's death. And even if that were not the case, I have every confidence that the most honorable man will win."

Falling silent, Sarah had to agree. Lord Spencer moved with undeniable grace and agility, while Mr. Denison looked terribly clumsy. She watched as Lord Spencer leapt back, easily avoiding Mr. Denison's blade as it struck the air beside Lord Spencer's chest. Circling around, Lord Spencer attacked boldly, his blade meeting Mr. Denison's as Mr. Denison defended himself with increasingly frantic movements, panting loudly from exertion. Still, Lord Spencer advanced, pressing his opponent backward and forcing him to respond swiftly to each of the blows Lord Spencer dealt him.

"Spencer's free hand," Sarah said as she studied

his closed fist. "It looks as though he's holding something. What is it?"

"A small frame containing a clover," Chadwick said.

Of course. A man with such deeply ingrained superstitious beliefs would never engage in a duel without bringing a bit of luck with him. She was glad she'd been able to help him with at least that much, especially since it appeared to be working.

Spinning around, he made a more abrupt movement, forcing Mr. Denison to leap aside, causing Mr. Denison to stumble as he did so. It became clear that Lord Spencer had been going easy on Mr. Denison until now, for he gave him no quarter this time. With a rapid stab, he punctured Mr. Denison's jacket and jumped back, his stance still ready for an oncoming attack.

But the attack never came. Instead, Mr. Denison dropped his rapier and clutched his arm, his expression dark as he ignored Lord Spencer's outstretched hand with more rudeness than Sarah had ever witnessed before in her life. Not bothering to pick up his rapier, he approached Sarah. As he came closer, she could see that his face had turned an alarming shade of purple and that tiny droplets of sweat covered his forehead in a wet sheen. He was practically trembling as he came to a halt before her, completely ignoring Chadwick's presence at her side.

"Never in my life have I been so humiliated," he snapped. "To be subjected to such mockery by a man who's undoubtedly—"

"Sir! I would caution you about your choice of language lest you find yourself called out again," Chadwick said.

"Very well," Mr. Denison said, albeit reluctantly. He licked his fleshy lips and swallowed with apparent difficulty. Leaning toward Sarah, he then said, "I plan to procure a special license today, allowing us to marry no later than the day after tomorrow." Leaning closer still while Sarah stiffened, he whispered, "I cannot wait to make you heed my command."

Heart slamming against her chest, Sarah took a step back. There was another option now, and while it didn't exactly appeal, it was certainly better than becoming Mr. Denison's wife. "Thank you for your offer, sir," she managed with remarkable dignity, "but I will not be marrying you."

He stared at her for a moment as if she'd gone mad. "But . . . you *have* to!"

"You cannot force her to the altar, Denison," Lord Spencer said as he came to stand beside the man he'd just beaten. His eyes met Sarah's, and there was a brief sadness within his gaze that was swiftly banished by an unforgiving hardness as he turned his eyes on Mr. Denison.

"I'll tell the world about your precious secret," Mr. Denison sputtered.

It was the one threat that Sarah could not ignore. She thought of her sisters.

"You will do no such thing," Lord Spencer said calmly. "If we are to play at blackmail, sir, I would caution you to consider that my power and influence are far superior to your own. I will crush you with them."

Sarah could have jumped for joy. Even though he hated her, Lord Spencer had chosen to be her champion and help her out of the mess she was in.

"I have no secrets or wrongdoings with which you may threaten me," Mr. Denison said.

Lord Spencer tilted his head, and Sarah realized that she was holding her breath. "Perhaps not," Lord

Spencer said thoughtfully, "but you do have two daughters whom you'd like to find suitable husbands for. If any rumors get out about Lady Sarah, however, I can assure you, sir, that your daughters will become unmarriageable faster than you can blink."

Mr. Denison paled. "This . . . this is an outrage!"

"I couldn't agree more," Lord Spencer said. Crossing his arms, he stared Mr. Denison down until Mr. Denison took a step back, wobbling a little as he did so. "If I might make a suggestion, it would be for you to put any thoughts of forming an attachment with Lady Sarah from your mind as quickly as possible."

"I will not stand for this!" Mr. Denison blustered.

"And yet it seems as though you must," Chadwick said with an exaggerated note of pity.

Jerking his head back and forth as he looked from one to the other with furious eyes, Mr. Denison eventually turned on his heel without further comment and strode off.

"Thank you," Sarah said, addressing both Lord Spencer and Lord Chadwick.

"You're welcome," Lord Spencer said, his face set in a serious expression that equaled the one he'd worn when she'd first met him. It had softened a bit during their acquaintance, and he had even allowed himself to smile and laugh on occasion, but that was difficult to imagine, looking at him now. "You should know that I would never spread unjust rumors about undeserving people, but Mr. Denison doesn't know that. I had to threaten him with something he cares about."

"I know," Sarah said. She gave him a weak smile, which he failed to return, reminding her of just how badly she'd hurt him. "I'm sorry," she said again, even though she felt it made no difference.

Lord Spencer acknowledged her apology with a

curt nod that sent her heart plummeting. "I trust I can rely upon you to escort her ladyship back to Thorncliff?" he asked Chadwick.

"It would be my pleasure," Chadwick said.

With one final glance in her direction, Spencer strode toward a horse that stood tied to a tree on the edge of the field. Standing beside Chadwick, Sarah watched as he swung himself into the saddle, kicked the horse into a canter and rode off across the field. He'd fought a duel for her and had even backed her up against Mr. Denison, but Lord Spencer had not forgiven her deceit, and that knowledge hurt like the thrust of a blade to her belly.

Chapter 17

"May I join you?" Lady Duncaster asked as she approached Sarah that afternoon.

Wishing to be alone, Sarah had taken refuge in a more secluded part of the garden where Greek statues standing in various corners offered some distraction from her turbulent thoughts. "I'd be honored," she said, gesturing to the vacant spot beside her on the bench.

Taking her seat, Lady Duncaster spent a moment arranging her skirts. Companionable silence followed until Lady Duncaster eventually said, "You haven't been yourself since the ball last night. Whatever it is that's troubling you, I'd be happy to help."

Inhaling deeply, Sarah expelled a heavy sigh. "I just wish I would have been wiser. Instead, I've hurt people I never meant to hurt, yet I find that I still want to be happy even though I have no right to be."

"You're being very harsh on yourself."

"I'm not being harsh enough," Sarah said, staring straight ahead. "Mr. Denison and I were supposed to become affianced last night, but I turned him down because of foolish pride and because I dared hope that another option might present itself. It did, but it's far from what I dreamed of. Frankly, I don't know what I was thinking to suppose Lord Spencer might . . ." Her breath quivered upon her lips, and her chest contracted. She closed her eyes. "I shall go to my uncle in Cape Town instead, where I shall become a governess to his three children."

"When do you depart?"

"Papa hasn't told me yet, but I suppose it will be as soon as I return home. Juliet will have her debut next Season, so my parents will want me gone long before then."

Lady Duncaster harrumphed. "Men can be such fools."

"Lord Spencer is right to forget about me now that I've told him what I've done. I'm completely unsuitable for him and have known so all along." She dropped her head in her hands. "Stupidly, I allowed myself to dream even though I knew how pointless it would be, and in so doing, I swept him along with me, deceiving him in the most selfish way."

"I don't believe all this self-deprecation will help," Lady Duncaster told her firmly. "You did what you did and that's that. Clearly you regret your actions, but I am also not entirely convinced that you are the only one to blame for the way things turned out. Now, I still don't know the specifics regarding your ruination, but I'm not so old that I cannot piece it all together either. If you did what I think you did, then your parents are to blame as well for not offering better protection at a time when you clearly needed it. You must also consider Lord Spencer's own fault in all of this."

"He has no fault."

"Ha!" Turning her head, Lady Duncaster regarded Sarah with great sympathy. "He knew quite well that you were supposed to marry Mr. Denison, yet he pursued you anyway. I'm not saying he was wrong to do so, because I truly believe the two of you are very well suited, but at some point along the way he must have wondered at your insistence to marry a man as unappealing as Mr. Denison is."

"I doubt he imagined the reason to be as awful as it turned out to be."

"Perhaps you're right," Lady Duncaster said. She paused a moment. "It is possible he might still come to his senses."

"Who? Lord Spencer?"

"Who else?"

Sarah pondered that. She loved him with all her heart, which only made everything so much more difficult. Soon she would be half a world away from him. "What if I give him a choice?"

"I like the idea," Lady Duncaster said. "Do go on."

"I've no desire to go to Cape Town. Better, then, to seek refuge in a French convent, knowing the choice to do so is my own."

"You plan to run away?"

"It's the only thing that makes any sense to me at this point, and perhaps the only one that might win me Lord Spencer if such a possibility still remains." Sarah doubted it. The sense of loss that gripped her, weighing down her heart, attested to it. Still, she had to try. "If I fail, then at least I will have decided my future on my own."

Lady Duncaster scrunched her nose. "I can't envision you in a convent, Lady Sarah."

"I think it might grant me the peace of mind I seek."

"Have you considered how to get there? I trust you have enough funds to allow for a comfortable journey?"

Sarah bit her lip. "I was actually hoping you might

be willing to lend me a horse to take me to Portsmouth. Once there I can pawn my jewelry and—"

"Stop right there," Lady Duncaster said. "This idea of yours is sounding more and more desperate by the second, not to mention potentially dangerous. I would be completely remiss in my duty toward you if I allowed you to do such a thing."

"But—"

"Allow me to make you a better offer." Steepling her fingers, Lady Duncaster pressed the tips to her mouth. "I think you had the right of it when you suggested that running away might spur Lord Spencer into action. He will either do nothing, or he will realize he cannot live without you and take up the chase. Hopefully it will be the latter, but to head off to France with barely a penny . . ." Lady Duncaster shook her head with obvious distaste. "It simply won't do, but since it does make a viable tale, we'll make it work. Rather than Portsmouth, you'll journey to Plymouth."

"Plymouth?"

"It's farther away, allowing Lord Spencer more time in which to catch up to you before your ship sails."

"So I will be sailing to France after all?" Sarah was getting confused.

"No. You'll be sailing to Portsmouth."

Sarah frowned, her confusion complete. "Forgive me, but I don't quite follow your reasoning."

"Well, obviously you must sail somewhere. Portsmouth is the closest port to Thorncliff, which makes it a most convenient destination. It will allow you to return here with relative ease, for if Lord Spencer still refuses to come to his senses, I will offer you a position as my companion."

Sarah stared at Lady Duncaster in amazement. "Are you certain?"

Lady Duncaster arched a brow. "I like you a great deal and have no issue with whatever mischief you got up to in the past. It's my impression that the two of us will get along quite nicely, if you agree, that is."

"Thank you, my lady, that is a most generous offer," Sarah said.

"And one that is made in vain, since you will be marrying Lord Spencer."

"I fear you may be wrong about that."

Lady Duncaster rose, so Sarah did the same. "We'll know soon enough," Lady Duncaster said as they started back toward the house. "We'll make the necessary preparations immediately—no need to linger—so that by tomorrow you may be off. Hopefully with Lord Spencer in hot pursuit."

Sarah grinned. "You make it sound so romantic."

"I hope it will be," Lady Duncaster said as they wound their way along a graveled path. "My own marriage had a very romantic beginning to it—I dearly wish the same for you."

Chapter 18

"It's chillier tonight than I expected," Juliet said that evening at dinner. As promised, Lady Duncaster had arranged for her guests to dine on board the *Endurance*. Though the air was regrettably cooler than it had been on the previous days, the setting was splendid, with globular lanterns strung along the rigging. Trays filled with water, on which roses and candles had been set afloat, were placed in the middle of each round table, while music drifted forward from the stern, where the orchestra played.

"You should have worn your spencer as I suggested," Lady Andover told Juliet.

"But Mama, it would have spoiled the entire effect of my gown," Juliet said as she looked to her sisters for support.

Sympathizing with her, Sarah said, "She does have a point, Mama. A spencer would crush those puffy sleeves to an indistinguishable mess." She looked at Juliet, who appeared quite pleased with Sarah's defense. "However, you could have brought a shawl. I'll fetch one for you if you like. Perhaps the pink one?"

"Oh, would you? I'd be ever so grateful," Juliet said, her smile widening into a happy grin.

"And since you're going anyway," Lady Andover said, "perhaps I can convince you to bring my lorgnettes? Unfortunately I cannot see as well as I'd like to in this dim lighting."

Hiding a smile, Sarah agreed to return with the items as quickly as possible. She made her way toward the gangplank leading down to the lawn, passing several footmen as she went. It seemed so strange to think that she'd be leaving in the morning. Stepping onto the springy grass, she hastened toward the house, determined to return before dinner was served. Thankfully, the seating arrangement had placed her at the opposite end of the deck from where Lord Spencer was seated with his family, saving her from having to endure a strained atmosphere with awkward conversation.

Reaching the glass door leading back inside, Sarah considered Lady Duncaster's offer. It was extremely generous of her, promising Sarah a comfortable life without marriage to a man she detested, and without leaving England either.

Passing a couple of footmen in the hallway, she started up the stairs. Turning down the corridor that would take her to her bedchamber, she paused at the muted sound of footfalls on the carpet behind her. Turning to see who was following her, she didn't quite complete her rotation before a heavy hand covered her mouth and she found herself pushed through a doorway and into a room filled with darkness. The door swung shut behind her. Panic rose up inside her as a strong arm grabbed her firmly about the waist, holding her arms in place and preventing her from lashing out, leaving her with no other option than to kick.

"Hold still, you little bitch," a harsh voice growled when the heel of her foot connected with a leg.

Mr. Denison.

However concerned Sarah had been for her safety a moment earlier, she was now terrified. Mr. Denison's words, coupled with the fact that he'd been seriously humiliated by her, did not bode well. Neither did the strong whiff of brandy on his breath. She tried to speak—to ask him why he was doing this, but his hand made that impossible.

"This is all your fault," he said in a gravelly tone. "Why the hell couldn't you just agree to marry me? I need that heir you were going to give me. But you think yourself better than me—that you deserve more. Well, you're not going to get more than what I've got to offer you now that his lordship knows you for what you are. Considering all the time and effort I've invested, I daresay it's time you paid your due." Reaching up, he pawed at Sarah's breast. Her blood ran cold. "If you'd protected your virtue, men like me would not be so tempted, but knowing you've already been had . . ." He grunted while he tugged at her nipple. "I daresay you've provoked the wildest imaginings."

Squeezing her eyes shut, Sarah tried to block out the painful words—the reminder of her stupidity and the nausea that threatened in response to Mr. Denison's touch. It made her sick to think of what she'd done—of what she'd given away in a moment of youthful folly—and what she'd denied Lord Spencer as a result.

Aware of what was likely to happen if she did nothing, she stepped down hard on Mr. Denison's foot. He muttered an oath. "Try that again and I'll make this painful for you," he sneered. He then chuckled and licked the side of her neck, making her shudder with disgust. "I wonder if Lord Spencer has had his chance to sample you yet," he continued as his hand left her breast and drifted lower, across her belly and toward the juncture between her thighs. Sarah struggled against him, but her attempts were futile. He merely laughed in response as he tried to force his hand between her legs. "You're not quite as willing today as I suspect you've been in the past," he said. "I find I rather enjoy it."

Locking her knees together with all her strength, Sarah fought to deprive him of what he was now after, though she feared she would not be able to do so much longer. He was stronger than she was, and she could feel her body weakening as she struggled against him. She tried to scream, but it was to no avail. Nobody would hear her or know of what was about to transpire. That was when the tears came. Sobbing, she reached out and tried to grab for something—anything—she could use as a weapon, but in the next instant, the door to the room crashed open. Mr. Denison muttered an oath, followed by a loud groan as he dragged her to the side. His hand left her mouth and Sarah gulped for air as she fell toward the floor, landing on top of Mr. Denison, who'd grasped hold of her gown in his own attempt to stay upright.

Sarah still wasn't sure of what had happened until she felt firm hands upon her arms, lifting her away from Mr. Denison and removing her to safety before dealing the vile man a hefty blow to the nose that produced a loud cracking sound. "I'll kill you, you despicable cad," Lord Spencer growled.

The room grew brighter, and Sarah saw to her horror that two footmen had arrived, alerted by the noise. "Lord Spencer, that's enough," she told Lord Spencer urgently as he punched Mr. Denison again. "Please stop."

But there was no stopping Lord Spencer's attack. He was like a man possessed with only one goal—to beat Mr. Denison until there was nothing left of him.

With rigid expressions, the footmen stepped forward and pulled Lord Spencer back, almost taking a hit themselves in the process as Lord Spencer flailed to be free from their grasp so he could finish Mr. Denison off. Or so it seemed to Sarah as she watched the scene unfold. Never before had she seen a man attack another. There was a mad brutality to it—a deep fury that seemed to consume—and although she knew Mr. Denison deserved a thrashing, she was glad the footmen were there to put an end to it, since she feared for Lord Spencer and what might happen to him if he managed to kill Mr. Denison.

"My lord," one of the footmen said, "Lady Duncaster is quite fond of her carpets. It would be unfortunate if you and your . . . er . . . friend were to get blood on it."

Panting heavily from the exertion, Lord Spencer stared down at the mess he'd made on the floor. Eventually he nodded and shrugged himself free of the footmen's grasp. "My apologies," he said. "If you'd please see Mr. Denison back to his bedchamber, I'll inform Lady Duncaster that he's feeling slightly unwell."

The other footman grunted. "I daresay that's an understatement, my lord." He hesitated briefly before saying, "May I ask what brought this on?"

"It was merely a quarrel," Lord Spencer said as he straightened the cuffs of his shirt and rearranged his jacket. "We just got a bit carried away. That's all."

"As you say, my lord," the footman replied as he stepped toward Mr. Denison, no doubt preparing to hoist the man back up to his feet.

"Come with me," Spencer told Sarah as he offered her his arm.

She went to him hesitantly, not liking the anger that lingered in his eyes. But she was grateful that he'd arrived as quickly as he had, and she therefore allowed him to escort her out of the room.

"Are you all right?" he asked her as soon as they were alone.

"I've had better days, I must admit, but I'll be fine. Thank you for rescuing me," she said, her entire body trembling in the aftermath. "The thought of what might have happened if you had not arrived when you did is too unbearable to consider."

"Shh . . . you're safe now." Placing his free hand over hers, he squeezed her fingers. "I'm just glad that I saw him following you when you left the ship, though I do wish I'd found you sooner."

"You mustn't berate yourself for anything, my lord. You saved me, and that is all that matters."

"Perhaps you should stay in your bedchamber and rest. I can inform your family that you have taken ill." His expression was set in hard lines, reminding Sarah of the breach in their friendship.

"If you don't mind bringing my sister her shawl and Lady Andover her lorgnette, I think that your idea is a good one." She hated the way her voice shook as she spoke.

Arriving at the suite of rooms Sarah shared with her sisters, Lord Spencer waited outside while Sarah went in to fetch the shawl, and then again while she went in search of the lorgnette. After she handed him the items, they stood facing each other in silence for a drawn-out moment. Sarah wondered if he was mourning the loss of their previous camaraderie as much as she was. "Thank you again," she eventually said, suddenly eager to be alone so she could prepare for her departure the following day. The sooner she left, the better.

He sketched a stiff bow. "I'm just glad I could help." He stepped back, fists clenched at his sides. "Until tomorrow."

Sarah watched him walk away, then quietly closed the door behind her. If only she could leave Thorncliff this instant. Entering her bedchamber, she knelt down and watched the soothing rhythm of Snowball's tiny body rising and falling as he slept. "He won't come for me," Sarah whispered. Lady Duncaster was wrong. Lord Spencer had done his duty toward her this evening as a gentleman, but he had put all thought of sharing his future with her from his mind. Acknowledging this, the last of her hopes crumbled.

"What will you do?" Chadwick asked Christopher later that evening as they each enjoyed a glass of after-dinner brandy in the library. They were seated in a secluded corner, while other groups of gentlemen were scattered around the exceedingly long room.

"I don't know," Christopher said. Staring into his tumbler, he suppressed a shudder. The image of Lady Sarah being assaulted by Mr. Denison still shook him. "I didn't imagine finding a bride when I chose to come here with my family."

Chadwick snorted. "No. I don't suppose you did. But Lady Sarah will make a fine wife for you, Spencer, if you can muster the courage to ask her, that is."

Looking up, Christopher met Chadwick's gaze. "It's not that simple."

"The devil it isn't." Chadwick took a sip of his brandy. "If what I said about Harlowe is affecting your decision, I urge you to reconsider. After all, we played cards with Harlowe, caroused with him, invited him into our homes, not one of us aware of his true character. If he was able to fool the lot of us, then it goes without saying that he was capable of charming a young lady."

"I don't know . . ." Chadwick's comment didn't make Christopher feel any better. He wished he could tell his friend what the real issue was, but that would be dishonorable, so he glowered instead.

"Forget Harlowe," Chadwick said.

Christopher raised a brow at the impossibility of that request. What he'd started to feel for Sarah was more than just a passing fancy. He'd genuinely liked her, admired her, longed for her company . . . to his consternation, he found that he still did. She had done the honorable thing by telling him the truth and he had understood her reluctance to do so, but he couldn't seem to forget about Harlowe. The man seemed to be haunting him from beyond the grave in the most disturbing of ways.

"Think of her character instead. She's a good person, Spencer, and more than that, she is good for you. Don't be a fool and pass up this chance at happiness."

Christopher considered his friend's words. Chadwick didn't know what Sarah had done, and Christopher was unsure of whether or not he was capable of accepting her mistake no matter how much he cared for her. Having thought of little else since the duel against Mr. Denison, Christopher had concluded that the incident was unlikely to harm his own family, now that Mr. Denison had been made aware that Christopher would use his influence to discredit him completely if he chose to spread malicious rumors. "I don't know . . ."

"Then perhaps I should make it easier for you by pursuing her myself," Chadwick said.

Christopher gripped the armrest and leaned forward, his brandy almost sloshing over the sides of his glass in response to the jerky movement. "You will not."

"So you won't stake your claim to her and you won't allow another man to do so either? Honestly, Spencer, I think there's something wrong with your head."

"My head is perfectly fine," Christopher grumbled.

But he couldn't help but wonder if perhaps he was being too hard on Lady Sarah—that he was allowing the ingrained rules of Society to guide him instead of considering his own opinion on the matter. Was her mistake really so severe that it should alter all his feelings for her? He still trusted her, more so now that she had told him everything. A lesser person would have avoided the truth until he discovered it for himself on their wedding night. Searching his mind, he considered all the other ladies he had ever known. None had affected him as much as Lady Sarah. None had made him as happy. Not even Miss Hepplestone. Dragging in a breath, he met Chadwick's speculative gaze. "You're right," Christopher said.

"I'm glad you think so," Chadwick said with a wide grin.

"I'll make her an offer tomorrow."

But when Christopher arrived at breakfast the following morning, eager to see Lady Sarah again and hoping to suggest they go for a picnic later, she wasn't there. Disappointed, he decided to wait, which resulted in a lengthy conversation with Lady Duncaster about her travels to India and how she once rode an elephant. "There aren't many ladies who can make such a claim," she said proudly. "Society has so many rules, most of which I've broken at some point or other. But I have no regrets, Spencer. You see, while all the other matrons here were dutifully doing their embroidery and producing children, I was out in the world, living. I'll never wonder what might have been, because I always followed my heart, though my parents were scandalized by some of the choices I made." She shrugged slightly. "Well, my life has been full, and I have known great love and happiness. What more could I possibly ask for?"

What indeed?

"You make a fine point," he told her as he met her steady gaze. "In fact, I've recently arrived at a similar conclusion—that living a happy life is of greater importance than constantly seeking to please others."

Lady Duncaster's smile was knowing, leaving Christopher with the distinct impression that she saw things others did not. He doubted anything escaped her. "So you will also follow your heart?" she asked.

"Edward the Fourth did when he married that impoverished widow in secret, and he was a king, whose choice of bride would have had a political impact on the entire country. Why, then, shouldn't I marry the lady of *my* choosing?"

"I can't imagine," Lady Duncaster said.

Christopher nodded. "Then that is what I shall do."

"I'm very happy to hear it."

Finishing the remainder of his tea, Christopher rose. "Thank you," he said, offering her a respectful bow.

"You're welcome."

Christopher prepared to turn away when Lady

Duncaster halted him by saying, "If I may, I would like to suggest you make haste, Lord Spencer."

The back of his neck prickled. His heart stilled. "Any particular reason I ought to know about?"

"Lord Spencer!"

Drawn by the sound of his name being called, he looked toward the door to find Lady Andover hastening toward him. She was red-faced and breathless.

What now?

"Thank goodness I found you," Lady Andover wheezed.

"My lady?" Christopher's brows knit together with uncertainty.

"At first I thought she might have eloped, considering Mr. Denison's departure this morning."

"What?" Christopher's heart slammed against his chest. Surely she couldn't be speaking of Lady Sarah. Not now, when he'd finally realized he wanted her no matter what—that he couldn't live without her. It would be too tragic for words. Bracing himself, he said, "Who are you referring to, Lady Andover?"

"To Sarah, of course," she practically shrieked, confirming Christopher's worst fears.

"I have since been assured by the groomsmen and servants that Mr. Denison was alone when he departed," Lady Andover said. She drew a shuddering breath.

"Calm yourself," Christopher told her. He felt only mildly placated by the knowledge that Lady Sarah had not left Thorncliff with Mr. Denison. In spite of his impatience to know what had happened, he pulled out a chair for Lady Andover and asked her to sit. "Perhaps you should start at the beginning," he suggested.

Nodding, she dabbed her handkerchief against

her forehead. Christopher gritted his teeth. "This morning, after dressing, I went to check on her to ensure she hadn't caught some nasty ailment that might prove harmful to the rest of us. As you know, my lord, she wasn't feeling well last night. When I thought about it, I realized she'd been a bit odd since the day before last."

"Your attention to your daughter's state of being is admirable," Lady Duncaster said dryly.

Christopher felt like applauding the comment, while Lady Andover herself seemed quite oblivious to the sarcastic criticism that had just been directed at her.

She nodded. "But when I arrived at her bed-chamber, I discovered that Sarah was nowhere to be found. Nowhere, I tell you! Her sisters claim they haven't seen her since last night, so I can only assume that she must have snuck out while they were sleeping, leaving behind an empty glass case filled with straw and twigs—most peculiar that—and most of her clothing." There was a very distinctive clip to her tone that sounded entirely too accusatory for Christopher's liking. He steeled himself. "Now, I don't care what silly notion has gotten into her head this time, but I will not allow her to do something rash that might potentially embarrass our family. Please, Lord Spencer, you must help me find her!"

"Of course," he said, even as his mind reeled with the news that Lady Sarah had run off and what that might mean for their future.

He fought for control. *Calm yourself.*

"Did she leave any hint of where she was going?" he asked.

"Not much," Lady Andover admitted, "but there was a note on her escritoire addressed to you."

Accepting the paper Lady Andover handed him, Christopher paused before unfolding the missive. He studied the elegant *S* that curled flamboyantly as part of his name. The message was brief, no more than a couple of sentences, really, saying simply,

During our brief acquaintance, you have become my dearest friend, which is why it pains me to know how grievously I have wronged you. Hopefully, you will one day find it in your heart to forgive me. Please know that I wish you every possible happiness and that I will forever cherish the time we shared together at Thorncliff.

Yours always,
Sarah

Christopher stared down at the piece of paper in his hand. *Dearest friend . . . forgive me . . . yours always.* Uncertain of his feelings and of what to do with them, he'd pushed her away, hurt her, yet her kindness flowed through the black ink.

He hadn't given her any reason to think they stood a chance anymore, had scarcely spoken to her at all for the past couple of days. When he had, he'd been curt and distant with her. Last night, when she'd needed comfort the most, he'd turned away from her, fearing that he would expose her to the overpowering rage that Mr. Denison's attack had evoked in him. And now she was gone, convinced no doubt that he hated her.

"Do you have any idea where she might be?" Christopher asked bluntly.

Lady Andover shook her head. "None at all. Indeed, I cannot imagine what might have gotten into that silly head of hers this time."

Squaring his shoulders, he stared down at his future mother-in-law. He didn't care for her in the least. "You have a dislikeable tendency to think the worst of your daughter, Lady Andover, offering her no support at all. Your constant berating of her, your unwillingness to forgive . . . it's been extremely painful for her. She knows she made a mistake, and I do believe she's likely to regret it for the rest of her life. The least you can do, as her mother, is to offer her some measure of comfort to help ease her suffering, but for some unfathomable reason, you cannot bring yourself to do so. Why, even now you insist on being critical of her."

"Lord Spencer," Lady Andover blustered. "You go too far!"

"On the contrary, I fear I don't go far enough," he muttered.

"Enough!" Turning, Christopher met the glowering gaze of Lord Andover, who'd joined them inconspicuously. "I will not tolerate such a tone, Lord Spencer. Especially not when you're addressing my wife."

"I shall address her with politeness as soon as she agrees to treat Lady Sarah with civility and respect," Christopher snapped, his patience running thin due to the ugly company he was presently keeping.

"Respect?" Lord Andover snorted. "I hardly think—"

"Choose your words wisely, my lord," Christopher said as he narrowed his eyes on Lady Sarah's father, "lest you give me no choice but to call you out—a notion that grows more appealing by the second."

Lady Andover gasped, while Lord Andover grew visibly pale. He tilted his head in acquiescence. "Forgive me, Lord Spencer. It is clear that my wife and I have overstepped our bounds." Christopher doubted the words were sincere, but for Lady Sarah's sake he said, "I suggest you consider what you're going to tell your daughter when you see her again. The last thing she expects from you is understanding or acceptance."

"As to her whereabouts," Lady Duncaster said, drawing Christopher's attention, "you might want to try the road to Plymouth."

"Plymouth?" Christopher's eyes narrowed as he recalled Lady Duncaster's words from earlier. *I would like to suggest you make haste.* "You knew she left and failed to tell me?"

"Highly inconsiderate of you not to inform me of her absence immediately," Lord Andover said.

Ignoring the earl, Lady Duncaster focused on Christopher. Again, she looked as though she was peeling away his outer layers until she stared straight at his soul. He flinched marginally in response to the direct scrutiny. "What sort of hero would you be if you were in constant need of guidance, acting only when others instructed you to do so?"

"You wished for me to decide whether or not to go after her on my own?"

"This is preposterous," Lord Andover said.

Lady Duncaster tilted her head. "She left because she couldn't bear the thought of staying and because she wanted an opportunity to decide her own fate. In so doing, she has also given you a choice, my lord. You can either let her go, or you can chase after her. As it is, she doesn't think you'll make the effort."

Christopher's throat tightened. "Where does she intend to go?"

"Does it really matter?" Lady Duncaster asked.

No. It didn't.

"I cannot believe this," Lady Andover said.

"Your collaboration in her flight is most disappointing," Lord Andover agreed. "Sarah was supposed to go to Cape Town as soon—"

"Cape Town?" Shocked, Christopher almost spat the words. "You want to be rid of your daughter so badly that you would send her halfway across the world? What sort of parents are you?" He composed himself. "Forget I asked that question, for indeed I already know the answer, as regrettable as that is. Now, if you'll excuse me, I intend to fetch Lady Sarah so I can ask her to be my wife." He then strode off, not granting the Andovers a chance to say anything more. Lord help him, he was furious!

Chapter 19

With the twenty pounds Lady Andover had kindly given her tucked away in her reticule, Sarah leaned back against the squabs of the carriage as she tumbled along the country road toward Plymouth. Lisa, the maid Lady Duncaster had insisted Sarah take along with her, sat opposite, her hands busy with a bit of mending she'd brought with her. It was almost two hours since Sarah had left Thorncliff behind, so she supposed it was possible that Spencer and her parents had discovered her absence by now. There was no question in her mind that her parents would be furious with her again, but this seemed insignificant compared with her concern over how Lord Spencer might react. Would he realize he couldn't live without her and come after her as Lady Duncaster envisioned, or would he choose to let her go? She wanted to believe in him, but she couldn't help the all-consuming doubt that filled her, strengthened by his cold distance from her for the last couple of days.

Lacing her fingers together in her lap, she closed her eyes and dreamed of him. God, how she loved him: his kindness, loyalty, sense of honor and ability to make her laugh. It broke her heart to run away like this, but it was the only thing she could think of that offered them both a choice, for although she'd told Lady Duncaster that she was grateful for her offer, Sarah wasn't entirely sure she wished to accept it. If Lord Spencer failed to be the hero she needed him to be, returning to Thorncliff would be both painful and shameful. She wasn't sure her pride would allow it, which was why she still toyed with the idea of journeying to France—if she could somehow convince the captain to veer from Lady Duncaster's orders. Yet another difficult task.

The carriage slowed, then came to a halt. "First stop of the day, my lady," said the footman who'd ridden in front with the driver. He opened the door, reached out his gloved hand to help Sarah alight, then offered Lisa his assistance as well.

"We'll change the horses," the driver said. "Shouldn't take more than ten minutes. Fifteen at most."

"Thank you, Michaels. We'll use the time to stretch our legs," Sarah said as she looked around. A narrow path led past the inn toward a small brook. "Shall we take a walk, Lisa?"

"Certainly, my lady, though I would advise you to make use of the inn's facilities first, since you may not get another chance before luncheon."

Agreeing, they sought out the privy, which, to Sarah's relief, turned out to be cleaner than she would have expected. When they were done, they walked down to the brook, where Sarah, spotting a flat stone upon the embankment, picked it up and flicked it into the water.

"I wouldn't have thought you could skip stones, my lady," Lisa said, sounding thoroughly impressed.

Sarah's chest tightened. "I only learned to recently. Lord Spencer taught me one day by the lake at Thorncliff."

"I think he's a fine gentleman," Lisa said as they turned back toward the awaiting carriage. "Very unpretentious, from what I've gathered."

A smile tugged at Sarah's mouth as she recalled him sinking onto his knees in a field of clover and racing across the lawn with her at dawn. "Yes. I suppose he is." Whatever else happened, she would always remember him fondly.

Christopher arrived at the Blood and Hound at ten o' clock with a horse in desperate need of rest. "Did a fair-haired lady pass by here this morning?" he asked the groomsman as he dismounted.

"About this tall?" Christopher nodded as the man held his hand up to his shoulder level. "Aye. I'd say she stopped here about an hour and a half ago."

Christopher allowed a sigh of relief. He was gaining on her, thanks to his lack of a cumbersome carriage. "Give me the fastest horse you've got."

"Now that might be a bit tricky," the groomsman said, catching up the reins and leading Christopher's horse toward the stables. "The carriage her ladyship was riding in took the last of our Thoroughbreds, and the ones they left behind aren't ready for the road yet."

Hell and damnation.

"What are my options then?"

Guiding the horse into one of the stalls, the groomsman held a bucket of water up so the animal could drink. "There's a gelding a few stalls down that the innkeeper uses to plow the vegetable garden out back. A few children from the village also come and ride him on occasion. He's a fine and gentle horse, but he ain't fast."

"Are you suggesting I borrow him?" Christopher asked as calmly as he could. His previous feeling of victory had been cast from him, replaced by a sense of impending failure.

"Don't see what choice you have if you wish to be on your way. The next posting inn's about twenty miles away. Hopefully you'll have better luck there."

If Christopher took the gelding, it would probably take him twice as long to get there as he'd hoped, but it would take even longer if he didn't. Dallying certainly wouldn't hasten his progress, so he accepted the horse he could get, determined to make the best of it.

After two more stops during the day, they reached Exeter when it was growing dark. "We'd best stop for the night," the driver said as the footman helped Sarah alight. "Wouldn't want to risk an accident or, God forbid, being held up by highwaymen."

Sarah agreed. "Thank you, Michaels. I'll see to it that rooms and supper are made available to you."

With Lisa by her side, she then entered the timbered building comprising the Hog's Head Tavern. She had diminished hope for Lord Spencer's arrival. It didn't look as though he would be coming after all, for if he were, he would have caught up with her by now, surely. Pushing the melancholy thought from her mind with the knowledge that she had servants to care for, she looked around the establishment.

The interior was dimly lit, with low ceilings held

upright by roughly carved beams, providing both a rustic and intimate atmosphere that Sarah found oddly appealing in its simplicity. "Excuse me, sir," she said, approaching a slender man with a balding head and graying whiskers who was seated at a table with a tankard of ale and what appeared to be a ledger. "Are you by any chance the innkeeper?"

Raising his gaze, he examined her for a moment and finally nodded. "That I be." He closed his book and got to his feet with unhurried movements, his eyes drifting from Sarah to Lisa and back again. "Would you like a room for the night, or just supper? Molly's got a fine stew boiling in the kitchen."

"Actually, I should like two adjoining rooms if at all possible, as well as accommodations for my driver and footman. There are four of us in total, so we'll require four meals as well. The stew sounds like a fine suggestion."

The innkeeper scratched his chin. "Not sure I can manage adjoining rooms, my lady, but I can place you across from each other if that's acceptable to you."

Sarah looked hesitantly at Lisa. Sarah had always enjoyed a private bedchamber, and although she quite liked Lisa, she especially felt the need for privacy now after being cooped up in a carriage all day. "That will be fine, thank you."

"As for your driver and footman, I can offer them a room to share above the stables."

Again, Sarah agreed.

"Each room will cost ye a shilling," the innkeeper said, meandering toward a row of numbered hooks on the wall where a collection of keys was hanging. Snatching two of them, he called for a young woman to show Sarah and Lisa to their rooms. Sarah suspected she might be his daughter.

"Supper is ready whenever you are, my lady," the young woman said after showing Sarah up to her room. Her cheeks were round and her smile was welcoming.

"Thank you," Sarah said as the door closed. Once alone, she studied her surroundings, deciding that she was extremely pleased with the room she'd been given. It was far more comfortable than she'd imagined it would be. Removing her kidskin gloves, she untied her bonnet and set it on a small round table. Smoothing back a few loose strands of hair, she crossed to the washbasin and poured water into it, reveling in the soothing freshness as she soaked a small cloth, wrung it and placed it against her face.

Fleetingly, she thought of her parents and how angry they would be with her for causing them further humiliation—the embarrassment of having to tell people they didn't know where their daughter was. Either that or they simply wouldn't care. Perhaps they'd even be relieved to find her gone, happy to be rid of the burden she presented.

A sigh crept across her lips as she thought of her sisters. She was going to miss them terribly if she didn't return to Thorncliff. She decided to post a letter to them before continuing her journey tomorrow.

The decision to do so eased some of her pain, the majority of which was related to Lord Spencer. It seemed increasingly unlikely that he'd come, but even if he did, could she really allow herself to accept his hand in marriage if he proposed? She couldn't bear the thought of him being constantly aware of how imperfect she was, which she'd no doubt he would be. How could he not, when she'd carelessly squandered the one thing that would bind her to him, and him alone? There was no doubt in her mind that whatever he said, however prepared he was to over-

look it, a part of him would always resent her for
allowing another man—worse than that, a man who
cared nothing for her—the right to her virtue.

As much as she longed for him to come rushing
after her, she suddenly wondered about her answer
if he proposed. Could she ignore the guilt she would
feel in denying him a proper wife? Could she live with
the knowledge that she wasn't quite good enough,
and that she never would be?

Doubt began to settle, increasing as she went
downstairs to supper with Lisa. By the time their
meal was over and Sarah returned to her room, she
knew her worries had been unfounded. Lord Spencer
wasn't going to come, which, as much as it saddened
her, also pushed aside the nervousness that had
clutched at her stomach the entire day. She no longer
had to wonder what to say to him or how to explain
her actions. Only one decision remained: whether to
go to France or return to Thorncliff.

Christopher was at his wit's end and very, very annoyed. An hour and a half after leaving the Blood
and Hound, the gelding had gone lame due to a
poorly shod shoe. After removing the shoe, Christopher had clutched his clover in his hand and walked
the remaining five miles to the next posting inn while
the poor horse had limped along beside him.

"I need to change my horse," he'd told the groomsman upon his arrival.

"I can see that," the groomsman had said, eying
the gelding with a pitiful expression. "Luckily we've a
fast stallion available. I'll ready him for you straight-
away if you like."

Finally, a stroke of luck! Christopher's spirits brightened and his hopes were restored until, halfway between Honiton and Exeter, it started to rain.

What began as a light drizzle quickly evolved into a steady downpour as clouds drew together, darkening the sky from a dusky indigo to pitch black. Christopher cursed as he pressed onward. When he'd left Thorncliff that morning, the sun had been shining, promising nothing but brilliant weather. He wasn't prepared for this—had even forgotten his hat in his haste to be on his way. Now he was caught in the dark, racing along a country road with water pelting in his face, his clothes as wet as they'd been after he'd jumped in the lake to rescue Mr. Denison. Thinking of Sarah, he urged his horse to run faster until, blessedly, a glow emerged in the distance, brightening as he drew closer. He could finally see the faint outline of the inn ahead.

Feeling victorious, he slowed his horse to a trot and entered the courtyard, where he leapt from the saddle and called for a groom to assist. "Go on inside, my lord," the man said as Christopher dropped a shilling in his hand.

Thanking him, Christopher strode toward the front door, his boots sloshing through puddles as he went. Once inside, he wiped the water from his face with the palm of his hand.

"Welcome, sir," an older man said by way of greeting. He introduced himself as Mr. Garison, the innkeeper. "Might I offer you a room? I can have a bath brought up and ask one of the maids to see to your clothes—make sure you get dry and don't catch a chill."

As tempting as the offer was, Christopher had not traveled all day to the point of near exhaustion so he could waste additional time away from Sarah. He wanted to see her—*needed* to do so—and had no intention of waiting one more second. "In due course," he said. "First I'd like to know if a lady arrived here earlier by carriage. She's quite distinctive looking due to her light blonde hair and bright blue eyes. She would have been accompanied by a maid."

Mr. Garison's eyes turned wary. "I cannot confirm or deny that, sir, since I don't believe in handing out information about people to anyone, unless they've committed a crime and the constable happens to be inquiring about them."

Drawing himself up to his full height, Christopher leveled Mr. Garison with the most quelling look he could muster and said, "I am Viscount Spencer, the Earl of Oakland's son. The lady I am seeking is the Earl of Andover's daughter. Lord Andover has charged me with the task of finding her and bringing her home, but if you require further incentive to inform me of her whereabouts, I can promise you that you will be well compensated for your assistance in this matter."

Mr. Garison looked neither impressed nor influenced by Christopher's authoritative tone. "If you think my moral compass can be swayed so easily, think again, my lord."

Frustrated, Christopher looked past Mr. Garison at the staircase beyond. He could make a dash for it and proceed to pound on every door upstairs, but the hour was late, and in spite of the sense of urgency that filled him, his manners as a gentleman did not allow for such a selfish course of action. Raking his fingers through his hair, he decided to make another attempt at convincing Mr. Garison to help. "I will confess that I am personally invested in the search for her ladyship." Mr. Garison's expression softened a little, urging Christopher to continue. "It's my intention to ask for her hand in marriage and to tell her that . . . that I've been the greatest fool and that I love her."

"Now that's the sort of thing I like to hear, my lord," Mr. Garison said as he leaned back on his heels. "World's too full of scoundrels these days. It's quite refreshing when a romantic comes along."

"So you'll tell me where she is?" Christopher asked hopefully.

"Aye," Mr. Garison said, "she's here all right, but she retired over an hour ago, so if I may make a suggestion, it would be for you to wait until morning before making any attempt at seeing her. In fact, I insist upon it."

"Do you have any idea how hellish my day has been?" It was as if Mr. Garison had yanked away the last of Christopher's enthusiasm for this journey. With little promise of seeing Sarah that evening, something flat, uninspiring and decidedly dull settled within him.

"Nevertheless, she *is* a lady, my lord. It would be most uncivilized, ungentlemanly and utterly inappropriate to disturb her now."

However much he hated having to do so, Christopher conceded the point. "Perhaps I'll have that bath you mentioned after all."

"A fine idea, my lord," Mr. Garison said as he snatched a key from a hook on the wall and crossed to the stairs. "Follow me and I'll show you to your room."

Unable to ignore her concerns about Lord Spencer, her parents and the uncertain future looming before her, Sarah found it impossible to sleep. Deciding that cooling the room would probably help, she opened the window to a heavy downpour and remained standing there for a moment, enjoying the feel of a gentle breeze whispering across her skin while water drummed against the roof. *Wine.* That would make her drowsy. Reaching for her robe, she flung it across her shoulders and tied the sash at her waist, then went to the door. Opening it, she stepped out into the hallway just as footsteps sounded on the stairs. Instinctively, she turned to see the innkeeper approaching and was just about to make her request known to him when she caught a glimpse of the man behind him. Her heart stilled before leaping into a full gallop. He'd come. Lord Spencer had actually come! Unable to speak, her throat unusually dry, she remained completely motionless as his eyes settled upon her with the sort of gravity that sent a rush of nervousness rippling through her.

"My lady," Mr. Garison said, arriving before her first. "Is there anything you need?"

"I . . ." Sarah blinked, heart fluttering in her chest as she looked to Lord Spencer, her cheeks flushing when his lips curved in a mischievous manner suggesting he knew precisely what she needed.

She cleared her throat, not liking the state of discomfort she was in. After no sign of him bothering to pursue her all day, Lord Spencer's arrival had taken her completely by surprise. "Some wine," she managed, deciding the drink would no longer be required merely to induce sleep. She needed it to calm her nerves.

"I'll send someone up with it as soon as I've shown his lordship to his room," Mr. Garison said, his expression hard as he continued down the hall with the request that Lord Spencer follow him.

Moving past her, Lord Spencer allowed his hand to brush against hers as he whispered, "Wait for me."

A cacophony of nerves erupted in the pit of her belly, spearing her with heat and leaving her quite breathless as she watched him go. It had taken him but a split second to undo her completely, her legs trembling as she pushed the door to her room open behind her and fled, his words echoing in her mind. *Wait for me.* Her heart thumped wildly as she leaned back against the wall and took a steadying breath. All day, in spite of her doubt, she'd hoped he cared enough for her to give chase, but now that he had, she felt an overwhelming degree of apprehension over being alone with him, speaking to him and explaining her actions. And then there was the issue of whether or not she could actually allow herself to accept an offer from him in the event that he made one.

A knock at the door startled Sarah out of her reverie. "Who is it?" she asked, her voice sounding weak to her own ears.

"Your wine, my lady."

Sarah breathed a sigh of relief and opened the door, welcoming the maid and accepting with much relief the jug she brought. Alone again, she wasted no time in pouring herself a large glass, which was emptied completely, along with an additional one, by the time Lord Spencer scratched at the door.

Seated by the open window and soothed by her drink, Sarah called for him to enter, but as the door eased open and he came into view, her fingers tightened around the stem of her glass. She swallowed hard as she took him in—his large frame clad in a white linen shirt that had not been tucked into his fawn-colored trousers. His hair was damp and his feet were bare, which appealed to her in the strangest of ways.

He closed the door gently behind him, and for the longest, most unbearable moment, he just stood there, watching her with an infuriatingly serious expression. He raised an eyebrow, and she lost her patience. "My lord," she said, bursting with the need to release all the thoughts that had churned around her head all day, "if you've come on behalf of my parents to fetch me back to Thorncliff, you'll have to gag and bind me, for I shall not go of my own free will."

"As alluring as that image is, I did not come on your parents' behalf, though they did ask me to find you. Rest assured, however, that I am here for my own . . . personal reasons."

The way he said *personal* practically curled her toes. "I am honored," she said, setting her glass aside on a table. "When I left Thorncliff, I'd hoped you would decide to choose me in spite of my shortcomings, that you would return my affection unconditionally and stop me from leaving. But I've had an entire day since then to consider our situation, and I've come to the realization that I cannot ask you to deny yourself the opportunity to marry the sort of woman you deserve." It pained her to say this, but she had to, for his sake. "Realistically, my lord, you deserve better than me—a woman whom you can gaze at fondly for the rest of your life without hating her for denying you her most precious gift."

"You think too little of yourself, Sarah," Spencer told her, his gaze softening as his shoulders relaxed. "And don't forget, I've had an entire day to consider my future with you at my side. It's what I want, if you'll have me."

"Make no mistake that this is my fondest wish,

but I would urge you to reconsider," she told him defiantly. "You think too much of me if you imagine I'd make you a good wife."

Pushing himself away from the door, Spencer closed the distance between them. "I beg to differ," he said as he raised his hand to brush his knuckles against her cheek. Instinctively, she leaned into the caress. "You forget I've had some experience with the marriage mart and that the only woman I found there to catch my interest was an imposter, so please don't think I haven't thought this through, because as a man once fooled, I've become very determined to find a bride on my own terms."

"But I'm not an innocent." Bitterly, she forced the truth upon him. "You cannot possibly ignore that."

A tentative smile tugged at his lips. "I'll admit that I didn't think myself capable of accepting it. Indeed, I thought the worst of you after you told me, and I blamed you for denying us the happiness that should have been ours if Harlowe hadn't charmed you."

Her chest squeezed as uneasiness rolled through her. If he wasn't here because of her parents or because he wanted her, then . . . "Why did you come?"

"Because I was a fool, Sarah, influenced by the artificial ideals of Society without considering who you truly are. But as soon as I pushed all the rules aside and focused on you alone, everything became clear. When I woke this morning, it was with the intention of asking for your hand. Imagine my disappointment when I found you gone."

"But you came after me," she whispered, still unable to believe he was really standing before her in the flesh.

"No small feat, considering my horse went lame. I had to walk five miles and managed to get caught in a rainstorm, but I was determined. I still am. Which is why I'm going to tell you a secret," he said as he gazed down at her. "You wouldn't be my first lover either."

She couldn't help the small laugh that escaped her in response to his unexpected confession. "That's entirely different! You're a man, after all—you're expected to have a few liaisons before you settle down and marry."

"Perhaps," he agreed with a nod, "but does it really matter to you that I've taken other women to bed? As long as I didn't do so after we met and that I swear to be faithful to you from this day forward? Isn't it enough for you to know that the women in my past are completely insignificant now that I have found you? They don't matter, Sarah. Not when it's you that I love. Don't you see? The same applies to you. Yes, I was shocked when I discovered your indiscretion, but that's because it went against everything I've been raised to expect from a lady of breeding."

"I hope you're not suggesting the rules of Society ought to be less stringent on that score, because I'm afraid even I would balk at such a notion. I do have sisters, whom I intend to stop from making the same mistake I made."

Christopher's direct gaze remained unwavering. "I'm not planning a rebellion, Sarah. I'm just trying to make you see that you're not a bad person because of what you did and that you deserve to be happy. Since you are willing to overlook my past indiscretions, I think it only fair that I should overlook yours."

She shook her head. "I just . . . I fear it will always be there, looming in the background and casting a shadow upon our happiness."

"Tell me," he said as his hands went to her shoulders, holding her firmly in place. "You said that marrying me would be your fondest wish, but is it really? If you'd never met Harlowe and your virtue was still intact, would you accept my offer of marriage then?"

"In an instant," she said, unable to be anything but completely honest with him. "I love you, Spencer, with all my heart."

"Then that is all that matters, Sarah. The rest is in the past. What you need to do now is look to the future and accept that what I feel for you is more powerful than any misgivings I might have about your lack of innocence. You are sweet, kind, considerate, generous, and you have punished yourself enough these past two years. It's time for you to stop suffering, when the truth of the matter is that there are people among us who've done worse things in my opinion. Why you should be denied marriage and children when several peers are openly committing adultery without anyone batting an eyelid defies logic. Besides, nobody need ever know about your history, since there's little chance of your parents mentioning it, and Mr. Denison has every reason to keep his mouth shut if he wants his daughters to marry well. But even if word were to get out by some misfortune, you ought to know that I will stand by you, no matter what."

It was a beautiful speech that tugged at Sarah's heart, tempting her to surrender, yet she couldn't seem to shirk the apprehension that filled her. "You are the most generous of men, my lord, and I am humbled to know how greatly you revere me. Please know that I reciprocate your affections, but even though I do agree with your views, I just can't help feeling as though it would be selfish on my part to accept—that I would be benefitting far more from our union than you."

"That you would even think something like that would be an obstacle is yet another reason why I admire you, but I'd like you to consider that if we don't marry, it will only be because of your reluctance and your fears. Nothing else is standing in our way, Sarah."

Looking back at his imploring eyes, Sarah realized how right he was. The only thing stopping her from leaping into the future with Spencer was her own guilt and cowardice. But perhaps her guilt was misplaced. After all, he already knew her darkest secret and was willing to overlook it so they could be together. And her fears . . . did she really wish them to deny her the chance of a happy family filled with children and the company of the man she loved? "I was planning to seek refuge in a convent if you failed to find me," she confessed.

Spencer stiffened. "Where?" he asked.

"In France."

He expelled a deep breath. "I'm glad I caught up with you then, because I do believe you would have been making the biggest mistake of your life." Bowing his head, he kissed her gently on the forehead. "You don't belong in a convent, Sarah. You belong with me." And as he tipped her chin with his fingers and lowered his lips to her mouth, she knew he was completely right.

Chapter 20

When they broke apart a short while later, Spencer met her gaze with such earnestness that she could practically feel his love enveloping her like a blanket. "I've spoken of marriage repeatedly," he said. "You know what's in my heart, and I daresay it matches the contents of your own. Please tell me that you will agree to be my wife, for I can think of no other woman with whom I'd rather spend every moment of the rest of my life."

The answer came to her quickly. "Yes," she said. "I will marry you today or any other day of your choosing."

"I wouldn't wish to deny you a proper wedding in London with your family and friends present," he said as he hugged her against him, his arms securely wound about her midsection, allowing her to savor the warmth emanating from the solid frame of his body.

His scent clung to his shirt and Sarah breathed it in, delighting in its familiarity and the knowledge that the man it belonged to would soon be hers. "I don't care about any of that," she said as she looked up at him. "All I want right now is to be your wife. The sooner the better."

Spencer grinned as he placed brief kisses all over her face until she was laughing with him. "I know precisely how you feel," he told her a second before his mouth captured hers. All playfulness vanished, replaced instead by an urgent hunger that Sarah eagerly encouraged, her hands clutching at his shoulders while inviting him in, sighing in response to the feel of his tongue stroking against her own, tempting her to follow his lead. And follow she did, until she found herself breathless.

"Your secret," he said, wishing for only truth between them as he leaned back a little so he could take her in. God, she was beautiful, with that wispy hair and those clear blue eyes. "My brother knows of it as well."

Concern marred her face as he said it. "Your brother?"

"I know I promised not to tell anyone, but I was furious after you explained to me the reason for not being able to pursue you. I needed an outlet for my frustration, along with a stiff drink to calm my nerves, so I sought out my brother. He won't tell anyone. I can assure you of that."

"How can you be certain?" Uneasiness filled her voice.

"Because the only person he's willing to speak to is me. Nobody else has been allowed near him after he returned from the war." He swallowed convulsively before adding, "His face shows severe scarring."

Understanding dawned in her eyes. "And yet he came with you to Thorncliff?" she asked softly. "How very curious."

"Considering the extent of the work being done at Oakland Park, he hardly had much choice." Christopher paused for a moment before saying, "When we are married, would you mind terribly much if he were to come and live with us at Hillcrest? I've yet to move there myself, since I never fancied living alone and away from my family. It's an odd notion, when I've always been used to being surrounded by people."

"Then we shall make it our home together," Sarah said, her eyes warming as she gazed up at him. "Of course your brother will be welcome."

It meant the world to him to hear her say that, for he knew how difficult it could be having Richard beneath the same roof. "It won't be easy for you," he added, deciding it would be best to lay all the cards on the table immediately rather than allow her to be surprised. The dark cloud Richard carried with him was not the sort of surprise most people would care for.

"It doesn't matter," she said in earnest. "He is your brother. If he would like to live with us, then I will happily assist in making the arrangements for him to do so."

"You are remarkably kind, Sarah. It's one of the many reasons I adore you."

"Do you truly?"

There was a hopefulness about her, but there was also a measure of doubt—as if she scarcely dared allow herself the possibility of him feeling deeply for her—that almost broke his heart.

"You told me you wouldn't be able to offer me love," she explained to him quietly.

"I was a bloody idiot, unaware of my feelings for you and more than a little afraid of welcoming such vulnerability. But I can no longer deny what's between us. More importantly, perhaps, I do not *want* to. I love you, Sarah, most ardently." And to cement the notion, he lowered his lips against hers with a possessiveness he'd never felt toward another. She gasped, startled no doubt by his urgency, and Christopher took advantage, conquering her mouth as he pulled her fiercely against his chest, his arms a band of solid iron around her slim waist.

It took only a moment for her to gather her senses and join him, her tongue meeting his stroke for stroke. Soft murmurs occasionally slipped from her throat, increasing his ardor. There was no doubt that he burned for her. Hell, his very soul was afire with the need to join with her—to be as one, a single creature sharing a heartbeat.

Shocked and concerned by his wayward thoughts and where they would surely lead if they weren't immediately dampened, he stepped back, placing distance between them and trying desperately to ignore the mess her dressing gown was in, having slipped off her right shoulder and parted in the middle. "Sarah," he murmured, stunned by the gravelly tone of his voice, which seemed to convey every wicked desire that welled up inside him. He was having a devil of a time holding them in check. "I should leave."

"Don't." Her chest rose and fell in response to her labored breaths, drawing his attention to her breasts.

His groin responded with instant alertness. "If we continue down this path . . ."

"Were you sincere when you asked me to marry you?"

"Of course!"

"In that case, I should like to avoid the torture of sleeping in separate beds. Especially since I have no innocence to protect." Her eyes glistened. "Please, Spencer. I appreciate your wish to do what is proper, but as things stand, Harlowe remains my only lover. I'd like to change that before we say our vows."

He grimaced, the reminder tarnishing the moment.

"Harlowe is dead," he clipped, more harshly than he'd intended.

Her eyes widened a little, but then she nodded, accepting his anger.

Feeling like an ass, Christopher began to apologize, but she cut him off, saying, "When I come to you on our wedding day, I want to be yours in every possible way, Spencer. I don't want anyone or anything between us, which is why I would like you to banish Harlowe from our lives forever by claiming me as your own. Right now."

"Christ, Sarah." Did she have any idea what she was doing to him by saying such things? Her words were most provocative, and in return he found himself uncomfortably restrained by the tight fit of his trousers.

Rising up on her toes, she wound her arms around his neck, pressing the entire length of her soft body against his. "Make me yours," she whispered right before she kissed him, stripping him of any remaining resolve.

Inflamed by her touch, he deepened the kiss, savoring the faint sigh that escaped her when his hand stole inside her robe to cup her breast. His thumb swirled across the tight peak of her nipple, evoking a soft groan from her throat. By God, he'd never felt a keener need to divest a woman of her clothing. He needed to see her, feel her, without restriction.

But her hands were already pulling at his shirt with a desperation to match his own, and before he could protest, she was pushing it over his head, baring him to her perusing gaze.

For the first time in his life, he found himself concerned about his physicality. He wanted to be everything she wanted, but the way she was looking at him . . . he couldn't decide if it was lust or pain or perhaps something else altogether. "Do you approve?" he asked, his confidence hinging on her response.

"You're so beautiful," she murmured, her voice cracking a little, "so perfect."

Christopher's spirits soared. "So are you," he said as her hands slid toward his waistline. *Damnation!* If he didn't pull himself together, he'd soon be standing before her as naked as the day he was born while she remained fully clothed. He could not allow that. Not when he was as desperate to see her body as she apparently was to see his.

Grabbing her wrists, he slowed her progress, even as his fully aroused manhood jerked with the anticipation of her touch. "Not yet," he murmured, lowering his mouth to hers, his tongue licking along her lower lip before thrusting inside the wet warmth she so willingly offered. If she touched him now in his present state of hunger, he feared he wouldn't last.

"Don't move," he told her gruffly, returning her hands to her sides. Leaning back so he could take her in, he pushed her robe from her shoulders, loving the sensual way in which her eyes widened and her lips parted. A rush of embers spread across his skin, increasing in heat at the sight of her breasts, outlined to perfection beneath the flimsy fabric of her nightgown, their hard centers thrusting toward him. Unable to resist, he lowered his head and took her in his mouth, his tongue flicking across her nipple as he drew her to him.

"Oh God," she sighed, her hands clutching at his shoulders while he dampened the fabric between them. Kissing his way back up, he made his way along the curve of her neck while she splayed her fingers across his back. His lips moved carefully over her delicate collarbone until he reached the edge of her neckline. "Turn around," he said as he gently nipped her shoulder. She did as he bade without question, her breath shuddering in response as he ran one hand along the length of her spine, down and over the curve of her bottom, delighting in the faint outline the delicate cotton of her nightgown offered.

When he squeezed her gently, she arched in response, as if he'd commanded her to do so. Reveling in the bold reflex, he did it again and was this time rewarded with a deep mewling sound as she pushed back toward him, her hips tilted in a most provocative manner. "Bloody hell," he murmured as he pulled at her nightgown, bunching the fabric as he hoisted it up over her hips, along the length of her torso and finally over her head. His breaths came in short bursts as he stared at the image she portrayed—her body lean, yet curved in all the right places. By God, he'd never wanted a woman as much as he wanted her now—beneath him, moaning his name as he thrust himself inside her. A groan escaped him at the mere thought of what was about to transpire, while hot desire raced to his groin, hardening him to the brink of despair. He needed release, but first he would have to free himself from his restrictive trousers.

"Don't move." Reaching down, his eyes fixed upon Sarah's delicious body, Christopher unbuttoned the fall of his trousers and allowed himself to spring free. Relief surged through him, but it was swiftly replaced with an urgency that forced him out of his clothing with remarkable speed.

Straightening himself, he fought for discipline, knowing how vital it was that he make this good for her. His heart was hammering in his chest as he stepped up behind her, his hands going to her hips as he pressed himself against her. She gasped in response to the contact, and Christopher smiled with wolfish satisfaction. There was no doubt she could feel the firm insistence of his manhood pushing between her thighs. Slowly, he ran his fingertips up toward her waist, across her belly, where her soft flesh fluttered beneath his touch, and up over her breasts. "You're perfect," he murmured in her ear as he rolled her nipples between his fingers. Her head fell back against his shoulder on a sensual sigh of pure pleasure. Christopher grinned as he bowed his head to lick her earlobe. If only she knew the extent of the pleasure he planned on giving her.

Never before had Sarah felt as wanton as she did now, standing there in a state of complete deshabille while Spencer did the most delightful things to her body. Oh Lord, it felt good as he gave his complete attention to her needy breasts, tugging and squeezing that plump flesh until they grew seemingly fuller. Between her thighs, she could feel the hard length of him gloriously brushing against her most intimate part each time she tilted her hips. It stirred an ache in her that seemed to have come alive with sizzling embers. Heaven above, it was most indecent, but she now longed for him to touch her there with greater insistence. Tilting her hips again, she hoped to encourage him to do so without the need for words. Almost immediately, one of his hands released her breast and came to rest upon her hip. With deliberate firmness, he urged her bottom closer still, until she was pressed up hard against his groin. "I get the impression you'd like to feel my fingers somewhere else on your body," he murmured in her ear.

All coherent thought fled her brain at those words. She could only manage a weak nod, to which he chuckled before kissing her shoulder. "Spread your legs further apart," he said. "Yes, like that. Christ, Sarah, do you have any idea how much I want you?"

"I can feel it," she whispered, attempting a tone she hoped would not sound quite as inexperienced as she felt.

Behind her, Spencer emitted a sound not entirely dissimilar to a growl as he swept his fingers between her legs, stroking her in a feather-soft caress at first, then more insistently as he parted her, his fingertips circling a part of her that brought intense pleasure to her entire body. "You're so wet," he murmured as he pushed a finger inside her, "so ready."

Closing her eyes, Sarah gave herself up to the spectacular sensations he wrought. She could feel him moving in and out of her, stoking a need within her that soon took the form of extreme pressure. It was both wonderful and torturous all at once. Her body begged to feel something more—to grasp the pleasure he offered. Clenching her muscles, she embraced her desire until the pressure exploded through her, dazzling her senses as she trembled in the midst of the most extraordinary storm. "God help me," she sighed when the last of the tremors abated and she sagged back against Spencer's warm chest.

"Does that mean it was good?" he asked with a hint of a smile to his voice.

Turning toward him, she flung her arms around his neck in adoration. "You know it does, you beastly man. What you just did was absolutely incredible."

Chuckling in response, he kissed her for a long, joyful moment. "Just wait until you see what else I have in store for you this evening," he said, waggling his eyebrows. Scooping her up, he walked across to the bed and set her down gently amidst the cushions. "You and I are far from being done with each other."

Sarah had no doubt he spoke the truth, for the proof of his desire was still very much apparent. "Tell me what I can do for you."

Spencer groaned, while his face took on an expression of sheer anguish. "I can think of a number of things, Sarah, but for now, the best you can do is welcome me into your warmth." His throat worked as he swallowed harshly. "If you still wish it, that is."

Lying back, Sarah spread her legs apart and offered him a tempting smile that she hoped would do the trick. He was upon her instantly, touching her and kissing her wherever he could until she squirmed beneath him, desperate once more for his touch. He did not disappoint, stroking her tenderly as he'd done before until she begged him for more.

More came soon enough as he rose up onto his elbows and positioned himself at her entrance, the tip of him nudging her flesh apart until she could feel him inside her, filling her with his strength and vitality. The sensation was incredible—so much so that tears sprang to her eyes. Whatever her experience with Harlowe, it would never hold a candle to this awe-inspiring moment of becoming one with the man she loved. There was no doubt. She loved Spencer with all her heart, and as she held him close, moving in time to his thrusts, she only wished they could remain like this forever—trapped in this moment, where their hearts and souls merged.

Swiftly, the familiar pressure began to build within her once more, coiling itself into a tight ball that carried her upward, teasing her with the expectancy of what would soon follow.

"Tell me you're ready," Spencer muttered between clenched teeth, his muscles rippling in response to the strain of his movements.

"Yes," she breathed, the sound hoarse as she gazed up into his imploring eyes, seeing there the moment when he abandoned his restraint. His final thrusts were harder, and then, on a spark of light, the pressure burst, scattering through her body like stars. Faintly, she heard Spencer groan as he found his own release, his hands clutching the pillow on either side of her head while his body shuddered above her.

As the moment subsided like an ebbing tide, Sarah felt her body relax until it was overwhelmed by a calm she hadn't known in years. Pulling out of her, Spencer sank down beside her on the bed and hugged her against him, pressing a tender kiss against her cheek before snuggling his face against the curve of her neck. Moments later, they were both fast asleep, wrapped in each other's arms.

Chapter 21

As they drove onto the graveled path leading up to the Thorncliff stables the following afternoon, Christopher lowered his head toward Sarah's ear and said, "If anyone asks about your absence, just tell them you went to visit the modiste in Portsmouth and were forced to remain there until today due to inclement weather and a lame horse."

"At least part of that story is technically true," Sarah said with a smile. Seated beside him in the carriage, she'd enjoyed her return to Thorncliff a great deal more than she had her departure.

"And if you agree, I'd like to announce our engagement at the first available opportunity. The sooner we get on with planning our wedding, the sooner we'll be able to live together as husband and wife." He pressed a kiss against the curve of her neck, sending delicious sparks across her skin and down her spine.

"Then I suggest we announce it immediately."

"I couldn't agree more," Christopher said as the carriage rolled to a stop. Opening the door, he stepped down and turned so he could help Sarah, soon to be Viscountess Spencer, alight.

But before she reached the ground, Christopher

placed his hands upon her waist and pulled her into his arms.

"What on earth are you doing?" she asked when he failed to put her down and started toward the house.

"Precisely what it looks like, my love. I'm carrying you."

"But you can't possibly! It isn't seemly!" She kicked her feet in protest.

"If you think I've any intention of letting you go again, then you are quite mistaken." Lowering his head to her ear, he whispered, "Since we're already weaving a Banbury tale, you may include that you just now twisted your ankle when you alit."

Chuckling, she relaxed her head against his shoulder. "You're absolutely incorrigible, my lord."

"And you are quite delightful," he said, pressing a kiss to the top of her head as he strode up the front steps. As soon as they entered Thorncliff, Lord Andover was upon them. "Sarah! Are you all right? Why on earth are you being carried?"

"I misstepped, Papa," Sarah said.

"Well, it wouldn't be the first time, I suppose."

Christopher frowned at the double entendre, to which Lord Andover responded with an uncomfortable laugh. "No harm intended, my lord. I'm just glad she's been found, although I cannot imagine what you were thinking, Sarah, running off the way you did. Lady Andover is quite beside herself, you know. She feared you might have decided to do something just as foolish as . . . well, we needn't discuss your past indiscretions."

"We most certainly do not," Christopher agreed as he tightened his hold on Sarah.

"Quite a delicate matter, to be sure," Lord Andover remarked. "But now that you're back, I hope to assure her ladyship that she needn't worry about you any longer. You'll do your duty, won't you, Sarah?"

Christopher winced, hating the condescending tone with which Lord Andover addressed his daughter. Drawing himself up, Christopher prepared to rebuff it, when Sarah spoke instead.

"You may rest easy now that Lord Spencer has returned me to Thorncliff, for I shall trouble you no further. But if you imagine that I will submit to any of the plans you've contrived to rid yourselves of me, please know that I don't accept."

"But you must," Lord Andover blustered.

"On the contrary, Papa, I shall follow my heart."

Lord Andover's face reddened. "Have you learned nothing from your idiocy?"

"Have a care, my lord," Christopher bit out. Had he not been holding Sarah, he would likely have dealt the earl a blow to the face. Christ, he was feeling protective.

"I have learned that you and Lady Andover were capable of tossing me to the wolves without much consideration, that you were completely unsympathetic and uncaring. I know my actions were dishonorable, but I had hoped that your love for me as my parents would allow for better treatment of me as a person."

"Love must be earned, Sarah."

"And yet I still love you and Lady Andover, in spite of everything."

Christopher's chest swelled with pride. She'd just bested her father by dealing a staggering blow to whatever conscience he might have left. Lord Andover's eyes widened, surprise evident upon his face as he drew back.

"You should also know that Lord Spencer has proposed and that I have accepted," Sarah continued.
To Christopher's satisfaction, Lord Andover's mouth
fell open. "However, I think it prudent to point out
to you that when I marry him, it won't be out of duty
or because I have no other choice. It will be because I
love him and can think of no other man with whom
I'd rather spend the rest of my life." With a smile
brighter than the sun, she beamed up at Christopher
with adoration in her eyes.

Lord Andover's transformation was immediate. A
smile lit his face, his eyes bright with the satisfaction
of a man who'd just unearthed a vast treasure. "Well,
whatever your reasons, I certainly consider it wonderful news, Sarah. Congratulations," he said, leaving Christopher with the distinct impression that in
spite of his positive words, the man still cared more
about the prospect of getting his eldest daughter off
his hands than he did about the fact that she'd made
a love match. Locking his jaws together, Christopher
chose not to comment. "And to you, Lord Spencer.
You've made an excellent choice for yourself. Heavens, Sarah, just wait until Lady Andover hears about
this. She'll be thrilled! Absolutely thrilled!"

"I don't doubt it for a second," Christopher murmured. Setting Sarah down, he offered her his arm
and began leading her down the hallway, while Lord
Andover followed behind them, still wishing them
well.

He was so loud in his exclamations, in fact, that
there was no need to go looking for Lady Andover at
all. She soon found them, saying, "Sarah! There you
are! Where on earth have you been? Oh, I was so terribly worried about you after—"

"She went to Portsmouth as you suggested, to visit

the modiste," Christopher said, stopping her tongue before she said something stupid. Other guests could hear their conversation. "Unfortunately, the weather and a lame horse resulted in the delay and she chose to remain there until she was certain of returning safely. Quite wise of her, wouldn't you say?"

"Oh yes! Yes of course," Lady Andover agreed, abandoning whatever reprimand Christopher suspected her of having had on the tip of her venomous tongue. "But tell me, is it true? I was just having tea with Mrs. Penbrook in the Chinese salon when Viscountess Eagelton arrived to tell us that she'd heard my husband hollering about his daughter marrying Viscount Spencer. Has an offer been made?"

"I wasn't hollering, my dear," Lord Andover said dryly. "Her ladyship has completely exaggerated the details."

"Frankly, I don't give a toss about the details," Lady Andover said, sounding just as mercenary as Lord Andover had earlier. "All I want to know is whether or not Lord Spencer has finally proposed."

"Finally?" Christopher asked, raising an eyebrow.

"Well, when you hurried after her the way you did, I knew you would probably do so eventually. The only question was whether or not she'd accept," Lady Andover explained, her expression suggesting that she was struggling not to elaborate on that point. Christopher decided his glower was probably having the intended effect.

"I have," Sarah said.

"Oh, my dear girl," Lady Andover said as she threw her arms around her stepdaughter. "You've finally made a wise decision."

Lord Andover coughed. Christopher stepped forward, intent on defending his fiancée's intelligence, but he was prevented from doing so when Lady Andover released Sarah and, looking at her, said, "Whatever our differences may have been in recent years, I do wish you happy." Her stiff tone suggested it was a chore for her to say as much. While Christopher wished Lady Andover would apologize to Sarah for the way in which she'd treated her, he accepted that this was as close as Lady Andover would probably ever come to admitting she'd done anything wrong.

"Thank you, Mama. Your approval means a great deal to me," Sarah said.

Christopher's heart swelled. Sarah's ability to address with such kindness the woman whose love for her should have been unconditional was not only remarkable but also a powerful reminder of why Christopher loved Sarah as much as he did.

"Of course I approve," Lady Andover said, clearly determined to ignore that she'd recently made a very deliberate effort to force Sarah into a distasteful marriage with Mr. Denison. "Why on earth wouldn't I? He's an eligible gentleman—a fine-looking one too, I might add. No, I have no cause for complaint. I'm sure the two of you will be exceedingly happy together and that your children will be the handsomest ones in England."

"Mama!"

Christopher chuckled in response to the blush that rose to Sarah's cheeks. She was looking adorably self-conscious. "May I suggest we celebrate with champagne later?" Christopher asked. "I'd like to tell my own family the good news, and then we can all meet in the . . . conservatory in, say, one hour?"

"The conservatory?" Lord Andover grumbled. "Won't it be horribly hot and humid in there?"

"Most likely," Sarah said, "but it's where Spencer and I first met. I can't think of anything more fitting."

Happily, they found Christopher's parents and sisters gathered on the terrace, where they were having tea with Lady Duncaster and Chadwick. "Ah! There you are, Spencer," Christopher's mother said as he and Sarah made their approach. "We were quite worried when we discovered you and Sarah missing last night, but Lady Duncaster assured us that it was probably just a question of a broken-down carriage and that you would bring Lady Sarah back to Thorncliff safely." Looking to Sarah, she said, "I trust you're all right?"

"Of course she's all right," Lady Duncaster said. "Just look at her, Lady Oakland. She's practically glowing!"

"Thank you for your concern, Lady Oakland, but Lady Duncaster is quite correct. I'm perfectly fine," Sarah said, accepting a vacant seat next to Laura while Christopher grabbed a chair belonging to another table and brought it over, placing it where there was most room, next to his father. "I took a carriage to Portsmouth with the intention of doing some shopping and got caught in the rain with a lame horse."

"Oh, how awful!" Fiona said.

"Accidents do happen," Rachel pointed out.

"Fortunately I found her and was able to escort her back to the house this morning," Christopher said.

"I'm sure you were," Lady Duncaster said with a sly grin.

"That aside," Christopher said, determined to prevent those present from dwelling too long on the information he and Sarah had just supplied or the question of how they'd spent the night, "there's something I'd like to tell you all. In fact, it's more of an announcement really." He could see on their faces that everyone had guessed what he was about to say, yet he was still overwhelmed by the squeals of delight from his mother and sisters, as well as the well-wishes from his father and Chadwick, the moment he told them that Sarah was going to be his wife.

Sarah received her fair share of attention too. Of course all his sisters and his mother began crowding her with questions about the sort of gown she'd like to wear, her preference for flowers and a slew of other things pertaining to a wedding. Christopher sat back and watched the spectacle with amusement, coupled with a small degree of pity for Sarah. Evidently, she had not fully considered what she was getting herself into when she'd agreed to marry him, which was really just as well.

"This is madness," Christopher heard his father mutter after a good five minutes of chattering about various types of cake. From the other side of the table, Chadwick served Christopher a look of clear exasperation, which was understandable, since he'd been stuck between Fiona and Christopher's mother.

Christopher chuckled. "It's only just the beginning, Papa. Don't forget you have one more son and five daughters."

Lord Oakland sighed. "God help me!"

A short while later, the entire Heartly family, accompanied by Lady Duncaster and Lord Chadwick, followed Spencer and Sarah into the conservatory, where footmen had been ordered to bring champagne and glasses. "Lord Montsmouth," Sarah said as she rounded a corner and found the earl crouching beside the fountain, as if searching for something. "What on earth are you doing?"

Looking up with an irritable expression, he said, "I was startled when I heard the door open, and I accidentally dropped my snuffbox. I'm beginning to think it might have rolled into the shrubbery."

"Getting startled in here is apparently a common occurrence," Sarah said. She smiled as she looked at Spencer. "Perhaps we can help you?"

"Thank you, Lady Sarah," Lord Montsmouth said. "I'd appreciate that a great deal."

"And once we've found it, I hope you'll join us for a celebratory glass of champagne," Spencer added.

"Oh, what's the occasion?" Lord Montsmouth asked.

"My engagement to Lady Sarah," Spencer said, straightening in a manner indicative of his pride. "We're making the formal announcement tonight."

Sarah's heart expanded, filling her with warmth from her head down to her toes.

"I say, that certainly is wonderful news," Lord Montsmouth declared. "Felicitations to you both!"

"Oh look," Lady Fiona said just as Sarah's parents arrived. "There's something shiny over there. Could that be it?"

"Ah, yes. Well done, Lady Fiona," Lord Montsmouth said as he peered down between the leaves of a large fern. "I do believe you've found it. Thank you ever so much!"

"I'm just happy I could help," Lady Fiona said while Lord Montsmouth stepped forward to retrieve his snuffbox.

"Do be careful," Lady Duncaster said. "I'd hate for you to crush my beautiful plants."

The expression on Lord Montmouth's face mirrored that of the rest of the men. Clearly they couldn't comprehend why Lady Duncaster would describe the plants as beautiful when there wasn't even a flower in sight.

Thankfully, Lord Montsmouth managed to complete the task without damaging the foliage and without getting dirt on himself in the process. The footmen readied the glasses of champagne, while Sarah's father tugged at his cravat. He was clearly suffering from the heat in the room but was considerate enough toward Sarah and Spencer not to mention his discomfort, for which Sarah was most grateful.

"A toast!" Spencer said as soon as everyone had a full glass in their hand. "To Sarah, with whom I look forward to spending the rest of my life."

"And to you, Lord Spencer," Lord Andover said somewhat dryly, "for ensuring her happiness."

"Hear, hear," Lord Chadwick and Lady Duncaster chanted in unison while Sarah leaned closer to her father and pressed a kiss to his cheek. "Thank you, Papa," she whispered in his ear, grateful for whatever support her parents were willing to give.

"I think it's time for you to meet my brother," Spencer said to Sarah when the last of the champagne had been drunk and the party began to disperse. "He's not very sociable, but I know he'd like to make your acquaintance."

"Are you certain of that?" Sarah asked. "It was my understanding that he doesn't want anyone to see him because of the disfigurement." She regretted her phrasing when Spencer winced. "Forgive me. I spoke without thinking."

"It's all right," Spencer said, "but in future, I'd appreciate it if you'd avoid that word, since Richard isn't any such thing. What he is, is living proof that war encourages evil unlike anything you and I can possibly comprehend. To think that I was out for a pleasant ride or enjoying a cup of tea while he was being tortured is sickening, to say the least."

"You cannot blame yourself for what happened," Sarah said, anxious at the vehemence in his voice.

"No?" The pain emanating from him reached across the distance between them so powerfully that Sarah felt she might be able to hold out her hand and touch it. "I'm his older brother, Sarah. It isn't right that he was made to suffer—that I was safely home in England instead of being there to protect him."

"As your father's heir, it would have been irresponsible of you to go to war, Spencer. You have a duty to your family to protect the legacy your father has been upholding for generations."

"Richard has told me the exact same thing, but it just seems so wrong and so cowardly."

"There is nothing cowardly about watching your younger brother head off to war, uncertain of what might happen to him and unable to help him in any way. I know you worried about him each waking hour—that you undoubtedly had countless restless nights wondering if he was all right."

Expelling a shuddering breath, Spencer quietly said, "As it turns out, I was right to be concerned. The things they did to him . . ."

"Try to focus on the positive rather than the negative. Your brother's alive, and whether he wishes to show his face in public or not, he's still in possession of all his limbs. Some of the men who returned weren't quite so lucky." Reaching out, she took his hand and gave it a little squeeze, aware that the guilt Spencer felt wasn't going to disappear anytime soon, if indeed it ever did. But he had her by his side now, and she was determined to help him through these difficult moments. "Come, let's go visit your brother."

When Christopher entered Richard's room, he didn't feel nearly as bad as he usually did. He had Sarah to thank for that. It was still hard to stand there in the dark, gazing at Richard's back and knowing why he wasn't allowed to approach, why lights were never lit in Richard's room and why the mirrors had been covered up, but at least Richard was still alive and physically able to do as he wished. There was a measure of hope to be found in that. "I came to tell you that Lady Sarah has agreed to marry me. I have brought her with me, since I thought you might appreciate meeting your future sister-in-law."

There was a short pause before Richard spoke. "I've heard good things about you, Lady Sarah, though I must confess I was a little concerned after that other . . . forgive me, I—"

"It's quite all right," Sarah said. "I know all about the horrid Miss Hepplestone, so I cannot say I blame you at all for taking an interest in your brother's choice of bride—especially since his decision to marry has, from my understanding of the matter, been even hastier this time."

Richard chuckled. "Yes, he does have an ingrained need to strike while the iron's hot, but I think he made the right decision in this instance. Welcome to the family, Lady Sarah."

"I think you should just call me Sarah, since we're soon to be brother and sister."

"Then you must call me Richard." He turned the unblemished side of his face toward her and offered a smile that warmed Christopher's heart.

"Will you allow me to come closer, so I may see you properly?" Sarah asked quietly.

The question practically knocked the air from

Christopher's lungs, it was so startling. In truth, he could scarcely comprehend what Sarah had just asked. Hell, he wasn't even certain of how to react to such a situation. Instinct told him to apologize to his brother for her forwardness, while another part of him warned he might inadvertently offend both Richard and Sarah by doing so. Thankfully, Richard saved him from contemplating the situation any further by saying, "Why? Because you feel the need to satisfy your own curiosity?"

"As a matter of fact, yes," Sarah told him boldly.

Christopher closed his eyes on a groan.

"Well," Richard said somewhat nonchalantly, "you're refreshingly straightforward and honest." A moment went by. "And since you're apparently feeling brave, then by all means, come closer and take a look. Just promise me you'll still agree to marry my brother."

Christopher opened his eyes in dumbfounded amazement. Nobody had seen Richard's face since his return to England, except for Christopher and Lord Oakland. Not even Lady Oakland had been permitted to do so, yet he was allowing Sarah? It was incomprehensible.

Watching as she made her way toward his brother with tentative footsteps, Christopher waited for her reaction—some startled response when her eyes finally settled upon the burned flesh that rippled across the right side of Richard's face. But when Sarah halted no more than two feet from where Richard was standing, her expression registered neither pity nor horror. On the contrary, she appeared to study him for a while, her brow creased to signify deep contemplation until she finally said, "It's not nearly as bad as I expected."

Christopher's jaw dropped. She was a lady accustomed to living a protected existence. How could she not be affected by Richard's appearance? Even Christopher, who loved him dearly, had to admit the scarring was ugly. Then again, Sarah's kindness probably prompted her to look beyond the wound to the man as a whole.

"And what did you expect?" Richard asked.

Sarah shrugged. "I'm not entirely sure. A frightening monster, perhaps?"

"But you don't find my appearance the least bit frightening, do you?" Richard asked with interest.

"No, though I do understand your reluctance to venture out into public, since I'm sure there are many who would disagree with me—especially those who knew you before this happened. They will likely be shocked a great deal more than I." She hesitated a moment before saying, "Have you considered a half mask? I'm sure one could be molded to fit your face with precision—by a milliner perhaps."

"A milliner?" Richard echoed.

"They're accustomed to making fabrics adhere to any number of shapes, and with a wire running along the top, you could wear it in much the same way you'd wear a hat. It would be as though you were at a masquerade, which I do believe would work to your advantage."

"How so?" Richard asked.

"Well, it would add that air of mystery to you. I'm sure the ladies would be terribly intrigued."

"Thank you for your suggestion," Richard said as he turned away from her, "but I have no desire to attract any woman's attention. Now, if you'll please excuse me, I'd like to be alone with my thoughts."

"But—" Sarah began.

"Congratulations once again, Kip. I've enjoyed meeting Sarah, but it's time for both of you to leave now."

The hard tone that Richard applied warned Christopher that his brother was at the end of his patience. "Come along, Sarah. We must respect his wish for privacy."

"Yes, of course," she said weakly as she walked back to where Christopher was waiting. Her features were drawn in tight lines that marked her concern. "I just—"

"Not now," Christopher told her firmly as he took her by the arm and guided her back out into the hallway. "Thank you for your time," he told his brother, receiving no response in return before he closed the door behind him.

"I'm so sorry," Sarah whispered as soon as they were alone. "I should never have implied that wearing a mask might lead to a romantic attachment."

"No, you shouldn't have," Christopher agreed, "but you did so because you want him to have a normal life and to be afforded the same chance at happiness that you've been given. Realistically, however, it's unlikely that will ever happen. His confidence has been crushed, Sarah. I doubt he'll ever be the same again."

"One can always hope," she said, "because without hope, what point is there?"

"It certainly shouldn't be discredited, but it's of little use to a man if he doesn't have luck on his side," Christopher said. Looking down at her, he could see the goodness of her soul reflected in her eyes, and as he bowed his head to kiss her, he considered for the millionth time how fortunate he was that she'd come into his life.

Epilogue

The moment Sarah said, "I do" in response to the vicar's question of whether or not she, Sarah Elizabeth Argisle, would take Christopher Maxwell Heartly as her lawfully wedded husband, it was announced that the groom was permitted to kiss the bride. Christopher swept Sarah into his arms with not only overwhelming joy but also a good measure of relief. She was finally his, to have and to hold until death did them part.

Kissing her, he poured all his love for her into that one spectacular moment, while a few friends who saw no need for restraint within the small Thorncliff chapel actually clapped and cheered. "Happy?" Christopher asked in a deep whisper as he eased away and gazed into her watery eyes.

"Overjoyed, my lord."

The smile gracing her lips was one of beatific beauty, and it warmed Christopher's heart to know that it was intended only for him. "Shall we head on back to the house?" he asked. "The sooner we get the wedding breakfast over with, the sooner we'll be afforded the privacy we crave."

"An excellent idea," Sarah said, visibly struggling

to keep a straight face. "After all, we have much to discuss with each other under the circumstances— plans that need to be made . . ."

It was difficult for Christopher to contain his laughter, but somehow he managed as he drew Sarah away with him, determined to get through the tedious formalities awaiting them at Thorncliff as hastily as possible.

Seven hours later, they were finally able to retire to Christopher's bedchamber. "It will be more comfortable in London when we return there," he said, undoing his cravat. Stopping next to his bedside table, he opened a small box and pulled out the earring that Sarah had found in the tunnel. "I do hope we find the one to match."

"For your family's sake, I hope so as well."

He met Sarah's gaze, drawn by her sincerity. By God, how he loved her! Carefully, without looking away from her, he returned the earring to its box. "I've decided that if you think my models are good enough, I'll try to contact an art gallery or museum— see if they'll be willing to put them all on display."

Sarah's eyes seemed to come alight. "Really?" she asked with excitement.

"You've managed to convince me it might be a good idea."

She smiled at him then—a smile filled with love and adoration. "I've no doubt you'll be a smashing success!"

His heart expanded. Nobody had ever believed in him so blindly before or with such enthusiasm. It was dizzying in a way. He shook his head, amazed by how fortunate he was to have married her. He'd give her the world if he could. "Once we get to London, you'll have your own bedchamber as well, with a maid readily available to help with your attire."

"What need do I have for a bedchamber when I can think of nothing better than to spend each night with you?" Sarah asked.

Christopher's pulse thrummed in response to her saucy tone. "I certainly have nothing against such an arrangement. And I must confess I'm quite pleased with the prospect of acting as your maid for as long as we're here."

"In that case, perhaps you'd care to unbutton my gown?" she asked as she turned her back toward him. "I'm finding it uncomfortably restrictive."

"Is that so?" His voice had dropped to a low timbre with a trace of gruffness to it. Stepping up behind her, he went to work on the buttons as she'd requested until it gaped open, affording him a view of her tightly bound stays and her thin chemise. With the tip of his finger, he traced a line along the length of her spine, producing a shiver. "I don't believe the trouble is with your gown, Lady Spencer, but with these horrid stays you're wearing. I suggest we remove them immediately." Pushing her gown from her shoulders, he waited for it to pool on the floor before untying the laces that confined her.

A tantalizing sigh escaped her when he finally pulled the stays away. Christopher wasted no time in divesting her of the chemise as well, leaving Sarah gloriously naked in his arms and with her firm bottom pressed provocatively against his groin. "How adventurous are you feeling, my dear?" he asked as he stroked his hands along her thighs.

"If you're suggesting something new, my lord, I'm more than happy to oblige."

Her words made his every muscle strain against his tightly wound control. He was finding it difficult to breathe, much less concentrate. "Go to the bed, but don't climb onto it and don't turn around." He watched her go until she was close to the edge. Then he said, "Stop! Spread your legs apart . . . a little further . . . yes, like that. Now bend over so your hands are resting on the mattress."

She did as he asked, offering a delightful view of her most intimate part. "Is this how you want me?" she inquired softly.

God yes! It was his favorite fantasy come to life. "It's exactly how I want you. Are you comfortable?"

"Aside from feeling rather exposed, I must admit I am—surprisingly so."

With his gaze fixed upon her welcoming beauty, Christopher shrugged out of his jacket and soon rid himself of his waistcoat, cravat and shirt as well. His shoes were swiftly kicked from his feet until all that remained to be done was to pull off his trousers. This too was accomplished with haste, until he finally stood as naked as she. "Are you ready?" he asked, determined not to pounce on her like an animal but to wait for her to offer an invitation.

"Desperately so," she murmured.

Her words tugged at his manhood—hardening him to the point of despair. He stepped up behind her, leaned forward and trailed the tip of his tongue along her spine while his hands sought her breasts—full and heavy with desire.

Arching her back in response to his caress, Sarah emitted a low groan when Spencer's fingers found her nipples, tugging and squeezing until she could scarcely stand the torture of waiting for what she really wanted—to have him inside her. Pushing back her bottom, she was momentarily rewarded with the touch of his hardness against her. It sent a pulsing heat to her core while fluttering embers streaked through her, arousing a fever that threatened to drive her mad.

Spencer groaned—the sound deep and throaty. "Not yet," he said as his hands moved to her hips, holding her steady.

Sucking in a breath, Sarah waited with tightly wound expectation while his fingers crept lower, brushing against her sensitive flesh and encouraging sparks to whirl up inside her. "Please," she gasped when he failed to probe deeper.

A seductive chuckle stirred the air. "Like this?" he asked as he parted her folds.

"Yes . . . God yes!"

With agonizing slowness, he drew one finger along her sleek center while she shuddered in response. "You're so wet," he rasped, "so ready."

Pushing against her, his body sought for entry, but instead, he inserted a finger while Sarah did her best to remain upright as the need for release crested. Words failed her, replaced instead by a choked whimper as he added another finger, increasing the fullness while his thumb stroked across her pleasure point. It was as if he was fine-tuning her body to ensure an immediate response when he took her completely. Which was probably why the blasted man drew his fingers away when the first tremor began to seize her, denying her the climax she so desperately longed for.

"Soon, my love," he told her tenderly when a sob of despair was wrenched from her throat.

One hand pressed gently but firmly against her back until she arched further, lowering her arms until her bottom was completely upturned and her torso rested against the silk coverlet of the bed. Closing her eyes as she clutched the bedspread with her hands, Sarah waited for Spencer to fill her and was quickly appeased by the feel of him pressing against her, warm and thick as he drove slowly inside her until she encased him completely. "You feel incredible," he breathed as he pulled back out, leaving her bereft for only a moment before thrusting back inside her, his hands gripping her hips to better control the movement.

Sarah gasped as long-suppressed quivers danced up her legs while the sensual stroke of her nipples against the silk beneath her teased her into a cluster of sensitized nerves. "Please . . . I need . . . more."

Increasing his speed, Spencer's thrusts turned hard and deep, reawakening the tremors he'd allowed to fade earlier. "Touch yourself," he demanded, and she readily complied, her fingertips stroking the fully aroused flesh that would send her soaring.

"If only I could see you better." His voice was gruff as he slammed into her from behind, driving her toward the peak where her climax awaited. "Soon . . . I want to watch you, your legs parted while you take your own pleasure . . . Would you like that, Sarah? Would it thrill you to have me watch as you stroke yourself into a frenzy?"

His suggestion and the wicked image it evoked sent a tremor straight through her. "Yes," she said, her breathing quickening and turning to labored pants. So did his, until on one final plunge, a shuddering climax tore its way through both of them, uniting them in physical bliss as they soared together before finally collapsing in a tangled heap on the bed.

"I must say," Spencer told her a short while later, when they'd fully recovered and were lying in each other's embrace, "I'm really thrilled with the prospect of being able to do that over and over and over again—as many times a day as we choose."

With a chuckle, Sarah rose up onto her elbows and stared down at her husband. "And just so you know, I have some very wicked ideas of my own that I'll want to explore."

"Well," Spencer said, eyes darkening with lust, "there's no better time than the present."

"I couldn't agree more, my lord," she said as she lowered her lips to his, the kiss indicative of a love more grand than she'd ever thought possible, the best part being that she knew he loved her equally.

Author's Note

Research is always a fascinating part of the writing process, so for those of you who are interested, I've included a bit of extra information on some of the historically accurate references in the story. For instance, the first balloon flight in England was performed by the Italian Vincent Lunardi, on September 15, 1784. James Sadler, whom I mention in the book, was a balloonist during the Regency period. He made his first attempt shortly after Lunardi's, on October 4, 1784, and while he did enjoy several successful flights, he was sadly devastated by the death of his son, Windham Sadler, in a ballooning accident in 1824.

Doctor Hill, on the other hand, whom Lord Spencer mentions during his card game with Denison, Lady Duncaster and Sarah, was a physician during the 1700s, and the first to note the dangers of inhaling snuff. In 1761, he published a study (*Cautions Against the Immoderate Use of Snuff*) in which he wrote, "The Acrimony of Snuff is able to produce in those Parts, with which it immediately or accidentally comes in contact, Swellings and Excretions, which, in some Kinds, require the severest Operations of the Surgeon to extirpate them; and in others become fatal, because they lie beyond his Reach . . ." But since the dangers of *smoking* tobacco weren't known as early as 1820, Lady Duncaster happily enjoys her cheroot until Sarah's mother makes a fuss for social reasons.

And for an added bit of fun, since I do mention Spencer's ability to skip a stone twenty-five times and some of you may think this unlikely, the current world record is actually an astonishing fifty-one skips, set by Russell Byars on July 19, 2007. His impressive attempt can be found on YouTube.

The Casebook of Barnaby Adair novels from
#1 *New York Times* bestselling author

WHERE THE HEART LEADS
978-0-06-124338-7

Handsome, enigmatic, and deliciously dangerous, Barnaby
Adair has made his name by solving crimes within the
ton. When Penelope Ashford appeals for his aid in solving
the mystery of the disappearing orphans in her care, he is
moved by her plight—and captivated by her beauty.

THE MASTERFUL MR. MONTAGUE
978-0-06-206866-8

When Lady Halstead is murdered, Barnaby Adair helps her
devoted lady-companion, Miss Violet Matcham, and her
financial adviser, Montague, expose a cunning killer. But will
Montague and Violet learn the shocking truth too late to
seize their chance at enduring love?

LOVING ROSE
978-0-06-206867-5

Rose has a plausible explanation for why she and her children are residing in Thomas Glendower's secluded manor.
Revealing the truth would be impossibly dangerous, yet day
by day he wins her trust, and then her heart. But when her
enemy closes in, Rose must turn to Thomas to protect her
and her children.

Don't miss these passionate novels by #1 *New York Times* bestselling author

STEPHANIE LAURENS

Viscount Breckenridge to the Rescue

978-0-06-206860-6

Determined to hunt down her very own hero, Heather Cynster steps out of her safe world and boldly attends a racy soiree. But her promising hunt is ruined by the supremely interfering Viscount Breckenridge, who whisks her out of scandal—and into danger.

In Pursuit of Eliza Cynster

978-0-06-206861-3

Brazenly kidnapped from her sister's engagement ball, Eliza Cynster is spirited north to Edinburgh. Determined to escape, she seizes upon the first unlikely champion who happens along—Jeremy Carling, who will not abandon a damsel in distress.

The Capture of the Earl of Glencrae

978-0-06-206862-0

Angelica Cynster is certain she'll recognize her fated husband at first sight. And when her eyes meet those of the Earl of Glencrae across a candlelit ballroom, she knows that he's the one. But her heart is soon pounding for an entirely different reason—when her hero abducts her!

At Avon Books, we know your passion for romance—once you finish one of our novels, you find yourself wanting more.

May we tempt you with . . .

- **Excerpts** from our upcoming releases.

- Entertaining **extras**, including authors' personal photo albums and book lists.

- Behind-the-scenes **scoop** on your favorite characters and series.

- **Sweepstakes** for the chance to win free books, romantic getaways, and other fun prizes.

- Writing **tips** from our authors and editors.

- **Blog** with our authors and find out why they love to write romance.

- **Exclusive content** that's not contained within the pages of our novels.

Join us at
www.avonbooks.com

An Imprint of HarperCollins*Publishers*
www.avonromance.com

*G*ive in to your Impulses!

These unforgettable stories only take a second to buy and give you hours of reading pleasure!

Go to *www.AvonImpulse.com* and see what we have to offer.

Available wherever e-books are sold.